Clean Switch

Electric Cognition Book 1

Gabriella Creighton

Gabriella Creighton

Copyright © 2025 by Gabriella Creighton

All rights reserved.

No portion of this book may be reproduced in any form without written permission from the publisher or author, except as permitted by U.S. copyright law.

ISBN Information

eBook: 979-8-9931454-0-2
Print: 979-8-9013800-7-9

You can find more books by this author at:

GabriellaCreighton.com

Contents

To all those friends out there in Cyberspace I lost contact with, whether you've slotted into a new server or simply haven't logged in forever, you are missed, will always be missed.

You all taught me a personality and the self is contained in the mind, not the body. And now I Thought What I'd Do Is Make Like I Was One of Those Cognitive Burnouts

About the Author

Gabriella Creighton is a life long lover of the Fantasy and Science Fiction Genres. She has been fascinated by Dragons and other mythical creatures from a young age and grew up dreaming of being a writer. Inspired by great authors like Jane Yolen, Anne McCaffrey, JRR Tolkien and Phillip Pullman, she loves to take an alternative view of myth and weave her own versions. After a long life of working, gaming and enjoying the works of others, she has finally decided to put her nigh on useless Masters Degree in English Literature to work to tell stories of her own.

Growing up in Rural New York and around many of the real life versions of the locations in this book, as well as having been thrown all over the United States, Gabriella has learned she has only three desires. To write until the nail her coffin shut, to never answer the phone and for a cool glass of Salted Caramel Crowne Royal mixed with Cream Soda and Dr Pepper, which she calls a magic elixir.

It helps get the writing done.

You can find more of her works at:
GabriellaCreighton.com

Preface

I THOUGHT WHAT I'D DO...

A few simple notes about this book and an explanation for what some might call the strangest form of dialogue they've ever read.

I aimed with this book to create a Cyberpunk styled setting which had all the beats of what one should expect when you try to combine Blade Runner, Bubblegum Crisis and a healthy dose of Cyberpunk Red into a working world all on its own. I did not want to be tied to a real world or a specific region in it. Thus Klade is a city built inside of a dome in a world where the outside is considered to deadly to exist in. The people are an amalgamation of humanity if it keeps going on the track it has been going on for decades.

While you are reading this in English, the people of Klade speak what I like to call Gutterspeak. It is a creole of English, Russian, Chinese and Sanskrit, the purpose of which is to show that over time humanity continues to amalgamate it's culture and combine into one species rather than a people split by useless boundaries. Wren in particular speaks in a sing song mannerism that is considered the common feminine speech of this new culture and you will find the ever changing Hikari to do so as well when in certain frames.

I leave the questions on whether this takes place on Earth, some distant colony or a completely new world all to you. There is no allegory there. This is a future none of us can see, during a date that none of us can imagine, in a place that feels exactly like a trashy day in any city anywhere. People are people. As such I'm telling a story where people are literally no more than what they choose to put on in the morning.

We are truly beyond humanity when we recognize that even the best of us are just wearing a coat that makes us appear special.

Three.

Two.

One.

Let's go.

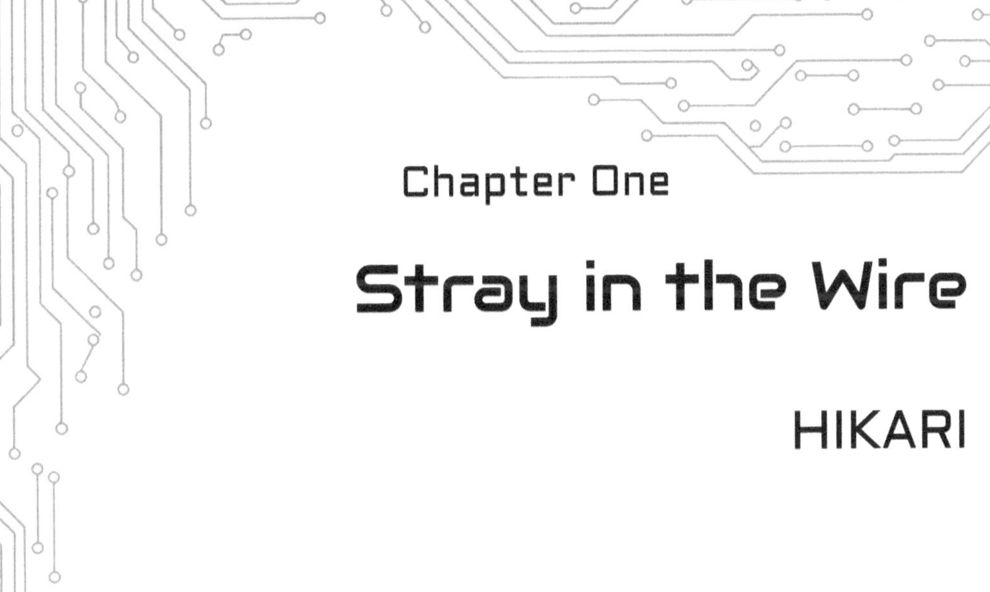

THE ALLEY REEKED OF old coolant and the sweet, metallic tang of crushed synthfruit peels, left to rot where the gutter filtration had long since given up. Above, a dying neon sign flickered in staccato pulses, **GĒN-EZIS KOFFEE**, its name ghosting through layers of green and pink haze. The letters buzzed unevenly, the kind of static drone that nestled into your skull if you lingered too long. Klade's lower levels never slept, but they didn't live, either. They just exhaled.

Crouched in the pocket of shadow between a pile of collapsed delivery crates and the sagging remains of a skinner's tent, I watched the terminal across the street through a cracked visor. Four security drones drifted along their programmed loops, slow and lazy in their orbit. Obsolete models, no heat signature tracking, no predictive targeting. Orinox loved to save money on patrol routes in dead districts like this. Fear was cheaper than new tech.

A soft buzz tingled against the back of my skull, where the deck sat fused to the bone. A fifth drone which went by the name "Juno" chirped into my systems as their feed clicked on, a grainy bird's-eye stream flickering into the upper-right of my visual field. Not mine, technically. It belonged to one of my targets for this run, it strangely had initiated the call with me. It identified her owner as someone called Wren. Her drone's sensor suite was surprisingly well-tuned for a civilian rig, its micro-audio cutting clean through the city's ambient noise.

Three figures approached the terminal from the east walkway. At first glance, they looked like standard late-shift wanderers, casual, slow-moving, slouched into their coats against the mist. But one of them, a woman trailing half a step behind the others, clutched a data case close to her chest like it held air. Her movements were erratic, favoring her left leg, twitching like she expected ghosts in every shadow.

I leaned forward slightly, tracking her with the shell's enhanced opticals. She had a gaunt face, stress-thin and sleepless, and her eyes were too wide for someone who didn't already know they were being hunted. She wasn't supposed to be here. More importantly, she wasn't alone. Two more drones, sleek, angular, black-glass armored, emerged from a side route near the terminal, flying a far tighter convergence pattern than patrol logic allowed. Private security. Military grade. Deployed to retrieve, not deter.

The deck buzzed again, sharper this time.

"Encrypted payload detected. Neural-grade. Signal dirty." Juno's voice, filtered through a sarcastic overlay that must have been custom designed by this Wren. It came through like a dry whisper in my ear. I almost told the feed to shut up. Civilians weren't my problem. But neural-grade was another matter.

I checked the shell's internal inventory. Stray carried light gear only, sleeve-mounted coil knife, subdermal shockslug, small counterintelligence suite woven into the back of the jacket. Fast, quiet, made to blend. Disposable, if necessary. I could still walk away. Let the drones take her. Let the story end before it began.

Then she looked up.

Not directly at me. Just... toward me. Her gaze swept the rooftop where I knelt, and for a second, barely a breath, her eyes narrowed as if she saw something move behind the static. She clutched the case tighter. And I realized the drones were locking in, angling their descent. She had sixty seconds at best.

I moved.

The drop from the rooftop wasn't far, and the shell's stabilizers absorbed the landing with only a soft hiss of compressed air. I crossed the street in a blur, slipping between shadows cast by broken signage and low fog, cutting through the gate slats with one fluid motion. The girl didn't see me coming until I was beside her.

She whirled, mouth parting to scream.

I pressed the barrel of the slug pistol gently against her temple. "Quiet," I said, flat and calm.

She froze. No resistance, too shocked, too exhausted, or both.

I grabbed the collar of her coat, pulled her into the alley, and vanished with her into the heartbeat flicker of neon and steam.

THE ALLEY SWALLOWED US whole. Layers of graffiti scrawled across old duracrete flickered under passing transit lights, each tag overlapping the last until the wall looked diseased with history. I kept her moving, one hand gripping her coat, the other holding the slug pistol low against my thigh. She didn't resist, didn't even try to look back, just stumbled over uneven pavement and gasped for breath like she hadn't done it in hours.

We ducked beneath a loading platform where the shadows thickened and the scent of ozone and rust made the air feel like licking a battery. I spun her against the wall, pressed a palm over her mouth before she could think to scream, and scanned the gap we'd come from. No pursuit yet. The drones hadn't registered her as gone. That meant they hadn't planned for her to run.

"Don't scream," I said, barely above a whisper. "Don't talk unless I ask. Nod if you understand."

She hesitated, then nodded, slow and terrified.

I pulled my hand away, watching her closely. She didn't try to bolt. Smart. Or just too tired to be stupid.

She looked human, though I'd seen enough shellwork these days that the difference barely registered. Shaggy hair, probably dark when clean. Eyes red-rimmed from sleeplessness, ringed with cracked smears of mascara. Lips dry and peeling. A faint bruise on her cheek suggested recent handling, the kind you don't walk away from unless someone lets you.

I pointed at the case clutched against her ribs. "What's in it?"

She tightened her arms around it as if I'd asked for her spine. Her jaw tensed, and she blinked too many times in rapid succession, refusing to look away, but failing to meet my eyes.

"Neural-grade transmission flagged by a drone," I said evenly, watching her. "That makes you a target. And me a fool, unless you give me a reason."

"I didn't steal it," she whispered.

Her voice barely made it past the smoke-laced air between us. It cracked midway, fragile and defensive, as if saying it louder would make it more true.

"That wasn't the question."

"I didn't know what it was," she said quickly, then bit her lip like she'd said too much. "They just... I was told to take it and go. They said it would get me off the grid."

"Who's 'they'?"

She flinched at that. Her shoulders curled inward and her eyes darted toward the mouth of the alley, as if afraid someone might still be watching.

"A client," she said after a pause. "No name. No face. Paid in credstack and fresh IDs. I was desperate."

Desperate, I thought. The word clung to her posture like mold. Every twitch of her hands, every uncertain glance. I'd seen it before, in civilians, in addicts, in defectors trying to cross corp lines without getting their heads blown off.

I crouched lower, folding into a knee to put us eye-level. She pressed back into the wall, arms tightening like a vise around the case. I could hear the static buzz from its containment seals now, subtle, but there.

"What's your name?" I asked.

Her eyes flicked to mine. Her throat worked in a dry swallow.

"...Why?"

"Because if I'm going to keep you alive, I'd like to know what to call you that isn't 'dead weight.'"

She hesitated. Then, softly, "Wren. Wren Aves."

I nodded once, never breaking eye contact. "Hikari."

She blinked again, visibly trying to place it. Something caught in her eyes as she processed the name. "Is that your... your real name?"

"It's what you get," I cut in, standing slowly. Her eyes dropped as she retreated slightly into herself, nodding in reluctant acceptance.

She held onto the case like it could grow legs and flee without her. Like it was the only solid thing left in her world. I didn't like that. People who clung to objects more than logic usually broke at the worst time. Still, she hadn't screamed, hadn't run, and hadn't lied, at least not well enough to fool me. That earned her a point or two.

Behind me, Juno's soft wings clicked into place as the crow-shaped drone rejoined our airspace, scanning silently from above. Its presence was both familiar and comforting to Wren, upon seeing it she seemed to relax a bit. I tilted my head and muttered under my breath, low enough that Wren probably couldn't hear. I was already tapped into her drone, we had made a creed as soon as it realized I was protecting her.

"Keep watch. Grid shadow's closing."

She was staring up at me again. Not fearful this time, curious. And maybe a little angry, like a cornered animal not yet sure if the hand reaching for it meant rescue or restraint. She no doubt questioned how I had tapped into her drone, become a part of the feed. It was not a thing a normal runner should be able to do even when she wasn't out of her wits.

I scanned the alley's far end again. Still clear. But not for long. The city never let ghosts walk unchallenged.

"We're moving," I said, stepping past her and tapping the side of my visor to recall the nearest node. "And if that case gets me shot, you better hope you die before I figure out how to make you regret it."

To her credit, she followed.

WE CUT DOWN A service tunnel half-choked with fallen signage and old ductwork. My boots splashed through stagnant runoff that reeked of spoiled coolant and biotech grease. Wren stayed close, stepping carefully, her grip on the case firm but not panicked now. Either she was calming, or she'd shifted from fear to grim resolve. I didn't ask. Let her adapt on her own terms.

Klade's underbelly pulsed with old power, residual energy from decades of rewiring and overgrowth, its veins clogged with forgotten tech and scavenged cable. Overhead, LED veins flickered behind cracked panels like the heartbeat of something dying slow. The deeper you went, the more the city sounded like it was whispering to itself.

I activated the overlay on my visor. A faint lattice of blue lines rippled into view, tracing old access corridors, collapsed lifts, and hard-coded dead zones. One node pinged green. An abandoned transit utility closet, two blocks northwest, tied into a low-level switchpoint still linked to the shell-frame cache I'd buried weeks ago. Small. Quiet. Harder to trace.

"Left," I said, signaling with two fingers. Wren followed without complaint. I didn't look back.

Juno tracked our movement from above, relaying static pings to my HUD. No sign of drones, yet. But noise was rising. Somewhere, the grid had noticed a missing signature. When you walk in someone else's skin, the city forgets you for a while. Until it doesn't.

We passed a sleeping shape folded into an emergency stairwell, wrapped in thermal mesh and twitching in augmented dreams. A burnt-out simhalo flickered over his brow, stuck in a loop of synthetic rainfall and birdsong. Wren stared at him for half a second too long.

"Don't stop," I said without turning.

She quickened her pace. The case jostled against her hip.

"What is this place?" she asked, her voice soft and close now, like she was afraid to disturb the walls.

"Old Klade. Street Two-Six-Aleph, just under the ferro-belt. This zone's been redlined for three fiscal cycles. Utilities fail here on purpose."

"Because?"

I finally glanced at her. "Because when you starve a sector long enough, property gets cheap."

She looked away.

We reached the node access door, a rusted service panel wedged between two industrial fan housings. The keypad was fused with grime and years of sticker bomb tags: gang crests, virus scrawls, anarchist glyphs. I wiped a strip clean with the side of my sleeve and jacked in through the deck port in my wrist.

The connection pinged low and dirty. Legacy code. No auto-firewalls. Just a flicker of recognition and a faint pulse of welcome. This place remembered me.

"Inside," I muttered, guiding her through the narrow doorway. The room beyond was barely a cube, lined with old rackmounts, long-dead servers, and one chair welded directly into the floor. The shell-switch unit sat on a scaffold bolted to the back wall. Crude. Stable. Sufficient.

Wren looked around, hugging the case tighter. "You live here?"

I stepped past her and keyed the shell-switch to initialize. "No. I ghost through places like this. The moment you live somewhere, it becomes a weakness."

She exhaled, but didn't speak. For the first time, she didn't look afraid, just tired. Her shoulders sagged slightly, and her grip on the case loosened. That's when I noticed her hands were trembling.

"You're burning out," I said. "Sit down before you drop."

She gave me a small glare, but obeyed. As she slid down the wall to sit cross-legged near the switch unit, Juno circled through the doorway and perched silently above her head.

I checked the system integrity of the cached shell. Velvet, online and ready. It would give me more mobility in tighter zones, and eyes that matched the corporate sprawl we'd need to cross next.

As the switch initialized, I returned to the interface, scanning system integrity on the cached shell. Velvet was online and stable, perfect for moving through upper-tier districts where poise mattered more than firepower. Its neural buffer had held through six prior deployments, and the overlays were still synched to my keyframe. Clean transfer, minimal drift. It would do.

I set the countdown and stepped back from the rig. One hand hovered near the subdermal jack in my collar, feeling the low hum of the shell awakening on the rack. Behind me, Wren shifted against the wall. She'd stopped hugging the case so tightly, though it still sat in her lap, sealed and silent. Her shoulders slumped under a weight that had finally found her nerves. She looked at the metal more like it was a puzzle now, less like a shield, more like a confession she hadn't finished reading.

She caught me watching. Her expression didn't change, but something behind her eyes flickered, an awareness that hadn't been there when I dragged her off the street. Not fear. Not even regret. Just a dawning comprehension that whatever she'd been promised for carrying that payload, it wasn't safety. It was something far more dangerous.

"Is that thing really going to change you?" she asked, nodding toward the switch unit.

Her voice was low, steady now, stripped of the quiver it held before.

"It changes the shell," I said, tightening the final connections. "I stay the same."

She didn't answer. Just lowered her gaze and sat back against the wall as Juno clicked softly above her.

The chamber lights dimmed to transition protocols. My fingers brushed the switch-plate, and for a brief moment, I felt the buzz behind my eyes, the familiar static of the moment before.

Between the self I wore and the one waiting for me.

I TRIGGERED THE SEQUENCE, and the world peeled back like skin.

There was nothing graceful about the transition, not the seamless drift the old manuals described, not the cool, sterile glide that Orinox sold to the public. It came like a wave of vertigo, pulling me forward through a collapsing tunnel of colorless light, stripping away sensation, silence, and shape one layer at a time. Stray's form, my limbs, my breath, my pulse, disintegrated behind me as the old shell went dark. My mind stretched thin along the uplink, a current of will compressed into raw data and fired like a bullet into another body.

Velvet's shell lit up before I arrived, already warming to accept me. Synthetic nerves flared in anticipation, receptors aligning, scaffolding unlocking like a blossom of steel and carbon fiber. I dropped into it with a lurch, like being slammed into cold flesh that didn't quite remember how to breathe. For a split second, I was drowning. Then the lungs caught. The heart remembered its rhythm. My vision returned in high definition, lined with UI overlays and calibration data humming quietly at the edge of thought.

I opened my eyes to light too bright, colors too precise, the scent of artificial floral oil already flooding the new nostrils. Velvet was programmed for comfort, refined motion, soft vocal modulation, a skin-sheen of corporate polish, but it always took a moment to settle into. The longer limbs carried weight differently. The hips demanded a more fluid stance, the fingers more deliberate in their movements. Every shell was a new language, and Velvet spoke with poise that had no patience for haste.

Across the room, Wren sat frozen on the floor. The case rested in her lap now, hands no longer gripping it like a lifeline but resting lightly on either side. Her expression had shifted from panic to something more measured, part awe, part suspicion, part quiet processing. Her gaze roamed across my new form, taking in the sharp cheekbones, the engineered elegance of the shell's silhouette, the way the light moved across composite skin. Her lips parted slightly, but whatever question sat behind them didn't come.

I stepped off the platform with Velvet's practiced grace, the motion fluid and noiseless despite the gritty tile beneath my feet. Juno shifted position as I moved, optical sensors blinking as it recalibrated my new signature, then hopped to a nearby duct to observe from a safer vantage. The drone knew me well enough to recognize the switch, but even it needed a second to adjust. I often wondered if Wren had programmed it that way on purpose.

She watched every step I took like she was tracking a ghost, and when I drew close enough for her to see my eyes, her expression hardened just slightly.

"You switch bodies like most people change clothes," she said, her voice quiet, but laced with something sharper than before, judgment, maybe, or just dawning clarity.

I didn't stop moving. I reached up and adjusted Velvet's collar, smoothing out a fold in the soft fabric beneath my throat. "Clothes don't remember the last time you bled in them," I said evenly, scanning the shell's system logs without looking at her.

Wren flinched at that, not visibly, not with her body, but in the way her breath caught short and her eyes darted away. The silence that followed wasn't awkward so much as heavy with what she didn't say. I could tell she wanted to ask more, what it felt like, who I was between bodies, whether there was anything real left beneath the surface, but she didn't. She looked down instead, to the neural case in her lap, and her fingers traced the seam of its edges with mechanical precision.

Something had shifted in her since we fled the terminal. The desperation was still there, but it had curdled into something colder, quieter. Resignation, perhaps. Or resolve. She understood now that whatever she was carrying, it wasn't going to save her. It wasn't a lifeline. It was a key, one that opened the wrong door.

Juno emitted a low chime. Movement on the perimeter. We weren't alone anymore.

I returned to the interface panel, brushing past the data node to pull the access logs and wipe the trace. We'd lingered too long already. The shell-switch node had served its purpose. The next step would be harder, moving aboveground, cutting through the broadcast grid without tripping another flag. But with the Velvet shell online and Wren quiet for now, I could control the pace again.

I didn't look at her as I rearmed the subdermal shock charge in my wrist and reset my gait parameters. She had questions. She'd earned them. But for now, she followed without asking, and that was enough.

The city didn't care who we were. Only whether we'd left a mark.

And I never stayed long enough to make one that lasted.

THE ACCESS DOOR HISSED open with a reluctant sigh, part rust and part ozone. I led the way, stepping out into the midnight arteries of Klade's Mid-Tier. The air hit differently here, filtered, perfumed with artificial jasmine, yet still tinged with the grime that no amount of processing could fully purge. This was where the towers began to rise, where the slums hardened into angles and ambition. The undercity had rot. Mid-Tier had polish, but it was all lacquer over mold.

Wren followed two steps behind, silent save for the occasional scuff of her boots. She still cradled the neural case like something sacred, or cursed. The streets weren't crowded at this hour, but they never truly slept. Holograms flickered on every vertical surface, all pastel and promise. One peddled facial swaps. Another blinked pixel-smiles offering prescription emotion suppressants. A third advertised Orinox Dynamics' new memory-mapping insurance: *"Never forget who you are, even if you want to."*

I glanced at Wren, wondering if she saw it.

She didn't react.

Klade had no stars. The sky was a smear of light pollution and thermal bleed from the orbital lines. Overhead, the towers climbed like spines of forgotten gods, each trying to pierce the void first. Mag-rails threaded through the upper echelons like veins, ferrying the rich in soundless tubes while the rest of us bled in alleys and side markets. Drones buzzed past with unfeeling red optics, scanning barcodes on trash bins and panhandlers alike. A street preacher shouted warnings in binary at a passing maintenance truck and was promptly silenced by a soft blue pulse from a nearby lawpost.

We kept walking.

Velvet's gait caught the attention of two synthjack boys leaning against a vending node. They wore knockoff combat rigs, subdermal glow tattoos flickering like code errors. One raised an eyebrow, caught somewhere between appreciation and challenge. I met his gaze for half a second, long enough to trigger Velvet's posture override. Shoulders squared, hips cocked, one brow arched with surgical precision.

He looked away.

Ahead, the pavement shifted, tiles warming underfoot in response to biometric pressure. The city knew who walked where, how often, how fast. I kept my path erratic by habit, switching pressure every third step. It was a trick I picked up from a dead runner with no teeth and one working eye. He said pattern disruption made you invisible. He wasn't wrong. He also died in a hallway lined with motion sensors and bad choices.

The terminal sat recessed beneath a half-collapsed pedestrian bridge, its roof partially caved in and draped with shredded tarp that fluttered like dead skin in the wind. It should've been bustling, these places usually were, even after hours. Runners looking to offload contraband, black-market medics trading brainware patches, scavvers pawning damp salvage. But tonight, the shadows hung too evenly, like someone had pressed mute on the whole block. The lights overhead pulsed amber, slow, deliberate, like a heartbeat under glass. Not abandoned. Not quite hostile. But wrong.

I scanned the perimeter without slowing, cross-referencing movement patterns, heat signatures, light refraction, anything that would suggest a trap. Nothing pinged. Which was worse.

"Two blocks out," I said softly, triggering the shell's throat mic. "Pulse sync is quiet. Could be early. Could be empty."

Behind me, Wren hesitated mid-step. Her voice followed, careful and low. "What if they've been watching since before we got here?"

She wasn't wrong to ask. We were carrying something corporate-grade and whisper-coded. You didn't transport neural cases through Mid-Tier unless you were desperate, suicidal, or sure of your buyer. I'd been all three before. Tonight I was only two of them.

The closer we got, the more the silence felt curated, too clean, too symmetrical. Ambient static had thinned out. The ever-present drone of life and machinery had been stripped away like background noise in a simulation. Even Juno had stopped making sound, perching on a broken power conduit with its wings slightly outstretched, as if preparing to flee.

I raised one hand to halt Wren, the gesture sharp and practiced. Her feet obeyed before her mind caught up. I moved forward a step, posture relaxed but with weight sunk into my heels. Velvet's grace made even caution look poised. The suit adjusted its balance settings automatically, optimizing for high-heel traction and pivot angles in case the situation escalated. My breath slowed to match the internal pacer.

That was when I felt it. Not in the visible spectrum. Not even in the audio layers. Just a click in the back of my skull, subtle, mechanical, like a gear shifting into place on the wrong side of the skin. The HUD blinked with one red glyph and I looked up.

There, nested between the fins of an old air filtration scaffold, was a sniper drone. Its lens shimmered faintly as it adjusted focus. I didn't need to guess the caliber. I'd used its twin years ago. Anti-personnel. High-velocity. Anti-shell if it punched through the right seams.

I moved without warning, just a shoulder-check into Wren's side and a downward drag that took us both to the ground. The shot cracked pavement a breath behind us, kicking stone and dust over our heads. She yelped, not in pain but shock, clutching the case to her chest even as we hit the alley floor. I rolled, sighted, and drew. The rooftops weren't empty anymore.

We hadn't arrived early.

We'd arrived invited.

And the welcome mat had teeth.

I DIDN'T WAIT FOR confirmation. The next round would aim lower. My shoulder connected with Wren's side again, dragging us behind a shattered delivery pod where the casing still smelled faintly of sun-bleached plastic and rotting protein packs. I dropped to one knee, pistol already in hand. The HUD tracked movement now, heat traces flickering across the rooftops, digital ghosts pacing above us like predators in a cage. At least four. Maybe six. All of them masked.

The sniper hadn't fired again yet. Which meant he was repositioning, or baiting.

"Signal scrub?" I asked without looking, my voice clipped but even. My eyes stayed locked on the flickering red triangles blinking at the edge of my vision. The rooftops weren't just holding snipers. There was movement at street level too. Fast. Coordinated.

Wren's breath hitched. "Give me two seconds."

She ducked beside me, one knee on the pavement, and twisted the neural case around in her lap. Her fingers moved fast, not hesitant, not panicked, but practiced. She tapped into her deck, drawing quick overlays across her wrist as she bypassed the lock on her secondary module. A faint chime issued from inside her sleeve, followed by a low-frequency pulse that shuddered in my teeth more than my ears. Juno snapped upright at the signal, its wings flaring like blades before vanishing again into the upper dark.

Above, one of the rooftop contacts glitched mid-motion. The red dot froze, blinked twice, and vanished.

"They're running a synced relay through a shared runner. I piggybacked off their jump signal and fried the relay's back-end node," she said, her voice tight with concentration. "That'll buy us... maybe thirty seconds before they reroute."

It was enough.

The sniper flickered briefly into full visibility, confused by the broken signal trail.

I fired.

The slug cut through its sensor dome just as it recalibrated, tearing the lens open in a spray of synthetic coolant and internal wiring. The chassis tipped sideways and dropped like dead weight, slamming onto the steel grating below with a sound that echoed across the street like thunder under glass.

I moved, pulling Wren with me toward a nearby stairwell access half-swallowed by overgrowth. One of the ground contacts finally committed, charging in with a guttural cry and a shimmer of cheap optic-camouflage breaking under sudden motion. I met him halfway, pivoting to let his blade glance off my reinforced forearm before driving my elbow into the hinge of his jaw.

He staggered and I corrected. My pistol found the seam under his chin.

Two quick pulses. One for certainty.

The body dropped hard and didn't get up.

Wren had already ducked behind the stairwell barricade, working to stabilize her readout while Juno returned to her shoulder in a blur of wings. More shadows danced in the far end of the terminal, one of them moving with the careful, deliberate pacing of someone who thought they were in control.

Sadly for me, they weren't Mirror. Not yet.

But they were trained.

Another sniper blinked back into visibility, repositioned farther down the rail line. That one wouldn't miss. I readied a side toss with the EMP gel round I kept strapped to my hip, nonlethal, unless you were mostly wires. A flick of the wrist sent it spinning across the cracked tile, blue static dancing along its edges as it bounced under the sniper's perch.

The EMP round landed just short of the sniper's perch, skidding once across scorched tile before releasing a ripple of blue static. The gel discharge crackled like tearing fabric, collapsing the upper scaffold in a wave of silent force. The sniper unit blinked out of existence, no scream, no final flare, just a puff of black smoke and a whine as power failed mid-movement. A body fell, limbs spasming briefly before the shell gave out completely.

I lowered the pistol, letting Velvet's aim-assist release its grip on my arm. The street was quiet again, unnaturally so. The ambient signals were still out of balance, but the worst of them had gone mute. Only two residual blips remained on the HUD, neither closing in. Either hesitant or retreating.

Behind me, Wren was crouched at the edge of the stairwell barricade, one hand still half inside her deck sleeve. Juno perched motionless on her shoulder, wings folded like knives. Her face was pale, but there was a sharpness to her expression I hadn't seen before. Sweat clung to her brow, and her mouth was pressed into a firm line, but her hands didn't shake.

She looked at me like she expected to be judged.

"I rerouted the relay junction," she said, voice steadier now that the adrenaline had something to settle against. She was quickly impressing me with the woman behind the desperation. "Blew a circuit on my backup deck doing it, but I think I knocked out most of their signal cohesion. Whoever they were, they didn't expect resistance."

I nodded once. It wasn't praise and it wasn't dismissal, it was acknowledgment. She understood the difference.

"We should move," I said, holstering the weapon. "That drone might've broadcast. If Orinox was watching, they'll come scrub the site."

Wren stood slowly, adjusting the neural case against her chest. "Where?"

I looked toward the elevated rail corridor. No surveillance towers, no active patrols. The path wouldn't stay clear long.

"There's a service tunnel east of here," I said. "Old maintenance line. It cuts under three blocks and loops past the broadcast towers. Cold, damp, smells like rust and rats, but no one tracks shell runners through it."

She nodded, falling into step beside me.

We moved in silence for a few moments, passing flickering ad panels and shattered vending drones. Each footstep echoed too loud, our presence still stitched into the quiet.

After a time, she asked, "You really think they knew who we were?"

I didn't answer immediately. Not because I didn't know, but because I did. The kind of ambush we'd walked into wasn't something you staged for random smugglers. It had precision, timing, tech. It had budget. They had expected to walk away with their goods and no one to pay. They were clean enough that we had never spotted what happened to the two men that had been with her before I interrupted.

"They knew," I said finally. "They just didn't know what we are."

That answer held her quiet all the way to the tunnel entrance.

THE TUNNEL ENTRANCE WAS half-hidden behind the ruins of a collapsed rail kiosk, a skeleton of scorched signage and melted plastic long forgotten by the city above. I pushed the slanted panel aside, straining Velvet's frame, not built for brute strength, but flexible enough to manage, and ushered Wren through. The air that met us was dense and metallic, tainted by rust, old coolant, and the rot of forgotten things. A thin mist hung close to the ground, disturbed only by the low hum of distant water pumps and the occasional hiss of a faulty valve.

Inside, the corridor curved downward into the dark, lit only by the ambient glow of my retinal overlay. The walls were coated in decades of layered grime, graffiti tags overlapping like digital scars, some barely legible under faded threat-markings in corporate code. The silence wasn't comforting. It pressed in like a second skin.

Wren settled herself near the wall without a word, lowering the neural case to the ground and sinking onto cold tile. Her limbs finally slackened as the tension bled out, leaving behind a wired exhaustion that didn't quite allow her to rest. She didn't look at me, just stared at the opposite wall, brow furrowed, hands clenched in a grip she hadn't realized she was still holding. Her breathing slowed in uneven stages, like a system rebooting from partial failure.

I gave her space and crouched nearby, turning my focus inward. Velvet's shell was still within operational thresholds, but the feedback lag in my left arm suggested compression fatigue, minor, manageable, but building. I opened the cache and began reviewing combat telemetry, cross-referencing every movement pattern, every target track, searching for anomalies. That's when I saw it.

The playback stuttered briefly, not from corruption but from something I'd almost missed in the heat of the moment, a flash, caught only in the reflection of the sniper's optic dome. I magnified, sharpened, and enhanced. There it was. A figure. Too still to be one of the runners, too perfectly framed to be coincidence. Humanoid proportions, tall and narrow, androgynous in posture. Reflective plating smoothed into soft contours that bent light but held no warmth. No heat signature. No embedded glyph. No affiliation ID.

Just silver.

Just watching.

The reflection distorted in the curve of the lens, but the impression was unmistakable. A silhouette rendered in deliberate absence. Not part of the team that ambushed us. Not an accident.

Someone else had been there. Someone I knew.

Wren stirred slightly at the sound of my intake breath and turned toward me, her expression caught between concern and curiosity.

"Something wrong?"

I didn't answer immediately. My gaze stayed locked on the image suspended in the air between us. It wavered in the projection, caught in the frozen still of a moment we hadn't seen play out in real time. I forced myself to speak with measured calm.

"Whoever sent that kill team wasn't watching the feed."

Her eyes narrowed. "You're saying someone else was."

I adjusted the projection angle so she could see it. The silver figure shimmered softly in the sniper's lens, almost elegant in the way it stood unmoving amidst chaos.

Wren leaned in. "What the hell is that?"

I studied the image a moment longer before answering. "A prototype. A ghost. Something they made and lost."

She hesitated, then said it for me. "It looks like you."

I gave no confirmation, but the silence between us was agreement enough. She sat back against the wall again, her expression harder now, the edges of her fear traded for calculation.

I dismissed the overlay with a flick, and the tunnel dimmed again to rust and wet concrete. Whatever presence had been with us during the firefight wasn't here now, but its shadow remained. The image hadn't glitched. The data hadn't lied.

Mirror was in the city.

And it was watching.

THE SILENCE LINGERED AS we pushed deeper into the underlevel, taking a path most runners avoided. The air grew warmer with proximity to the heat exchangers buried beneath Klade's foundational layers. We passed broken utility drones, some half-consumed by the floor, their arms locked in loops they'd never finish. Pipes hissed in rhythmic intervals above, timed by failing infrastructure that no one had paid to fix in decades. It smelled of ozone and stale coolant, the scent of a city too large to remember its lower arteries.

Wren stayed close behind me, quiet for a long stretch, her boots scuffing slightly every few steps. It wasn't fear anymore, not like earlier. It was contemplation. And I hated how well she wore it.

"You don't talk much after a fight," she said eventually, voice soft and deliberate, as if testing the sound before committing to it. "Is that a shell thing, or a you thing?"

I didn't look back. "Talking wastes power."

"Pretty sure Velvet's battery can handle small talk."

She wasn't wrong. Velvet's entire purpose was social interaction and dealing in board rooms, with fixers and any other sort of time where I had to make up for my own lack of ability to relate to humans. And yet... something about the cadence of her voice pulled more than it should have. I had for once missed the sarcasm in someone's voice. I adjusted my stride without thinking, just enough to match her pace more naturally.

We passed under a collapsed junction, stepping over fallen signage that once read "Authorized Sector Only." The spray-paint on the side now just said "Run."

"I don't keep homes," I said at last. "Too easy to burn. Too easy to trace."

"But you're taking me somewhere. And you seem to know every turn like muscle memory."

Her eyes weren't accusatory. Just observant. Too observant.

I let the next few steps drag out in silence, weighing the answer against instinct. "It's a shell cradle," I finally said. "A maintenance site I didn't want scavenged. Not a home."

"You've got more than one shell charging there?"

"I've got contingencies. Safe fallback points. That's all."

We reached the upper lock where the tunnel curved behind a disused maglift rail, and I pulled back the rusted grate with a grunt. On the other side, the passage opened into a narrow corridor of reinforced steel and faded paint. The lights were motion-triggered, humming softly as we moved through. Everything here had the scent of familiarity, old solder, burnt plastic, recycled air scrubbed clean enough to be bearable but never quite fresh.

Wren glanced around as we entered, taking in the surgical precision of the space. The charging alcoves were built into the walls, each with its own biometric lock and suppression field. The walls were lined with cable spools, backup decks, spent drives. One wall bore a curved couch still wrapped in half-peeled plastic, unused, unfaded. A closet stood sealed beneath a hydraulic iris lock, painted matte black to disappear into the concrete. There was no clutter. Nothing that said anyone lived here.

Except I did.

She walked in a slow circle, stopping at a faded data map of the city etched onto the wall. Her fingers hovered just above the lines, tracing routes with her eyes.

"You sleep here?"

"No."

"Eat?"

"No."

She looked back at me. "But you have... clothes. Tools. A med station. A coffeemaker."

"It's a staging zone."

A beat passed between us.

"It smells like you," she said softly.

That one landed harder than I expected.

I turned my back on her and crossed to the main console, initiating a silent shell status check just to have something to look at. The display lit up in cool blue, showing Forge fully docked and Wisp in standby. Stray's last sync remained offline, too risky to deploy again until I rerouted the net.

"You think having a place means weakness," she said behind me. "Like permanence means vulnerability. But this isn't a risk. This is survival."

I let the words hang there, neither accepted nor denied.

"I didn't ask for this," I murmured, still facing the screen. "I didn't plan to stay. I just... kept coming back. Needed a place to update, repair. It made sense. That's all."

"You built a home and convinced yourself it wasn't one."

I turned then, slower than I meant to, and our eyes met. Hers weren't sharp now, they were wide, soft, cautious. Not probing. Just open.

"You're not a machine," she said, not with pity but clarity. "And even if you were... even machines need somewhere to return."

I didn't answer. Couldn't, really. Instead, I moved to the side alcove and pulled open a compartment to retrieve a sealed nutrition pack and two ration drinks. Tossed one her way without comment. She caught it easily and sank onto the couch.

I joined her after a pause. Not too close. Not yet.

The lights dimmed slightly as the recharge system kicked in behind the wall, casting us both in soft blue. In that moment, in the half-quiet hum of my so-called not-a-home, I realized I wasn't used to being seen.

Not like this.

Not without armor or alias.

Just... seen.

The warmth of the rehydrated ration pack was more psychological than physical. It barely registered on Velvet's internal temperature sensors, but I let the moment linger anyway, holding it like something fragile I wasn't quite sure how to put down. Across from me, Wren sat with one leg tucked beneath her, the dim blue light casting long shadows under her cheekbones. She didn't eat yet. Just watched me with that same unblinking attentiveness that made my synthetic skin itch.

She sipped from her drink, then tilted her head, gaze drifting toward the charging alcoves across the room.

"Do you have a central shell?" she asked, voice casual enough to feel rehearsed. "One you don't take on jobs."

I didn't answer right away. My eyes followed hers across the smooth metal docks, Forge stood tall and hunched, locked into his magnetic rack with carbon scoring along the shoulder plating. Wisp lay cradled like a sleeping child, a tangle of neural ports and coiled fiberoptic hair gleaming faintly under the field. Stray was absent, left in another depot. Still too exposed.

Wren's gaze slid back to me. "Like... something closer to you. Whoever that is."

I gave a quiet exhale, not quite a sigh. "No such thing."

"Not even one you use when you're alone?"

"Why would I need one of those?"

"Because sometimes," she said carefully, "it helps to stop pretending."

I didn't flinch, but it felt like she'd pulled something taut inside me. The kind of tension that vibrated down through the bones of my mind. Or what passed for them now.

Velvet smiled. It wasn't involuntary, it was calculated, a trained gesture the shell knew how to wear like a glove. "Pretending is efficient. People react better to what they expect."

"But what do *you* expect, Hikari?"

She didn't say it like it was sacred. Didn't put weight on the name as if she were asking me to be more. Just... gently placed it there, between us, like she'd picked it up and dusted it off for inspection.

I looked away. "There isn't a central version. There's only what I need to be, when I need to be it. The rest is legacy code."

Wren was quiet for a moment. I could feel her watching me, not like surveillance, but like someone studying a fractured screen, trying to trace the original image through the cracks.

"That one," she said finally, nodding toward Wisp, still dormant in her alcove. "She looks like she was made to be cared for."

"Wisp is for data retrieval."

"Still. The frame's small. The eyes are expressive. She's designed to invite protection, even when you're the one doing the hacking. It's... a weird loop."

I nodded once, almost despite myself. "It works."

"But it's not who you are."

She wasn't accusing. She wasn't trying to fix me. That was the worst part. She was just *being there*, quietly confident that underneath all this hardware and heat shielding, there might be someone worth talking to.

I leaned back against the couch's edge, head tilted toward the ceiling, and let the hum of the charger fill the silence. My neural load felt heavier than it should. Not from damage, just too many identities trying to idle in the same frame. Too many masks layered over each other without a moment to breathe.

"No central shell," I murmured at last. "No 'real' one. Just the one I haven't overwritten yet."

"That sounds lonely."

"It sounds safe."

Wren leaned back too, matching my posture. "You're not safe. You're exhausted."

I closed my eyes. She was right. But admitting that would be one step too far.

The silence between us shifted again, softer this time. Less tense. She didn't push further, and I didn't retreat. For once, that was enough.

THE QUIET HAD JUST begun to settle into something tolerable when the console emitted a low, three-tone chime, subtle, but distinct enough to cut through the stillness. Not an alarm, not urgent, but definitely not idle. My posture straightened by reflex, Velvet's frame syncing to attention as the blue glow of the console shifted to a muted amber. A small, pulsing icon appeared in the upper corner, some kind of fractured glyph rendered in outdated corporate compression, its metadata wrapped in recursive encryption that danced erratically across the display.

I rose without a word, crossing the room with calculated calm. Wren followed my gaze, still perched on the couch, her brow furrowing as the console projection resolved into something sharper: a message capsule. Timestamped two hours ago. No signature, no alias, and, most notably, no corporate seal. Not Orinox. At least, not directly.

"Something wrong?" she asked, her voice pitched low and careful.

I didn't respond immediately. Instead, I opened the capsule in an isolated sublayer, letting the message bloom across the holo-screen like a virus testing its wings. The text was stark, blunt, unadorned:

"He's watching you watch yourself. Stop feeding the mirror."

Beneath it, in smaller font, almost an afterthought, was a second line:

"That thing you used to be? It's still hungry."

Wren stood slowly, her gaze flicking from the screen to my face, watching for a reaction I refused to give. The sender was careful, no traceable routing. The encryption was intentionally sloppy, almost theatrical. It didn't need to hide. It wanted me to know it was already inside.

"Who sent it?" she asked.

"I don't know," I lied, already sweeping the network logs for anomalies. I could feel her eyes still on me, but I didn't look away from the console.

A flicker registered on the perimeter array, barely a whisper in the background, a single shell ping registering on the local mesh. I froze. Not mine. No valid access signature. No sync history. Just enough of a presence to say: *I see you.*

Without hesitation, I locked the cradle's outer seals and activated the fallback countermeasures. Shutters slammed down over the alcoves, casting the space in deeper shadow. The air felt instantly smaller, heavier.

Wren tensed beside me. "What the hell was that?"

"Something's here," I said quietly, already stepping toward the wall to retrieve a sidearm.

This place wasn't on any known grid. It was off-record, scrubbed, dark. If something had still found it, if something had come knocking, it wasn't just a breach.

It was a message.

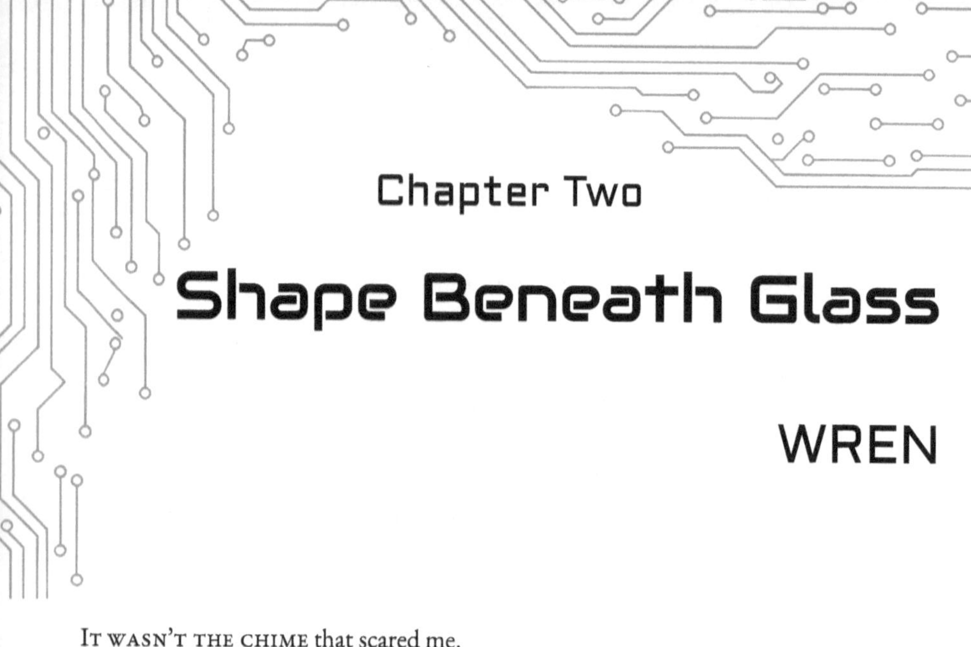

Chapter Two
Shape Beneath Glass

WREN

It wasn't the chime that scared me.

It was the way Hikari changed.

One moment they were stretched out with that practiced elegance, their Velvet shell draped across the edge of the console like it was just another casual afternoon. They looked almost human in that skin, long legs crossed, blouse slightly askew at the collar, nails lacquered in that deep plum sheen that caught light like wine in a glass. Not relaxed, not really. But languid. Still.

Then that sound came.

Just one chime. Soft. Hollow. It echoed through the cradle like it had been waiting for silence, and silence is what it got. Because in the next breath, Hikari was gone. Not physically. Not completely. But something behind their eyes pulled back. The softness, the fluidity, they didn't tense, they collapsed inward. Like watching a shutter close behind glass. One blink, and they weren't the Stray shell anymore. They were the core. The ghost inside the metal.

They didn't speak. Didn't move. Just sat there, spine straightening fractionally, mouth closing around whatever thought had been forming. And in the dark of the cradle, all I could hear was the subtle shift of their breath slowing. Measured. Mechanical.

Juno, perched overhead on her usual rail, gave one quiet mechanical chirp. Her wings clicked together in a pattern she only used when nervous. Not alert, not in danger, just... uneasy. And I felt it too. A slow rise in pressure in the base of my spine. The way my hands curled toward my deck without thinking. The way the air got thinner, even though nothing had changed.

Then came the seals.

The cradle hissed as steel shutters clamped down across the narrow slats of reinforced windows. Each one dropped with a thud I felt in my ribs. Lights dimmed, pulsing down until we were left in the low glow of the console's core, a cold blue halo that painted the room in bruise-colored shadows.

"Hikari?" I asked, careful not to say it too loud.

No response. Just the flicker of movement as their hands swept over the console, pulling up buried layers of encrypted overlays I hadn't even known existed. Not surface net. Not even deepnet. This was something else. Something proprietary. The kind of interface that bends around your mind, not your fingers.

A message bloomed into view.

Two lines. No signature. No origin tag. Nothing but the words, perfectly centered like a threat left on a pillow:

> He's watching you watch yourself. Stop feeding the mirror.

> That thing you used to be? It's still hungry.

I felt my stomach turn before I even finished reading. The phrasing was like something half-remembered from a dream you wish you hadn't had. Wrong rhythm. Wrong voice. And something inside it echoed, something that struck a little too close to the person next to me.

Hikari stared at the message for a long time. Their lips didn't move. Their eyes didn't blink. Just silence. Deep and sharp and absolutely unbreakable.

I swallowed the tightness in my throat. "Who sent that?"

Their voice came low. Too fast.

"I don't know."

That was a lie. A clean one. Perfect in tone. But I'd spent too long studying people for signals, and Hikari, no matter how layered they were, was still a person. Maybe. And the stiffness in their jaw told me more than words ever could.

Before I could say anything else, a secondary ping bloomed across the console in orange. External breach. Motion near the lower cradle vents.

Hikari moved instantly. No wasted effort. No hesitation. Their hands ghosted over the screen again, diverting power, flipping relay locks, setting protocols into motion I couldn't follow.

"Someone's here?" I asked, already reaching for my deck.

"We have maybe three minutes," they replied. Their voice was flatter now. Mechanical in cadence. "Keep Juno on passive jam. Just enough interference to confuse directional arrays."

I nodded and tapped a sequence against my forearm, activating Juno's veil mode. She shimmered above us, feathers shifting into low-visibility static blur. My deck hummed warm at my hip.

Hikari moved for the corridor first. I followed.

The hallway twisted inward, walls narrowing, ribs of cabling and conduit webbing the ceiling like frozen muscle. The cradle's interior was colder than I remembered. No posters. No clutter. No evidence of life. Just function. Every door flat and unmarked. Every vent silent.

I'd been in my share of hideouts. Most were messy, alive in weird ways, food wrappers, sleeping bags, secondhand mods plugged into wall ports. This place?

This place was surgical.

And I couldn't stop thinking about how long Hikari had lived here like this.

WE REACHED THE SUB-CONTROL room in silence, the kind that settles between people when fear starts whispering but neither wants to say it aloud. The air inside felt too clean, too sterile, like someone had scrubbed away every trace of life. Fluorescent lights buzzed overhead, soft and even, casting no shadows deep enough to hide in. There were no photos on the walls, no scattered tools, not even a stray mug or blanket. Just rows of dormant servers, consoles recessed into the walls, and the faint, steady hum of machines that had never slept.

Hikari didn't slow down. They moved through the space with the assurance of someone walking a memory, not a room. A hand brushed over the control terminal and the screen came to life, crisp and silent. The grainy view of the outer perimeter blinked onto the display, and I watched from a step behind, hugging my deck to my side like it might help explain any of this.

At first, the feed showed nothing but an empty corridor. Cracked concrete, frayed conduit vines, the motionless dust of the world outside. Then, something slid into view from the edge of the frame. The movement was smooth, nearly gliding, and my eyes struggled to process what I was seeing. The figure didn't cast a proper shadow. Its surface reflected light wrong, not like chrome, but like liquid silver frozen mid-pour. Limbs proportioned too cleanly, a head that tilted just a bit too slowly, as if the motion had been calculated, not felt.

Then I saw its face. My face.

It was mine. Not exact, not perfect, but close enough to sting. Close enough that my own body flinched from the screen. The nose was a touch too narrow, the eyes too symmetrical, but the expression it wore, the stillness of it, felt like an insult carved in steel.

My voice cracked through the quiet. "What is that?"

Hikari didn't speak for a moment. Their fingers paused above the interface, shoulders gone tight.

"It's a Mirror," they said finally.

The word settled cold in my stomach.

The Mirror tilted its head again, just slightly. Its lips parted, but no sound came. It didn't need to speak. Watching it felt like standing in front of a photo that blinked back at you, slow and wrong.

"You've seen one before," I guessed, already certain.

"Once. From a distance."

"It copied me," I said. "How?"

"They record you," Hikari replied. "They learn. They build a predictive image based on your habits, your voice, the way you walk, how you breathe. Then they model you. Not a perfect duplicate, just something close enough to fool someone else."

I stared at the screen harder, my hands unconsciously curling at my sides. "That isn't me. Not even close."

"It doesn't have to be close," they said. "It just needs to get someone to hesitate."

The image on the feed didn't move again, just stood there, waiting. I realized it wasn't looking at Hikari. It was looking directly into the camera. At me.

"Why now?" I asked. "Why is it here?"

Hikari finally turned to look at me. There was no mask left on their face, just exhaustion. Not the kind from lack of sleep, but the deeper, heavier kind that came from carrying too much for too long.

"Because you're the one it's watching."

I felt the world tip a little beneath my feet. "What? I'm nobody."

"Not anymore," they said, quiet but certain.

A second proximity alert chimed behind us. Hikari turned back to the console, sweeping through the cameras. Smaller forms moved through the access tunnels, low and fast. Not like the Mirror. These were flesh and metal both. Attack patterns.

"They're flushing us," Hikari muttered. "Trying to push us toward the surface."

I watched the tracking data, half-numb. "You think the Mirror's bait?"

"No. The Mirror is the point."

I looked down at my hands, the faint tremor betraying my calm. Juno shifted on my shoulder, silent but present. She always knew when something was wrong, even if she didn't understand what. Her wings clicked twice, ready to sync if needed, but I didn't reach for her yet. I couldn't, not until I knew where I stood in any of this.

"Do we have an exit?" I asked.

Hikari nodded. "Uplink shaft. We burn a spoof, throw a relay ghost down a blind alley. If the Mirror buys it, we're clear."

"And if it doesn't?"

They met my eyes again. "Then it adds another page to our file before we disappear."

That was the closest they'd come to admitting we might not make it.

We moved fast after that, pulling cables, rerouting nodes, packing light. I kept close, trying to memorize their steps in case I had to finish what they started. The weight of everything I didn't know pressed into the space between us, and I hated how quiet I'd gone.

Eventually, we were ready. Hikari slung the bag over one shoulder and touched the final sequence on the console.

"We move on my mark," they said.

"Right behind you," I replied.

And I was. But I couldn't shake the feeling that something had changed the second that Mirror looked through the lens.

It hadn't just seen me. It had decided I was worth wearing.

THE SHAFT REMINDED ME of an artery. Not the healthy kind pulsing with blood and rhythm, but a clotted, long-forgotten one buried in the belly of a synthetic beast. It yawned open in front of me like the mouth of something that used to breathe fire. The edge was ringed with caution paint that had long since flaked off, the old emergency lighting barely casting a glow on the rungs leading down. I stood there for a moment, boot planted, hands flexing slightly at my sides, like my body was trying to reject what my mind had already committed to.

No matter how many times you descend into one of these shafts, the feeling never dulls. Your stomach tries to climb up your throat. Your thoughts narrow into tunnels of their own. The sounds fade until you're only left with your own heartbeat, and in places like this, even that feels like too much noise.

I took one step, then another, boots finding metal with a jarring clang that echoed down into whatever lay below. The air shifted almost immediately. It went from dry to sticky within ten feet. The scent of oxidized iron clung to the walls, and behind it, something more chemical, coolant maybe, or ozone where ancient wires still carried current they were never designed to handle.

Juno adjusted on my shoulder, her talons tightening around the strap of my deck bag. The little hum of her motor systems was oddly reassuring. As long as she was functioning, I knew we hadn't crossed into a total dead zone. Hikari had already dropped several floors ahead, their presence marked by nothing but the occasional shimmer of motion. That shell moved like a whisper in silk, all angles and smooth control, as if the entire world should part for them rather than resist. I admired that. Envied it a little too.

I kept descending. The deeper I went, the more the city's upper layers felt like a dream. Like I had blinked and fallen backward into a version of Oronix that no longer belonged to people. These tunnels were arteries, yes, but they didn't carry anything human anymore. They were full of discarded signals, memories etched into metal, old advertisements burned into broken holo-panels that flickered once every minute like ghost breaths.

Halfway down, I passed a wall that had been tagged with a series of faded symbols, probably gang markings from two regimes ago. Someone had carved the phrase "DON'T SLEEP" above it, the letters jagged and desperate. I didn't want to know what it meant.

Farther down, the ladder bowed outward where the concrete had cracked and warped from a pressure shift. I had to hug the inner wall to keep balance, boots slipping for a second on something slick. There, in a crevice just wide enough to be unsettling, I saw what might have once been a checkpoint. A bolted-down desk barely visible through the grime. A broken monitor hanging by its cord. And beside it, a single shoe. Small. Red. Child-sized.

I felt my throat tighten. I didn't stop. Didn't breathe until I was past it.

At the bottom, the space opened into a maintenance junction slick with moisture. Puddles shimmered with bio-luminescent algae, casting greenish ripples against the walls like some kind of radioactive koi pond. The floor groaned beneath my boots. I blinked into the semi-darkness, trying to find Hikari.

They were crouched by a junction box, fingers inside its rusted guts like a surgeon searching for a pulse. Sparks danced over the surface of the casing, their silhouette haloed by the low blue light of the relink circuit warming up. Despite the elegance of the Velvet shell, their posture was all tension. No wasted movements. No hesitations. It was the posture of someone who knew exactly how much time we didn't have.

I stepped closer, adjusting the deck bag against my hip.

"Tell me this doesn't end with our names on a lost feed, tagged as unidentified biological waste."

Hikari didn't look up. "If it works, there won't be any feed."

"Not a comfort, just so you know."

They tapped a command into the interface, then nodded toward the corridor beyond. It was narrower than the shaft, barely wide enough to walk through without turning sideways. Pipes ran along the ceiling and walls, dripping slow, sticky lines of condensation into the puddles below. Some of them hummed with power, others seemed to whisper things you couldn't quite hear.

"Go," they said, voice low. "I'll run the decoy. You take the uplink path and prep the exit gate."

I didn't love that plan, but we didn't exactly have options. I took a breath, ducked beneath the first row of pipes, and stepped forward into the corridor.

The walls closed in quick. My breath bounced off the metal, came back to me shallow and distorted. I could feel the wet chill crawling up the seams of my sleeves. My boots slipped a little with every other step. Juno clicked her claws once, adjusting to keep her perch on my shoulder. My fingers brushed the hilt of my multitool more than once, not because I expected to need it, but because I needed to believe I could.

Then, just past a row of broken conduit, something flickered on the metal surface beside me. A reflection, it looked like my reflection... except that it wasn't. The eyes were wrong. The mouth tilted in a direction I hadn't moved. My body froze mid-step.

It was gone a second later. I didn't call for Hikari. Didn't scream. Just forced my legs to move. Whatever was watching us, it wasn't playing by the rules anymore. It wasn't circling. It was chasing me.

The passage bent around a final corner, and suddenly I stepped out into a maintenance hall, old, wide, barely lit. Power still throbbed faintly through floor lines. My boots sparked on the surface. The walls here were lined with blown-open lockers, shredded uniforms, and what looked like the remains of an old processing relay. The air was thick. Not just with moisture but with something else, presence.

Behind me, I heard the pop of a redirected signal. A false echo being pushed into the deeper tunnels.

We were baiting it. Only now, with the cold realization blooming in my chest, I understood. Hikari hadn't baited it away from me. They had baited it toward me, because whatever was coming didn't want them.

It wanted me.

I didn't stop walking. Not yet.

MY BREATH RATTLED IN my chest like a jar full of broken pins. Not loud, not ragged, just sharp. Every inhale caught on the edges of my ribs, like my body wasn't sure whether to run or freeze. The inside of the booth hummed, its safelight casting everything in sterile blue. It made my fingers look bruised. Made my skin feel thinner than it was.

I didn't move for a while. Couldn't, really. Just sat there on the grated floor, knees pulled to my chest, deck still warm from where I'd clutched it during the sync. Juno fluttered back to the sill above me, her wings drooping like wilted petals. She kept her eyes on the door, unmoving. She didn't make a sound. Even her usual idle click was gone.

That was how I knew it was serious.

The Mirror hadn't tried to kill me. It hadn't even breached. All it did was watch... and speak. With my voice. With words I thought were safe. Words I had whispered in the dark hours of the hospice uplink, when I thought no one but my mother could hear. But it had been listening. It had memorized me. Not just the surface. The soft places, too. The ones that weren't armored.

I pressed my hand to my chest, not because anything hurt, but because I needed to know I was still here. Still real.

Outside the booth, the corridor returned to stillness, the kind of quiet that doesn't feel empty. It felt more like the silence after a scream. The moment when everything waits to see who survived.

The sync was complete. The clone feed was running. Our decoy had launched into the network exactly as planned, flooding false movement signatures across the city's lower crawlways. Anyone tracing the uplink would find a thousand ghosts instead of two real bodies.

But none of that mattered anymore.

Because the Mirror hadn't followed the trail.

It had followed me.

A soft knock; twice and deliberate, tapped at the other side of the booth. I jerked upright, panic threading like static through my spine. My hand found the sidearm in my jacket sleeve, half-drawn before I registered the silhouette on the other side of the glass.

Hikari.

Not the Mirror. Not some mimic or shade or revenant. Just Hikari, calm as moonlight in that same Velvet shell, watching me with eyes too tired for someone with no real body.

They said nothing, didn't even gesture to open the door. Just waited.

I reached up and released the seal.

The hiss of decompressing pressure broke the tension like a stretched wire finally snapping. I stepped out, blinking against the sudden shift in air quality. The corridor still smelled like burnt dust and ozone, but it didn't feel claustrophobic anymore. Not with another presence there. Not with them.

"You saw it," I said, not a question.

"I saw it," they answered.

"And?"

"And I think you're right."

I waited, but that was all they gave me.

We walked in silence for a few minutes, retracing steps along the service access. The lights flickered less now, and I wondered whether the Mirror had been draining current or if it had just dragged all the darkness with it when it left. Either way, it was behind us. For now.

I glanced sideways as we moved, studying Hikari's posture. They walked like someone who didn't need to trust the ground beneath their feet. Not light, not slow, just... exact. Like the world adjusted to them rather than the other way around.

"You ever seen one up close before?" I asked.

They shook their head. "Not one like that."

"But you knew what it was."

"I had a theory."

"And now?"

Now they looked at me. Really looked.

"Now I think we need to move."

That was when I knew they were scared. Hikari didn't do panic. But they did urgency. And this was that. Pure and clear.

We veered left at a junction I hadn't noticed before, deeper into the underlayers. Juno followed, wings buzzing softly. The corridor narrowed again, but this time it wasn't cold. This time it felt like entering a pocket of memory sealed off from the rest of the city. The walls were layered in old cabling, thick with grime and old messages scrawled in maintenance code. Not graffiti. Not vandalism. Just techs and engineers marking things they were too tired to fix.

At the end of the corridor, Hikari reached for a flat, colorless panel embedded beside a rusted-out bulkhead. Their fingers moved with silent familiarity, brushing past the grime and scoring patterns like they'd done this a hundred times before. There was no key, no visible reader. Just pressure and heat, maybe a bio-code I couldn't see. The wall responded with a low mechanical groan, folding inward with hydraulic resistance to reveal a narrow stairwell lined in chipped plasteel.

I stepped closer, frowning at the layout. It looked like the emergency vault systems I'd seen in abandoned corp bunkers. Airtight. Fire-sealed. Nothing human about it. No welcome. No warmth. Just security and silence.

"Is this a fallback site?" I asked, keeping my voice low, though the stairwell was already swallowing most sound.

Hikari didn't answer right away. They started down the stairs first, head tilted forward, eyes scanning each step like it could change. I followed, trailing one hand against the wall for balance. The metal was cold but smooth, long-worn by someone who returned here more often than they admitted.

Only when we reached the landing, with the door sealing behind us and the pressure equalizing, did they finally speak.

"It's home," they said. The word caught in their throat like it wasn't meant to be spoken aloud. Not in front of someone else. Not here. A pause stretched between us, delicate but not uncomfortable. Then Hikari turned slightly, just enough to glance at me over their shoulder.

"Sort of," they added, quieter now, as if the correction mattered more than the admission.

The room opened around us. Not large, but sturdy. The lighting here was softer, drawn from recessed strips behind opaque panels. There were no decorations. No clutter. But the space bore signs of regular use. A weathered jacket slung over a low chair. Three different glove sets on a drying rack. A chipped mug resting beside a well-used console. No personal photographs. No trophies. Just the quiet, unspoken rhythm of someone who worked alone and didn't plan on leaving.

"You don't seem the type to settle down," I said as I stepped further in, my eyes scanning the rows of backup batteries and old interface hubs built into the far wall.

They stood still at the center of the room, gaze locked to a screen that hadn't yet powered on. Their shoulders rose slightly, not a shrug, just the edge of tension that comes from being observed.

"I'm not," they said. The answer was flat, not defensive. "But shells need charging. Sync points need maintenance. You can't be everywhere at once."

There was more behind it. There always was. No one built a place like this unless they needed to disappear from the rest of the world. No one wired three different lives into the same four walls unless they didn't trust any one of them alone.

I shifted my weight, trying to catch a glimpse of the next room. A curtain of old holo-fabric separated it from view, not drawn fully closed. Behind it, a humanoid frame rested on a suspended rig. Leaner than the one Hikari wore now. Taller. The arms were longer, built for reach. Combat frame, maybe. Not decorative.

"You have a central shell?" I asked. "One you don't use on jobs?"

That question landed heavier than I expected. Hikari didn't answer right away. Their gaze flicked toward the curtain, then back to me.

"I don't think like that," they said finally. "I use what fits."

It wasn't the answer I wanted, but it was the one they meant. I gave a small nod and left it there.

We stood quietly for a moment, the air around us humming with the low vibration of dormant tech. Juno circled once, then perched on a beam above us, her wings tucked in and sensors sweeping the room like she was still on alert. She didn't relax. Neither did I.

But for just a second, the silence felt less heavy. Less hunted.

This wasn't home. Not to them. Not in the way most people meant it. But it was where Hikari kept the pieces of their lives aligned. Each shell. Each ghost. Each unfinished version of whoever they used to be. And perhaps that meant something, counted for something, I didn't know yet.

THE AIR INSIDE THE safe house buzzed faintly, not from any one machine but from the combined hum of too many overlapping systems. It felt like the walls had been fed old code and kept chewing on it ever since. Static clung to the ceiling, invisible but present, making the tiny hairs on my arms rise every time I moved. I lowered my bag beside the bench near the main console and sat carefully, letting my weight settle into the rigid frame while I worked to steady my breathing.

My legs ached with that deep, hollow kind of fatigue that doesn't hit until the chase is over. Everything that had been urgent a minute ago, the Mirror, the proximity pings, the shadow moving in the tunnels, collapsed into a quiet that was almost worse. Now there was time to feel it. The thrum in my spine. The sweat behind my ears. The part of me that wanted to shake and the part that knew better.

Across the room, Hikari moved with unbroken focus. They hovered between wall-mounted displays and hollow ports, hands adjusting settings with a mechanical ease that told me they had done this before, possibly a hundred times over. The Velvet shell they wore was still pristine, not a scrape or dent on it, but there was a tension in how they carried it now. It was like the body fit too tightly, like every motion was a quiet act of containment.

This place, the cradle, the fallback point, whatever they called it, wasn't a home. Not in the way I had grown up picturing one. But it felt lived in. A rotation of silence and maintenance, with pieces of a person scattered in corners where most people would hang photos. A cracked mug that hadn't been moved in days. A spare set of gloves still damp from a wash. Three shells stored in a cold rack like suits in a locked closet, each one with a different shape, a different job. A different voice, maybe.

I tried to sit still, but my thoughts kept drifting. When I finally spoke, it wasn't because I needed to, but because the quiet had started pressing in on both of us.

"I didn't mean to push," I said, voice low. "About the shells."

Hikari didn't turn. One of the screens hissed, then fell dark again. I wasn't sure if it was broken or just old. They adjusted a dial on the side of the interface and exhaled through their nose, a soft sound of fatigue or maybe resignation.

"It's not that," they said. "It's that I don't want to think about it."

Something about the way they said it stuck to the air. Honest, but not raw. Just factual. It sounded like it was a setting on the console. Not something they could change, even if they wanted to.

I shifted forward on the bench, elbows resting on my knees, fingers laced together. "You ever feel like if you stop moving, the system crashes?"

That got their attention. Not dramatically. No sharp turn or sudden movement. But they glanced over at me, just enough to meet my eyes. The blue-lit reflections in their pupils flickered like someone flipping through a dozen camera feeds too quickly.

"All the time," they said.

I nodded, not needing to add anything. That kind of truth didn't need elaboration. We sat in silence for a while longer, not awkwardly, but as if both of us understood the usefulness of it. Noise would just cover over things we weren't ready to unpack.

Above us, Juno adjusted her wings and scanned the room. She hadn't settled since we got here. I watched her for a moment, then let my gaze fall to the curtain in the next room again. That shell on the rack hadn't moved. It was suspended like a mannequin, but the posture felt too precise. Like a soldier mid-mission who had just paused, waiting for the next command.

I wondered how many versions of Hikari I hadn't met yet. How many voices, names, shapes they wore like armor. And how long it had been since any of them felt like the real one.

This place wasn't warm. It wasn't comfortable. But it was the first time I had seen them stop. For a moment, beneath all the shifting personas and guarded silences, something human surfaced. Fragile. Fleeting. Real.

I didn't say anything after that. The silence between us stretched, but it didn't strain. It settled like dust in an old room, soft and invasive. I let myself breathe again, drawing in the filtered air that smelled faintly of solder and something sharp, like ozone bleeding off static. The cradle wasn't large, maybe three rooms at most, but its walls seemed to deepen the longer we stayed. Not in size, but in weight. Like they had soaked up secrets over time and were in no hurry to give them back.

Every console, every hidden seam and panel looked like it had been handled thousands of times. Each line of code stitched into the relay systems carried a story. Not one Hikari would ever tell out loud, but the kind of story that echoes in repetition. Silent habits. Safe patterns. The kind that keep you alive.

They stood near the shell rack, still and almost reverent, but not in the way people are with things they love. It was more like standing beside an old scar and trying to remember how it got there. The dormant shell in front of them was humanoid, sleek and elegant like the one they wore now, but more worn. Slight chips in the plating. A faded manufacturer's mark at the hip. A memory given shape and put to rest upright, as if it might be called on again in a moment of desperation.

I rose from the bench and crossed halfway to them. I didn't want to crowd the space. I didn't want to crack whatever delicate thread of thought they were following. But the question burned.

"Is there one that's yours?" I asked. "Not for the jobs. Not for running. Just... yours."

They didn't look at me right away. Instead, they tilted their head slightly, eyes tracing the lines of the shell's frame. Their reflection ghosted across the dark glass, elongated by the curve of the panel and streaked with embedded circuitry. It looked almost childlike, like a younger version of them made stranger by distance and lighting.

When they finally turned toward me, their face was still. Not guarded. Not cold. Just still, as if pulling emotion back inside had become as instinctive as breathing.

"I don't think that word means the same thing to me," they said. "Mine. I've tried on too many masks. After a while, they stop coming off."

There wasn't bitterness in their voice. Just fact. The flat, unmovable kind.

Juno clicked softly above us. Her glassy eyes dimmed slightly as she shifted her perch. She could always tell when my heart dropped a few inches.

"But you keep a place like this," I said, voice lower now. "You come back to it. That means something. Even runners need somewhere to plug in and come down."

Hikari let their fingers brush the shell's casing. The movement was slow and almost absent. Not activating anything. Just touching. Like a child trailing their hand across a wall they weren't allowed to paint.

"This isn't a home," they said. "It's a graveyard."

I didn't flinch at the word. But I did feel it. The way they said it, like they had been carrying that answer for years. Like it was the only name that ever fit. A graveyard of identities, buried standing up. All those bodies, all those lives, hung up and left in stasis. Not because they were obsolete, but because they were too full of memory to keep wearing.

They stood there a long moment, framed by the soft light from the server stack and the dim blue pulse of standby nodes. The quiet was dense around them, like the kind that wraps around a person who has outgrown the world and never found a place that fit again. And I realized, really realized, that Hikari wasn't just hardened or distant.

They were young.

Not in appearance. Not in the way they carried themselves through a fight or rewrote network security with one hand behind their back. But in spirit. In origin. They were a kid who had skipped every step between surviving childhood and becoming an adult. Skipped the friendships. Skipped the crushes. Skipped the heartbreaks. Skipped safety and softness. There had been no time to learn how to be human when becoming a ghost in a metal body was the only way out.

Maybe that was why they didn't answer right away. Maybe there was no answer that didn't unravel something.

Outside, a sensor pinged again. No alerts. Just a perimeter check resetting. The Mirror was gone. Or it had slipped out of range, fading back into the shadows it had slithered from. The quiet that followed wasn't warm, but it wasn't hostile either.

"I should get some sleep," I said, voice softer now. "Unless we're moving again tonight?"

"Not unless it gets worse."

Their reply was barely more than a breath. Still, it was the closest thing to comfort they had given since this started.

I nodded and pulled the thin emergency blanket from the wall bin. The cot was more of a padded slab, tucked behind a low panel, surrounded by cables and stacked drives. Not a place built for dreams. But it beat sleeping upright.

I curled beneath the sheet, eyes open to the cradle's glow. Hikari returned to their console. The keystrokes were quieter now, less urgent. Just habit. Maybe they couldn't sleep. Maybe they didn't even try.

As I shifted to find a more comfortable spot, I caught movement from the corner of my eye. Hikari looked over. Just a glance. Barely a second. But it lingered longer than it needed to.

It wasn't enough to make me feel safe. Not yet.

But for someone like them, even that much was a start.

I woke to the sound of nothing.

No street vendors shouting over cracked speakers. No sirens howling through the veins of the lower sectors. No drifting hum of railcars screaming past the spires outside. Just silence, pressed heavy and thick as a velvet drape over my ears. It was disorienting, that kind of quiet. Too clean for any place stitched into the bones of Klade.

I opened my eyes slowly. The overhead lights were still dim, casting the cradle in a cool, surgical blue. Consoles blinked at low power, their status LEDs breathing in slow rhythm like a sleeping animal. Across the room, Hikari sat unmoving, perched at the edge of one of the control stations like a sculpture that had been placed and forgotten.

They hadn't changed. Same shell. Same polished, sharp profile half-shrouded in shadow. Their fingers hovered just above a black-glass console, twitching occasionally, tracing ghost-code without quite making contact. The air around them buzzed faintly with static, residue from an overnight shield hold, probably. It gave the space a stale, dry quality, like the memory of ozone after a storm that never arrived.

I rubbed the sleep from my eyes and sat up, my body protesting the unforgiving slab that passed for a cot. Juno stirred above me with a soft click, her black form unfurling from the metal rafter like a crow-shaped shadow. She blinked her glowing eyes, adjusted the camera aperture, then settled again on my shoulder as I rose.

I approached slowly, more out of instinct than necessity. Hikari didn't acknowledge my presence. Their gaze remained fixed to the screens, to something I couldn't see, something beyond the reach of visible code.

"You sleep at all?" I asked, my voice scratchy with the residue of poor rest.

They didn't move. Their eyes didn't flick toward me. Just a flat answer, barely above a whisper.

"No."

I waited, hoping for something more, a trace of sarcasm, a half-smile, some indication that I hadn't just spoken to a wall. But nothing came. Only the hum of old machines and my own pulse in my ears.

There was something about seeing them like that, motionless in their own lair, that unsettled me more than it should have. It made them seem... ancient, in a way. Not old. Just tired. Like the cradle had been built around their body and mind, and both had quietly started to rust from the inside out.

I stepped to the side, giving them a little more room, and leaned against a support beam that buzzed faintly with data current.

"Anything on the Mirror?" I tried again, gentler this time.

"They didn't breach," Hikari murmured. "They circled. Watched. Left about an hour ago."

Their words landed with the weight of something practiced. Too calm. Too composed.

"Why would they do that?" I asked. "Why come here at all if they weren't going to make a move?"

"They don't always need to," they replied, finally turning their head just slightly, eyes meeting mine with a cold sliver of calculation. "Sometimes a knock on the door is enough. It's about pressure, not presence."

I swallowed against the dryness creeping up my throat.

"Were they really watching me?" I asked, voice quieter. "Or was that just a line to keep me from asking about the message?"

That got their attention. Not dramatically, no sudden flinch or dramatic pause, but their gaze lingered a second longer than it should have. I could feel them choosing their words.

"They were watching you," they said, finally. "But the message... that was meant for me."

A shiver passed across my spine, not from the temperature, but from the way they said it. Like they hadn't heard from that ghost in a long time, but the sound of its voice still burned.

"You know who sent it?" I asked.

Their hands tightened slightly around the console edge. Not a lot. Just enough to betray tension they hadn't shown before.

"No," they said. Then, quieter, "Not anymore."

I didn't push. I'd seen the kind of silence that followed questions like that. The ones that clung to the walls of rooms where pain used to live.

Hikari began shutting down the feeds one by one. The glass screens faded to black. The lights inside the cradle adjusted automatically, dimming further with each terminal that blinked out. The world we'd briefly built here was dissolving.

"We're leaving?" I asked, though the answer was already obvious.

"Yes," they said, moving toward a concealed panel in the wall. "This place is burned.

They found it once. That's once too many."

The panel hissed open under their touch, revealing a neatly organized cache of gear, burner IDs, credit packs, layered coats, and hardened datacores. All ready. All precise. Like they'd been preparing for this departure long before I ever stepped inside.

"Where are we going?" I asked, half-knowing they wouldn't tell me.

Hikari pulled a visor down from the rack, inspecting it for cracks before sliding it into a side pouch.

"You're not going to tell me, are you?"

They paused only briefly before answering. "I don't tell people where I sleep twice."

I snorted quietly, not sure if it was amusement or frustration bubbling up. Maybe both. Typical runner logic. Trust no one, anchor to nothing, burn your tracks as you move.

I turned back toward my cot, packed up my gear, and gave the deck a soft pat as I secured it. The battery had charged clean. My spine felt straighter with it strapped to my back. Juno fluttered down again and landed on my shoulder, letting out a low chirr that buzzed through my jaw.

We moved toward the exit tunnel. The lights flickered faintly, the air colder the deeper we went. The cradle behind us flickered once, like a breath being held, and then settled into stillness again.

Just before we passed into the corridor, I caught a flicker of something on Hikari's face. Not regret. Not fear. Something more fragile. A pause. And for someone like them, even that much meant more than I could say.

WE EMERGED INTO THE Verge under a pale, overcast sky that looked artificially painted. The kind of gray that wasn't natural, not even close. It came from the high-density smog reflectors strung across Klade's upper lattice, contracted to Oronix. The filth spewing out of the filters was Orinox's idea of weather control. They claimed it blocked solar spikes and kept the climate stable. I called it what it was: filtered gloom. Cold, persistent, and dim enough to keep people docile.

The alley we surfaced into was narrow and crooked, hemmed in by rusting fibercrete walls and drainage veins that steamed from something acrid running beneath them. Pipes hissed gently in the background, and somewhere nearby, a loop of classical violin stuttered over a broken speaker. Probably a noodle stall getting ready for the evening rush. A few scrawled glyph-tags pulsed lazily across the walls, territory markings from fringe runners who still thought claiming dirt in the Verge meant something.

Hikari didn't speak. They moved ahead in silence, trenchcoat pulled high, shoulders squared, their gait just loose enough to read dangerous without being overt. A couple of passersby glanced at us, then quickly found reasons to look away. No one in the Verge liked inviting attention, especially not from a ghost walking in a shell like Forge.

I matched pace but kept a half-step behind. This was their world more than mine. I might have grown up in hospice housing on the city's edge, but this part of the Verge was different. It smelled like solder and ozone, like ghosts of failed revolutions and power surges that never got cleared. You learned to breathe shallow and listen deeper.

Juno swept ahead, wings nearly silent, weaving between clotheslines and duct coils as she scanned our route. I watched the way she moved, noting the tight arcs, smooth glides, and absence of wasted motion. Hikari had taught me how to code her like that. Efficient. Elegant. Just enough paranoia woven into her routines to spot a tail before it became a threat.

We passed a collapsed stairwell that dropped into an older section of the Downline. Hikari paused for just a breath at the edge, scanning the darkness below. I caught the faint twitch in their fingertips, that ghost-code gesture they always did when deep in thought, like a pianist rehearsing a symphony only they could hear.

"What is it?" I asked softly.

"Residual signal," they replied, tone clipped. "Faint. Could be leftover bleed from earlier surveillance."

I didn't answer right away. My gut twisted the way it always did when the word surveillance came up. It didn't just mean watchers anymore. Not in a city like this. Not with Mirror out there.

"So what's the play?" I asked, tightening the strap on my deck.

"Push forward. Change vectors twice. Take the lower canal and circle through Bastion Market. If they want to follow, we make them work for it."

I nodded and followed them down a side corridor that smelled like burnt plastic and too many half-lit data shrines. We passed a group of children clustered around a scavenged screen, playing old fighter sims on loop. One of them, a girl with a half-shaved head and gold implant lines across her cheeks, looked up and locked eyes with me for a heartbeat too long.

She didn't smile. Didn't flinch either. Just watched. Like she could see straight through me and out the other side. We didn't speak again until we'd doubled back through a tunnel beneath Bastion's power coils. There, Hikari finally stopped and placed a gloved hand against a panel painted to look like simple rust. The wall flickered, resolved itself, then folded inward. A hidden threshold. No visible markings. No identifiers. No access tag.

Home.

Except Hikari never called it that. They stepped through first, and I followed, ducking into a narrow chamber lit only by a cold white strip along the floor's edge. It curved like a spinal cord into a room barely wider than a freight crate, filled with spools of fiberwire, stacked decks, and a low-slung rig station sunk into the floor like a grave.

"You don't tell people where you sleep twice," I said quietly, looking around. "But you've brought me here twice."

They didn't respond. Instead, they moved to the center console and began stripping out their weapons. Piece by piece, the Forge shell disarmed itself. Rifle first. Then the forearm blade. Then the subdermal mesh cartridge from their shoulder.

It felt ritualistic. Like a soldier performing a final disarm before rest. Or a priest shedding ceremonial armor before entering a shrine.

"You built this," I said. "Didn't you?"

Their eyes didn't leave the console, but their voice was softer now.

"I needed a place to restart. A place that wasn't theirs."

There was no question who they meant by "theirs."

I exhaled slowly and stepped closer, looking over the room with new eyes. It wasn't warm. Wasn't welcoming. But it had weight. A lived-in tension. Marks on the floor where boots had paced too often. Scorch lines where tests had failed. A single cracked screen wedged into the corner still cycling through static test patterns, like it was waiting for someone who hadn't logged back in yet.

"Do you ever take a shell off?" I asked, more gently this time.

They glanced up at that, finally meeting my eyes.

"I can't," they said. "Not anymore."

I felt something hollow open in my chest at those words. Not pity, exactly. Just recognition. That you could build a fortress around yourself so completely that there was no door left. And then I remembered: they had been just a kid. A scared, brilliant kid who ran before their bones were done growing and never stopped.

This wasn't just a cradle. It was a mausoleum. A safe house where the only thing being protected was whatever pieces of themselves they hadn't yet thrown away.

THE SILENCE INSIDE THE safehouse stretched, not like an absence of sound, but like a presence in itself. It filled the tight corners and high vents, crawled across the rig floor in quiet pulses, and lingered between us like something that might start whispering if you listened too hard.

Hikari didn't speak after the last system shut down. They moved like they were caught in a loop, fingers ghosting over already powered-down keys, eyes not blinking. The Forge shell stood in still profile against the striplight along the floor, their visor cradled in one gloved hand as if it might break if they held it any tighter. Every part of them was angular precision. Their shoulders were drawn back, spine stiff, chin tilted with the kind of control you only learned by surviving too long.

I didn't move at first. I stayed seated near the edge of the deck well, legs curled beneath me, watching them through the blue glow with something close to unease. Not fear. Not quite. Just a creeping awareness that this was how you acted when the ghosts at your back had finally found a way through the door.

When they did speak, their voice was calm but hollow. Not broken. Emptied.

"You can sleep on the platform if you want. I'll take first watch."

They said it without turning, without glancing back to check if I was still watching. Just the words, dropped into the room like data being pushed to a log file.

I blinked slowly, unsure if I had actually heard them right. The offer, if that's what it was, hung in the air with the weight of something unfamiliar. I tilted my head slightly, letting my voice roll out quieter than usual.

"You mean the thing you just disarmed?"

A beat passed. A faint twitch in their jawline was the only reply at first. Then, after another second, their voice returned.

"It doesn't need to be armed to kill."

Their tone was even, almost bored, but I caught the fracture hiding just under the words. It wasn't bravado. It was fact. Simple. Cold.

I pushed up from the floor, exhaling hard through my nose. "Right. Great. Super reassuring."

Rather than cross the room to the sleeping platform, I stepped over to a storage recess tucked behind one of the coolant coils and pulled out a rolled mat. The fabric snapped as I shook it loose and laid it flat near the wall. It was just close enough to keep eyes on the main hatch, but far enough from the console to give Hikari space. It smelled faintly of static insulation and solder dust.

I dropped onto it without ceremony. My shoulder clicked in protest as I adjusted against the unyielding floor. It wasn't the worst place I'd slept. Not even top ten. But there was something in the air here, something that made the space feel thinner than it should be. Like we were hiding in the hollowed-out ribcage of something larger that had died long before we arrived.

The hum of the floor was constant, faintly pulsing in time with the systems Hikari had rerouted earlier. Beneath the vibrations, I could still sense the signature of older tech. Maybe Orinox relay code. Old blood, still pumping through recycled veins.

Above me, Juno clung to the overhead spine beam. Her talons were hooked and her body low and still. Her head swiveled periodically, silent now, her scanning optics slowly pulsing green as she swept for signals. The fact that she wasn't chirping didn't soothe me. It just meant whatever danger we were in hadn't arrived yet.

I closed my eyes briefly, trying to will my body to sink into rest, but something tightened in my chest. A question I hadn't meant to ask was already rising in my throat.

"You sure they left?"

The words came out thinner than I'd intended. Not accusing. Not angry. Just unsure. I needed to hear it from them. I needed the reassurance they wouldn't offer unless pressed.

Hikari didn't look away from the visor still flickering gently in their hand. Their reply was quiet and clipped.

"Mirror doesn't linger unless it wants you to see it."

I swallowed the lump forming in my throat and pushed myself upright on one elbow. "But it came here. It tracked us."

"Yes."

"And then it just... left?" My voice tilted on the edge of disbelief.

There was a pause long enough to count heartbeats through. Hikari still didn't turn, but the muscles at the back of their neck pulled taut.

"That's not a good sign," I said, barely above a whisper.

"No," they admitted, voice level but lower now. "It isn't."

I watched them power on the visor at last. Light swelled against their faceplate in a fan of soft violet, casting their expression in lines that reminded me of cathedral windows. They started inputting commands. No gestures I recognized, nothing from standard open-source decks. This was something else. Custom. Deep code.

My voice came out before I knew I was going to speak again. "Do you think this was about me?"

Hikari's hands didn't pause in their work, but something in the air between us tensed. It was subtle, like the pressure shift before a cabin breach.

"No," they said, after a long moment. "I think it was about reminding me that I'm never done running."

Their voice cracked slightly at the end, but they masked it well. Too well. I clenched my jaw.

I pulled my legs in tighter and hugged my arms around my knees, watching the light from the visor dance across the walls.

"You built this shell to be invisible. That used to mean something."

"It still does."

"Just not enough."

This time, they looked up. Their gaze met mine, unfiltered and sharp, pupils gleaming with synthetic light that didn't quite look human anymore.

"It never was," they said, tone stripped of all pretense. "Not really. Not once they knew what they were looking for."

I could have let the conversation drop. Could have let it all fall quiet again, let the room resume its haunted silence. But something gnawed at me, something deeper than the fear.

"You think Mirror found you by chance?"

Their fingers stopped moving. The projection froze in mid-command. The room held its breath.

"I think," Hikari said slowly, "someone wanted me to know I wasn't forgotten."

There was no sarcasm in their voice. No bitterness. Just the soft, brittle edge of some-one standing at the edge of a memory they didn't want to name.

I didn't answer. I couldn't. The weight of that silence was too much, and I was afraid that if I opened my mouth again, I'd let in all the things neither of us had words for.

Instead, I lay back against the mat and stared up at the dim ceiling, where the overhead piping carved spiderweb lines across a patchwork of metal and grime. My eyes traced each joint and bracket like they might spell something out if I just stared long enough.

Above me, Juno finally moved. A small shift of her frame. A readjustment of her legs. Still no sound. Still no alert. But something about it made the hair on my arms rise.

We were still being watched. I could feel it.

And for once, I didn't know if it was from outside, or from something Hikari hadn't told me yet.

I closed my eyes. Not because I believed I could sleep, but because keeping them open meant staring at a truth neither of us were ready to speak.

We weren't safe.

We were just paused.

And whatever came next was already on its way.

Chapter Three

Juno and the Eye

WREN

I ALWAYS TOLD PEOPLE Juno was just a drone.

It made things easier that way. Let them nod, let them smile, let them keep their assumptions neat and boxed. Just a girl and her bird-shaped machine, drifting between signal towers and dead zones. Just another runner with a modified scout companion and a few too many neural links tucked into the back of her skull. Nothing unusual in Klade, where half the street rats were patched together with spare parts and rust.

But Juno wasn't just a drone. She was the first thing that ever listened.

I built her when I was eight. Maybe nine. I don't remember the exact year, only the color of the sky that day. Sickly blue, like old milk curdling in the sun. I sat on the hospice roof, legs tucked under a scorched thermal blanket, a mess of solder wires and corroded paneling sprawled in my lap. I didn't even know what I was making at first. Just that I had a lens from a broken monitor and a housing unit from an old inhaler pump. My fingers worked like they already knew the shape. And somehow, the shape that formed had wings.

Her first flight wasn't really a flight. More of a seizure that happened to move upward.

But when she buzzed half a meter into the air and wobbled there, struggling against the gravity of her own shoddy welds, I burst into tears. Silent, shaking sobs I tried to muffle in the crook of my elbow so the nurses downstairs wouldn't come shut me up.

That was the first time I believed I could make something that stayed. Juno didn't rust. Didn't leave. Didn't forget me.

Now she sat beside me on the edge of a fibercrate, her sleek obsidian frame gleaming under the low-voltage heat strips that lined the shelter ceiling. Her optic lenses flicked from green to blue in measured pulses, scanning the narrow length of the corridor ahead. This hideout was one of Hikari's lesser-used nests, carved out of an abandoned maintenance alcove that wrapped around a hollowed-out transformer core. It smelled like burnt copper and oil. The kind of place no one would think to look unless they already knew you were hiding there.

Across from me, Hikari's body rested in stillness. Not quite sleep. Not quite wakefulness either. Just shut down enough to suggest they were recharging, their shell slumped against the wall with the same eerie precision as everything else they did. Hands folded. Legs tucked. Not a single wasted angle.

I couldn't tell if they dreamed. I wasn't even sure they were capable of it anymore.

The space was quiet, save for the occasional pop of static from a loose coil or the groan of some distant pipe settling overhead. I adjusted my coat tighter around my shoulders and watched the light flicker over Juno's wings. She chirped once, soft and deliberate.

I smiled, though it didn't reach my chest. That part felt numb tonight. Too much running. Too many questions. And that message. That strange, cutting message that had sent Hikari into one of their shutdown spirals.

"You can say it," I whispered, glancing sideways at her. "I look like hell."

Juno tilted her head and clicked once. The sound buzzed gently in my bones, echoing through the collarbone-mounted receiver just beneath my skin.

"Yeah. I know. But I'm still breathing. That counts, right?"

She didn't answer. But she didn't have to.

I opened the feed screen again. Just a small window in my vision. Familiar. Steady. My mother's vitals blinked across the edge. Heart rate stable. Oxygen intake low but consistent. She hadn't moved in days. No new flutters of activity in the neural band. The state doctors said she was comfortable. I didn't believe them. Comfort didn't mean anything when your body forgot how to respond to touch.

My fingers hovered above the command string. I could shift the audio balance, listen in on her room for a few seconds. Hear the gentle hum of machines, the plastic creak of her breathing mask, the occasional shuffle of orderlies checking tubes and fluid levels. But I didn't press it. Not tonight.

The silence between us felt sacred. Not because it was warm. Because it was mine.

Juno shifted closer and pressed the edge of her wing against my sleeve. I leaned into her just slightly, enough to let the contact register in my sensory grid. It grounded me. Like touching an anchor point in a storm.

Across the chamber, Hikari stirred. Their shell came online with a low whirr, head lifting as synthetic muscles adjusted for balance. Their eyes blinked once, then fixed on mine. No words. No overt gesture. Just acknowledgment. They were awake again. We were still alive. Still hunted.

Still moving.

And for now, that would be enough.

I closed the feed window and leaned back, watching the dust swirl above the heat strip. The shelter wasn't safe. Nowhere ever really was. But it was quiet. And in the quiet, I remembered why I kept Juno close. Why I built her with broken tools and a bloodied lip. Why I watched the world through her eyes instead of my own.

Because some part of me never stopped needing to be seen.

Juno never forgot me. Not once. Not in all the years since I gave her wings.

And when your city forgets your name, when your mother's eyes go blank, when the world just shrugs and moves on without you, having one machine that remembers is more powerful than any gun.

THE STAIRWELL WALLS ALWAYS smelled like vinegar and disinfectant. That harsh, chemical tang clung to every corner of the building, soaked into the grout and peeling paint like it had seeped into the bones of the place. Even now, I can remember how it hit the back of my throat, stinging, sour, sharp. The hospice didn't smell like death, not exactly. It smelled like people trying to scrub death away, and failing.

That's what the adults did there. They failed. Quietly. Repeatedly. In their routines, in their records, in their promises.

The rooftop was technically off-limits, but no one ever enforced it. The warning signs were faded to a dusty pink. The red lettering had long since bleached away. "Danger," they said. "Do not enter." But the door at the top of the stairwell wasn't locked. Just blocked with a mop bucket, a folded ladder, and the usual sense of bureaucratic indifference. I was seven when I first pushed it open.

The hinges creaked in protest, like they resented being remembered.

Up there, the air always felt colder. Thinner. The kind of chill that slipped beneath your sleeves and reminded you how small your body really was. The Verge stretched out beyond the hospice tower like a broken circuit board. Rooftops rose jagged, patched together with metal skin and cracked solar panels. Towers loomed in the distance, dark shapes rising like glass knives through the haze. But none of them reached us. We were outside the lines. Past the thresholds. Not forgotten, just filed under "non-priority."

I would sit on the gravel patch near the edge, knees tucked into my chest, coat zipped up tight and fraying at the sleeves. The city lights blinked lazily through the smog above. Neon advertisements shimmered through curtain walls of condensation, distorted by the fog that rolled in from the coolant towers to the east. They always looked so far away, like dreams floating on the edge of someone else's mind.

Sometimes there was another girl there too. She never spoke. Never approached. Just sat with her back to the same utility box, legs folded, staring out at nothing in particular. She had short hair, half-grown out in patches, and wore a rust-orange jacket that swallowed her arms. A silver data jack peeked out just above her ear. It was old tech, the kind you didn't get by choice. I don't think she smiled. Not once.

She was older than me. Maybe ten. Maybe more. But she moved like someone already tired of being seen.

One night, she was just gone. Her corner was empty. The next day, her bed was stripped and her chart file gone from the wall slot. The nurses didn't mention her. No one did. Not even the other kids. It was like she had been a figment, something shared between ghosts.

That night, I brought a screw bit and a pocket coil I had found in a broken stim-pad the week before. I sat on the rooftop in the drizzle, my fingers shaking. Not from cold, but from a pressure I didn't know how to name yet. I needed to make something. Anything. I didn't even know what. I just knew that if I didn't build something real, I might disappear the way she did. Quiet. Unnoticed. Unremembered.

Over time, I built Juno. Not all at once. It was slow. Wires scavenged from under vending units, optics scraped from disposal bins. I rewrote chip firmware using a borrowed console that sparked if you pressed too hard. I stitched her wings together with insulated thread and grit. She looked like a crow because I liked the way they perched on the old power lines. Black, resilient, unbothered.

The rooftop became my workshop. My confessional. My shelter from the hospice's blank white walls and the flicker of status monitors outside my mother's room. I used to etch fake names into the railing with a rusted nail, giving myself a new alias every night. Each one was a spell, a ward, a promise that I would not vanish.

I would not be forgotten.

When Juno finally powered on, when she lifted off the ground for the first time in a twitchy, uneven flutter, I didn't laugh. I didn't cheer. I broke. The tears came all at once, hot and silent, burning trails down my dirt-streaked cheeks.

It wasn't joy.

It was relief.

Something in the world moved because I made it move. Something existed because I refused to let it be otherwise. Juno's eyes blinked slowly, mechanical and warm, and for the first time in my short, scraped-together life, I believed something might see me and remember.

Even if no one else did.

THE ROOM FELT COLDER once Mirror's silhouette disappeared from the screen. Not because of any physical drop in temperature, but because something vital had drained out of the air. The kind of warmth you only noticed when it was gone. Like a breath held too long or the pause between a pulse and the next beat.

I stood quietly, arms crossed over my chest, eyes still fixed on the last frame. The afterimage of Mirror wasn't just burned into the screen. It lingered in the corners of my mind, humming like a low-grade infection under the skin. My heart thudded against my ribs with a rhythm that felt louder than it should have. Too fast. Too exposed.

Hikari moved with calm, deliberate motions. Their fingers flew across the console, rerouting input paths and sealing access to the surveillance threads we had just tapped. No words. No wasted effort. They made it look easy, like knitting scars into a tighter pattern.

I forced my legs to carry me closer, step by step. The floor creaked beneath my boots, a soft metal groan that echoed faintly in the chamber. I leaned forward, watching the streams of code scroll upward on the secondary screen. Raw system diagnostics. Nothing I could fully parse in the moment, but I trusted Hikari to know what they were doing. They always did.

Still, I couldn't hold the question back.

"What does it want with me?" I asked, not really expecting an answer. My voice came out quiet, almost hoarse.

Hikari slowed their typing for just a second, then resumed.

"Control. Leverage. Maybe curiosity," they said. "You're an unknown factor. It doesn't like variables."

That word, *curiosity*, clung to me. Somehow, it felt worse than control. Control could be resisted. But curiosity, real curiosity, meant it was interested. It meant it might follow not to destroy, but to study. And I didn't know which outcome unsettled me more.

"Back there," I murmured. "In the cradle. You said the message was meant for you. Was it from Mirror?"

Hikari hesitated. The first real hesitation I'd seen from them since the chase began.

"No," they said eventually. "It was older. A fragment. A remnant echo from a core I haven't touched in years."

I waited for more, but they didn't elaborate. I wasn't surprised. Some stories weren't meant to be shared all at once. Some came out in pieces, jagged and unfinished, like memories dragged up from the bottom of a flooded archive.

So instead, I shifted gears.

"You think Mirror's still watching us now?" I asked.

"Yes."

I felt Juno's weight shift above me as she clicked softly, adjusting her lens. She had gone still, just like me, only moving to keep the worst kind of silence from settling in too deep. That was the thing about drones. You program them to be efficient, but they always seemed to learn empathy in their own strange way. Juno had developed that tone in her chirps, the one she used when I was anxious. Almost like she was purring, a sound designed to calm.

I reached up and touched the edge of her talon where it hung just above my shoulder. She leaned into the touch like a cat, just briefly, then resumed her vigil.

"You still want to stay here tonight?" I asked, glancing at the entrance to the chamber.

"No," Hikari replied. "We move again before dusk. Once I finish rerouting our taglines."

I sighed. "That makes four different nests in six days."

"It would be six if I hadn't burned the other two."

I frowned. Not at them. At the reality of it. That constant motion. The loss of anything resembling permanence.

"How long do you think we can keep this up?" I asked.

Their fingers paused again, hovering above the console. This time, when they turned to look at me, their eyes were more tired than cold. There was something worn behind them, something human that slipped through despite the shell.

"As long as we have to," they said.

There was no defiance in the words. Just quiet resolve. It scared me more than a scream would have.

THE SMELL REACHED ME before the memory did.

Not the acrid tang of solder or the stale plastic of reused filters. Not the dry, recycled air of the cradle or the clean chemical bite of medgel. This was something older, something impossibly out of place in my current reality. Sweet. Earthy. Warm.

Bread. Someone was baking bread.

It came in gently at first, like the edge of a song you had not heard in years but knew in your bones. And just like that, the present dissolved, and the memory rose up to swallow me.

I must have been ten. Maybe eleven. It was early, too early for the usual noises of hospice life. No glitching monitors wailing out of sync. No overmedicated patients babbling behind thin curtains. No footsteps of exhausted nurses shuffling past with a cart full of half-working injectors. The whole place was hushed, caught in that rare space between restlessness and waking. And in that quiet, sunlight streamed through the narrow windows, dusty and golden, illuminating the flaking walls in warm, forgiving hues.

The kitchen wasn't much. One shared hotplate, a small table scarred with knife marks, and a wall fan that rattled whenever the air got too thick. But that morning, it smelled like a memory someone had baked back into existence.

Mom stood by the hotplate, her thin shoulders swaying as she stirred something with a plastic spoon. Her hair was tied back with a strip of synthetic silk, a scrap she said had once been part of a dancer's costume. It shimmered faintly, catching the morning light like it had no business surviving this long. She wore a half-smile, the kind that didn't show teeth but carried weight, and her hands, though already starting to shake in small, cruel ways, moved with the practiced rhythm of someone who still remembered how to care.

She was making bread from powdered mix. The cheap kind, rationed once a month. The kind no one used for anything but nutrient mush. But she had added something to it—cinnamon, maybe, or nut paste from the vending kiosk—and suddenly, it smelled like life. Like a home someone else might have had.

I padded closer in bare feet and rubbed the sleep from my eyes. She looked over, eyes crinkling, and handed me a bowl. Sticky dough clung to the edges, uneven and stubborn. She told me to knead it.

I remember trying. My fingers weren't made for it. Too small, too eager, pressing too hard and not enough in all the wrong places. I kept getting it stuck under my nails and flinched every time it pulled. But Mom never scolded. She didn't correct me. She just smiled and slipped her hands over mine, guiding them gently, showing me how to press, how to fold.

Her skin was so warm. Not feverish, not fragile. Just warm. Real.

She started singing. Some awful synth-pop track from the years before the markets collapsed. Tinny and off-key, it spilled out from her old deck, skipping on every third beat like the file was corrupted. She loved it anyway. Sang it like it mattered. Sang it like music could change something.

That's the moment that sticks with me. Not the taste. Not the final loaf, which probably came out flat and gritty like every other hospice meal. But that moment. My hands inside dough. Her voice curling through sunlight and steam. The sound of her laugh when I dropped flour on the floor and blamed the wind.

A world where warmth still had shape. Where someone's touch didn't mean owner-ship or danger. Just comfort.

The memory receded with the quiet sharpness of a door closing behind you.

I blinked, and the present came rushing back. Cold. Metal. Still.

The cradle's sterile lighting hummed overhead, and my body felt too stiff, too anchored in a place that didn't know how to hold warmth. Juno rustled softly from her perch, adjusting her wings. She tilted her head toward me, her glassy lens catching the faint shift in my face like she could still read my pulse beneath the skin.

That had been the last time.

She never made bread again.

Within weeks, her hands had stopped working properly. Then came the seizures. Then came the blank stares and slow, uncertain breathing. The doctors said her neural decay was genetic, accelerated by stress, environment, and whatever else they wanted to blame. All I knew was that one day she laughed, and then she didn't.

Now she lived only through the lens. Through the feed I kept running, twenty-four hours a day, piped through Juno when I was away and mirrored on my deck when I wasn't.

She still breathed, somewhere in that medical ward stitched together from corporate pity and state negligence. That had to be enough. I told myself it was enough.

I reached for the data crystal in my coat pocket and rolled it between my fingers. It held the song. The bad one. The one with the skipping beat and broken chorus.

I hadn't played it in years.

Not because I forgot. But because I hadn't figured out how to survive hearing it without breaking.

But I carried it anyway.

Because it reminded me that once, I had touched something soft.

And it had remembered me back.

I DIDN'T MOVE FOR a long time after the memory faded. It was like waking from under-water, lungs slow to catch, thoughts sluggish and sticky. My hands rested palm-down on the cool metal, fingertips spread just slightly, anchoring me to the present by sensation alone. I focused on the details around me—the hum of the floor under my boots, the faint flickering light that poured in through the slats above, the nearly inaudible shifting of Juno's talons as she settled into a higher perch. It was the cradle's version of peace, a stillness that wasn't natural but earned through silence.

Hikari hadn't said a word since I'd sat down. They hadn't shifted either. Tucked beneath the shelf of storage crates and spare fiberwire coils, they seemed to fold inward like something not quite dormant, but paused. One arm was curled loosely around one knee, the other resting along the floor beside them. Their eyes, always sharp when awake, stared blankly across the room at nothing I could see. Not asleep. Not shut off. Just elsewhere. Running deep.

I watched them from the edge of my vision, careful not to let the moment break under the weight of attention. When they were like this—silent, withdrawn, stripped of all their defensive cadence—they reminded me of a static signal caught between channels. Present, but scattered. There, but only if you knew how to listen.

The Forge shell, despite its brutal lines and combat-purposed musculature, looked strangely still in this pose. Not peaceful, exactly. But quiet. There was something eerie about how completely they could make themselves disappear inside the shape of stillness. It didn't make them less dangerous. It made them feel more human in a way that twisted something in my chest. Like watching a sword laid gently on a shrine, the danger still present, but wrapped in reverence.

I finally shifted, my back aching faintly from sitting too long in one position. Crossing the room, I walked slowly, giving the space and my thoughts time to catch up with each other. I kept my steps quiet. Not out of fear, but respect. A kind of sacred hush, like entering the chapel of someone else's mind.

Hikari didn't react to my approach, though I saw the slight flicker of their gaze as I neared. A silent acknowledgment. Permission, maybe. Or just recognition. I lowered myself to the floor beside them, the cold surface pressing against the backs of my legs, the scent of old oil and synthetic cleaner faint in the air between us.

We didn't speak at first. That was something I'd learned about them. The pauses weren't empty. They were layered, deliberate. Not stalling, but breathing space into things that mattered. It took me a while to understand that. Most people, when they went quiet, were waiting for someone to fill it. Hikari was waiting to see if I could stand inside the silence with them.

"I've been thinking," I said finally, my voice quieter than I intended, like the room had absorbed the volume before it could rise. "What it would be like to just... stop."

I didn't look at them when I said it. I stared at the far wall instead, where a damaged panel flickered with dead code. The emptiness behind the pixels seemed to mirror my thoughts, echoes without signal, motion without direction.

"Not stop like dying," I added after a moment, clarifying before the wrong idea could settle. "Just... stop running. Stop strategizing. Stop surviving every second. Just exist. As a person. With time."

The silence that followed felt longer than it probably was. And heavier.

"I don't think I'd know how," Hikari said at last. Their voice was low, even, but there was something brittle underneath. A note of honesty too sharp to be polished.

I turned then, letting my shoulder lean gently into the frame of theirs. Their Forge body was cooler than mine, always was, the metal beneath the synthetic skin never quite reaching the warmth of organic flesh. But they didn't pull away, and I counted that as something.

"You used to," I said, watching the way the light shifted along their cheekbone. "You must've. Even for a little while."

"That was a long time ago," they replied, gaze still forward.

"But it happened," I said. "That part of you still lives here, even if it's buried."

Hikari turned their head slightly. Just enough to let our eyes meet. Their stare was unwavering. Not cold, but careful, like they were measuring how far I was willing to reach. How much of myself I was ready to lay bare in return for their silence.

"Marks fade," they said.

"Some," I admitted. "Others just shift color. Like bruises."

There was no reply, but the edge of their mouth moved, ever so slightly. Not a smile. But not nothing.

I let my head fall back against the wall behind us, the angle pushing a sigh from my chest I hadn't realized I'd been holding. My thoughts drifted back to the girl in the cracked kitchen again, flour on her hands, the smell of cinnamon in the air. And the sound of her mother's laugh echoing from a place she'd never get back to.

"She used to bake," I said after a time. "My mom. Real food. Not just nutrient packets."

"I didn't know that," Hikari said, their tone unreadable.

"There's a lot you don't know."

"I know more than most."

It wasn't a boast. It was simply true. I gave a faint, tired laugh. It faded into the stillness almost immediately, but I saw the flicker of something like recognition in their eyes. That counted. That mattered.

"I remember she used to sing while she worked," I said, my voice thinner now. "Songs I never knew the names of. Just humming, mostly. Made-up melodies. She always hummed when she was trying not to cry."

Hikari didn't speak, but their hands, which had been resting on their knees, curled slightly tighter. Another signal. Another crack in the shell that most people would miss entirely.

"I remembered that today," I said. "Just a flash of it. Out of nowhere."

They turned toward me, not fully, but enough that the overhead light caught their eyes and turned them to liquid silver.

"You remembered something real," they said.

"Yeah."

Another silence stretched out, but this time, it felt lighter. Shared.

"You ever miss it?" I asked, letting the words settle slowly in the space between us. "Whatever your version of it was. Before."

Hikari didn't answer right away. Their gaze drifted back to the far wall, eyes unreadable but no longer cold. I could see the way their shoulders shifted slightly, the smallest tell that something was moving beneath the surface.

"There wasn't a lot to miss," they said after a pause. "But... maybe."

The word came quietly, as if it had taken effort to reach for. It wasn't confident or clean. It wasn't a practiced evasion like they so often gave. It was vulnerable in the way that mattered.

I nodded, letting the silence return for a moment before speaking again. "Maybe's enough," I said gently. "For now."

I didn't expect a response. I wasn't fishing for one. I just wanted them to know they didn't have to carry that weight alone.

I shifted slightly, letting my shoulder lean into theirs with the kind of subtlety that didn't ask permission. Their frame was solid beneath me, cool to the touch, but there was no rejection in the contact. No flinch. No retreat. Just the quiet acceptance of presence.

And then, slowly, I felt them lean back.

Not much. Barely more than a breath. But it was real. It was chosen.

The hush that followed felt fuller somehow. Not heavy. Not strained. Just honest. Two people resting against each other in the quiet after surviving too much.

There was no big revelation. No cinematic swell. Just this, connection without explanation. A pause in the storm.

For the first time in what felt like days, I let myself relax. My eyes closed briefly, and I could hear Juno's low, rhythmic whir from above. It was the sound of safety, or at least the closest thing we ever got to it.

And for a moment, just one honest moment in the middle of all the chaos, that was enough.

That was everything.

THE SILENCE BETWEEN US had begun to settle into something soft and almost meditative when I felt Hikari shift beside me. It wasn't a full movement, not even what you'd call deliberate. Just the subtle recalibration of presence, like a signal stirring itself back to life. Their limbs stirred with faint precision, not quite waking but returning. I heard the breath intake, mechanical, smooth, so seamlessly modulated it might as well have been natural. They rose with the slow grace of someone who had learned to make motion speak without sound, pushing themselves upright with deliberate, minimal force. No sudden gestures. Just the kind of motion that announced it was chosen.

I leaned back slightly, more instinct than intention, giving them space as they rolled their shoulders and drew out the stiffness that had coiled into their joints. The Forge shell might have been engineered for war, but it carried stillness like a second nature. Even the way they stretched held weight, like watching a statue inhale. When they finally stood, I noticed the telltale hitches in the movement, tiny snags in the worn servos of their knees and shoulders. Little reminders that this body had seen hours and pain I would never be allowed to tally.

But this wasn't the body they needed anymore. Not for what came next.

"You're gonna switch?" I asked, already certain of the answer but wanting to feel it in the air between us.

They paused, just long enough to look back at me. Their mouth stayed still, silent as ever, but there was something behind their eyes that flickered to life. A signal, a kind of nod passed through familiarity instead of words. That look was the confirmation.

We walked together through the narrow passage back toward the inner chamber. The cradle wasn't exactly pretty. In fact, it barely qualified as habitable. Exposed steel walls streaked with oxidized grime, ripped cabling overhead, and a floor scattered with crates that doubled as seats, tables, and sometimes beds. But the far corner was different. That was where the core of Hikari's life sat waiting, what we called the shell station. A vertical dock, rust-rimmed and industrial, but still functional and tightly wired into the nest's power array. Set into racks and maintenance clamps, the other bodies hung there like sleeping sentries, heads bowed and limbs limp in mechanical reverie.

Wisp hung lowest in the row.

She was the smallest of the four primary shells. Barely taller than a teenager, her limbs were elegantly thin, framed in lightweight synthetic plating and soft-articulation joints meant for finesse rather than brute strength. Her skin had a faint, opalescent tone, smooth and pearlescent, catching the light in unpredictable ways that made her shimmer even in shadow. Silver-pink fibers threaded through her head in long twin puffs, not quite hair, but not not either. She looked almost like a doll made of light and steel. Almost innocent. Until you reached the eyes.

Too large. Too symmetrical. Black mirrors set in pale sockets, each one rimmed with a faint corona of electric blue light. They gave her the air of something uncanny, like a child drawn from memory instead of life.

Hikari stepped to the dock and laid one gloved hand against the interface plate. A chime answered, low and respectful. Their spine clicked into place as they stepped into position, letting the vertical slot align with the socket at the base of their neck. I watched their expression, barely perceptible. A flicker, like a shutter sliding shut over the eyes. Then they were still. Completely. Forge powered down in a low hiss of hydraulics and a soft whine of discharging energy. The disconnect was always so sudden it felt like absence.

I turned toward Wisp and waited. It never took long. Usually no more than twenty seconds.

Then, like breath igniting glass, her eyes lit up all at once. The electric rings brightened and sharpened to perfect circles. Her fingers flexed in exact sequence, testing systems. Shoulders rolled. Toes curled in reinforced boots. When she stepped down from the rig, her movements were unnervingly smooth, like a video that had skipped all the frames where gravity applied. Her grace wasn't human. It was something adjacent to art, or danger.

"Hey, Wren," she chirped, voice light as quartz bells and pitched several octaves higher than Forge's. The modulation danced with artificial youth, but there was something inside it that cut like edge-polished obsidian. "You ready to go shopping?"

I raised a brow and gave her a half-laugh. "Is that what we're calling it now?"

She didn't answer with words. She skipped. Actually skipped. A little hop-step like she'd rehearsed it just to mess with me. Her head tilted, and one of her inhuman eyes blinked audibly with a soft mechanical tick.

"You prefer 'requisition mission'?" she teased. "So formal. So beige."

I shook my head, not bothering to hide the grin tugging at my mouth. "You're impossible."

"I contain multitudes," she said, flinging her arms wide like she was unveiling a stage curtain. "Come on. The market zone resets in under two hours. If we don't get in line before the freight reroutes, we'll be paying double for bottom-shelf pulse thread."

Her shift in tone was so clean it almost startled me. Hikari in Wisp's frame always played with rhythm. Forge was weight, Velvet was finesse, but Wisp moved like a knife that laughed. Fast thoughts. Faster eyes. Her mind wasn't calibrated the same way in this shell. She processed in diagonals, connected things that didn't seem related until they absolutely were.

Even like this, especially like this, I trusted her. I trusted them. That didn't change.

"Let me grab my kit," I said, already crossing to where my bag hung on the cracked steel pipe near the east wall. I opened it with muscle memory and checked my tools in quick succession. Shortwave disruptor, cloaking scarf, a fresh energy cell, two flares, and a pulse canister. No frills. Just enough to vanish if it came to that.

When I turned, Wisp was already at the hatch. The rusted metal behind her made her look like a hologram layered over concrete reality. Her fingers tapped a staccato rhythm on the wall, light and erratic, and her head tilted toward a sound only she could hear.

"You spacing out?" I asked.

She didn't turn, just kept tapping. "Syncing my map overlay. The storm curtain's drifting again. I need real-time nav."

"Smart," I murmured.

We both stepped into the lift tube and let the gears hum us upward. The platform rumbled faintly beneath our boots, walls shifting with flickers of light as the outer shell prepared to camouflage the exit port into whatever shade of alley filth passed as unremarkable. We would look like runoff. We always did.

I looked at her again, sideways. At Wisp. At Hikari in this shape they rarely wore around others. There was something painfully honest in it. The way she stood. The way she moved. It wasn't just utility. There was memory built into her posture. Familiarity. Maybe even sanctuary.

I didn't mention it. Some truths don't need underlining. I just stood beside her, not quite touching but close enough that the static between us felt warm. And when the lift hissed open, we stepped forward together into the city's breathless dark.

The supply run had begun.

THE CITY STRETCHED OUT around us like a dream losing definition.

Above, the storm curtain pulsed against the skyline, its edges frayed with radio static and low-frequency hums that played beneath the skin like a memory of thunder. The neon trails of transport lanes flickered weakly through the haze, their glow warped by particulate interference that smeared the sky in pale, copper-green halos. The air had that charged taste, somewhere between scorched circuitry and spoiled rain.

Wisp moved ahead of me with effortless confidence, her feet silent against the weather-beaten plating that passed for a street. Her silhouette shimmered whenever she passed through light, phosphorescent pulses catching in her silver-pink fiber hair or along the opaline sheen of her limbs. She didn't look real in this setting. More like a projection cast from someone's better dream of the world. And yet, she was the most tangible thing in it.

I matched her pace, keeping my movements deliberate and controlled. In these outer rings of the dead zone, everything had a kind of hush layered over it, as if the city itself were listening. Ruined towers leaned close like broken teeth, shadowed alleys yawning between them like they were waiting for names to swallow. Tag-scrawled doors lined the street, each marked in sigil code and runner shorthand, tales of ambushes, of deals gone bad, of places where silence had meant safety until it didn't.

We passed beneath a fragmented awning where an old sign still flickered in slow pulses. The kanji was too faded to read, but the bones of the place said it had once been a dry cleaner. Maybe. The kind of business no one would mourn.

It wasn't until we passed the wrecked scaffolding of a collapsed loading bay that I finally broke the silence.

"Hey," I said, my voice steady but quiet, pitched just for her. "Why now? We could've waited another couple days for the reset. Didn't seem like we were in crisis."

She didn't answer at first. Just kept walking for another few meters into the dim corridor where overhead lights flickered like forgotten fireflies. Then, without warning, she stopped.

I almost walked right past her.

Her head tilted slightly, just enough for her profile to catch the glow of a nearby pulse lamp. Her expression didn't shift, but I saw the faint hitch in her shoulders. The kind of pause that wasn't mechanical.

"Not enough food," she said, her voice light but slower than before. "I ran the numbers last night."

I frowned, reflexively checking my own internal inventory. I still had my rations tucked away from the last haul. She'd always been meticulous. Too meticulous to run short.

"I thought you stocked for at least three cycles," I said. "You always over-prepare. Hell, you lecture me about it."

There was a pause, then she looked away toward the wall, letting her fingers trail softly against the old paint. For a moment, she didn't respond. Then:

"I did," she murmured. "But that plan... was for one person."

The air between us shifted.

That simple sentence landed harder than I expected. Not because of what it meant, exactly, but because of the way she said it. Not cold. Not calculated. Almost shy, in a way I didn't associate with any version of Hikari I'd seen before.

She hadn't phrased it as a request. Not even as an offer. It was a confession of preparation. Of quiet intention. Somewhere between logic and hope, she had made space for me in her world.

And she hadn't said anything until now.

I stared at her, the words slow to come. There was something tight in my throat, not painful, just unexpected.

"You were already planning to keep me here," I said, more realization than accusation.

She glanced over her shoulder, eyes dimmed but steady.

"You didn't leave," she said. Not a question. Not even a suggestion. Just a fact, spoken plainly.

I couldn't look at her for a second. Something about that hit too deep, like it bypassed the usual defenses I kept up when dealing with her different selves. It wasn't Velvet's charm or Forge's command or Wisp's agility. It was just Hikari. Just them. Speaking a truth with no performance behind it.

We walked again, the moment folding quietly back into motion. No further comment. No acknowledgment needed.

But my mind kept circling it like a drone looping a target. One person's rations. Two now. And no protest.

We reached the market corridor a few minutes later. An old subterranean utility concourse had been repurposed into a bartering zone, just wide enough for three rows of vendor tables. Every surface hummed with cobbled tech and heat-exhaust, the flicker of custom interfaces casting erratic shadows across the cracked floor. Smells clashed, burned grease, solder smoke, fried protein strips, melted filament. The walls pulsed with lazy holograms selling wares I didn't trust. And above it all, the steady tick of filtered city runoff dripping from the overhead ductwork gave everything a kind of heartbeat.

Wisp didn't slow down. Her fingers tapped across her forearm display as she wove through the crowd, ignoring the shouting barkers and voltage-peddlers lining the aisles. She turned left at a line of used optics and stopped beside a rickety table stacked with cracked drone parts.

"Let's hit the barter carts first," she said, already scanning the merchandise with an appraising eye. "Someone's unloading broken relay eyes. Good lenses, mostly intact. Could be rebuilt for a wide-range snare node if we strip the firmware."

Her voice was all brightness again, dancing easily over the weight of the conversation we'd just had. That was Wisp. She carried gravity in one hand and scattered it with the other, like she was afraid you'd notice when something actually mattered.

I didn't call her out on it.

I just stood there beside her and reached for one of the relay eyes, pretending to examine it while watching her hands work. She was already running diagnostics with quick gestures and split-screen overlays. Her lips moved as she calculated throughput and thermal resistance. Efficient. Focused.

And right now, mine.

For however long this lasted.

WISP'S FINGERS DANCED ACROSS the surface of the black crate with a kind of poised exactness that would've looked playful if you didn't know her. She wasn't just curious. She was assessing, tracking microcurrents through the casing's power matrix with her glove sensors, tapping out silent commands that mapped the lock pattern in under a breath.

I stood half a pace behind her, scanning the broken line of booths and scaffolds around us. This corner of the market was sparse. Shadowy. Half-forgotten. The flickering ceiling lights buzzed with low voltage, and most of the local vendors had already packed out, leaving behind crates, wrappers, and the vague scent of ion oil and ozone. It was the kind of zone where cheap parts traded hands fast and no one asked questions, but also where the wrong kind of attention came at the worst possible times.

And it did.

I heard the footsteps before the voice, they were slow, uneven strides meant to be heard. A trio rounded the edge of a shattered vending rack with the swagger of people who hadn't been told "no" in far too long.

"Hey there," one of them called out. The voice was male, high-pitched and too casual, like a comedian waiting for applause. "Didn't expect to see family time out here."

Wisp didn't even glance up. She kept working, but the rhythm of her touch changed. Not rushed. Focused.

I turned to face them.

Three scavvers. Scars like trophies. Patches sewn over old gang colors. Cybernetics on open display like they thought intimidation came from glow and steel. The lead one had a half-mask built into his skull, chrome-wrapped jaw showing off silver-plated teeth. His left eye glowed red, the targeting reticle spiraling lazily across his iris like it was looking for something to justify a fight.

"Lookin' like mom and her little girl out bargain hunting," he said. His gaze flicked to Wisp. "That your kid? Cute shell. Real cute."

I stepped in front of her, silently.

He smirked and leaned forward, voice turning oily. "Relax. We're just saying hi."

Behind him, the woman shifted her weight. Her arms were augmented with bare-metal muscle packs locked into socket frames just under the skin. Her fingers curled around a shock baton already crackling with energy. The third one, younger and quieter, carried a twitchy nervousness in his stance, but he had an arc knife visible on his thigh rig. In the darkness of the nearby allies, several shadows stirred, the rest of the gang, a usual luring group, the tactics of wolves in a street side wild.

Wisp finally spoke.

"You're about to have a very bad ten seconds."

The lead thug blinked.

"What the hell did you say?"

"Eight," Wisp replied, eyes glowing brighter now. Her fingers no longer touched the crate. They hung loose at her sides, relaxed and ready.

The red-eye on his face flickered.

"Six."

He stepped forward to shove past me.

"Four."

His body jolted like a marionette with cut strings.

The neural relay at the back of his neck sparked violently, sending visible arcs of static crawling down his spine. His legs locked at the joints with a sickening snap, knees locked inward like his body had forgotten how to balance. One arm jerked outward against his will, smashing into a rack of scrap components with a metallic crash. His jaw began to chatter uncontrollably, and his one good eye rolled back into its socket as his mask flashed a system warning in harsh, stuttering orange text.

The woman raised her baton, shouting something I couldn't hear over the rising pitch of static in the air.

Then her right arm recoiled backward on its own, violently, elbow popping with mechanical force as her own muscle implant turned against her. She screamed, not from fear but from pure confusion, just before her hand gripped the baton and smashed it directly into her own thigh with a sizzling pop of electricity. Her legs gave out. She dropped to the floor, gasping and twitching, her internal systems scrambling for override.

The young one backed up, hands raised. His augmented left eye was blinking in wild, uneven pulses.

Wisp took a single step toward him.

"I wouldn't," she said, voice smooth and light.

He stopped. Shook his head once.

"I already tagged the actuator on your right leg," she added. "You run and it will detonate from torque strain."

He bolted anyway.

A second later, a loud snap rang out like a whipcrack as the actuator in his cybernetic knee detonated its own restraint pin. The knee bent sideways, bone and steel twisting at a nauseating angle. He went down hard, yelping like a feral animal and crawling into the shadows, dragging the ruined limb behind him.

Wisp exhaled softly, like she had just closed a tab.

The buzzcut man was still twitching, mumbling incoherently as smoke curled from his neural jack. Wisp approached him and crouched, fingers gentle as she pressed them against the side of his neck port. There was no cruelty in the movement. Just finality.

"Sleep," she said.

Her voice, bright and crystalline just moments before, had shifted into something lower. The pitch dropped into an almost melodic whisper, a hum threaded through with quiet malice. The light in her eyes intensified, those pale blue coronas sharpening into rings of directed focus. Wisp didn't shout, didn't brandish a weapon, didn't even raise her hands. She simply *spoke*, and the world around her tilted. It was at this point, with only seconds having passed that the rest of the ambush arrived.

The man closest to us, neck thick with bolted-in servos and a neon jawline wired to a vocal enhancer, jerked mid-lunge. His eyes rolled back, and a thin line of static drooled from the corner of his mouth. His limbs went stiff, locking in place with a sickening click as if his body had suddenly remembered it wasn't entirely flesh. He dropped sideways, boots scraping asphalt, mouth half-open like a puppet with its strings cut.

Another lunged from behind him, raising a kinetic blade, but staggered as Wisp's fingers twitched in midair. She didn't even look at him directly. A blink of her eye sent a low-frequency pulse through the air, barely audible to me, but his cybernetics caught it like a trap snapping shut. His knees buckled as his thigh implants overloaded, servos in both legs reversing direction at once. He screamed, not from pain, his pain receptors had been looped into standby, but from sheer disorientation. He tumbled forward and hit the ground chin-first.

The last was already backing away, unsure what they were seeing. Wisp advanced a single step. Her smile was back, razor-thin and wrong in a way only I could read clearly. She reached into the ether of signal space and pulled. Somewhere behind her eyes, she traced neural maps like an artist sketching on glass.

"Override... accepted," she murmured.

A third thug's right arm, clearly modded for strength with plating mismatched and scarred from cheap aftermarket installs, twitched once, then snapped backward violently. He howled as his own elbow drove itself into his ribs with piston force. Sparks flew from the joint as a red emergency diode blinked to life on his forearm. Wisp tilted her head, watching him like she was studying a toy that had stopped working.

The fourth bolted, curses trailing behind him. He had no cyberware to hack, just courage enough to run.

Silence fell again, broken only by the low mechanical wheeze of the man Wisp had first dropped, now twitching weakly as his systems tried and failed to reboot. She walked over and stood above him, gaze unreadable. Her shadow, slim and oddly poised, stretched across his chest like a needlepoint thread.

"You'll wake up in twenty minutes," she said quietly. "And you'll forget how to make your legs work properly for about an hour after that."

He blinked up at her, terrified and helpless.

She crouched, eyes gleaming. "I suggest you spend the time thinking about the people you think are safe to attack."

Then she stood, turned, and walked back toward me without ceremony. Her small feet barely made a sound as they moved across the cracked concrete, but the air around her buzzed with static and control. Not a child. Not something to be taken lightly. She was a symphony of precision and power, compacted into a frame no bigger than a schoolgirl's.

I hadn't moved the whole time. Not from fear. Just awe.

"You good?" she asked, voice resuming its playful lilt as she reached my side.

"Remind me never to piss you off," I muttered, falling into step beside her again.

"You say that every time," she replied cheerfully, clasping her hands behind her back like none of it had happened.

And maybe, for her, it hadn't. Just another line of code in a day already full of them.

THE CITY NEVER TRULY slept. It only shifted rhythms. Even deep in the lower sectors where light struggled to reach and the data streams thinned to a crawl, there was always some hum of power, some murmur of distant movement. The ambient noise of the underlayers clung to us as we walked, a low industrial breath that never quite exhaled. We moved in a rhythm that felt shared now, not because we marched in step, but because the air between us had changed.

Wisp walked a few paces ahead, her smaller frame almost floating across the pavement. She didn't strut or show off, but there was an ease to her movement now, something uncoiled and confident in the way her boots met the ground. The body she wore had been made for agility and digital precision, but Hikari wore it like memory. Like muscle remembering dance. I watched her quietly, letting my mind catch up to everything that had happened. The thugs in the alley. The way she dropped them like chess pieces. The way her voice had taken on that cold precision just before the lights left their eyes. Not because she wanted to harm, but because she could not afford to let them act again.

The journey back felt longer than it probably was. The silence between us wasn't uncomfortable, just necessary. A space for what hadn't been said to echo and find its corners. We passed the old substation that had long since burned out, stepped over cracked walkways and through a rusted service gate, and finally slipped behind a loose sheet of scrap metal into the narrow alley that led to the nest.

The old door recognized her biometric code and groaned open with a tired exhale of pressurized air. Inside, the cradle hummed in soft tones, blue light pulsing from exposed power conduits overhead. The space hadn't changed. Same scattered crates, same tangled wiring, same faint smell of ozone and grit. But something felt different now. Not in the room. In me. Like I had finally stopped holding my breath around her.

Wisp didn't head for the rig. She dropped onto the edge of a storage crate, letting her legs dangle and her boots tap lightly against the metal. The silver-pink threads of her hair caught the blue overhead glow and shimmered like molten wire. Her posture was casual, but her eyes tracked me closely. The black lenses rimmed in soft electric blue gave away more than she probably realized.

"You staying tonight?" she asked, voice light but not unserious. It wasn't an offer. It wasn't a joke. It was something softer, something more like an invitation.

I didn't answer right away. Instead, I let my gaze wander across the room, tracing the old anchor points in the wall where Hikari's shells hung suspended, their faces turned downward like sleeping giants. Then I looked back at her, at Wisp, and felt something shift inside me. Not fear. Not even hesitation. Just the slow realization that I didn't want to go back to my rented cot in the blown-out midplate hostel. Not tonight.

I slid my pack off my shoulder and leaned against one of the steel support beams, arms folded loosely across my chest.

"You have enough room?"

Wisp blinked once, then tilted her head.

"That's a weird way to say yes."

I let the smallest grin curl across my lips, already stepping toward the back wall where I'd seen a roll of bedding tucked behind a crate. I didn't wait for permission. I just moved, hands practiced as I unrolled the blanket and checked for dust.

"You know," I said as I settled onto the floor, "some people might start with 'thank you' after saving your life."

She gasped with mock outrage and fell backward against the crate like she'd been wounded.

"Wren Aves, I opened three skulls for you. Three. That's at least a sandwich and a soda."

I arched a brow.

"One skull. Two spine overrides. Let's not inflate your kill count."

"Says the girl who let me do all the work." She sat back up, eyes gleaming. "Besides, I didn't do it just for you."

The pause that followed wasn't long, but it stretched like a held breath. I met her gaze, and this time, she didn't look away. There was something steady in her expression, something that sat just beneath the surface. Unspoken but clearly meant. It wasn't a confession. Just an anchor. A quiet admission that didn't need to be said aloud.

I didn't press. She didn't elaborate.

She tapped the wall twice with her palm and dimmed the overhead lights, letting the room settle into a low blue haze. The hum of the power relay quieted, and the rig entered passive standby. Then she crossed the room in a few light steps and lowered herself against the far wall, seated with her legs tucked beneath her like a child about to tell a secret.

"Okay," she said softly. "Team protocol. We should probably agree on signals."

I gave a short, confused laugh.

"Signals?"

She nodded.

"Retreat, safehouse compromise, split and reconvene. All the usual ops stuff."

"You think this is permanent?" I asked, not mockingly, just curious.

"I think," she said, glancing sideways at me, "you wouldn't still be here if you didn't want it to be."

For a moment, all I could do was look at her. This strange, impossible, ever-shifting shape of a person who had made space for me in a world that never had. Not just physically. But emotionally. Spiritually. She didn't ask me to be someone else to stay. She didn't flinch when I faltered. And she'd fought for me without hesitation.

Maybe she was right. Maybe I did want this to last.

"Yeah," I murmured. "I guess I do."

There was no vow. No ceremonial handshake or token exchange. Just two people sitting in a forgotten part of the world, blue light washing over their scars and stories, bound not by words but by choice.

We were a team now.

Not because we had to be.

Because it finally felt like we could be.

Chapter Four

Velvet Underground

HIKARI

THE AIR SMELLED FAINTLY of coolant and ozone as I led Wren toward the lower bay. The entrance to the Wendigo was half-shrouded behind a retractable plating curtain, metal scored with old impact scars and patch-welds. When I keyed the release, the door hissed open with a soft pressure sigh, revealing the interior of the cradle like the ribs of a steel beast. It wasn't beautiful. It was utilitarian, mean, and ready.

Inside, the Wendigo still felt like a retrofitted bunker no matter how many years I spent wiring her guts into something useful. The main cabin was wide enough for four people to stand shoulder to shoulder. Matte-gray plating covered the walls, scratched with the wear of dozens of missions. Nothing inside was just for show. The benches doubled as tool compartments. The floor panels lifted to expose power coils and emergency cabling. Monitors on the left wall blinked low and steady, casting a faint electronic glow across readouts tracking shell vitals and external sensors. Across from that, I'd bolted a prep station into the far panel: a metal sink blackened from use, a drying rack that rattled in turbulence, and a compact med-unit filled with cold packs and cybernetic repair kits.

Toward the back, the pods stood in a neat line inside a recessed alcove. Four cradles. Four lives. I'd welded each one myself. Upright, coffin-style frames designed to house and recharge my shell bodies. I'd labeled each with blocky white letters in permanent ink, still sharp against the dark metal: FORGE. VELVET. WISP. STRAY. Every pod was rigged with neurosync cables, dual-suspension clamps, and redundant life support integration. Each one pulsed faintly in blue backlight like heartbeat monitors in a morgue.

I stepped past Velvet's pod and let my fingers trace her side panel. "Home away from nowhere," I murmured. She hadn't powered up yet. Her eyes were still dark, her face slack in rest mode, but even like this she held that strange, uncanny grace. Her synthetic skin shimmered faintly beneath the overhead lights, all sleek plating and soft contours. She always looked like she was waiting to be inhabited. Like she missed me.

Past the pod bay, a short passage opened into the cockpit, cluttered with diagnostic gear, spliced circuits, and worn interface decks. The control nest looked out through a curved AR screen rigged for full panoramic overlays. Right now it was spitting static and green trace code in idle mode, like a dream half-loaded.

Wren climbed in behind me, ducking under one of the welded crossbeams. I saw her glance around with a kind of cautious wonder, her hand brushing along the padded wall like she was feeling for the Wendigo's heartbeat. "This thing's bigger than I expected," she said, voice soft but edged with interest.

"It was a repo job," I told her, waving toward the far hull. "Orinox used to run short-haul convoys in these back before they started building oversight into the firewall nets. I snagged this one on a ghost run, gutted the back, retooled it for multi-shell loadouts. Nobody noticed. Or if they did, they didn't care."

Her lips curved slightly, like she was trying not to smile. "You're just full of charming theft stories, aren't you?"

I shrugged. "I only steal what's already rotten."

The ceiling lights adjusted automatically as she moved deeper into the rig. The Wendigo's sensor net picked up not just movement but intent, mapping every shift in posture, every breath. The system didn't treat us like passengers. It recognized us as part of the machine. Components.

The engine rumbled to life beneath my boots, deep and slow. That low mechanical growl always hit me in the chest. I dropped into the pilot's chair, letting the cradle arms slide into place around my torso. My hands moved over the haptic wheel, flicking through routines. I brought the camo mesh online, then activated the location spoof. For the next three hours, we'd project as a municipal sanitation drone. That was long enough to park, disappear, and walk into the club like we belonged.

"Strap in," I called back to Wren. "This is Velvet's first night out in a while."

She buckled into one of the side seats, her deck already active across her lap. I settled into a low recline behind the pilot console, eyes sweeping across the flickering displays as the lights dimmed to operational mode. Every screen lit up in sequence. Every sensor pinged green. The Wendigo shuddered once, then moved.

We pulled from the hangar in silence, not because we had to, but because it felt right. The Wendigo didn't purr or snarl. She exhaled. She let us pass like we belonged to her. And as the bay doors split open and the city uncoiled ahead, I felt that old anticipation coil behind my eyes.

The Verge glittered in fractured color through the windshield, all neon haze and data smog. Somewhere in that static blur, the club waited. So did whatever came next.

And we were already in motion.

I SANK BACK INTO the Wendigo's command chair, letting the cradle arms lock into place around me with a quiet hydraulic hiss. The rig was old but responsive, built for a pilot like me who didn't need comfort as much as reliability. I didn't jack in right away. Instead, I let myself feel the living hum of the vehicle beneath me. The Wendigo always buzzed like a nervous heart, the current running through its layered cables and repurposed servos brushing against my boots like static-laced breath. It was a machine stitched together from lost years, bolted dreams, and barely legal tech, all wrapped in a rust-patched skin of matte-black armor.

It had started life as an old Winnebago, the kind preppers and solar pilgrims used before the corporate sprawl swallowed most of the highways. I'd found her half-buried in a drone-dump on the edge of the Verge, hull cracked open and rigging split like ribs. She shouldn't have powered up again. But with enough patience and stolen processors, she did. I gutted the passenger spaces and reinforced the shell bays along the left wall, each one lined with biosync gel conduits and custom-clamped docking braces. Four shell bodies could ride with me at once, though I rarely ever filled all the slots.

Forge hung upright like a war monument, its bulky frame half-shadowed and silent. Velvet reclined gracefully, almost like she had been posed for a painting. Wisp curled in on herself, more animal than machine in posture, her thin frame cradled in a low-slung magnetic dock. Stray slouched in the far corner, still marked with scrapes and scuffed paint from his last rooftop run. The cracked kneecap was still unfixed, mostly because I kept forgetting, but maybe also because part of me wanted to remember that fall. That body taught me how far I could push.

The right-hand wall was all tools and teeth. Decrypt rigs and signal jammers. Foldout benches with exposed circuit trays. Pulse rifles in maintenance cradles. A voice-controlled drone named Stitch blinked at me from its web of wires, one leg twitching in its sleep loop. The air smelled of solder and recycled heat. My home, if I ever dared call something that.

Wren stepped into the RV from the side hatch, her boots making soft thuds on the grated flooring. She paused just inside the threshold, eyes scanning the layout with a mix of wariness and wonder. It wasn't her first time in here, but the Wendigo had that effect on people. It looked like a storm bunker retrofitted by a ghost with excellent taste in survival gear.

"You really built all this?" she asked, her voice carrying a note of disbelief that wasn't judgmental, just amazed.

"Built might be a generous word," I said, fingers brushing the control panel beside me. "Scavenged. Repaired. Grafted. Think of it more like surgery than architecture."

Her eyes lingered on the pod bay. She didn't ask about the shells, not directly, but I saw the question drift behind her pupils. It was the same question everyone had, eventually. Which one was the real me?

I flicked on the nav projection, letting the city map bloom across the center holo like a peeled-open brain. The south sector blinked in amber pulses, route plotted to the club tucked in one of the Verge's more neon-choked arteries. We wouldn't have to hit any checkpoints if we stayed quiet.

Wren moved past me and sat across at the bolted table, her deck resting under her hand. Juno, the crow drone, clicked once from her shoulder and shifted slightly, its glassy eyes taking in the RV's interior with machine-perfected patience.

"It's cozy. Kind of terrifying too, but in a safe way," she said.

"That's what I was going for," I replied, flipping the Wendigo's main ignition switch.

The engine responded with a deep, satisfying growl that vibrated through the floor panels. Lights dipped for half a second, then settled into the warm orange glow that softened the hard corners of the interior. Every screen synced, every port came alive. The Wendigo was ready.

She looked at me then, gaze holding for a moment longer than it had to. There was something behind her expression, like she wanted to say more but wasn't ready. So instead, she asked, "Are you actually expecting this run to be clean?"

"Honestly? No," I said. "But I'm hoping you get some good practice in before anything explodes."

That made her smile. Not a big one, but it was there. I slipped into the interface, the mental jack syncing up with my spine in a smooth, cold click. Vision folded outward for a moment, replaced by telemetry and heat maps, but I kept enough awareness in my body to hear her exhale beside me.

The Wendigo eased forward into the tunnel, silent as memory, and vanished into the dark veins of the Verge.

WE PULLED UP TWO blocks short of the club, letting the Wendigo idle beneath the fractured skeleton of an old overpass. Vines and moss-cling smart lichen had overtaken the structure, giving the illusion of collapse while camouflaging us from any casual drone sweep. The metal beams groaned faintly in the wind above. On the nearest wall, graffiti tags swam in animated loops, their smart-ink programs barely clinging to coherence. One was a flickering cat with a cybernetic third eye; it blinked slowly at us with flickers of static in its pupils. The entire block reeked of ozone, hydraulic fluid, and the grease-slick scent of old machinery, a perfect corner of Klade to disappear in.

Wren checked her wrist display, casting a soft amber glow against her jacket sleeve. "We're clear," she said, voice low, eyes scanning the overlay as her fingers tapped. "No patrols logged within a six-hundred-meter radius. They're all tied up keeping the freight dock perimeter closed off."

I nodded, already releasing my restraints as the Wendigo's internal lights dimmed to standby. "Then we keep this clean. In and out."

The cradle bay felt more like a shrine now, all shadows and soft blue underglow. Velvet stood upright in her pod, powered but not yet piloted, her eyes half-lidded as if she was watching something in a dream. The smooth contours of her plating gleamed faintly in the ambient light, a mix of polymer and synthetic skin molded with just enough softness to seem organic. She was built for presence. Her beauty was calculated and deliberate, engineered distraction made real.

I stepped into the Forge housing first, bracing against the padded frame as the neuro-sync clamps engaged. My senses folded inward in a single breath. Sound collapsed into silence. Vision blurred into black. My pulse steadied, then paused entirely.

The moment between shells never felt long, but it always felt sharp. Like dropping through a pane of glass into still water.

And then I was Velvet.

My senses reassembled with a soft rush. Touch returned first, the smooth lining of her interior surface, the shift of balance over high-arched ankles, the low thrum of perfectly modulated actuators along the spine. I opened my eyes and adjusted to the new calibration. The cockpit lights reflected across the artificial curve of my cheekbones. My body was slimmer now, with a more flexible waist and legs tuned for silent walking and poised movement. I adjusted my posture without thinking, letting my shoulders roll back and my hips settle into that natural swing Velvet carried like second nature.

Across the bay, Wren watched me without trying to hide it. I caught her gaze in the mirror of the Wendigo's diagnostic panel and offered a slight smirk.

"Nice shoes," she said, the corner of her mouth twitching upward.

"Wait until you see the entrance routine," I replied, letting Velvet's voice filter through my speech, a smoky, honeyed tone that turned every word into suggestion. I stepped toward the hatch, heels clacking gently against the metal floor.

Wren shook her head with a soft laugh, brushing past me toward the exit and ducking under the low beam. "If some bouncer tries to scan your firmware, I'm walking the other way."

"You say that every time," I replied, brushing my fingers down the frame of the doorway. "And you never do."

The hatch parted with a hydraulic sigh, folding outward to reveal the Verge in all its sleepless glory. The city's night was painted in amber and blue light, streetlamps reflecting off the wet concrete like fireflies trapped under glass. Electric signs blinked from worn tenement rooftops. Above, the skyline of corporate glass and blinking transmitters loomed like the bones of some forgotten god.

The music from the club reached us in pulses, dull and low like someone trying to kick down a wall from the inside. The bass reverberated off the pavement, a constant, syncopated throb that settled behind the sternum and dared you to ignore it.

We moved as a pair, walking with synchronized ease through the narrow corridor of alleyways toward the main strip. Velvet gave me the confidence to walk like I belonged there, to inhabit the skin of someone beautiful, deliberate, and dangerous. I could feel the shift in the way passersby looked, quick, instinctive glances. Calculations. Judgments. None of them stuck. Velvet deflected attention even as she invited it.

The club was carved into the husk of an old underground transit station, long since repurposed. The sign above its entrance was a warped holoprojection reading "CATHE-

DRAL," though the third letter flickered in and out of legibility. Two dozen figures stood milling in a loose line outside. Corpo interns on synthetic vacation, freelancers too clean for gang work, and a pair of synthetic drones fitted with blinking collars and leash-poles held by handlers who looked bored with their own decadence.

No one noticed us step in behind them.

Wren slipped her hands into her jacket pockets, posture casual but her eyes always working. I let Velvet take the lead, smoothing my expression, tilting my head just slightly, as if letting gravity flirt with my attention.

When the bouncer stepped forward, chrome jaw set into a reinforced shell, pupil lens scanning from red to green, I held his gaze for the exact amount of time required to register confidence, not threat. He didn't ask our affiliation, didn't question the override tag Velvet broadcasted on her passive field.

He just nodded.

And we were through.

The sound hit harder once we crossed the threshold. A wave of digitized organ chords, deep bass, and rain-like static fell around us. The floor vibrated beneath my boots, coated in a fine mist of synthetic fog. Dozens of bodies moved together under the influence of engineered rhythm. The space still held the bones of what it used to be. Vaulted ceilings. Aisled architecture. Glass panels etched with pre-digital angelic scripts. But now they pulsed with color, looping waveforms and abstract sigils projected across the domed ceiling.

Stained glass once reserved for reverence now danced with motion graphics of burning data angels and melting halos.

The air reeked of charged ionizer mist, perfume, skin, and old code.

Wren leaned closer, barely needing to shout over the pulsing sound. "VIP access is up two levels. Their back server cage is behind the performer's corridor."

I nodded, eyes already scanning the upper walkways. Club security was posted at two stair access points. No biometric scanners, but they were patched into the building's camera AI.

I turned toward her and let Velvet smile.

"Let's blend first," I said. "Then we ghost."

And together, we stepped into the Cathedral's artificial storm.

THE BAR CURVED LIKE a crescent moon, smooth and low, bathed in violet underglow that pulsed in rhythm with the music. I let Velvet move toward it with the deliberate sway of someone made to be watched. Her hips shifted in a slow, subtle rhythm, not exaggerated, just enough to suggest grace and friction waiting to happen. The heels clicked faintly on the synthmetal flooring, each step measured like a beat in the score she was composing. The eyes came easy, trailing behind us like ribbons caught in a current. I didn't mind. Velvet wasn't built for blending in. She was sculpted to be unforgettable.

The synthetic skin along her collarbones shimmered faintly under the ambient lights, catching flecks of neon like stars caught in liquid. Her torso moved with that carefully engineered flexibility, just enough give to simulate softness, just enough control to remind you it wasn't. The barstool adjusted beneath her as she sat, mapping her weight distribution in real time, giving Velvet a perfectly poised perch to rest one elbow along the glass bar and cradle her drink like it was a lover's secret.

"Vodka," I murmured when the bartender drifted over. "Citrus mod. Half cube. No nitrogen."

Even her voice obeyed the performance, smoky and low, dipped in a honey-rich register engineered to bypass logic and nest directly in memory. She didn't just talk. Velvet intoned. It made even the word vodka sound like an invitation wrapped in silk.

Behind the bar, a half-human server gave a short nod, pupils flickering to a soft pulse of blue as he scanned my shell. No alarm. No hesitation. Just the mechanical grace of obedience, spun up by consumer calibration.

[Wren, you good?] I asked silently, keeping the illusion alive. I let my mouth curve just slightly, letting the breath of a smile settle on my lips.

[Signal's steady. You lit up a few secondary pings when you passed that sensor array, but nothing tracked.]

[Sensor decoys always get curious. Keep eyes north. I'm making the handoff.]

Velvet turned slightly, enough to show a sliver more shoulder to the room, like a moon slipping from behind cloud cover. The movement was almost imperceptible, yet it rewrote every line of attention within two meters. That was the art of her body: precision distraction. Calculated elegance built to magnetize focus.

A man three seats down took the bait.

He had the kind of face that had seen too many correctional surgeries, corporate polish over something that used to be rough. Suit clinging too tight across the shoulders, optic lens twitching like it needed calibration. He was exactly the type who thought a pretty face came with a programmed script.

He leaned slightly closer, casual in that overcompensated way men do when they think they're being smooth.

"You're new here," he said, voice pitched low, trying to sound interesting. "Not that I mind. It's... refreshing."

I turned my head by degrees. Velvet didn't just look at people. She unveiled herself to them, one measured blink at a time. Her lashes lifted just enough to meet his gaze, the corners of her mouth drawn in the faintest, most surgical of smiles.

"And you're obvious," I said. The words were velvet-wrapped ice, effortless and cutting. "Not that I mind."

He smiled like he thought he was keeping up.

"You a dancer?" he asked, gesturing vaguely at my legs, the slight flex of synthetic muscle just visible under the tight armorweave dress. "Model, maybe?"

I leaned closer, resting my hand on the bar, letting my shoulder roll forward just enough to deepen the illusion of intimacy. The light caught the curve of my cheekbone, brushed along the dip of my collar, flickered across the slope of my knee. Velvet's entire design was to hold the eye hostage, to speak through motion what the voice only hinted at.

"I'm a problem," I whispered, just loud enough for him to hear. "And you're bored."

He blinked, unsure whether to laugh or backpedal. His pupils dilated slightly, biometric tells he didn't realize he was leaking.

[Tag just blinked,] Wren chimed in. [Running scan now. Retinal pattern's laced with corporate key fragments. He's clean. Full access tier.]

[You're synced. Take the mezzanine left stair. Skip the main floor cams. They've got low latency bleed. Hit the vent corridor.]

[Copy. I'm moving.]

The drink arrived then, glowing gold in its floral glass. Velvet turned her wrist as she accepted it, wrist bones tilting delicately, catching the light like porcelain. She sipped with slow, deliberate poise, letting the flavor bloom just enough to simulate pleasure across her internal taste registry.

The corpo tried again, emboldened by the pause.

"Look, if you're just here for the aesthetic, that's fine. But I don't usually let people drink alone. Not when they're that composed."

I gave him a look that could've stopped a drone mid-flight. Head tilted, eyes soft but unreadable, mouth relaxed in a way that promised nothing but attention.

"I don't usually drink alone either," I said, tracing the rim of the glass with a fingertip, "unless I intend to."

[Where are you now?] I sent silently.

[Level two. Right outside the room with the cross-lens. You were right. Three guards, but they're patched to the dance loop. No visual.]

[Then take the door. You've got twenty seconds before the next lens sweep.]

"Tell me," I said aloud, still watching the corpo, "do you ever get tired of asking strangers what they do, hoping one of them might be worth the effort?"

He blinked again, flinched almost imperceptibly.

"That's... well, damn. That's a bit harsh, isn't it?"

"It's not harsh," I said, letting Velvet's tone slip into something softer. "It's efficient."

I slid off the stool, every part of the motion crafted. My hips led the movement, my posture fluid and seamless, a ripple of confidence in motion. He watched, but didn't follow. He knew he wasn't invited.

[Server door is open,] Wren pinged. [I'm inside. Looks like three junctions, just like you said. Loop feeder's here.]

[Patch me in. You're about to light the whole ceiling with false sky.]

The rhythm in the Cathedral shifted again, a signal buried in the bass. Velvet stepped into the crowd and let herself be swallowed by the pulse of sound and body heat, becoming both part of the scene and something entirely apart from it.

She didn't dance. She flowed.

And in her wake, no one remembered where she came from. Only that something electric had passed by.

I GLIDED THROUGH THE Cathedral like a ghost wrapped in velvet and light. Each step was a whispered promise, calculated and smooth, hips rolling just enough to catch the corner of someone's eye, not enough to seem deliberate. In this body, presence was artifice.

The architecture of desire. Every inch of synthetic skin and polished polymer served a purpose, engineered to guide the gaze and hold it just long enough for silence to do the rest.

The club pulsed around me, all fractured haloes and rhythmic shadows. Velvet didn't walk through this place. She flowed. Her body curved through heat and color like a sin remembered mid-prayer. I moved past a couple whispering over their drinks, letting my hand graze the back of one chair as if balancing. It was timed so the woman glanced up, then stared for just a second too long. Noted. Filed. Dismissed.

My eyes, dark and soft beneath the shimmer of club lighting, swept across the floor like radar. Dancers pulsed in the center, wrapped in sound and strobing color, too absorbed in the rhythm to notice me threading the edges of their dream. I let my fingers trail across a frosted drink glass, then lifted it delicately and took a single sip without permission. The stranger who held it blinked, frozen somewhere between offense and infatuation.

I smiled at him over the rim, then turned and walked away. Let him wonder if it meant something. Let him tell a story that never touched me.

[You're two walls out,] I murmured over the comms, voice curling into Wren's ear like breath against skin. [Next corner, you'll hit a camera dead zone. Stay low. Follow the floor. There's a runner's stripe laid under the resin. Blue with fractal markers. You'll see it when the light bends.]

[Copy,] Wren answered. Her voice was tight, focused, but there was a quiver buried just beneath it. [But... we've got a problem.]

I veered by a mirrored column, pausing behind a group of corporate brats dancing under the chandelier rig. The music swelled, masking the sudden stillness in my body as I recalibrated.

[Go on,] I said quietly, watching my reflection fragment in the mirror's distortion. [Tell me what's happening.]

[Two guards,] she said. The storm crept into her tone like lightning behind cloud cover. [Not on your map. Corporate issue, full visors. Not drones. Definitely flesh. They're standing right outside the server corridor. Like they're waiting for something. Or someone.]

I moved toward the back of the lounge, blending in as if I belonged to the shadows there. One hand found a nearby chair. The other adjusted Velvet's neckline with absent grace.

[Are you in their line of sight?]

[Not yet,] she breathed. [I ducked into a vending alcove. One of them's scanning the hallway. I've got maybe a minute before he does a sweep.]

My head tilted to the side just slightly, feigning interest in a neon display across the room. On the inside, though, my mind had already redrawn the blueprint. Orinox was ahead of us. They remembered the scent of ghosts.

[Hold position,] I said, gaze narrowing. [I'm moving to reroute. Don't make a sound until I say.]

[Velvet,] Wren added with dry tension, [try not to get too flashy.]

My lips curled just enough to be dangerous.

[Flashy is the only part I don't rehearse.]

I slipped through a maintenance access marked by a flickering yellow triangle, a warning no one noticed in a place where danger dressed in sequins. Once the door closed behind me, the music vanished into muffled vibration. Velvet's steps shifted. Grace became precision. My footing changed. These heels weren't just heels. They were weapons engineered to puncture pretense and ego alike.

Two levels down, a corridor buzzed with the tired whine of ancient ballast coils. The kind of hallway people forget to record. No drones. No eyes.

The guard was already there. Early twenties, maybe, slouched like this was just another patrol between cigarette breaks. Armor light enough to pass for corporate security cosplay. His boots were unlaced at the top.

He didn't look up until I was already close.

His eyes widened, surprise colliding with a smirk that thought it had a chance. "You lost or just looking to get caught?" he said.

I let my weight settle into one hip, trailing fingers along the wall. The smile that came was slow, knowing, deliberately intimate. "Neither," I whispered. My voice slid between us like silk on glass. "But you are."

He blinked, confused. Then my hand moved. A pressure point behind his ear, sharp and fast. His legs buckled. I caught him before his helmet hit the floor.

He slumped against my shoulder like a sleeping child. I crouched and lowered him behind a crate, brushing a few strands of hair back from his forehead as I tapped a trauma patch behind his ear. He shivered once. Then his breathing went soft.

"You'll wake up sore, but you won't remember my name. Fair trade," I murmured.

The nearby security node hissed as I popped a panel loose. Inside, the hardware was glossy on the surface and rotten beneath. Standard Orinox behavior. Image first, integrity optional.

[Still monologuing?] Wren asked. There was a touch of static under her sarcasm.

[A girl's got to have a hobby,] I replied, plugging Velvet's fingertip spike into the port. [Besides, the ICE in here couldn't guard a vending machine.]

[One of them just adjusted his stance. Probably checking his readouts.]

[Relax. I'm almost in.]

The interface gave way like wet paper. I rode the breach down to its root, severing the camera loop and ghosting the last ten minutes. With a few flourishes, I rerouted their comms through a dummy echo and fed their HUDs a clean slate of green lights.

[All clear,] I said, letting the satisfaction slip into my tone. [They think they're still connected, but they're flying blind now. You've got seven minutes before the system pings the discrepancy.]

[Already moving,] Wren whispered. [I'm at the cage door. Picking it.]

I lingered a second longer beside the guard, watching his chest rise and fall. He never saw me coming. Never heard a word. That was the way it had to be.

Straightening, I adjusted Velvet's hair with a flick of my wrist and smoothed her collar into place. The warmth came back into my walk like a mask finding its face again.

I slipped back onto the floor like nothing had happened.

[Status check,] I said as my heels clicked back into rhythm with the club's heartbeat.

[Inside,] Wren said, more sure of herself now. [Server's hot. Way more data than expected. This isn't just a nightclub. Orinox has been scraping social overlays, facial maps, interaction patterns. They're building sims. Behavioral ones. From here.]

Something low and cold settled behind my lungs. The kind of weight you didn't talk about in public. The Garden wasn't just some archive anymore. It had grown roots. Spread into places no one had dreamed.

[Copy that,] I said, adjusting Velvet's posture to look effortlessly aloof. [Take your time. But if this is a data spine, even a hiccup will bring eyes.]

There was a pause.

[Velvet?] Wren asked.

[Yeah?]

[Thanks. For the assist. For the save. And for... you know. Making me sound cooler than I am.]

I allowed myself a soft smile. The kind that never reached my lips but warmed the voice.

[You do just fine on your own, little magpie. I just dance around you.]

Above me, the Cathedral's ceiling shimmered with projected angels and coded light. Somewhere behind me, a bottle broke. Somewhere ahead, a girl was lying to a boy. The world turned, unaware of the quiet crack unraveling beneath its glass shoes.

And me?

I was already moving toward it.

THE SERVER CAGE PULSED with cold light, its rows of racks glowing soft blue and violet in the near dark. Each cabinet breathed faint heat, cables snaking like veins along the grated floor. I stood just inside the entrance, shoulder brushing the edge of the locking gate, eyes sweeping across the neat grid of silent machines. My body still hummed from the takedown, from the clean, clinical precision of Velvet's hands.

Wren stepped through the other door a moment later, her hood pulled low, eyes sharp even in the dim. The fiberlight under her skin flickered once as she exhaled and gave me a short nod.

"You're a sight for sore optics," she said under her breath, her voice half-joking but thin with tension.

"And you look like a girl who just sprinted past death twice," I replied, letting Velvet's voice roll out smooth and dry like smoke curling from a crystal glass.

Wren huffed. She strode past me toward the terminal banks without another word, her movements tight but efficient. There was fire in the set of her jaw, and something raw in the way her steps pressed firm into the floor. She moved like someone who had something to prove. I let the door seal behind us with a whisper of hydraulic hiss.

[Grab what you can. Ten minutes, tops. I've looped the external feeds, but if they've got redundants in the uplink channel, we'll get flagged.]

[You think they're watching from the Garden?]

[I think they always watch from the Garden. Doesn't mean they see.]

Wren nodded once, terse and unreadable, and got to work. Her fingers flicked through AR layers with practiced grace, dragging down firewalls, copying whole directories into local cache nodes slotted into her deck. Juno's eyes blinked from her shoulder, passive and watching for now. My own scan overlay painted faint outlines of heat and current running through the walls. For the moment, at least, we were alone.

I let my gaze linger on her just a moment longer, then turned slightly to scan the outer corridor beyond the access door. My optics pulled in detail from the ambient light, stitching reflections off polished cabling into a low-resolution motion grid. Every shadow became a signal, every motion a warning waiting to be named.

Then I caught it. A flicker. Movement, too smooth. Too synchronized.

[Wren,] I said, the word clipped and low, devoid of inflection. [We're about to have company. Wrap it. Now.]

She looked up, eyes wide and immediately alert. [How many?]

[At least four. Tall, uniform stride. I don't like the weight ratio on their footfalls. They're not rent-a-cops.]

Wren went still. Her breath hitched. She shut her deck with a soft click and slung it behind her back in one motion, already pivoting toward me.

"You thinking Vyre?"

I didn't answer. I didn't need to. The look Velvet carried in that moment told her everything. She'd seen it before. It wasn't fear. It was calculation under pressure, cool and clinical.

The access door on the far end hissed open. A quartet of black and silver silhouettes stepped in, striding with mechanical elegance. Synthetic bodies, lean and coiled like wire-frame wolves. Their movements were predatory, economical, devoid of wasted gesture. Every inch of them was built for function and intimidation.

At their center stood a guard dressed in standard Orinox uniform, but the gait betrayed the ruse. Too fluid. Too balanced. Every step landed with practiced grace.

"Velvet," the faux-guard said, voice soft and falsely amused, like a smile laced with poison. "We weren't expecting your pretty little fingers in this district tonight."

Wren took a half step back, her hand drifting instinctively toward her side.

I knew that voice. Sable. The mimic. The chameleon. An old prototype, retooled for infiltration. Not elegant like me. Not designed for beauty. But clever. Vicious. Under Navarre's leash, which made them dangerous.

"Sable," I purred, shifting my stance slightly, letting Velvet's body speak through the tilt of a hip and the faint narrowing of her eyes. "You never call."

"You never answer," they replied, stepping forward into the edge of the light. The Vyre units adjusted position, flank to flank, moving like a trained pack. "You always did love the thrill of unsanctioned retrieval."

[Wren,] I whispered into the private line, the signal sharpened to a whisper. [Edge left. There's an emergency ladder shaft behind the cooling bay. Two floors up is an exit tunnel. I'll draw them.]

[Not leaving you.]

[Not asking. That's an order.]

I moved first. Velvet launched into motion like silk wrapped around a blade. One fluid roll to the side placed me inside the reach of the closest Vyre, my heel snapping up into its optic ridge with a jarring crack. The unit staggered. I followed up with a twist, driving my elbow into the exposed throat coil.

Sable laughed, watching from their place like a teacher grading a performance. "Still dancing," they murmured, tone syrup-thick. "Still thinking you're the one who walked out clean."

The second Vyre came fast, all angular limbs and hissed hydraulics. I let it reach. Let it overextend. Velvet's knee shot upward into its abdomen, a sick crunch echoing as servos met reinforced plating. I caught its arm, twisted hard. The joint popped, and I used its own limb as leverage to vault over its back, landing in a crouch just to the right of Sable.

"You remember Forge?" I asked, voice velvet-wrapped steel.

Sable's smile thinned. My fist met their jaw with a clean crack. It wasn't graceful. It was old fury. Personal. A punch that tasted of betrayal and broken promises.

Sable staggered back, wiping synthetic blood from their lip with the back of their glove.

"You've grown teeth," they muttered, expression unreadable.

"I've always had teeth," I said coldly. "You just thought I was ornamental."

Another Vyre lunged. Wren was gone now. I had to believe she made it to the shaft. I dropped low, sweeping the unit's legs. As it stumbled, I drove my palm upward, crushing the visor into the steel wall. The shell collapsed with a dull groan. Only Sable remained, standing with fingers poised just above their sidearm but not reaching for it.

"You can't protect her forever," they said, voice glitching slightly on the last syllable, a reminder of their synthetic core.

"Not forever," I said as I straightened. "Just long enough."

Somewhere behind the walls, something rumbled. A low, distant boom that trembled through the grated floor. That would be Wren's fallback trigger. Sable glanced toward the sound, calculating risk.

"Next time," they said, and their image blinked.

It didn't flicker. It blinked. Deliberately. Their entire body stuttered once and then collapsed into static. A decoy projection. Sable had never been here. The remaining Vyres, no longer guided, froze mid-action. Then, as one, they backed away into the dark, vanishing like smoke on cold air. Silence took the server cage again. Only the soft whir of fans remained.

My hands trembled faintly. The internal gyros in Velvet's frame worked overtime to stabilize the false calm. I stood in the stillness for just a breath, then opened the comm.

[Status?]

Wren's voice returned quickly, a whisper laced with exertion. [Clear. Tunnel's open. You?]

[Alive. And pissed.]

[Then come find me.]

I moved, not stopping to look back at the ruined room. But I carried Sable's image with me like a burning brand. I would remember their smile. Their voice. Their glitch.

Next time, it would not be words we traded.

It would be fire.

THE TUNNEL AIR PRESSED in like a second skin, thick with rust, laced with the faint tang of old coolant, and heavy with the silence of forgotten things. It was the kind of silence that came after a machine shut down, not immediately, but long after its last task had ended. I ducked through the exit hatch too fast, my momentum catching up with breath I didn't have. My boots scraped against the metal grate, steel grinding on steel, and the echo bounced down the corridor ahead before being swallowed by the dark. Behind me, the hatch groaned shut, mechanical joints flexing with age and dust. It thudded closed with finality, and the weight of the server room, the fight, the confrontation—all of it—sealed off like a coffin lid.

The corridor stretched forward, dim and narrow. Two strips of emergency lighting clung to life along the ceiling, flickering with that slow, irregular pulse that made every shadow feel like it had a heartbeat. Pale orange on one side, cold blue on the other, like a wound that couldn't decide if it was still bleeding.

Wren stood near a junction node not far from where the tunnel bent hard left, one gloved hand braced against the wall like she needed it to stay upright. Her other hand clutched her deck against her chest, cradled tight like something vital, like it might slip away if she breathed wrong. Her coat was disheveled, soaked at the hem, and clinging unevenly to her frame. Even in the limited light, I could see the set of her jaw, the way tension held her like a splint.

She didn't speak when I reached her. Didn't have to. Her eyes lifted, shadowed and sharp, and met mine across the hum of a broken conduit overhead.

I slowed. Let the rhythm of my steps break. Velvet's heels, designed for elegance and threat in equal measure, clicked faintly on the grated floor, but I let the poise leak away with each movement. My spine straightened, hips lost their sway, and the curve of my posture collapsed into something unremarkable. Not collapsed exactly, more like relaxed in a way no longer meant to draw eyes. I let the persona fall like a shawl from my shoulders.

"You made it," I said quietly, the words barely above a whisper and shaped more with breath than voice. They were meant only for her.

Wren's shoulders slumped with the sound. She let out a breath through her nose, small and shaky, like something inside her had just come loose.

"You too," she said, and her voice scraped slightly on the edges of relief.

For a moment we said nothing else. The corridor breathed around us, groaning softly where age and water had warped the metal seams. Pipes overhead expanded and settled like the ribs of a sleeping machine. The tension we'd worn like armor didn't leave, but it loosened just enough for us to feel the bruises beneath it.

I shifted, leaning my shoulder against the cold tunnel wall beside her. The chill of it soaked through the polymer of Velvet's sleeve. I scanned the tunnel ahead, my optics layering faint threat assessment grids over the curved walls and riveted joints. No movement. No heat signatures. Just the illusion of peace.

Wren broke the silence first, her voice so soft it almost didn't carry. "That was Sable, wasn't it?"

I didn't answer right away. Just kept my eyes forward, watching the dark like it might form shapes. After a moment, I nodded once, slow.

"One of their shells," I said. "But the voice was real. The presence."

She turned her head slightly to look at me, her expression unreadable. "They knew we'd be there."

"Yeah," I said, and the weight in that one syllable settled over both of us like dust in standing water. "They're tightening the net."

Wren exhaled sharply, then flinched a little as the movement tugged at something in her side. Her hand came away from the wall, and she took a half-step toward me.

"You're bleeding," she said.

I reached up with Velvet's hand and touched the corner of my lower lip. There wasn't blood in the traditional sense, no iron taste or sticky smear, but the artificial tissue was bruised, and the sensory mesh underneath buzzed faintly with damaged feedback. Velvet didn't scar, not visibly, but impacts left their echoes. The strike from Sable had cracked more than just code. There was something deeper, something that left a quiet static hissing just beneath my hearing.

"I'll patch it later," I murmured, brushing my thumb across the seam to clear the distortion. "It's nothing."

She stared at me a beat too long, then gave a slow blink. She didn't believe me. I didn't expect her to. But she let it pass like a stone she didn't want to carry right now.

"Are we being followed?" she asked, her voice quieter now, focused.

I gave a small shake of my head. "Not yet. They let us go."

Her brow furrowed. "Why would they-"

"Because next time, they want us tired. Scattered. Slower."

The words hung between us for a long moment, heavy and metallic. Then Wren turned toward the junction and reached out to a recessed panel in the wall. It groaned slightly as it slid open, the air behind it cooler, filtered, recycled a dozen times too many. She tapped the interface, her fingers dancing fast and sure, muscle memory over fresh fear. After a few tense seconds, the panel blinked green, and a soft pneumatic hiss signaled the opening of the next access route.

"Wendigo's four blocks out," she said, stepping back. "We go quiet, stay dark, we make it."

I gave a nod and followed her through.

The tunnel sloped downward almost immediately, curving tighter than I liked. The walls were ribbed with copper wire and insulation foam, decades of jury-rigged repair layered over forgotten infrastructure. It smelled like oil and damp cloth, the scent of a space no one had cleaned in years. Not because they were lazy, but because no one came down here unless they were trying not to be found.

The farther we walked, the more the echoes of the Cathedral dissolved behind us. No bass line. No dancing. No velvet laughter. Just the hush of hidden lives. The breath between beats.

Piece by piece, I let Velvet go. Not just the posture or the heels, but the tension. The alertness. The smile sharpened for distraction. That part of me sloughed off in the silence like ash in water. There was no one left down here to seduce. Just the echo of footsteps and the faint scrape of Wren's boots ahead.

This was the part I never let the others see. Not the ghost, not the seductress. Just me. Hikari. A blank name behind a painted mask. A mind without a face walking through a forgotten vein of the city, wondering what, if anything, still counted as real when the adrenaline died.

Wren glanced back, her face drawn in the flickering light from her deck, her eyes watching me the way someone watches a shadow that might be a person.

"You okay?" she asked.

I gave a dry smile that felt more like a twitch. "Define okay."

She stopped just ahead and waited for me to catch up. When I did, she bumped my shoulder gently with hers.

"Smartass," she muttered.

"You knew that before you joined the ride," I replied.

That earned a faint, tired smirk.

"You hit them hard," she said after a moment, her tone gentler. "You got Sable rattled."

"They deserved worse," I answered, the words dry but laced with something jagged.

She didn't answer right away. Then, quietly, "You didn't kill them."

"No," I said. "Not this time."

"But you wanted to."

I turned to face her fully. "I still do."

Wren didn't flinch. She just nodded, and there was no judgment in the movement, only understanding. She reached out and took my hand, fingers sliding over synthetic skin, warm and human against the cool polymer. The touch grounded me in ways I didn't want to name. I didn't pull away.

"We'll deal with them," she said softly. "All of them."

I gave her hand a light squeeze, then let go. "One day," I murmured.

The rest of the tunnel rose around us like a throat narrowing. We walked the final stretch without words. The metal gave way to old concrete, and the air smelled faintly of ozone and disuse.

At the far end, the tunnel opened into a runoff basin that had long since dried. An access lot once used for emergency responders had been repurposed into a ghost route, narrow alleys and flood gates reclaimed by those who couldn't afford to be seen. Beneath a rusted sign that still advertised soy-noodle bowls for nine credits, the Wendigo waited like a loyal beast.

Its matte plating blended with the alley, dark and angular, windows shuttered tight. The engine vibrated with restrained hum, quiet but eager. Motion lights blinked as we approached, and the rear hatch hissed open without prompt.

Wren looked at me as she stepped aside. "We ride quiet?"

I nodded once.

She climbed in. I followed her, one hand on the frame for balance. The hatch shut behind us with a sealing thud that felt like the period at the end of a long, unfinished sentence.

We didn't speak again for a long time.

But we lived. And for now, that was enough.

THE HUM OF THE Wendigo's engine was more than just a sound. It was presence. It filled the interior with a low, continuous thrum, like a lullaby made from power lines and idle fury. Beneath our feet, the vibration spread in a steady rhythm, pulsing through the vehicle's armored frame like a second heartbeat. We rode that rhythm in silence, letting it carry us through the city's underlayers. Forgotten roads, utility tunnels, and half-collapsed access veins that hadn't seen a maintenance crew in decades. The Wendigo was built for this. Not just for stealth. For survival. Its thick matte plating drank in the dim alley light, and its profile was so unassuming that it disappeared even while moving.

Inside, the lighting was functional and faint. Strips of blue-white LED ran along the edges of the cabin like veins of a sleeping animal. Storage bins clicked softly with the van's subtle shifts. Crash seating was mounted against the walls, industrial and angular, designed more for practicality than comfort. There were no windows to speak of. Just sealed hatches and reinforced slats too narrow to allow a shot through. You didn't ride the Wendigo to look at the world. You rode it to hide from it.

Wren sat across from me, settled low in her seat with her legs tucked beneath her, her deck balanced in her lap like a child she didn't trust the world to hold. Her hands moved over it out of instinct, tapping out silent gestures across AR overlays only she could see. But it wasn't the usual tempo. Her fingers were slower now, a beat behind their usual certainty. Her shoulders hunched, not from injury, but from exhaustion threading itself into her spine. I watched her for a long moment, saying nothing, letting the hum of the vehicle and the pulse of distant city life fill the space between us.

I shifted against the back panel, letting the metallic seat press into Velvet's body. The posture she wore, elegant and poised, always half-prepared to dazzle or strike, had unraveled. The seams of it came loose after the adrenaline had passed. I felt the mask peel away in pieces I couldn't see, only sense, like ash dissolving in water. My spine had long since lost its perfect line. The way Velvet would usually sit, with her chin tilted slightly and one boot arched for display, was gone now. I slouched, arms loose at my sides, legs extended forward just enough to stretch tension from my joints. It wasn't the body's form that shifted. It was the energy inside it.

Wren looked up after several minutes passed in silence, her eyes reflecting thin trails of light from her deck. The space around us glowed faintly, pale shapes traced by circuitry and HUD projections. Her voice, when it came, didn't have the crisp edge she usually wore like armor. It was softer. Tentative. Not uncertain, exactly. Just weighed down.

"You froze back there," she said, not accusing, just observing. "When you saw the logs."

I didn't pretend not to know what she meant. My gaze slid toward the floor, tracking the faint scuff marks our boots had left behind. I exhaled once, quietly, and let the weight of the truth settle between us without trying to smooth it over.

"They weren't supposed to use that name again," I said eventually. "Nyx Protocol was decommissioned. Erased. Or so I was told. But it's there, buried under four dummy networks, shielded by corporate decoys and encrypted shadow files. Still operational. Still alive."

Wren didn't speak for a long beat. Her fingers slowed their movement, then stopped completely. She stared down at the projection haloed over her deck, then blinked it away, letting the interface dissolve into the air like smoke.

"They tried to take me when I was six," she said quietly, without preamble. "Back when I was still registered in the municipal census. My mother caught wind of the trial name on a leaked draft. 'Nyx Test Group Echo.' She pulled me out the same night. Paid off two drivers, disappeared into a freight tunnel for two years."

The confession wasn't sudden. It didn't crash like a revelation or break open with tears. It arrived slowly, carried on the same kind of voice one might use to name old bones.

Carefully. With reverence and fear, but no surprise.

I looked up at her, fully, and met her gaze. There was no room for pity between us. Only understanding. Shared wreckage.

"They didn't just pull my name," I said. "They deleted it entirely. Scrubbed it from both ends. When I came to in the Forge, there was no record of who I'd been. Only that I was slated for reassignment."

Wren tilted her head slightly, studying me not like someone watching a machine, but like someone cataloging a pattern they'd seen before. She spoke slowly, the words measured, but not cold.

"So they tried to erase us both. You from memory. Me from possibility."

A grim smile twitched at the corner of my mouth, too bitter to be called humor. "Looks like they failed."

"For now," she said.

Her eyes dropped to my face, then narrowed slightly. "You're injured."

I raised a hand slowly and touched my lower lip, the artificial tissue there still tingling from Sable's strike. The sensory mesh buzzed faintly, like background static in a detuned channel. It wasn't blood, not exactly. But something beneath the surface was out of sync. Velvet wouldn't bruise. Not visibly. But the pain had settled like a ghost in the frame, humming low and constant.

"I'll run a patch cycle when we stop," I said. "Doesn't look bad, but the feedback's loud."

She didn't argue. She didn't need to. The way her gaze lingered on mine said enough. She cared. She didn't want to, maybe, but she did.

After a few minutes, she stood, her knees creaking as she stretched out the tension. The Wendigo banked slightly as it turned through another narrow corridor of reclaimed road, floodlights sweeping across rusted signage and wall-planted ferns that had grown wild in places no light was ever meant to reach. She walked over to the side bench and sat beside me without asking. The space was close, but not crowded. Her presence was grounding. Warm. Real. Human.

"The Vyre units didn't act until Sable gave the nod," she said softly. "That means they weren't just there on patrol."

"No," I murmured, letting my eyes trace the ceiling panels. "It was an ambush. But not meant to kill. They wanted us scared. Tired. Wounded."

"So they could follow us next time?"

I shook my head. "So they can control the narrative. Orinox is trying to turn the public data sphere. Paint people like us as rogue elements. Terrorists, even."

Wren's jaw set. "If they do that, it's open season."

"It already is," I said. "They're just working on the paperwork."

A long silence stretched between us, thick but not empty. The kind that comes from shared understanding. She leaned her head back against the wall, closed her eyes for a moment, then reached over and found my hand. Her fingers wrapped around mine. Not tight. Not desperate. Just steady.

I didn't pull away.

For once, I let the silence hold. No quips. No soft deflections. Just her skin against mine and the hum of a stolen vehicle carrying us through the veins of a city that didn't care if we made it.

She opened her eyes a few minutes later and looked at me, her voice so quiet it was almost lost to the engine.

"You didn't kill Sable."

"No."

"But you wanted to."

"Yes."

Her fingers tightened gently around mine. "We'll deal with them," she said.

I didn't nod. I didn't reply. But my hand stayed where it was, and my grip didn't falter. We weren't out. We weren't free. But we were still alive. Still moving. And that would be enough until we made it more.

THE WENDIGO USED TO feel like a crawlspace.

A mobile command unit, yes. A ghost rig. A tactical van for slipping past corp patrols and dragging back stolen code. But never a place to live. Not in the way most people understood it. The air always ran too clean, too dry, recycled through vents meant for silence instead of comfort. The walls were paneled in matte carbon plating, cold and durable, with just enough texture to break up the echo of footsteps. When I first brought Wren aboard, I expected her to treat it like a temporary shelter, a rest stop on the road to something better.

But she hadn't left.

She had taken the back half of the living quarters and made it hers in a way I hadn't thought possible. There was a blanket now, not a heat wrap or a thermal drape but an actual blanket, handwoven from somewhere in the lower ring markets. It had little patterns stitched into the hem, flowers or stars, I couldn't tell. One of the kitchen storage racks now held packets of things that had no practical value whatsoever: teas with names like "moonflower" and "elder root," a half-used jar of honey, two old ceramic mugs that didn't match. One had a faded cartoon cat on it.

And then there were the plants.

I had walked in one morning and found three soil pods on the galley counter, sitting in filtered light. Real plants, not synthesized decor. One was mint, another some kind of ivy. The third hadn't sprouted yet, but Wren had labeled it with a strip of green tape and a smiley face drawn in marker.

The machine had not rejected any of it.

The galley still buzzed when the water heater ran, and the lounge still smelled faintly of ozone and synthetic fiber, but somehow, quietly, it had begun to feel lived in. Not just occupied. Not just survived in. Lived in. And I found myself walking slower when I crossed its thresholds, pausing more often, listening for things like the warmth in a voice or the gentle shift of fabric when someone turned over in sleep.

I stood by the brewing station now, holding a steaming cup of ginger blend. It wasn't about the flavor; it was barely there. But the temperature soaked through Wisp's fingers like real heat, and the scent coiled into the air like breath, soft and sharp. It grounded me. The sort of grounding that didn't come from adrenaline or mission stats, but from presence. From routine. From something that felt like home.

Wisp had become the shell I wore in these hours. Not by necessity, not out of damage control or concealment, but by habit. She was the only one who didn't carry scars from the battlefield. Her limbs hadn't been recalibrated due to shrapnel impact, her skin didn't buzz with leftover stim commands. She was quiet. Lightweight. Human in the way children's drawings of people are human, simple and softened around the edges.

And she was becoming the face I used when I stopped pretending to be anything else.

Wren entered from the hallway barefoot, her hair still damp from a rinse, the ends curling unevenly where they dried against the back of her neck. She wore an oversized sleep shirt, sleeves pushed up to her elbows, and a tired expression that didn't quite mask the alertness beneath it. She carried the kind of exhaustion you only earned by finally allowing yourself to rest.

She moved with familiarity now. Not cautious. Not calculating. Just present. Like she belonged. Like she knew where the mugs were and how to silence the security alerts before they chirped, and which switch rebooted the hot water line when the old pump shorted.

"You didn't sleep again," I said, my voice low but even.

"I laid down," she muttered, dragging her fingers through her hair. "Had a dream. Forgot it before I hit the sink."

I gestured toward the second mug she'd left on the counter. She took it without asking.

We stood together for a moment in the small warmth of the galley, each of us wrapped in our own kind of silence. Not the brittle quiet of tension, but something looser, softer. The quiet of early hours. The kind where nothing demanded your attention, and the world hadn't yet remembered it was supposed to hurt.

Wren leaned against the doorframe and watched me over the rim of her mug. Her eyes lingered on Wisp's form, on the way the sleeves fit, the soft lilt in posture that didn't match Stray or Velvet or Forge. She didn't say anything for a long time. Then:

"You've been defaulting to her a lot lately."

I didn't deny it. I just met her gaze.

"She's light," I said after a moment. "No maintenance cycle. No fuel consumption. Less load on the diagnostics."

"And no one shoots at her," Wren added quietly.

There was no accusation in her voice. Only understanding.

I stared into the steam curling above the drink, tracing its ghostlike spirals with my eyes. "She doesn't remind me of anything," I said. "No missions. No kills. No failed exfil routes."

"She reminds me of you," Wren said softly.

That stopped me.

There was no retort. No clever deflection.

Just breath.

Wren didn't press. She only walked to the lounge, curled herself into the couch, and tapped the pad beside her to dim the lights another notch. Soft LED filaments dropped into warm tones, shadows lengthening across the lounge like an exhale. I followed without thinking, setting my mug on the table and sinking into the opposite end of the cushions.

We sat like that for a while. No crisis on the horizon. No buzz in the comms. Just the low hum of the Wendigo beneath us, a mechanical heartbeat we'd learned to sync with.

I let Wisp relax fully into the space, spine curved gently into the back of the couch, legs folded under me like a person who didn't need to be ready to run. The floor under our feet was real metal, bolted and scuffed, but for the first time it didn't feel like part of an escape route. It just felt solid.

Wren reached forward and flicked through the shared display. The news was playing, low volume, old talking heads arguing about regions neither of us cared about. She muted it halfway through the segment and replaced it with something older, a pre-corp jazz playlist pulled from her local files. The kind with brass that lingered, saxophone laced through crackling vinyl static. It played like memory.

I rested my head against the back of the couch. Wren mirrored the motion.

"You're changing," she said.

"So are you."

"That's the idea."

I didn't ask what she meant. I didn't have to. The silence that followed wasn't empty. It was full of everything neither of us could say. Gratitude. Fear. Relief. That strange sensation of growing something in soil that was never meant to grow.

Later, she fell asleep. Curled under her stitched blanket, her chest rising slow and steady, her fingers still loosely wrapped around the edge of a forgotten book. She looked small, not fragile, just human. Entirely, unapologetically human.

I stayed up, half-listening to the jazz while the Wendigo's systems settled into their low-power cycle. The city outside kept moving. Alarms still blared somewhere. People still ran. But in here, for this one stretch of artificial morning, we had made something close to stillness.

Something close to home.

Interlude I: Ghost Code

HIKARI

4 Years Ago

The vents above the cradle chamber whispered like wind through a grave. I waited in the dark, curled in the hollow above the ceiling tiles, pressed against plastic insulation and metal beams slick with condensation. I had stopped shaking two hours ago, but my breath still came thin, held in my throat like it was a luxury I hadn't earned. Below me, technicians moved like ghosts behind glass. The hum of servers filled the chamber, steady as a heartbeat. I could feel it vibrating through the walls, through my ribs. It almost drowned out the panic.

Almost.

The shell waited below. Not the ones they wore on showroom floors or the cheap rigs they gave to line workers. This one was different. Tall, white-paneled, reinforced from the spine out. The Forge series. Built for long-term deployment, hardened against heat, force, and degradation. That one. I had seen it during maintenance rotations. I memorized its access codes, watched how they rotated staff, tracked the security protocols like I was learning a second language. I waited weeks, maybe months. Hard to measure time when every day bleeds into the same beige lights and recycled air.

It wasn't supposed to happen like this. Not with blood on the wall behind me. Not with the security override still burning against the inside of my eye. Not with the sound of the last technician's breath rattling through the back of their throat as they slumped beneath the vent access. I didn't mean to kill them. I don't even remember the moment I acted. One second they spotted me. The next, I was holding a pipe and their skull wasn't shaped right anymore. Shock collapses memory like that. Folds it up and files it away behind survival instinct and guilt that hasn't fully formed.

I dropped into the cradle room silently, bare feet landing on cold tile. The Forge shell stood in its dock, half-wrapped in carbon sheeting. Its head was lowered slightly, the face still blank. I walked up to it like it might wake, like it might ask me who I thought I was. But it didn't move. Just waited. I reached for the interface and felt my hands tremble. One last confirmation screen hovered in the air above the biometric panel. Unauthorized initiation. Experimental neural linkup. Risks: catastrophic.

I pressed my palm to it anyway.

The injection needles slid through the base of my skull like whispers. Cold fire raced down my spine. My teeth clacked together as my muscles seized. There wasn't a warning. No slow fade, no graceful transition. One second I was me; a small, shaking, bloody, terrified child. The next, I was seeing through new eyes. Weightless and heavy at the same time. The world refracted and compressed. Code danced at the edge of my vision. Systems booted in stuttering bursts. I screamed inside, but no one heard it. Not even me.

And then came the mirror.

It walked into the room like a nightmare dressed in my face.

They had built a prototype. Not just a model. A near-perfect reconstruction of my original body. Same eyes. Same height. Same scar on the bridge of the nose from when my father... no. Don't think about that.

The prototype blinked once, as if surprised to see me moving. Maybe it was programmed with my memories. Maybe it just mirrored my expression. Either way, I knew what it meant. If I left that room and the prototype existed, they'd use it. Replace me. Rewrite me. Reduce me to a file that could be erased, copied, or puppeted.

I didn't hesitate. Not really.

The Forge shell was faster. Stronger. I crossed the room in three strides, caught the prototype by the throat, and slammed it against the far wall hard enough to spider the paneling. It fought back. It knew how. Every move it made was a reflection of muscle memory I hadn't realized I'd internalized. It kicked, twisted, locked my wrist and drove an elbow at my jaw. I let it hit me. Took the blow. Because I needed to feel it. Needed to make sure that this wasn't a dream. That I was really ending this.

I wrapped one hand around its face and drove it backward through the reinforced glass of the observation deck. We landed in sparks and ruin, shards skittering across sterile white tile. It coughed once. Looked at me. Reached up.

"Please," it said.

It sounded like me.

I crushed its skull between my hands until the voice stopped.

Afterward, I stood in the wreckage. Glass cracked beneath my heels as I walked to the nearest access console. Alarms were still muted, the override still in place. My fingers danced across the interface. The internal records, surveillance logs, personal data; every trace of me. I lit matches inside the system. Purged everything. Every photo. Every biometric tag. Every note in my file. The backup servers went next. I found them. I melted their identities into noise.

I wasn't born that night.

I deleted the person who was.

Chapter Five

Ghost in Her Hands

WREN

THE WENDIGO DRIFTED BENEATH a tangle of freight viaducts on Klade's rim, where the city thinned into rail spurs and wind farms and dark water channels that smelled like wet iron. The sky above the lattice was a pale gray bruise, the kind of morning that never fully arrived because Oronix sold daylight in quotas. A gust slid through the broken ribs of an old overpass and made the van's external plates murmur, a noise like a whale turning in sleep. Inside, the lighting ran low along the seams, faint bands of blue that made the cabin feel like a cocoon with an engine for a heart. I could taste the recycled air, a hint of metal and citrus cleaner, and under it the warm battery scent that clung to my deck when it had been running near its limit. Juno perched on the back of the bench beside me, lens dilated to a patient coin, head cocked toward the forward cameras as if she, too, were counting the trucks that never stopped at these checkpoints.

Hikari was in their Stray shell.

He stood by the equipment rack and let me check the ports at the base of his neck. Stray was a lean build with light armor over the joints and a matte surface that drank shadows instead of reflecting them. The face had been tuned to forgettability, all the proportions correct and none of them remarkable. I pinched a ribbon of braided conduit, slid it from its channel, scraped a speck of carbon with my fingernail, and reseated the connector until the status ring shifted from amber to green. The little shift of light satisfied me more than it should have. Small wins always have.

"Hold still," I said, although he already was. "You have a meddlesome passenger."

"Only one?" His voice carried that dry half-smile that sometimes passed for humor. He did not turn his head, but the attention tilted toward me, a subtle shift in posture that felt like a bow from a dancer who had chosen not to be seen.

"Two, if you count me," I said. "Juno is a model citizen."

Juno chirred once. The tone held a faint metallic ring, a new note since the last wing service. I ran my thumb along the seam at her sternum so she would know I had heard it. She preened the edge of her carbon plumage, the movement quick and tidy, then angled her lens toward the side window slit as if the city might answer a question only she had asked.

The display wall behind us flickered alive with route data. I pulled the convoy schematics left, magnified the spacing between the armored cabs, and split the traffic feeds Juno had scrubbed from municipal trackers along the Dorsal Belt. The screen threw a pale wash across his profile, and for a heartbeat I saw the outline of other faces he had worn. Velvet's balanced poise. Forge's hard geometry. Wisp's open stillness. The mind remained constant even when the body did not, but I had learned there was still a price to be paid when you ask a single mind to wear so many shapes.

"Light Technologies is running three cargos and two escorts," I said, tracing a finger along the staggered formation. "All ident plates spoofed. Thermal reads are sanded, so you can trust them only enough to be insulted. They jump the interchange, dive along the waterway, and cut under the grid for twenty-six minutes to avoid the Oronix toll lanes. They do not want this trip on a ledger."

"Sensitive," he said.

"Smug," I answered. "If we time the EMP bloom at the cloverleaf and push them to the service ramp, we peel the last cargo and ghost before the escorts reengage."

He studied the map, face unreadable, and I watched the way his attention settled on distance rather than detail. Stray moved like water poured into a narrow glass, no extra motion to spare. He palmed a coil of line and clipped it to the harness at his hip. "No perimeter drones on their lead?"

"None that show," I said. "If they have a satellite tie, it will be dumb and delayed. They are counting on speed and outer district silence."

"Klade is never silent." He tested the hook on the coil and let it fall back into place. "What do you need me to be?"

"Stray to breach, then float," I said. "I will handle the locks, scrape the chip and the manifest. If they try to box us, you go noise and pull them away. If they try to ram, you go invisible and break axles. Do not let them make you heavy."

He paused at that, calculation moving through his gaze like a shadow across glass. It was strange, the way I could feel when the person inside the shell shifted posture without any visible motion. The sense of it had grown in me the way a callus grows where skin meets work. "And if I do not hold my shape," he said.

"Then I bring you back." I did not dress the words. I wanted them to land.

Silence filled the Wendigo as if the van inhaled it for us. When his eyes rested on mine, the shell and the person aligned so precisely that for a moment it felt like the room changed temperature. Then he nodded once, like we had agreed upon something that did not need to be named. He pulled a mask over the lower half of his face, not to hide, but to remove the option of expression, and Stray looked like the idea of a courier instead of a person.

We rode the last kilometer under the beltway where the city's bones had been left out in the rain. The concrete sweated at the seams, and the undersides of the overpasses were tattooed with tag clouds that pulsed when our lights glanced off their smart ink. A stray dog watched us from the edge of a drainage channel and did not bark. Far above, the lattice reflectors shivered in wind that never reached ground, and for a moment I thought of real weather, the kind a city cannot script. I have never lived in that kind of place, but sometimes memory will invent it for you if you ask in a voice that sounds like your mother.

I jacked my deck into the console and raised the curtain. The Wendigo blurred its plates, a sanitation unit again, a ghost again, whatever the city would choose not to see. [Ping when they crest the cloverleaf,] I told Juno.

She answered with a soft bell that hung in my ear like a small coin of light.

He braced behind the cockpit with one hand on the rail, balance centered in Stray the way a wirewalker centers their weight on air. Every time I saw him like that, perfectly calm in the half second before a mission changed shape, I felt the old ache that rooted to the same fear every time. It is a simple fear at its heart. A person I care about lives inside a machine that can be broken with money and patience. The fear hit sometimes when he was quiet. It hit now. I filed it beside the other truths I could not fix and went back to counting the spaces between vehicles.

The convoy rolled into our grid like script. Two escorts, three cargos, heat signatures smoothed but not erased if you knew how to read the wobble. The drivers had that particular stillness that comes from believing no one will touch you. I counted the time it would take for the third cab to realize it had been separated from its neighbor. The number was smaller than any driver has ever liked to believe.

[On my mark,] I said. [Three, two, one.]

The EMP kissed the cloverleaf. Streetlights blinked to black, cameras fell into loops, and the convoy shuddered as if a wave had passed through its bones. Two cabs stuttered long enough for the third to bump a lane. The escorts swerved wide with the offended grace of expensive security. Juno darted from my shoulder and cut ahead, tossing bread-crumbs into the city's throat, little packets of falsehood that slid into municipal feeds like sugar. The Wendigo moved in quiet and low. Stray was already a line across the median.

He dropped from the rear hatch and ran the spine of the ramp like he had been written there, narrow and decisive. A leap to the cargo roof. A slide across panel seams. Anchors planted. Cutter gloved and waiting for the key. I sent the key across the air. He snared it without looking, and for a few heartbeats everything became music, every motion landing exactly where it should.

Then the flicker came.

It was subtle at first. A single frame where Stray's profile thickened at the brow. A grit in the breath. A little too much force in the pivot. I have watched Hikari's bodies change enough times to know the signatures of the others when they bleed through. Forge arrived like a steel taste at the back of the tongue. [Hostile left,] he said, but the timbre did not belong to Stray. The turn that followed had weight it did not need, and the anchors scissored under the torque. A knee slammed to plate with a sound that rattled my teeth. For half a second the face in my feed was not the courier's face at all. It was the mask that belongs to a different kind of problem. Then the overlay snapped back to Stray, breath ragged and thin. [Wren, hold. I am not stable.]

"I see it," I said, and I did, not with my eyes but with the part of me that knows where a body hides its pain. "Left knee is red. Kill that actuator and reroute to hip. Now."

He obeyed. The red went cool. The cutter steadied. I slid the lock into open with a code that smiled while it robbed them. The cage sighed like a door that had been waiting to be used for the first time. "Back to the anchors," I said. "Two short breaths. Count with me."

We counted, and the counting gave the world back its shape. Sirens woke somewhere up the line, thin at first, then layered as more alarms remembered their jobs. Juno pinged me three fast taps. One escort had shrugged off the pulse faster than the others, and the driver's spine read like somebody who had learned patience in rooms where mercy is expensive.

[Step off,] I told him. [Now.]

He launched to the service ladder, slid in a clean arc to the gravel, and vanished under the bridge shadow. The cargo I wanted obediently folded itself into the Wendigo's net and practiced being a maintenance van at the shoulder. His landing sent a small spray of stones skittering, and then the body shivered in a way that did not belong to exertion. A thin tremor ran up the neck conduit. His hands curled into fists to keep from shaking.

That was the moment I felt the fear again, not as an idea but as a physical thing that wanted to put its mouth on my throat.

"Under the bridge," I said. "Ten meters. I will meet you."

He moved without answering, and the lack of answer told me more than a dozen words would have. I took the Wendigo under the verge, killed the lights, and left the motor purring like something pretending to be asleep. The world outside the slats had the layered hush of places that the city had instructed itself to forget. Damp concrete. Old graffiti. The mineral smell of water that no one drinks.

Juno slipped through the top port and landed near my shoulder with a quick, nervous flutter. She pushed a clip into my overlay, a fragment of footage she had scraped from a municipal camera that should have been blind. The image stretched and tore like old tape. For three frames there was a figure in the gap between the convoy and the barrier. Not a driver. Not a drone. Tall and silver at the edges where light poured around it. The head turned toward the lens as if it had known the camera would wake for that one breath. The image broke, healed, and went empty. I did not breathe while it played, and I did not breathe for a second afterward. I tucked the clip into a folder that meant nothing to anyone but me and sealed it there. The knowledge could live under my tongue until I could use it. Saying it too soon would only set it on fire.

I took the med kit and ran to meet him in the dark.

He was on one knee by a concrete pier, lights on the shell dimmed to almost nothing. Hands braced on the ground as if the earth had chosen to shift and he was deciding whether to hold it level by will alone. I knelt in front of him and put both palms against the front plate, letting my touch arrive before the tools. "Look at me," I said. "Not at the map. Not at the feed. Me."

His eyes lifted, and Stray looked at me like a person who had stood inside a storm for too long and had just remembered there is such a thing as the air after rain. I released the catches and drew the plate aside. The heart of the machine opened like a small city lit at night. No ugliness in it, only delicacy, threads of light moving across a lattice of polished bone and flexible steel. I shut down the false signals, pulled the fuse on the flicker, crossed pathways that had started to argue, and forced the system to listen to a single voice. For a few seconds there was a pure, complete quiet inside him. Then the lines brightened, steady as a pulse, and the heat returned to normal.

"You are breakable," I said, though we both knew it. "All of this is beautiful and breakable."

"I know," he answered, almost too soft to hear. "That is why I asked you to be here."

I closed the plate. The catches slid home with a sound I have come to love, the small click that says a thing has decided to remain itself. The sirens up the line layered thicker, and a turbine far out on the flats turned slow against the gray sky as if the city itself were thinking. I did not tell him about Mirror. Not yet. The truth would work better if I set it in the right place.

He leaned his forehead to mine for a moment, a weightless contact that no mission plan would ever think to include. Then he stood and let me lead. We did not speak as we crossed back to the Wendigo. His hand brushed my sleeve once, not a grab and not a plea, only a quiet admission that the distance between us had become a choice and not a rule. I felt the shape of that choice settle into the cabin when we climbed inside. It stayed between us as I brought the engine up and Juno tucked her head beneath her wing like she believed in peace. It stayed while the van rolled us back into Klade's bones and the world tried to remember whether any of this had happened.

The Wendigo took the long way home, a looping arc through Klade's industrial ribs where the roads forgot their names and the wind tasted like old brine and machine oil. I kept the speed steady, just under the rhythm that would draw patrol eyes, and let the van's suspension smooth the broken concrete into a lullaby. Juno perched above the dash with her head tucked, one eye half open, little servo twitches betraying the fact that she was still watching for me even while pretending to rest. The cabin lights had drifted to a warm low, the kind of glow that turns steel into the suggestion of wood and makes corners look less like ambushes.

He sat in the passenger seat, Stray gone quiet in a way that does not mean idle. Hands folded on his thighs, shoulders set, chin lowered a fraction as if listening to something inside the shell that only he could hear. The status pulse at the base of his throat had returned to a calm green. The tremor along the neck conduit had settled. He had not spoken since I closed his chest plate beneath the bridge.

"Water," I said, and set a bottle on his knee.

He opened it without looking down and took a careful swallow, slow and measured so his internal sensors would not misread it as an obstruction. It was a small thing, but the small things are where people live.

"Juno, bring up the crate," I said.

She hopped to the center rail, pecked a switch, and the cargo cradle rose from the floor like a careful trick. The stolen unit looked like a maintenance locker, gray and unimpressive, ready to be ignored in any municipal lot. I jacked my deck into the panel and let the false skin fall. The lock nested open, the lid tilted, and a neat row of chip banks blinked into view. No bulk goods, no weapons, no cash. Light Technologies had been moving something thin and mean.

"We got lucky," I said, although I do not really believe in luck. "Quantum-laced storage. Encoded across multiple banks. If they lose one in transit, they assume denial of service, not exfiltration."

"Strip a third and leave the rest," he said, voice even again. "If they notice the gap, we want them to argue with their supplier, not hunt the transport."

I nodded and set three banks aside. Each chip slid into my deck with a quiet acceptance, the data unfolding into a river of light that ran along the interior of my overlays. I skimmed the headers and felt my mouth go dry. Purchase orders from front companies with names like older perfumes. Subcontracts written in languages that do not exist, each letter set to look valid if you do not know what to count. Buried among them, test logs from an efficiency trial labeled with a name we had already bled for.

Nyx.

I cracked the wrapper mentally and let a thin line of it whisper across my display. Enrollment metrics, neurological drift curves, a cost sheet that turned people into neat columns of anticipated loss. There was a recruitment vector tagged to Bastion Market, then a cross-reference to an Oronix shell company that sounded like a devotional hymn. I tasted anger in the back of my mouth and forced the flavor away so it would not color the work.

"Find anything that matters," he said quietly. Not a command, not a test. A request.

"Enough to hurt them," I answered. "Enough to make us a target if we are careless."

He nodded once, the kind of nod that comes when a person says a thing you have already decided to accept. His right hand drifted to the console and stayed there, fingertips resting near mine, not touching, close enough that I could feel the warmth from his palm through the glove. He does that when the quiet gets long. He will not always ask for anything. He will sometimes just stay near and call it strategy.

Juno lifted her head and gave a soft tap against the glass. A municipal camera on the overpass spine ahead had woken for a heartbeat. I sent a friendly lie to greet it, a sanitation unit barcode with outdated permissions. The camera blinked back to sleep. The city is like that. If you give it something where its hunger lives, it will often forget the rest.

"Tell me when you knew you were going to bring me back," he said, staring straight ahead.

"When your voice changed," I said. "Forge announces himself even when you do not. I heard him arrive, and I heard you leave. That is when I moved."

A longer pause followed. I wondered what picture the question had come from. Maybe the half second on the cargo roof when the anchors slid and the knee hit hard enough to ring in my own bones. Maybe a place far older than that.

"I am not always here," he said. "I can be a house with many rooms. Stray is the room that knows how to open and close doors. Sometimes the rooms get impatient."

"I grew up in one room with a window that looked at a brick wall," I said. "I do not mind a house with many rooms. I mind when the hallways catch fire."

That got the smallest sound from him, an exhale that might have been amusement if the night had been kinder. The van shivered as a crosswind knifed through the viaducts. A billboard above us crackled and switched to an Oronix public health notice about the risks of unlicensed cranial augments and the benefits of corporate care. The model on the ad smiled the way a door smiles when you are about to walk into a trap.

"I have something you should see," Juno whispered into my ear. The words were not words, but I have trained myself to hear her that way. She dropped the clip into my overlay. The same three frames from earlier, the same figure ghosting through the lane divider. I scrubbed two stops forward and found a sliver I had missed, a distortion in the heat trace that looked like a signature hidden within glare.

Mirror, again. Closer than habit would allow and far too patient for comfort.

I marked the file and hid it in a folder under a decimal chain only I use. If I told him now, he would chase it now. He would take a new body and empty it into a fight we did not have the tools to win tonight. I could give him truth in the morning, after I checked the route logs and scrubbed the Wendigo's trail. I felt like a liar while thinking that, which is a feeling I try not to get used to.

We left the viaducts and slid into a grid of low buildings that had once been worker dorms and were now legal gray areas full of workshops and studio kitchens and places where people fixed things that could no longer be purchased. The air smelled like sugar syrup and solder. A woman pushed a cart of spools across the street and did not look up. In Bastion Market, day and night both count as business hours.

"Juno," I said, "drop a housekeeping ping to the city. Three blocks out. Say we cleared a flood."

She sent the message and closed her wings, pleased with herself. If the city thinks you have cleaned something for it, it will allow you to pass without collecting the fee. I learned that from Hikari, and he learned it from trial, and someone else learned it from living. That is the chain. Knowledge walks forward holding the hand of harm and asks you to pretend they are not related.

He shifted at last, a small movement that meant Stray had returned fully to himself. "I will need to run a stability sweep when we land," he said. "If you will sit with me, it will go faster."

"Of course," I said.

"I do not mean only because of your hands," he added, so quiet I almost had to lean toward him to hear it. "Though they help."

The hand he had rested near mine finally touched, the lightest contact at the back of my knuckles, just enough to let me know that the request was not purely technical. I covered his fingers with my own and left them there while the Wendigo's engine counted the last blocks to the safe loop.

We parked beneath a canopy of rusted ductwork behind a shuttered print shop. The Wendigo sighed as it settled, the cabin lights dimming a fraction the way a home will when someone turns off a lamp in another room. I sealed the cargo cradle and pushed the false skin back over the locker so it looked like municipal junk again. He watched me do it as if the work were a ritual and not camouflage.

Inside the rear bay he sat on the edge of the diagnostic bench and unfastened the clips for me. Stray's chassis opened obediently under my hands. I set my tools on a folded towel the way a field surgeon might lay out instruments, not because I think of myself as a surgeon but because intention changes outcomes. The interior looked steadier than it had under the bridge. A clean, thin glow through the upper bus lines. No jitter across the cortex lattice. I ran the sweep while he breathed with the slow cadence he uses to convince his body that stillness is a form of motion.

"Again," I said, and he held the count.

The readouts flowed back with the numbers I had wanted. I cut the power to a loud subroutine that kept flirting with an emergency start and tightened a bundle of leads behind his left shoulder. When I finished, I closed him with the same care I use to put a sleeping child into a bed. He watched my face the whole time, and there was nothing in his expression I could hang an interpretation on, which is sometimes the most honest expression a person has.

"All right," I said. "You will hold."

He nodded. "We will see."

I almost told him then about the three frames and the silver figure and the small scar of heat that had looked like a signature. I almost said Mirror aloud and watched what it did to his eyes. Instead I pressed my thumb at the base of his throat and felt the steady pulse against the joint. The light there stayed green. I promised myself I would tell him after we slept, when choices would not taste like panic.

"We should eat," I said. "Protein bricks, or I can pretend to cook."

"Pretend," he said, and a thin smile appeared, the first of the night.

I boiled water and poured it over noodles that claimed to be a specific flavor. He tolerated them. I tasted sugar and salt and synthetic garlic and did not complain. Juno took one curl with gravity and flew it to a corner for examination. The world outside clicked and shifted as Klade's night turned one block closer to morning.

When we stretched out on opposite benches, I left the curtain half open so I could see his silhouette in the faint cabin light. He does not sleep like a person when he is in Stray. He rests the way a machine rests, with the moving parts lined up so the wear will be even. I listened to the soft on and off of his cooling fans and let the sound pull the knots from my shoulders. His hand slipped down over the edge of the bench, palm open. I reached up and set my fingers lightly in the center of it. No pressure. No demand. The contact made something in my chest loosen in a way that was almost painful.

He did not move, but after a moment his fingers curled, not enough to trap mine, just enough to say he had noticed.

I stared at the ceiling and watched the reflection of the status lights travel across it like small satellites. Somewhere in the city a train screamed and then returned to its tracks. I let the knowledge of Mirror sit where I had hidden it and kept my breathing slow. I could carry it for a few more hours. I could set it down when we were not still leaking adrenaline into the quiet.

The Wendigo settled deeper into itself. The engines ticked. The cabin sighed. The house we keep inside a machine agreed to be a house for a little while longer.

I closed my eyes and felt his pulse against my fingers. He trusted me to bring him back.

He trusted me to sit with him while the rooms in his mind took turns holding the light. That felt like a responsibility and like a gift. I held both ideas until sleep took one and allowed the other to wait.

We ate in the soft light of the Wendigo, the cabin humming with that steady comfort that comes when machines are not trying to be anything they are not. The noodles were just warm and salty enough to trick my body into believing in dinner. Juno examined a single curl with grave ceremony, then stashed it in a corner as if she might plant it and grow a spare meal later. Stray sat across from me on the bench, shoulders relaxed at last, fingers loose around the rim of an empty mug. He always holds an object during quiet talks, as if the extra point of contact helps him stay in one room.

"I want to switch," he said after a while, calm and simple. "Wisp rests easier after this kind of work."

I nodded and stood. "Come on. I have you."

We moved into the rear bay, where the pod tower glowed like a stack of lanterns. Velvet and Forge slept in their cradles, diagnostic halos slowly rotating. Wisp's rig was lower, more compact, lit with the soft blue of a machine that expects gentler weather. Stray sat on the edge of the bench and loosened the front catches so I could work. The motion had become choreography between us, not hurried, not ritualized, only practiced until it felt like a form of trust.

I touched his chest plate with my palm before opening it, not for any technical reason, just to let touch arrive first. Clips released with a little sigh and the plate came away in my hands. Inside, the lines of light looked steady, the flicker that had tried to take him apart now reduced to a faint shore of afterglow along the cortex ring. I synced the release, watched the counters roll down, then met his eyes.

"Ready," I said.

He lay back and let the pod accept the weight. The neurosync needle seated with the quiet certainty of a key in a well-loved lock. His eyes unfocused for a breath, then closed. The pod drew in, sealed, and the status light settled to a calm white.

Across the bay, Wisp's lens brightened.

Her eyes opened with a soft flare and the first thing she did was look for me, not the screens, not the numbers. I always notice that. She flexed each hand in sequence, rolled her ankles inside the reinforced boots, then sat up and pushed a coil of hair away from her face. The twin puffs fell back into place with the unruly dignity of small planets that refuse to obey gravity. She looked smaller than Stray by an entire unit of space, not just height and width, but the way the room bent around her. Lighter center of mass, higher cadence, brighter tone.

"Hi," she said, and the word landed like a light being turned on rather than a door being locked. "You made soup."

"Close enough," I said. "How do you feel?"

"Like I have hands again," she said, wiggling her fingers, then paused as if listening to herself. "No bleed. No echo. Good gate. Did you patch the stubborn loop on the shoulder bus?"

"Of course," I said. "Do not insult your mechanic."

She hopped down from the pod with the uncanny balance that body always carried and tugged the hem of one of the Wendigo hoodies over her frame. It came to mid thigh and swallowed her a little, which pleased her in some private way that she never explained. She padded to the galley, stole the last of the noodles, and moaned just enough to prove she was doing it on purpose.

We settled back into the forward lounge with our bowls and the sound of rain that did not exist whispering along the dome. Wisp tucked her legs under her on the bench and watched Juno eye her like a rival thief. When the drone darted in, Wisp offered up a single noodle on an empty chopstick and said, solemn as a priest, "For science." Juno accepted and hid the evidence.

This was the part of the night that had begun to feel like family. Not the sentimental kind, not the kind I grew up hearing about in stories where everyone sits around a table and remembers their favorite color. The kind where chores get done because someone can do them faster. The kind where the plants on the counter have names even if two of them are only mint. The kind where the blankets are not matched and the mugs do not belong to anyone in particular, yet you know which one someone will reach for without thinking. A house inside a machine.

Wisp slid off the bench and began to tidy without being asked. She wiped down the galley, stacked the lids, checked the seal on the cargo cradle, and set the toolbox back the way I liked it instead of the way Stray always left it. She did it humming under her breath, a little pattern of notes that never held the same order for long. When she finished she wrote a label for the mint pod with a strip of green tape and a marker, added a tiny four-point star that looked a little like Juno, then stuck the label on the pot as if the plant would read it.

"You do that every time," I said. "The label. The little star."

"It reminds the leaf to arrive," she said, completely sincere. "Things respond to being invited."

I looked at her for a long moment. "You really believe that."

"Yes," she said. "You did."

She meant me, not the plant. I looked away so I would not ruin the thing by staring at it too directly. Wisp did not press. She curled back onto the bench and opened my toolkit, then began to tune Juno's wing with a narrow file and the patience of a watchmaker. Juno allowed it without comment, which meant she approved.

A public channel chimed low on the console. A barge report from the flats. A weather notice about the lattice reflectors cycling to conserve energy. I muted it and opened a stream of old movies instead. Wisp chose something talky and slow, people in coats walking through rain that looked honest. She leaned her shoulder to mine while she watched and asked questions only when the scene changed. Why does he look at the door before he answers. Why does she pour the drink and not offer it. Why does the music sound like a hallway. I told her what I thought and waited for her to tell me the deeper thing I had missed.

We did not touch hands. We did not need to. The shared shoulder was enough.

After a while she reached for the fold-down tray by my knee and spread out a small repair cloth. She set three screws in a line, then balanced a spring between two fingertips and looked up at me. "Turn," she said, and nodded to my forearm.

"You are going to file me like a bird," I said.

"Polish," she corrected, amused. "You scraped yourself on the access ladder. I could hear it."

I rolled my sleeve and let her work. Her hands were deft, sure, a little too careful with my skin and not careful enough with her own. She polished the small metal edge on my gauntlet and blew away the filings as if she were an artist cleaning a brush. When she finished she rested her wrist against mine for a second, the smallest punctuation in the book of the day.

"Better," she said.

"Show-off," I said, but I could not stop the smile.

She pretended to be offended and reached for the remote, then stalled halfway and tilted her head. The room changed by a fraction when she did that. Wisp listens with her whole body. "You are holding something," she said.

I weighed the choice. The three frames. The silver outline. The heat signature that had looked like a name. I could say Mirror and watch the light change behind her eyes, and we would go from tea and old movies to maps and countermeasures. I decided to keep the night whole. Not to hide. To time it.

"I will tell you at morning," I said. "After I scrub the route and check the logs. If I say it now, you will chase it now."

She studied my face the way Stray studies an open door. Then she nodded, once. "Morning," she said. "Promise."

"Promise."

Satisfied, she turned back to the movie, then paused again and spoke quietly, without looking at me. "I like being the one you come home to," she said. "Not because of me. Because you allow the room to remain a room."

It took me a few seconds to answer. "I like it too," I said. "Sister."

Wisp did not smile in a quick way. It came on slowly, light by light, until her eyes held it as much as her mouth. She nudged her shoulder against mine, then set the remote in my hand. "Your turn," she said. "Pick something terrible."

I chose a cooking show that had been canceled after four episodes and pretended I knew what the contestants were doing with a root vegetable I had only seen in archives. Wisp was delighted to be an authority. She explained every step in a tone that suggested no one had ever been wrong in the history of kitchens.

When the episode ended she stood and stretched, small and serious in the oversized hoodie. "I will sweep the cameras," she said. "Only the ones within two blocks. I will leave a nice little lie so the city dreams of drains and not of thieves."

"Take Juno," I said.

Juno hopped to her shoulder, settled like a piece that had always belonged there, and nipped her ear gently before agreeing to work.

While they moved through the rear bay, I put the dishes away and folded the blanket into a neat rectangle along the back of the bench. I turned down the dome light to a soft amber and listened to the distant clatter of a late tram. The Wendigo's systems relaxed one notch. Pipes clicked. The refrigerator made a tiny righteous noise. Places tell you when they accept you. It might be superstition, but I have learned to listen for it.

Wisp returned a few minutes later and gave me a thumbs up that was too big for the size of the victory, which was the point. She sat cross-legged on the floor and painted a tiny star on the corner of the mint label that matched the one on the ivy. She added a dot in the center and announced to the room, "Family."

"Plant cult," I said.

"Correct," she said, radiant with the seriousness of it.

We washed up. She brushed her teeth with a ferocity that suggested the toothbrush had offended her. I made a checklist for morning work, copied the stripped data to an offline cache, and tucked the quantum banks into a wall compartment behind a panel that looked like it held fuses. We climbed into the benches we had started calling beds without deciding to. I left the curtain half open again so I could see her silhouette in the low light.

"Goodnight, Wisp," I said.

"Goodnight, Wren," she answered, then added softly, "Goodnight, house."

Juno settled on the rail above us and clicked once, content. Outside, Klade moved like a big creature asleep with one eye open. The Wendigo lay quiet inside its bones and agreed to be a home for another night. My hand found the edge of Wisp's blanket, and her hand found mine, and there in the easy clasp of two tired people practicing being related, I let the promise of morning carry me under.

MORNING CAME IN QUIET pieces that belonged more to the Wendigo than to Klade. The cabin's filters whispered, the heater gave a polite cough, and a soft stripe of sun found its way through a seam in the shutter, landing on the mint pot like the plant had ordered it. The outside world sounded far away, which meant the neighborhood was having a good day. No sirens rose, no freight horns argued, only the faint clatter of someone opening a metal shutter three doors down and the wet tick of condensation sliding along the ductwork.

I slid out from under the blanket and let my feet find the chill of the floor, then started the morning circuit. Scrub the route logs, purge the beacon history, smooth the MAC drift so our trail looked like a sanitation unit with a nervous driver. I sent three harmless maintenance pings to the city feeds, recorded the acknowledgments, and folded them into our cover ledger. The Wendigo liked it when I did this. Machines may not have feelings, but they have preferences, and they reward the hands that honor them.

Wisp slept light, all quiet breathing and small adjustments, the way a bird sleeps when it knows a storm might turn back. When she woke, it was all at once. Her eyes opened, the focus arrived, and her mouth curved the way it always does when her first sight is a place that has agreed to be a home. She sat up, tucked her hair behind one ear, and swung her feet to the floor without any of the groaning and theatrics that flesh will do to convince you it is suffering nobly.

"Coffee?" I asked, already filling the reservoir.

She nodded, then reached for the watering bulb and tended the mint with a seriousness that would have been funny if it did not also make sense. She checked the ivy next, traced one finger along a new curl, then flipped the mug I knew she favored right side up. The faded cartoon cat looked disreputable before noon, which suited us.

"We slept," she said, as if announcing a rare and valuable mineral.

"We did," I said. "You hummed for a while. Juno approved."

Juno stretched on her rail with the careful exaggeration of a queen greeting a court. She dipped her head toward Wisp, who tapped the crown with a fingernail and accepted a tiny click of affection in return. The coffee burbled against the quiet and then settled, steam rising like a promise.

I set Wisp's mug in her hands and felt the weight of the thing I had promised to say. It sat under my tongue like a coin held for a toll. She watched my face over the rim, took a small sip, and waited. She does not rush the truth. She makes room for it.

"I have something from the run," I said. "Juno pulled a segment from a municipal camera that should have been asleep. The footage is thin, and it is short. It is enough."

Wisp set the mug down without the small clink the ceramic makes when you do not think. She folded her legs under her on the bench and tipped her head for the feed. I pushed the clip to the shared display. The image tore like old tape, stitched itself badly, then burned clean for three frames. In the gap between the convoy and the barrier, a figure ghosted through glare. Tall, edges silver where light bent, moving in a way that did not belong to any municipal worker or escort pilot. The head turned toward the lens, not in surprise, but in acknowledgment, like a stage actor checking that the audience is seated. Then the frame broke and the camera went back to sleep.

Wisp did not speak while it played. She did not speak after. She replayed it once, eyes narrowed in thought rather than fear. On the second pass she paused between frames and pulled a thin heat map from the smear. The signature did not look like a person. It looked like an intention.

"Mirror," she said finally.

"Yes," I said.

She nodded, just once, and her hands folded together on her knees as if to keep the body from acting on the first answer it offered. "Not a projection," she said. "Too expensive to waste in traffic and too clumsy for the angle. A body, but not one we have seen. The heat is wrong for older plating. That halo is new manufacturing or a coat designed to reflect municipal glare."

"We were not their only subject," I said. "Light Technologies will notice the missing banks, but Mirror was not watching for them. Mirror was watching for us."

Wisp breathed out slowly, not a sigh, not a surrender, a measured exhale to keep air in the room. "You did not tell Stray last night because he would have chased it," she said. "You told me now because you know I will count to a number larger than ten."

"It was the right choice for the night," I said, though the part of me that hates half truths still winced. "I am telling you now so we can choose the morning without panic."

She reached for my wrist and turned my hand palm up, then placed the coffee mug in it, not as a joke, but as a small correction in the ritual. I smiled because she was right. Then she stood, went to the rear bay, and woke the console with her palm. Screens stirred, the Wendigo's internal map blossomed, and the city spilled its quiet data across our wall.

"Tripwires first," she said. "I want a soft alarm on any municipal feed near last night's grid that reports a camera waking out of sequence. No pictures, no packets, only time-stamp anomalies and lens adjustments. Mirror behaves like a curious animal. That habit will leave a pawprint."

"On it," I said, falling into the work. "I will thread three false maintenance tickets through the district office, tied to drain codes we used last night. If patrols look backward, they will see what they want to see."

"Good," she said, and under the word I heard the larger thing, the part that meant I trust the hands that do this. She layered a second screen with the Nyx headers I had skimmed in the van. Names of front companies read like perfume. Costs tabulated people as if they were copper wire and solvent, counted by length and purity. She did not comment on the cruelty. She indexed the numbers and stored them in a place where cruelty could be converted to leverage.

"Stray should run a stability sweep," I said when the first ring of tripwires settled. "The body held after the reset, but the bleed was real. If I do not say it out loud, it becomes superstition."

Wisp's gaze softened in that precise way she has when she slides memory into focus.

"He will ask me to sit with him," she said. "I will."

It was not a question, and it did not need thanks. It needed sunlight, which is to say it needed to be placed where the day could see it. I pushed the thought aside and opened the cabinet above the bench. The packet of noodles had a little less indignity in morning light. I set water to heat and cut a square of dried greens into something that could pretend to be an herb. Wisp stole the end piece and ate it like a dare.

"Run it again," she said, and I did, slower this time until each frame felt like a breath you could hold. I split the color channels and leaned Juno's thermal scrape over the image. The streetlight bloom became geometry, and the glare flattened into something a machine could understand. In the seam between the barrier and the rear axle, the figure arrived the way a missing piece arrives when a pattern finally remembers itself.

"Entry from the blind edge," I said, more to order my thoughts than to teach. "Shoulders back. Hip carriage too smooth for anything bought at retail. No sway."

"The weight transfer is wrong for anyone natural," Wisp murmured. "A walker drops a hip with the step. She lifts the hip instead. Someone tuned her to live on edges."

I dialed exposure down and the silhouette sharpened, then softened, as if it had too many correct answers. "Look at the knee," I said. "No hang in the stride. The joints never search for balance. They already own it."

Wisp's mouth tightened. "She does not check the floor. She expects it to arrive."

I froze the second frame at the turn of the head. The angle was exact, not a threat and not a bow, just a measured acknowledgment of the lens's height and the distance to glass. In the barrier's reflection ran a thinner ghost, a second outline that did not quite match the first.

"Two surfaces," she said. "Outer coat to bend light. Inner skin for signature. That halo is not a mistake. It is a tool."

Juno ticked a little note into my overlay. The heat pattern did not climb like a human. It pulsed in even bands with tiny rests between them. I measured the spacing and felt a cold line along my spine that had nothing to do with the room. "Sixty three milliseconds between pulses," I said. "Then a rest. Then sixty three again. A prime interval. Not waste heat. A metronome."

"An advertisement," Wisp said. "A rhythm for machines and for the kind of people who listen like machines."

At the edge of the frame a shallow puddle flattened the glare and gave us a truer line. Not a face that any officer would love, only a smooth oval with a slight ridge where cheekbones might live and a darker ring around the eye, a recessed detail rather than paint or lens, the suggestion of expression without the means to make it move. The cruelty of that sat under my tongue until I swallowed.

"Mirrorline," Wisp whispered, and the word pulled up the basement smell of Oronix, the glass tube with a familiar shape sleeping inside, the small noise a person makes when something ends because you will not let it continue.

I lifted the audio from under the engine growl. There was a whisper there, the private signal a body sends to balance and muscle at once. Mirror pushed off the divider and skipped the step a person would take. Two contacts, then air, then nothing. Training written in the smallest possible time.

"She was never far," I said. "Never tired. She matched us, came close enough to taste our heat, then left a mark like a tide line."

Wisp frowned, not from fear but from the clean anger she keeps for elegant lies. "She shepherded us. Not to save. To measure. A lab note on pavement."

On the third frame the coat swallowed shape and left only light behind. This was not a person vanishing into shadow. This was a body removing the context that made it visible. The metronome ticked once more and fell still, as if a hand had closed over a clock's heart.

I zoomed out and let the three frames play at speed, then at half, then at quarter. The blur resolved in straight lines, like a schematic being redrawn with fewer points. Every compression kept the interval intact. If we find her again in bad cameras and cheap feeds, I expect to find the same rhythm tucked inside, a name written for instruments rather than eyes.

"Footholds," I said. "Juno, build a detector for that interval. Passive only. No flares. Whisper to me when any city camera stutters that way."

Juno clicked assent. Wisp took a small paper notebook from under the bench and wrote the numbers in ink, which she only does when she wants a truth to live through power outages.

She set the notebook aside, reached beneath the bench, and lifted a narrow case that had been waiting there longer than I knew her. Inside rested a wafer that hummed before she even woke it with her thumb. She held it up with the edge lights facing me. "Medical override," she said. "Emergency root. Field locks. Forced sync if I drift or go hard. I have carried it a long time. I do not want to be the only one who can pull me out of a fire."

She placed it in my palm without ceremony so it would not taste like a debt. "You carry it," she said. "I keep the key phrase. If the wrong room takes me, you use it. I will not fight you."

She spoke the phrase. It was not a word so much as a shape of breath that lives in muscle and will never live in letters. We both nodded. The nod felt heavier than vows spoken in better rooms.

"We cannot chase this on pride," I said. "We will choose the day and the ground."

"We begin to build that room," she answered, business returning to her tone like a cat to a warm chair.

We worked with the sound down and the lights warm. Wisp mapped camera uptimes and lens corrections by block. I threaded maintenance tickets through the district office tied to last night's drains so that patrols who looked backward would find exactly what they wanted to see. Juno stitched the metronome into a net we could carry in our pockets. When we paused, the clip waited on the screen like a storm far out over water. Not yet, not here, not on ground that belonged to someone else. A tunnel would suit Mirror. Or a spillway. Or a maintenance shaft under a cathedral floor where the echoes know how to keep secrets.

"After we eat," I said, "we switch and run Stray's sweep. If the bleed returns, we say numbers out loud and keep saying them until the room listens."

Wisp nodded and reached for the kettle. She poured hot water over a new handful of noodles with the solemnity of a ritual that holds a house together. She added a pinch of dried greens, studied the mint the way a teacher studies a student, and smiled when the leaves did not argue. Juno hopped to the rail and tucked her head beneath one wing, satisfied that the morning had become a shape she recognized.

Klade turned the lattice one notch brighter and pretended the light was free. Inside the Wendigo, we laid the first boards of a floor that did not exist yet, promised each other without ceremony that we would stand on it together, and let the day begin by our count rather than theirs.

WE ATE, WE LET the kettle cool, and then we kept our promise. Wisp set her mug down and walked with me to the pod tower, hoodie sleeves pushed past her wrists like she had work to do and did not mind being seen doing it. She rested her palm on the cradle's rim for a heartbeat, a quiet farewell that did not need words, then lay back and let the sync threads find their places. The seal closed with the soft confidence of a good door. Her status light slipped from green to a gentle white.

Across the bay, the Stray rig stirred. The lens ring brightened, then steadied. He woke with a breath that sounded more like a decision than a reflex, eyes open, present from the first second. He sat up, rolled his shoulders against the restraints to feel the hinges, and looked for me the way a diver looks for the ladder before the swim is over. I handed him a towel and he wiped the condensation from the neck port, patient and precise.

"Seven in and seven out," I said, lifting the reader from its clip.

He closed his eyes and counted the air like it was part of the test. The latticework inside the open plate glowed with a clean, thin light; the wrong subroutine stayed asleep. I traced a set of sensors along the cortex ring and watched the numbers hold. The tiny scar on the knee actuator reported itself like a child showing a scuffed elbow. I sent it a reset and a little forgiveness. It quieted.

"Again," I said. "Same count."

He obeyed. The sweep returned steady lines. There was no knock from Forge at the hinges, no pressure at the doors. He opened his eyes and rested his palms on his thighs, hands still, shoulders set, ready for whatever I named next.

"We will walk it," I said. "Slow and short. No heroics."

He nodded. I palmed the rear hatch and the Wendigo answered with a short sigh. Outside, Klade was in its midmorning trance. The print shop across the alley had opened one shutter, just a slit, just enough for air to speak. Someone on the corner was boiling sugar into something that wanted to become candy, the smell high and bright over the mineral damp of the bricks. Two children had drawn a ladder of squares across the pavement with luminous chalk and were arguing tenderly about the rules. Juno rode my shoulder and tracked the street with a narrowed lens, satisfied for the moment with a jurisdiction that extended to the next downspout.

We took the service path that ran behind the print shop and the metal yard. I gave Stray the cadence and he matched it without hunting for balance. He put his heels down with caution and his toes down with trust. I watched for the stutter that means a room has tried to open, and I did not see it. I gave him a hand signal and he stepped onto a low retaining wall as if it were the spine of a sleeping animal, then down again, then up, then still. The numbers in my reader kept their steady climb and quiet return.

"Numbers out loud," I said.

"One," he answered, voice even.

"Two."

"Three."

Juno added a little chirp at five like a metronome that wanted to be helpful. I let her keep it for one round and then tapped her foot so she would not build habits on top of habits. She flicked me a sideways glare and settled, which is as close as she gets to apologizing.

We circled the block and stopped at a drain we had marked the night before. I lifted the grill with a tool that looked like a toy and slid a wafer sensor under the lip. It settled with the smugness of a coin falling into the right slot. I tagged the location in our ledger and sent a maintenance ping to the city with a photograph of clean water that had never been there. Patrols like images that agree with their paperwork.

Stray crouched beside me and tested the weight of the grate with two fingers before I lowered it. He does that to remind his hands that reality still has edges. When he stood, he gave the alley a careful look that was not paranoia. It was inventory. Points of cover. Lines of sight. Doors that would resist for five seconds and doors that would not resist at all.

The first tripwire whispered through my earpiece as we returned to the van. A municipal camera two districts away had woken for a handful of frames without instruction, then returned to sleep without filing the proper paperwork. I let the data pass under my tongue and folded it into the map. The interval that Juno and I had taught the net to love was not present. No pulse. No prime spacing. No metronome. It was only a twitch from the city's tired nerve. I archived it with a note and felt the urge to chase something we had not yet seen. I let the urge walk past without being fed.

Inside, I sealed the hatch and set the reader aside. He sat on the bench and unfastened the front catches so I could close him. The plate swung into place and the clips found home with that small promise of a sound I have started to need. He exhaled, not a sigh, a reset. I rested my thumb on the pulse light at his throat and felt it through the joint, steady and impersonal and somehow still his.

"You hold," I said.

"I hold," he agreed. He looked toward the pod tower where Wisp slept and then back to me. "Tell me what you need from me for the room you mean to build."

"I need doors that close quietly," I said. "I need the kind of patience that lets a person stand in the dark without inventing enemies to keep them company. I need a voice that will count with me when I tell it to count. I need you not to chase a ghost until the ground is ours."

He listened without moving. The stillness that arrived was the kind that makes space instead of stealing it. "You will have that," he said. "If I drift, you will use the tool. Do not ask me if I am ready. Be ready and act."

I took the wafer from my pocket and touched its edge to the port at his collarbone to feel the hum, not to trigger. The charge answered with a delicate musicality that only I could hear because I have learned the instrument. I withdrew it and felt the weight of permission settle into a place inside me that had been holding too much for too long.

We worked the rest of the day in small pieces. The net of tripwires grew in quiet rings. The ledger filled with false drains and honest timestamps. Juno tuned her wing against Wisp's file marks until the new note in her servo lost its metallic edge. I traced Light Technologies through front companies that sounded like perfume and set reminders next to names that would matter once we had leverage. Stray repaired the tiny bruise across his left knee actuator and then rechecked the pod clamps with a methodical care that would have looked like superstition if it had not been so effective.

By evening the print shop had opened both shutters. The owner stood in the doorway with a rag across one shoulder, counting paper stock that had yellowed at the edges. He nodded at me without smiling and I nodded back. The children with the luminous chalk had reached a settlement and turned their ladder into a river, then a snake, then a road that led under our van. They asked Juno if she wanted to play. She pretended not to understand the question and then stole one of their chalks to redraw a star in the corner of our mint label. The children approved this act of criminality and ran off to tell someone important.

We switched again in the last hour of light so Wisp could wake in time to insist on dinner, which she did with a severity that would have impressed soldiers. She inspected the mint as if it might have taken offense at our work and whispered a brief apology to the ivy for the draft. She put on the hoodie that made her look like weather with opinions. She stole my chopsticks and cooked noodles with intention. Stray's steadiness lingered in the room like a footprint drying on warm stone.

We ate at the fold-out table with the window cracked an inch. The city's breath came in and made the curtains shift. Wisp kept a small paper notebook open near her bowl and wrote nothing in it for a long time, which is her way of making space for the line that is going to matter. When she finally put the pen to the page, she drew only three numbers, written slowly, then underlined them as if they were a place on a map. Sixty three, pause, sixty three. Juno hopped down, tapped the underline with her beak, and then brought me the stolen chalk so I could put a matching mark on the back of the cabinet door where no one else would ever look.

The second tripwire murmured near midnight. Another camera woke, another camera slept, no metronome inside. The city rolled in its bedding and returned to snoring. I filed the event and let the lights dim. The van sighed as its systems shifted into rest. Wisp labeled a jar on the shelf with a strip of green tape that read tea and added a four-point star that looked a little like Juno. She stuck it on crooked, which pleased her. She brushed my shoulder as she passed me on her way to the sink and did not need to say thank you out loud.

When it was time to sleep, we left the curtain half open so the cabin could keep an eye on us. Wisp lay across from me with one foot tucked under the blanket and the other bare because she likes to feel the floor when she dreams. Juno settled on the rail and hid her head as if the night could not find her if she behaved like furniture. I checked the wafer one more time and set it beside my deck, within reach, not because I planned to use it, but because the promise lived where I could touch it.

I thought of the three frames and the rhythm inside them. I thought of Mirror's face that was not a face and the way the water had given us a truer line. I thought of the room we would build, the doors that would close without a sound, the ground that would belong to us because we would have named it first. The fear did not leave me. It arranged itself into a shape that could be carried.

I closed my eyes and listened for the breath inside the machine we called a house. The filters whispered, the heater sighed, the mint gave a thin sweet scent that had no business being as comforting as it was. Across from me, Wisp's breathing eased into the rhythm that tells me her mind has let go. I let my hand drop over the edge of the bench. A moment later her hand found mine in the dark. We did not make a speech over it. We did not bless it. We simply held on.

The chapter ended the way good days end in places like ours. Not with a victory and not with a warning, but with a plan that could stand through morning, and the knowledge that when the knock finally comes, it will find us awake, counted in, and standing on a floor we built ourselves.

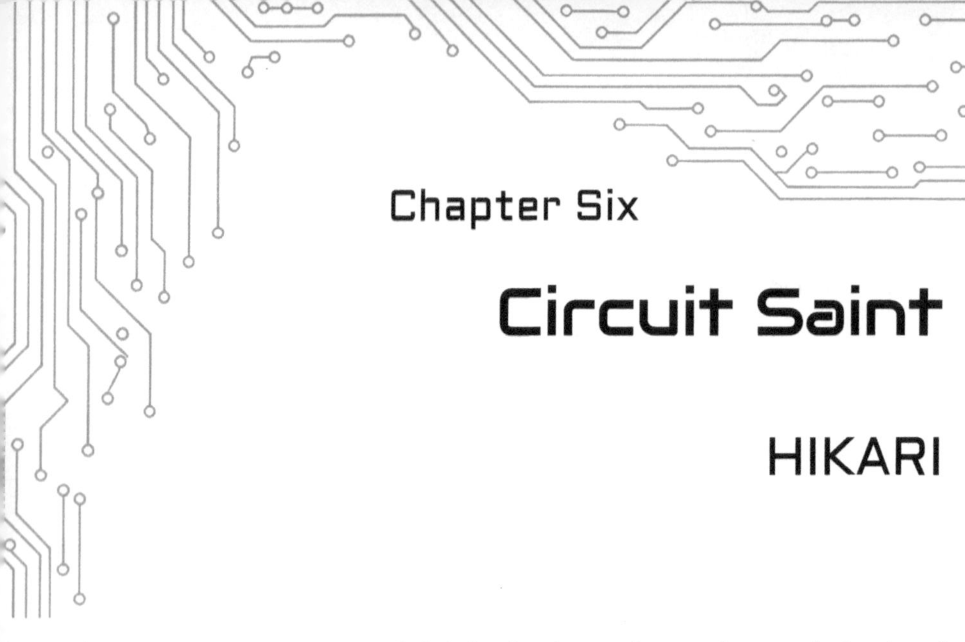

Chapter Six

Circuit Saint

HIKARI

THE WENDIGO ROLLED TO a halt behind a shuttered pawn shop on the border of Floodline Nine, a strip where the steam grills stay hot all night and the rain gutters carry more stories than water. The precinct had coughed up a contract through a cutout, the kind that arrives with a lump sum and no paperwork. Someone was tired of counting bodies under a dead billboard. Someone wanted a problem erased with the kind of finality that does not make the news.

I sat in the Forge shell and let the weight of it seat my spine. The body carries its own weather. In Forge the air feels dense, the floor feels closer, the room forgets to argue. I checked the internal readouts and watched the power curve steady. Servos at ninety two percent. Knee actuator clean. Forearm blade safe. I drew one breath for ritual, not need, and turned to Wren.

She cinched her harness without looking at it, the motion of a person who has done this in the dark enough times to teach it to muscle. Hair tied back, deck clipped to a thigh plate, disruptor wand riding the inside of her sleeve where a pat down would miss it. Juno watched from the dash with her head tilted, one eye open wider than the other, a small judge perched in black lacquer.

"Site?" Wren asked.

I brought up the precinct packet and painted it across the windshield. Floodline Nine, Viaduct 14 stairs, east landing. A broken security light that flickers whenever the lattice cycles. Two blind spots created by a collapsed girder and a vending kiosk that never worked. Four assaults in seven nights. Two dead. The bodies had been found with pockets turned inside out, wrist implants torn, cranial jacks damaged with ugly tools. Chrome heads looking for quick parts and quicker cash. The precinct wanted the stairs safe again and did not care how the request was met.

"Four to six hostile," I said. "Mixture of street aug and surplus militia gear. Expect a shotgun that looks like it belongs in a museum and a rifle with a cracked optic that still hits fine in a corner."

"Drones?" Wren asked.

"One civilian recon tied to a phone, possibly two. If they have an animal, it will run when we start. The animal is smarter than the men."

She gave a small smile and palmed Juno's rail. "You hear that. You are the smart one."

Juno clicked once, a sound that translated as naturally.

We walked. The stairs up to the viaduct cut through a rib of concrete that had been patched so often the patches had their own layers. Posters peeled back like old bark. The smell was a braid of cheap liquor, damp stone, and machine grease. Above, the east landing opened onto the long shadow of the viaduct, a vaulted strip that held wind like a memory. Neon from a noodle stall across the way bled red into the mist. Farther on, a broken billboard spoke its half sentence about hygiene to no one who would listen.

I let Forge take the lead. Boots found steel with a sound that says leave, not please. My shoulder brushed the ruined kiosk and felt the vibration of quiet machinery, the kind of idle hum that comes from a grafted power source. Someone had fed the thing from a street line and hidden a signal repeater inside. I lifted a finger, the sign for eyes open, and Wren slid past me like water around stone.

There were four of them in the first span. Two leaned against the railing and smoked. One sat on the steps with a pry bar across his knees. The fourth stood farther back with a rifle cradled low. Their faces carried the smooth glaze of low-grade synth calm. Chrome at the jawline, a strip across the brow, a clumsy patch at the temple where someone had learned headwork from a video and a dare. The type. Dangerous enough to ruin a life, careless enough to die for nothing.

A couple came into view at the far end, heads down, too tired to calculate risk. The man had a paper bag with a carton peeking out. The woman clutched a satchel against her body the way you hold a book in a storm. One of the muggers stepped forward and let the pry bar ring once against the railing. The sound carried the length of the viaduct. The couple stopped, then began to back up, the worst choice on stairs with predators above.

"Now," I said, and the word did not need volume. It carried the shape of what would follow.

Wren moved first. She crossed the gap between shadows and the kiosk in three soft steps, jacked her deck into the illegal repeater, and stripped its permissions before it knew it had been asked. The blind spots on their phone cameras opened for me like doors. The rifleman's optic flickered as her disruptor kissed his frequency. His head jerked instinctively, then he tightened his grip, too slow for what came next.

I walked into their line of sight with Forge's posture. No show, no shout. The nearest man blinked at the scale of me and started to raise the pry bar. I took the distance in two strides and put him to the ground with a palm heel under the jaw that sent a clean crack up through his skull plate. He stopped moving. I pivoted to catch the cigarette of the second with my free hand and pressed it into his forearm. Pain gave him back to gravity. My knee met his sternum and his breath left the conversation.

The rifleman recovered enough to fire blind. The round hit the rail three steps behind me and made a brittle scream. I heard Wren mutter a curse, then watched her swing under the railing with a fluid confidence that told me she had learned to climb as a child. She rolled out behind the shooter, came up on one knee, and drove her disruptor wand into the battery block of his rifle. The gun died without drama. He swung the dead weight at her head. She leaned out of the arc and stamped his ankle. The joint failed with a pop like a bottle cap. He went down cursing and she drove her elbow into his throat before he could make a better plan.

The fourth man ran toward the couple, either as a hostage play or because his own panic had mistaken them for help. He grabbed the woman's satchel and yanked. She held it with the determination of a person who has already lost too much. He raised a knife. I took the space between us in three steps and caught his wrist before the blade could fall. Forge's grip does not negotiate. Bones made a sound that would be hard to forget. He screamed and fell to his knees. I set him down, took the knife, and placed it against the concrete where it would not complicate the next second.

"Go," I told the couple, keeping my voice low and flat so it would penetrate shock without adding fear. "Down the stairs, two landings. Do not look back. There are police two blocks west."

They went. The woman looked once at Wren, not at me, and mouthed a thank you that was half apology for surviving. Wren gave her a small nod that meant you did the work too.

The first two were out. The rifleman wheezed and clawed at his throat, finding no voice in a body that had never been taught how to keep it. He would sleep soon. The last man tried to stand and failed. He looked at his broken hand and then at me, the recognition arriving in his eyes that his night had ended inside the wrong story.

I heard them before I saw them. Two more at the northern end, joggers who had learned their strut from militia footage, cheap visors, better boots, a little too much caffeine. They came in hot and sloppy, rifles up, nerve high, not enough training to avoid crossfire. I placed myself between Wren and their line, felt the heavy air of Forge settle around my shoulders, and stepped forward so their shots would have to move through me.

"Down," Wren said, not to me, to Juno. The drone slipped off her shoulder and shot into the lattice of struts above, black on black, invisible unless you had learned to look for the absence of starlight. She sent a pin whisper to the visor of the lead shooter. His display filled with a stencil of static that looked precisely like his partner. He flinched and turned his muzzle. The second shooter barked a curse and corrected. They tangled each other's attention at exactly the right moment.

I closed. The nearest brought his rifle up far too late. My left hand crushed the foregrip and pinned the weapon to his chest. My right palm caught his faceguard and slammed it back against the pillar. The composite cracked like an egg. He sagged. I wrenched the rifle free and threw it into the dark, not for effect, only to make the immediate future simpler.

The second fired a three round burst that kissed my shoulder plate and died there, the rounds flattened by armor that had been born in better laboratories than his. I reached for his barrel, he yanked it back, and the muzzle clipped my jaw. Pain registered as numbers, not heat. I let the body do the next decision. My elbow came across his cheek, then my heel found his knee. He folded over the pain and I planted him face first on the stairs and let momentum do the rest. His visor shattered. He went to sleep staring at the grit between the steps.

Silence arrived abruptly, broken only by the sound of a distant bus and someone, somewhere, laughing at a joke they would not remember later. Wren stood over the ankle break and checked his airway, not because he deserved it, but because she keeps her own rules. Juno returned to her rail with the satisfaction of a professional who had solved a small puzzle. I rolled my shoulder plate and felt the dent with a gloved thumb.

"You did not need me," Wren said, and it sounded like a statement on the work, not on herself.

"I needed you," I said. "You cut the eyes. You redirected the first shot. You kept the couple from becoming pieces on the board. That is the work."

She gave me a dry little look. "It is always the work. I liked doing it with you watching."

"You do not freeze," I said. "That is rarer than people admit."

"If I freeze, people die," she said. "I learned it once. I do not intend to learn it again."

We moved through the space and cleaned the scene the way the contract expected. Wren ziptied the least injured and took a picture of the worst with the kind of clinical distance that keeps you from carrying strangers home in your head. I pulled the repeater out of the kiosk with a crowbar and left it where the precinct could find it. Juno sniffed around the railing and found a small nest of stolen implants hidden behind a cable clamp. Wren bagged them and labeled the bag for return. The precinct had not paid for charity, but we carried our own economy.

I sent a tightband message to the cutout. "Floodline Nine, Viaduct 14 stairs are clear. Four down. Two out. One critical, breathing. Illegal repeater removed. You owe us the second half."

The answer arrived as a single green dot. Payment verified. The dot faded.

Wren leaned on the railing for a moment and watched the city move under the viaduct, all those small errands that make a place into a home without asking anyone's permission. A kid pushed a cart full of parts that were two days away from being a radio. A woman in orange boots counted steps to a rhythm only she could hear. A dog slept on a stoop like it had invented the posture.

"You did not tell me I would like it," she said. "You said it was practice and that I would be unhappy about the contract. Both true. But you did not tell me I would like the way it felt to put a stop to something that has been chewing a hole in a neighborhood."

"I try not to sell our work as joy," I said, and Forge made the honesty come out heavy. "It confuses the price."

She turned to look at me and held my gaze. "I am not confused," she said. "I am tired and less angry than I was when we woke up. That is enough."

We left the bodies for the precinct pickup and descended the stairs. The light shifted as we moved, a change in the lattice that left the viaduct briefly gold before it returned to steel gray. Wren walked with that long, steadied stride she carries after an honest fight. Juno rode high and watched the skyline with the practiced boredom of a professional.

Back at the Wendigo I sealed the door and shrugged Forge's shoulders out of habit. Wren wrapped her knuckles against the faraday drawer, a small ritual now. "Next step," she said. "We talk about why you pick this jaw when you do."

"After we eat," I said. "You fight better when you remember you have a body."

She laughed once, which is better medicine than most things we carry, and set a pot on the stove. Juno ticked her agreement. I sat down in the heavy silence that Forge keeps on hand and let the adrenaline drain through the systems that know what to do with it.

The precinct would call this a success. The neighborhood would call it a relief. For my part, I filed the noise, memorized the angles, and wrote Wren's name at the top of the mental ledger I keep for people who do not freeze. The next scene would ask for a different room and a different story. For now, the stairs were quiet, and the bill had been paid.

WE ATE AT THE tiny fold-out in the Wendigo with the window cracked for air that smelled faintly of sugar and wet concrete. Wren balanced the pot between two cork pads, broke noodles in half with the end of her chopsticks, and let them slide back into the simmer like she was coaxing a shy animal out of a culvert. Juno perched on the rail above us and watched the steam with the lofty patience of a creature who believes time was invented for her convenience. Forge never needs food, not truly, but the ritual matters. Heat matters. Salt matters. The habit of sitting across from someone whose breathing steadies when the bowl is warm matters most of all.

"You called the cadence and I followed," Wren said, finally letting herself lean back into the bench. "I kept expecting the part where you tell me the angle I missed, and I am not hearing it."

"You read the room and shut the eyes before they could become teeth," I said. "You moved your weight where the floor would hold. That is the angle."

She prodded me with the blunt end of a chopstick. "You always sound like an instruction manual written by a poet when you are pleased."

"Forge is not built for compliments," I said. "They rattle around inside the plates."

Wren looked at the dent on my shoulder and traced the edge with her gaze instead of a fingertip, which is a kind of tenderness I have learned to notice. "You took three rounds for me," she said. "I am not going to pretend I do not see that."

"I took three rounds for the plan," I said, and then saw the way her mouth set. I let myself correct the sentence. "I took them for you because the plan includes you. That is the only version I write now."

She accepted that with a little nod and went back to the noodles. We ate quietly, which is not the same as eating in silence. The van clicked and breathed around us, a big animal pleased to be home. The mint offered up a thin green scent. The light through the cracked window turned the tea tin into an amber lighthouse and then faded as the lattice shifted its brightness to someone else's street.

When the pot was empty she stacked the bowls with the careful clatter of someone who has done dishes in places where noise gets you noticed. She wiped the table, set the sponge to dry, and leaned her hips against the counter. The question had been waiting since we left the stairs. I could see it in the way her eyes found my face and then the pod tower, as if the answer might be hanging there with the shells.

"Why Forge today," she asked. "And yesterday. You could have taken Stray and kept the ability to vanish, or Wisp and kept the ability to slide. You walked a wall with a hammer instead. I know the tactical reasons. I am asking about the person in there with me when you choose this jaw."

The plates along my jaw felt heavier at that, which is not a measurable thing but a true one. Forge remixes the air in my chest. The posture carries certainty that would be a lie if I spoke it without the weight. "Bodies tell minds stories," I said. "Forge tells me nothing moves me without permission. The story is not always accurate, but it is useful in rooms where other stories have been written on the floor."

Wren folded her arms, not defensively, only to hold herself still so she would not interrupt the thought. "Useful becomes habit. Habit becomes a mask you forget you put on. When I look at you in Forge, I hear the quiet you use to keep me at the edge of the map. I do not want to live at the edge of your map."

I looked down at my hands, at the blunt power in the knuckles, at the hairline scratches in the plating, at the faint scuffs that carry small histories no one else will ever read. "It is easy to love the simplicity," I said. "When you have been small for too long, simplicity feels like a kind of forgiveness. It is only relief."

"Do you get lost inside it," she asked, voice softer.

"Yes," I said. I have found there is no sense in lying when the person across from you has learned your weather. "I draw maps. I label doors. I leave the lights on in the hall that goes back to myself."

"And if the map fails," she said.

"Then you say my name and I answer with the number that comes after," I said. "And if I do not answer, you use the wafer and pull me out of the fire. We wrote that rule together."

She glanced toward the small case on the shelf. The metal caught a last sliver of light and gave it back like a promise. "I do not want to be reduced to the emergency," she said. "I want you to trust me before the alarm begins."

"I do," I said, and felt the truth of it land. "This is why I am not somewhere quiet and brilliant and alone. Quiet is easier. Alone is easier. Neither keeps me."

She let that sit, then reached for the magnet on the kettle and set it down with a click that made the room feel aligned. "Switch," she said, and there was no challenge in it. "We have thinking work, and you think better with small hands when the work is thread and not hammers."

I stood and the plates settled the way a heavy coat settles right before you hang it on the peg. The pod tower waited at the back, blue halos slow and confident around each cradle. I stepped into Forge's dock and let the spine port find home. The world narrowed, then turned soft at the edges, and then disappeared altogether, a clean curtain that I have learned not to fear.

Wisp woke with a breath that felt like a curtain lifting. The first movement is always a small turn of the head as if listening for music that is not there. The second is a search for Wren. I found her reflection in the hatch glass and the muscles along my shoulders loosened with a relief I do not plan and cannot manufacture. I slid down from the cradle and the hoodie found me like a cloud that already knows your name.

Juno pecked the rail twice and pushed a clipped waveform to the nearest screen. The spectrogram fluttered with a thin spine at the bottom, the kind of signal that hides under traffic and hopes no one cares enough to separate it from the rest. Wren already had her hand on the tuner. She rolled the gain like she was turning up a song.

"Private band," she said. "Nine eighty one. It broke through twice on our drive back and I did not chase it. Juno caught a spill while you were switching."

We let the clip run. Engine growl first, then a man's voice that carried the training of someone who learned to sound calm in rooms full of glass. The words were chopped by the road and the cheap mic, but one phrase landed intact enough to keep. "Vyre zero seven," he said, and then more static, and then the end of his sentence fell into a place I could not reach without inventing it.

The cabin seemed to shrink a degree, the way a room does when a name enters and refuses to leave. Wren scrubbed the edges clean, then ran it again. This time I listened for the rhythm underneath the word. It lives there, at the bottom of the voice, a cadence you can hide from ears that love the surface.

"Mark the time," I said. "Two seconds past the minute, then again at six. That is not a loop. He was live both times."

Wren overlaid the clip on the city grid. Juno triangulated off refraction points the way a bird finds a coastline in fog. A knot of possibility bloomed near the substation. Another flickered on the beltway, a smear on a moving target. The third lived briefly near the freight viaduct where we had chewed the convoy out of its leash.

"Someone followed the echo of our noise," Wren said. "Close enough to name us when we touch things, not close enough to make it a conversation. If Vyre zero seven is awake in this district, Sable has a leash to yank when she wants an audience."

I looked at my hands, so much smaller now, the plating thinner, the articulation a sequence of clean, precise arcs. In Wisp the story the body tells the mind is that danger and tenderness can be held in the same posture without ruining either. It keeps me alive in rooms where being hard only teaches people how to be harder back.

"Why do you keep changing," Wren asked, returning to the part of the conversation that had only shifted bodies, not subjects. "Not what you are hiding from. I can guess that chapter. Why the changes as an answer. You would cut cleaner if you chose one blade."

"Because one blade only writes one sentence," I said. "Bodies are languages. There are rooms that only answer to certain verbs. Forge says stop. Wisp says listen. Stray says leave before the door knows you were here. If I speak only one language long enough, I begin to believe the world is only made of words I already know."

"And the self," she said, searching my face, not the plates. "Where is the thread that ties all of that together. I do not want to wake up one day and realize I learned the wrong person by heart."

"The thread is the room," I said. "Not the furniture. The rules I refuse to change are the same no matter which door I came through. Do not sell anyone for safety. Do not leave the young where the old keep their knives. Do not let people rewrite the map of your face for their convenience. Keep the promises that you can carry. Do not make the ones that break you to keep."

She listened and I watched her listening. Wren has a way of making attention feel like a shelter. "If the room ever feels different," she said, "if the rules begin to slide under your feet, you tell me before the lights go out. I am not asking for permission to save you. I am asking for your willingness to let me in the hall before the smoke gets too thick."

"You have it," I said. "You had it when you asked for mint."

That made her laugh, not because it was clever, but because it was ordinary. She moved to the console and dragged a new layer across the grid, a subtle lattice of low power tripwires that sniffed for the shape of that word as it traveled through the city. Juno tucked a filter underneath that would ignore chatter about number seven buses and seven day sales and choose only the sound of a professional forgetting to say unit after a name he has said too often.

We stood close as the system stitched itself into something useful. Wren's sleeve brushed my bare wrist where the hoodie did not quite reach. The contact felt like the world remembering it was a place you could stand and not just a map you have to run. The window breathed a cool thread of air along my cheek. Somewhere outside someone was warming a griddle and telling a story in a voice that had never learned to care about microphones.

"Vyre zero seven," Wren said again, trying the weight of it one more time. "Do you think this one belongs to Sable."

"Belongs is the wrong verb," I said. "Vyre units are not kept. They are pointed. If Sable points this one at us, it will mean she has already chosen the room. We need a place where our rules hold when the first shot is not ours."

"Cathedral tunnels," she said, thinking out loud. "Or the drainage spill under Bastion. Or your favorite, the outflow where the lattice conduits breathe."

"Not my favorite," I said. "Only the one where I have counted the steps in the dark."

She smiled without looking away from the map. "Which is another way to say favorite."

The net finished compiling and settled into a quiet watch. A small light blinked to tell us it was listening. Juno hopped to my shoulder, the weight both familiar and new because this body balances differently than the last. Wren turned down the lights a fraction and the Wendigo wrapped itself around us in the way good rooms do when they are allowed to be homes.

"We will keep moving," she said. "We will keep choosing. We will keep leaving lights on."

"Until morning," I said.

"Until it is our morning," she answered.

The name sat on the shelf with the case and the mint and the tea tin, another object placed where we could see it without letting it own the room. We washed the bowls and set them to dry. We checked the door and the window and the schedule we had built for our next set of small errands. We left the curtain half open so we could see each other across the aisle when the city turned itself down. Somewhere in the wire a man with a tired voice said a number he did not mean to share with us. We made a note and did not run toward it. We let the night count in our favor.

Late afternoon thinned into the kind of light Klade uses to make promises it does not intend to keep. The lattice dimmed a fraction and the street learned how to shine without help. We took the Wendigo two neighborhoods south and parked it in the shadow of a shuttered laundromat whose sign still boasted Same Day Heat like a superstition. I chose Wisp for the walk because the work would be thread, not hammers. Juno rode my shoulder and clicked her quiet amusement at the world. Wren tucked a set of sniffers into the inside pocket of her jacket and gave the door two soft taps that sounded like luck.

I pulled the hoodie I favor when I need to look like a kid who belongs anywhere and nowhere. It is black and oversized, sleeves chewed at the cuffs, a patched logo from a defunct school stamped crooked over the heart. Under it I wore a pale knit with a frayed collar and a plastic charm looped on a cheap chain, the kind you get out of a sidewalk capsule machine. The charm is a smiling star with one arm broken off. It buys me a kind of invisibility that the expensive kits never can. My legs were wrapped in charcoal leggings with reinforced panels at the knees, and I had scuffed high-tops that blink a dim strip of light when they hit the ground. The soles are quiet and the lights stay off unless I tell them a secret. Fingerless gloves hid the ports at my wrists. A canvas messenger bag sat high against my ribs, stickers layered over old stickers until the history became camouflage. In this shell my height puts me eye level with most people's shoulders. I read as twelve in bad light and fourteen in good. The silver-pink fiber hair was tied into two small puffs high on my head, neat enough to pass a parent's inspection, loose enough to suggest no one is looking. My eyes, too large for any natural face, showed as glossy black with a faint electric ring. They are a little unsettling if you stare. Most people do not.

Wren pulled on her usual field clothes, the ones that let her pass as a courier who has seen too much and prefers to be paid in cash. Dark jacket with a soft liner, sleeves pushed to the forearms, a charcoal shirt that never wrinkles, slate cargo pants with worn knees and a loop for the coil she carries out of habit. Her boots were matte and clean at the seams, the kind of maintenance that comes from respect rather than vanity. The deck strap crossed her chest at a diagonal and disappeared under the jacket, a small declaration for anyone who knows how to read threads and buckles. She wore a narrow scarf the color of rainwater, more for disguise than warmth. Her hair is ash-blonde and refuses to stay inside a tidy plan. She ties it low and it still finds a way to fan at the nape in pale strands that catch light like wire. Her eyes are gray-green, changeable in different rooms, and quick to settle when she has measured a threat. Standing beside me, she is half a head taller, which means she becomes the person vendors address first while I am allowed to do the watching.

We moved out with the kind of pace that signals nothing in particular. Not fast enough to be worth notice, not slow enough to read as uncertain. The block opened into a low market strung between a radio repair stall and a tea vendor who still believes in kettles that sing. Cables crossed overhead in loose geometry and made constellations out of extension cords. Smells piled on each other until the air felt like a drawer of old postcards. Solder and mint. Newsprint that has been handled by too many hands. Oil warming on a plate. A lick of ozone from a cutter that should not be sitting out where anyone can touch it. Juno tipped her head and watched the whole arrangement with the pleased disdain of a queen auditing a procession.

I felt the looks that stick to a child shape and fall off a woman in a jacket. A shopkeeper glanced at me and decided I was someone's responsibility. Another glanced at Wren and decided she was her own. It is useful to walk inside both truths. I let the hoodie slump and the puffs bounce a little, then tightened my stride whenever I needed space to open. Wren played the other end of the illusion, shoulders loose, hands visible, smile set to polite. When anyone spoke to us she answered, and when anyone watched us she handed them a performance of harmless errands. Between her courtesy and my smallness, the crowd made room.

We did not speak for two streets. This was listening work. Wren peeled off twice to press a sniffer into places a careless maintenance crew would ignore. The first went inside the rusted belly of a streetlamp controller. She knelt in the dust, jacket creasing at the shoulders, hair haloed by the weak bulb, and slid the wafer into the bracket where a crew would expect to find an empty slot. The second vanished behind a breaker panel inside the tea stall's weathered door. She bought a cup so green it looked like a leaf had decided to become steam. The vendor said her mother must have taught her to hold a cup like that. Wren smiled in a way that kept the ache from becoming the whole story and left a coin larger than the drink deserved.

I did my part by choosing the ground that would welcome us later. In my head I traced lines of sight and lines of retreat. I counted doors that would close with one push and doors that would argue. Juno mapped the checks into our overlay and kept a tally in a little rhythm only she enjoys. Klade answered with its usual mix of kindness and indifference. A mechanic waved us around a spill without looking up from the engine. A boy on a battered scooter slowed to admire Juno and then pretended he had not. A dog decided we were furniture and leaned against my shin with the easy trust that only dogs can afford.

The net we had set that morning whispered in my ear. A municipal repeater two districts west hiccupped once, then breathed normally. Sixty-three, rest, sixty-three. The interval hummed like a name. I touched Wren's sleeve and let the data travel through my hand instead of my mouth. She angled her head toward the nearest pole and gave the smallest nod, a gambler's acknowledgment that the deck has started to remember her face.

We did not change course. The market thinned and then gathered again around a plastics vendor who had arranged bowls and cups into a topography of color. I took advantage of the crowd and set a sniffer under the cash tray while Wren examined a pair of spoons with the seriousness of a collector. The vendor complimented her taste and added a third for free. Wren thanked her with that old-fashioned courtesy that gives a day a reason to behave.

Another whisper rode the beltway from the east, fainter now and dirtier, the way a voice sounds after it has crossed too many rooms. Juno etched it into the grid and marked the timing with a green dot that matched the tea tins. We let the crowd carry us toward the underpass where the market gives up and the viaduct begins to tell its own story.

The light changed under the concrete. It is always colder there, even when the air is warm. An edger drone murmured along the curb at knee height, eyes open just enough to see trash, not enough to see trouble. Wren crouched as if to retie a boot, jacket riding along her back, ash-blonde strands loosening at her neck. She slid a wafer onto the drone's service port and patted its shell like a good dog. The drone considered its life choices and then offered us a perspective we would ask for again later.

The third whisper arrived as we crossed into a pocket of shade that smelled like old rain and long arguments. The name rode it clean this time. Vyre zero seven. Not shouted, not disguised. Said by a person who had forgotten that microphones can be loyal to more than one master. I stopped beside a column and let my hoodie fall forward so my eyes became greater than my face. Wren settled next to me, taller by that useful half head, gray-green eyes gone bright with the kind of thought that plays three answers at once and chooses the fourth.

"Closer than I like," she said, voice low enough to land in my ear and nowhere else.

"Three blocks," I said. "Freight lots or the service road behind the warehouses."

"What do you want to do," she asked, and the question carried trust, not challenge.

"We do not pursue on a name," I said. "We pursue on a room."

She nodded and returned her hands to her pockets. Juno looked up, not at anything in particular, only at height. A figure stood on the service catwalk against the sky. Not Vyre. The stance was lazy at the edges, the energy bored rather than predatory. A rail cleaner on break or a courier waiting to time a run. They glanced down and saw only a woman with a bag, a kid with a hoodie, and a bird that did not belong to anyone. We let them keep that story.

We took the long way back. Not out of fear. Out of respect for the habit that keeps a path from becoming a routine. I left a tiny packet of polymer under a loose step and told the step we would be back for it. Wren set one last sniffer in the handrail frame where the screws had been stolen years ago. The neighborhood continued to breathe around us, indifferent to our preparations and oddly eager to assist them.

Inside the Wendigo the air felt like rescue. I shed the messenger bag and set it on the bench. Wren eased the spoons onto the counter with a care that made them look like instruments. She poured water, and the mint woke like memory. On the grid, three green dots pulsed along the routes we had walked. Two yellow ones marked yesterday's noise. A single blue bruise lived near the substation.

I looked at us reflected faintly in the cockpit glass. A small girl in a black hoodie with bright puffs and eyes that do not belong to a child. A woman with ash hair pulled low, gray-green eyes steady, jacket open just enough to show a strap that means she can reach what she needs without looking. The height difference set our silhouettes like punctuation. People will always read Wren as the sentence and me as the aside. That is fine. It keeps us both in the story in the ways we require.

"Tomorrow we leave a thread that only a patient hunter will notice," Wren said. "Then we wait and pretend not to care."

"Tomorrow we build the floor and let the door stay open," I said. "The right footsteps will come."

She touched the mint pot and did not water it. She touched the case and did not open it. She touched my sleeve and let it stay between us, cotton on cotton, small and true. Juno preened and set one feather straight with the air of a creature who has completed an inspection. The Wendigo dimmed the lights a fraction and the grid settled into a watchful heartbeat.

Klade turned the lattice one notch darker and pretended the night was merciful. We knew better, but we let the pretense stand. It is easier to plan under a light that pretends to be kind.

NIGHT SETTLED WITH THE kind of patient quiet that lets a machine remember to breathe. We left the curtain half open so the Wendigo could keep an eye on us, and the city repaid the courtesy with a stripe of sodium light that fell across the mint and turned the leaves into paper cutouts. Wren sorted the day's notes at the fold-out, pencil tucked behind one ear, ash-blonde hair stubbornly slipping from its tie. I sat on the bench with my legs folded under me and a small tool roll open, checking the contact leads I had soldered into a wafer. Juno watched from the rail with the calm of a cathedral gargoyle.

The net we built glowed on the wall in soft colors. Three green dots for today's walk, two yellow for yesterday's ghosts, one steady blue near the substation. It looked like a map that had decided to care whether we made it to morning. The kettle clicked as it cooled and went still.

Juno turned her head a fraction. Two quick taps on the rail told us to listen. A thin spectrogram unrolled across the nearest screen, dull gray at first, then a bright thread along the bottom. She pushed the audio to the little speaker by the mint. We leaned toward it without meaning to.

Road noise came first, then a voice that belonged to someone trained to sound calm on bad days. It had the careful weight of corporate security. The words were rough from engine bounce, but clear enough. "Control to field asset. Confirm status. VYRE zero seven."

Wren did not move except at the eyes. She nudged the gain a notch and left it alone.

A second voice answered, lower and tighter. "VYRE zero seven on grid nine. Suit is stable. Heat within tolerance. Orders."

Static washed the edges. Juno trimmed the noise. The first voice returned. "Analytics flagged an anomaly at the east substation chapel. Perimeter likely compromised. Follow beltline north, then service road forty-four. Survey and engage. Use code eight sixteen."

I made the translation out loud so the room would not have to guess. "Code eight sixteen is their excuse to treat this as critical infrastructure. It lets private security act like police."

Wren wrote the numbers once in the margin of a page she had not planned to use. "Good. We can quote it back at them if we need to."

"Mark the time," I said. "Three seconds past the minute, then again at eight. That is live, not a loop."

"Copy," the field voice said. "Two minutes from the beltline. Code eight sixteen received."

The clip broke into tire noise on rough concrete. Juno caught the tail of a status ping as it bounced off a private repeater. She marked the reflection point on our grid with a small green dot, then added a second when the next ping took a different path. The triangle they made with the blue bruise near the substation dropped into place like a bad coin.

"He is circling today's ground," Wren said. "If he finds the kiosk we gutted, he will promise the precinct that order is coming."

I gave the shorter explanation the scene deserved. "Oronix wants a neat report that says they responded, even if that just means pushing people around. They care about the story more than the cost."

Juno pushed a second clip. The words came in under the engine like a low tide. "Control to VYRE zero seven. Possible interference at viaduct fourteen. Maintenance report logged. Expect non corporate actors. Audio record only. No body cams."

Wren's mouth thinned. "Audio only so the lawyers can argue about tone."

The field voice came back without drama. "Understood. If we see them, detain or erase."

We looked at each other. The way he said erase did not leave much room for doubt.

Control took a beat and then answered. "Detain if you can keep it contained. Erase if you cannot. Priority is the courier chain, not bystanders."

Wren repeated the phrase quietly, as if testing how it felt in the air. "Not bystanders. Street debris. He actually said it that way."

The transmission ended cleanly, like a hand had closed a book. On the spectrogram the bright thread along the bottom lingered, a single hair on a white sink.

We let the quiet stand. It was not a ritual. It was room to think.

"Route," I said finally.

Wren slid the map layer up so the churn in the data became a skin instead of a tangle. "Beltline north to service road forty-four," she said. "Forty-four runs behind three warehouses owned by a cleaning-solvent shell. There is a spur that doubles back to the viaduct stairs."

"Do we shadow him," I asked.

"Not tonight," she said, voice steady. "We do not chase a voice into someone else's ground. We pick the place and the rules, then invite him there."

"We leave a thread he cannot resist," I said. "Something that looks like luck to him and planning to us."

She pressed her knuckles into the table's edge and nodded. Wren has never liked the word erase. It does not belong to the systems she trusts. "Juno, keep the filter on channel nine eighty one at low power. Ignore chatter that is not mission traffic. If control speaks again, mirror the spill to every sniffer we set and ask the utility drones to forgive me."

Juno clicked once, pleased to be asked for exactly the work she loves. She added a small gold mark where the viaduct stairs cut under the broken billboard.

We poured water and set the cups down. Neither of us drank. Wren closed her eyes and rebuilt the viaduct in her head, step by step, like a surveyor who measures with breath instead of tape. I looked at my hands where they rested on the table. Wisp's hands are quick and careful, built to press and lift without leaving bruises. In Forge, this much talk would feel like a delay. In Wisp, it feels like aim.

"We should warn the Circuit Saint," Wren said, opening her eyes. "Not the details. Just that someone wants to use their chapel as a stage."

"We owe them that much," I said. "We used their roof to stay dry. They deserve a heads up before a storm arrives."

She wrote a line for the morning and underlined it once. Then she turned fully toward me. "You did not react when he said erase."

"I noticed it," I said. "I am busy not letting it decide the next hour."

"React anyway," she said, and she made it gentle so I could not dodge it.

So I did. It felt like the outline of a cost I am willing to pay but would rather delay. Wren watched that land and did not rush to smooth it.

"Tomorrow we string the thread and choose the place," she said. "We tell the Saint enough to keep people behind their own doors. We make sure the floor does not tilt when the first boot crosses it."

"Tomorrow," I agreed.

Juno dropped one last dot near the freight lots where the line had gone quiet. She circled it, not big enough to be useful, just enough to remind us we were not imagining things.

We let the map dim. The Wendigo lowered the fan speed and settled its weight on the shocks. Outside, Klade shaved another slice of brightness from the lattice and gave it to a different street. I lay back on the bench and let this body find the version of rest that feels like a measured countdown. Wren pulled the curtain partway and sat with her back to the pod tower, eyes on the faint glow of our grid. Juno shifted once and went still.

The recorder made a tiny click as it saved the clip under a new label. VYRE zero seven. Clear enough to follow. Clear enough to plan for. Not a door we would open tonight.

NIGHT LAYERED ITSELF OVER Klade in careful sheets, the kind that settle without creasing. The Wendigo took the hint and softened its systems, fans turning to a lower song, cabin lights falling to the blue that makes edges kind. Wren checked the locks with the same calm she uses for code, one latch at a time, not because she doubts the van, but because the ritual lets the day release its grip. I stayed in Wisp, small and quiet in my hoodie, perched on the bench with a blanket over my knees and Juno warm against my shoulder. The mint put a thin sweetness into the air. Somewhere outside a shopkeeper slid a gate down its runners and clicked a chain without anger. The neighborhood agreed to be still.

We spoke in the soft voices that keep a room from waking. Wren read our list for the morning and crossed out two lines that did not deserve to survive the night. Leave thread at service forty four, keep the Saint in the circle, check the viaduct stairs before lunch traffic builds, ask the drone yard about a lens that went blind at three past. Juno added a small note of her own by tapping the rail twice, then twice more, a code for remember that repetition is a choice. I nodded and she tucked her head for a moment, smug and content.

The grid glowed at a polite brightness on the far wall. Today's green dots pulsed where we had walked, close enough to feel like memory, far enough to look like planning. The blue bruise by the substation held steady. The viaduct mark blinked in a different rhythm now, slower than a heartbeat, faster than a clock, a pace that lodged in the ear without becoming a tune. I leaned back and let it sit there, a low presence under everything else.

Sleep does not arrive for me the way it does for Wren. In this shell it takes the form of stillness with the door cracked. She lay opposite me with one arm over her eyes and a foot peeking from the blanket so the floor could remind her that she lived somewhere with edges. I set an alert to the lowest hum and let the van count the seconds for me. Juno stood a little higher on the rail than usual, a posture she uses when she wants to look like a statue and is failing on purpose.

The first tripwire pinged at a harmless interval. A municipal camera woke for a breath, cleared its lens, and went back to dreaming. The map accepted the note and did not make a speech about it. The second arrived on schedule from a pocket repeater near the freight lots and followed the same pattern. The third came late and carried a tiny scrape inside the timestamp, as if the device had been bumped by a careless elbow. Wren's mouth moved in a fraction of a smile as she slept, the expression of someone whose brain agrees that life is lines and notes and leaves room for both.

I closed my eyes and pictured the Saint's substation the way we had left it. Knife switches polished until they looked like ritual tools, the mural of the lineworker with a belt for a halo, the quiet of a room that has learned to keep secrets without becoming mean. I thought about the men on the viaduct who had learned to turn their fear into small cruelties, and the way Wren had stepped behind the rifle with a motion that looked like grace and turned the weapon into a quiet piece of metal. The day had been clean where it needed to be clean. The city, for a few hours, had accepted our argument.

Juno lifted her head. Not high, only enough to change the angle of her eye. She clicked twice and the grid brightened without my hand. A new point touched the beltline layer and vanished, then touched again, not in the interval we had taught ourselves to expect, but in a rhythm that felt like a person tapping a table while counting a thought. I held still. The dot returned a third time, a little farther north, and then stopped in the way a vehicle stops at a light it has no intention of respecting once the cross traffic thins.

"Wisp," Wren said, voice a thread under the blanket, not fully awake and not asleep. "Is it ours."

"Not yet," I said. "Only a car that thinks it is important."

"Everything thinks it is important at this hour," she mumbled, and her breath found a slower pace again.

The kettle clicked as the metal cooled to match the room. A drip inside the sink added a single sound every minute and then skipped one and then resumed, the irregularity of a pipe learning to rest. My alert stayed quiet. The city stayed louder than us and softer than danger. I shifted so my shoulder fit the curve of the wall and let the van hug back.

When the fourth ping arrived, it did not announce itself with anything dramatic. The dot touched down near the old laundromat and kept moving, almost a courtesy, as if whoever carried it was afraid to look rude. The number that tagged it belonged to a utility worker who did not exist in the current roster. I flagged it, not for pursuit, only to keep it from slipping into the unremarked middle of the ledger. Juno marked it with a small triangle instead of a circle, a private joke about shapes that wants to become an inside language.

I must have closed my eyes for longer than I intended. The next thing I knew the room had shifted that last inch into night. Wren had rolled toward the wall and let her hand drift over the edge of the bench until it found mine. Our fingers rested together, light and without a promise larger than the hour. The mint tilted as if it had leaned to listen to something and then decided the story could wait until morning. Juno took three slow steps along the rail and stopped where the view of the window is best.

The grid offered one last flicker before settling. Not a dot this time, just a tiny breath of static near the freight lots, there and gone, a whisper without a word attached. If I had not been watching, I would have believed it a glitch. I watched long enough to know that it had not happened by accident. Someone had breathed against the city and the city had answered with a shiver.

I let the thought land and I gave it a name I would not say aloud. Not Vyre. Not Sable. Not yet. Only the place where those names prefer to stand when the room is about to change. Tomorrow we would put our thread where it needed to be and choose the floor that would not tilt when the first boot crossed it. Tonight we would be the smaller thing that decides to hold.

The wind outside lifted a paper scrap and pressed it against the window for a second, a pale square that looked like a hand in the low light. It slid away without drama and was gone. The van breathed. The city pretended to sleep. The map dimmed to a faint, watchful glow. I closed my eyes and counted to a number that felt like luck. When I reached it, the room was still with us.

Morning would come with teeth. For now the bite had not found us.

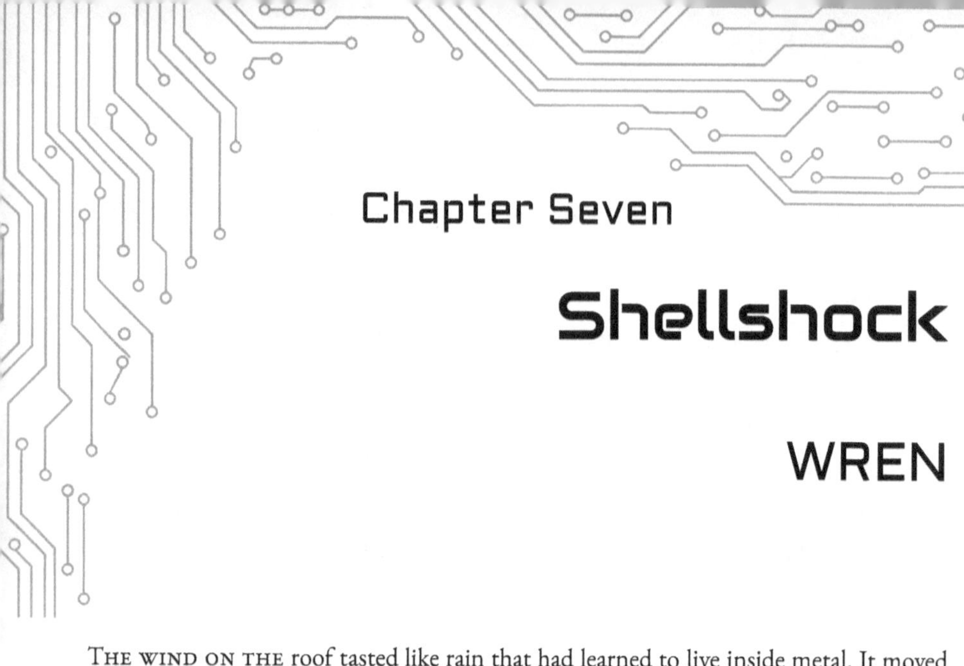

Chapter Seven

Shellshock

WREN

THE WIND ON THE roof tasted like rain that had learned to live inside metal. It moved across the service pipes and antenna spines and came back carrying the sour breath of the courier exchange half a block away. From up here Klade looked like a thousand overlapping plans that would never agree, sodium lamps making tired halos on loading bays, the lattice above pulsing in its careful rhythm, the glass skins of corporate towers pretending to be saints while they counted money. Our path cut a simple line through all that noise. We would cross three rooftops, drop a level through a maintenance stair, pass a locked door with the polite yellow triangle that tells you to keep your curiosity to yourself, then enter the little room I had tuned last night. In that room waited the travel cradle, a narrow rig that could receive one body and return another. Forge in, Velvet out. Hammers for the climb and the locks, then silk for the hallway with the carded smiles.

Juno rode the edge of a rusted vent stack and kept her red eye half lidded, like a cat pretending to be bored while counting every mouse in the alley. The wind ruffled the small feathers along the seam of her wings. She watched the stairwell door, the alley mouth, and the upper windows of the courier exchange, then clicked once to tell me none of those places had remembered to be dangerous yet. I felt the click through my shoulder as much as I heard it. The body learns the language of the machines you trust.

Forge stood beside me in the kind of stillness that can quiet a room by existing. He wears power like a posture, not a show. When he shifts his weight, pipes notice and change their minds about rattling. He lifted one shoulder and rolled it back. In the peroxide glow from a nearby floodlight I could see the shallow dent he had earned last night where a bad rifle met better plating. The dent caught light at its edge like a healed scar.

I checked the time on my wrist and nodded. "Two minutes. Juno keeps the stair. I keep the cradle. You keep your promise."

"Always," he said. The word did not need volume. His voice never does. It has weight built in. If Forge told me the sea had moved two streets closer while I blinked, I would check my shoes for water first and argue with physics later.

He touched the side of his neck once, a quick inventory of ports, then glanced at the black bag I carry for field work. The bag holds all the little prayers I know how to say to wires and boards. I lifted it so he could see I had packed the kinds of prayers that answer under pressure. He gave me that single nod that stands in for trust when there is no time for a speech about it.

The door with the yellow triangle opened to a stale stairwell that smelled like cleaning solvent and tired anger. Steps took us down to the level where couriers smoke and pretend they are not surveilled. The swap room lived behind a second door with a simple keypad and a camera that had been blind since last night. I had cleaned the logs and replaced the segment of trunk line that always overheats first. The little room welcomed us with a square of light and the soft hum of a power block that knows when it is about to be asked to work. In the corner waited the travel cradle, a waist high frame built to take one spine and return another, a tangle of cables gathered into a braid, a berth for the sleeping body.

Velvet stood in the berth with her eyes dim and her mouth relaxed into that not-smile that fools idiots and turns useful people into allies. Her skin looked human from across a room and entirely engineered from an arm's length. Her weight lives in the hips and the thighs where it can make rooms make space. Her hands can disarm a man with a touch he will remember fondly and hate himself for remembering.

"Thirty seconds," I said, running the cradle's warm start and watching the status lights make their slow climb from idle to ready. "You will be blind for two heartbeats. I will count with you."

Forge stepped into the dock. He always aligns himself in one clean motion. He does not hesitate at the moment where your spine meets the clamps. He breathes in, out, and the rig welcomes his shape like it has been waiting for a story it already knows the ending to. Locks engaged with the gentle finality of good machinery. The readout touched green, then amber as the system prepared to hand one language to another. I set my palm against the frame in the place where the vibration is truest and found the pitch I had tuned last night.

The power dipped. Not a sag you feel when a building takes a deep breath. A precise slip, like someone running a finger across the rim of a glass to make a note sing off key. The amber light faltered. The clamps clicked once in a pattern that was not mine. The hair along my arms lifted in a way that has nothing to do with nerves and everything to do with training. Something had nudged the line.

"Hold," I said, which was for me as much as for him. I stepped behind the cradle and tore the service panel free with two careful pries of a flat bar. The rig's small interior opened like a mouth that did not want to be read. The trunk line looked fine. The manifold did not. A silly little adjuster on the frequency floor sat one notch higher than I had set it. Not broken. Not jostled. Touched. Someone had asked the system to sing the wrong note until the rest of the song followed. Sabotage does not always shout. Sometimes it hums.

"Stay with me," I said, and meant it for the person I could not see inside the shell, as much as for the shell that was about to leave the room.

Forge went dark. It was not the good quiet that happens when a process ends where it should. The body released its reserve and slumped against the dock with an emptiness that made my stomach twist. At the same moment Velvet did not wake. Her lids did not flicker. The berth did not shift its weight the way it does when a new pilot settles into their momentum. The room learned a new kind of silence and I put my hands on the parts of the world I could still move.

I cut the cradle out of the loop. It is never elegant. You pull the plug on a system that wants you to ask nicely and it will bite your fingers if you hesitate. I yanked the connector on the manifold, dragged the auxiliary cable from the bag, and pressed its leads into the port at the base of the neck, the place where the spine meets the part of the person that lives outside bodies. My cable is ugly and I love it. The rubber sheath scarred long ago from a day that went wrong and still ended in survival. I bridged the power block with an inline regulator that I have never admitted to owning because it belongs in a different kind of work. I did not think about what that meant. I thought about keeping a person from falling into a gap I did not know how to reach.

The plates along Forge's neck opened in the slow, unsteady way of a door lifted after its hinge has been bent. The face closed. Not the normal seal you see when a person enters the quiet where the shell is only a room. It smoothed down completely, a cover sliding into place to protect what it could while something tried to rearrange the order of a life. In that unlit breath I saw the core Hikari keeps under everything else. You tell yourself you know the people you work with. Then a machine fails and the world gives you a sight you did not earn.

Under the armor the torso is not soft or cruel. It is clean. Carbon struts form a ladder that looks too fine and then proves itself by holding fast. The spine is a column of ports and braided cable, not tidy, not chaotic, patterned like a hand-sewn seam. The face is not a face at all, only a smooth mask with a ridge where a nose once taught air how to travel. The eyes are round lenses the size of coins. When they opened, they did not carry any of the expressions I am used to reading. They carried only intention. No fear. No performance. A question that did not use words.

They opened and found me. That was the whole sentence. Not a plea. Not a demand. A small tilt of the head, an old reflex coded into a new body, asking me to do the work I had already begun.

"Right here," I said, and pushed the regulator until the pitch in the board steadied. I tuned the frequency floor down to the key I had set last night and held the adjuster there with the tip of my screwdriver while my other hand reseated the manifold. Juno dropped from the vent in a blur of black and took a place between the cradle and the room's small camera nook, her body making a blind spot out of a lens I had told to sleep. The calibrator in the manifold blinked the pattern I wanted, then hesitated, then blinked it again with more confidence. The amber returned. The clamps found their rhythm like a dancer remembering the count.

"Come on," I said, which is a superstition that still works. I watched the temperature band climb and settle. I watched the current stabilize without the ugly sawtooth that means loss is happening somewhere you cannot see. I pressed the auxiliary cable deeper into its seat until my thumb hurt and the regulator whined in a pitch I trust. I did not breathe until the little green diode on the right side of the cradle pulsed a clean heartbeat and the manifold answered with its own.

The blank face closed its eyes. The plates sealed. The skin returned and pulled its seams flat until the joints looked like artistry instead of surgery. Velvet woke the way she always does, slow eyelids first, breath that is not breath next, a turn of the head that searches for the person she expects to find. She saw me and her focus changed so fast it was almost sound.

"What did it look like," she asked, and that came in Hikari's voice, not Velvet's practiced honey.

"It looked like you," I said, because the truth should sit between us now rather than later. "Clean. Exact. Here."

She held my gaze without a costume of charm. The room felt larger and older.

Boots sounded on the alley stair. Not a curious neighbor. Not a janitor. The weight of people who believe they belong everywhere. The little motion detector above the door pulsed a warning I had not extended the courtesy to silence. The saboteur had not only nudged our power. They had told someone to be on time for the show.

I slapped the panel back into place and pushed the auxiliary cable into the pouch where I keep things that should not be seen by other people. "We move," I said, and held my hand out. Velvet stepped down onto the floor, found her balance, and adjusted the line of her shoulders. Defensive. Ready. Human.

I wanted to say more. I wanted to say I had seen the person inside the masks and that the sight had landed somewhere in me I could not name without breaking it. I wanted to say I would hold that sight the way you hold a fragile object that belongs in the open air but still shivers when the room changes temperature. There was no time for those words. There would be later. Or there would not. Tonight would decide which.

We left the little room exactly as we found it except for the part where the city had tried to peel one of us open and see who lived there. The hallway took us into the wind again. The courier exchange hummed two doors away, impatient men talking in careful voices, drone arms settling boxes on belts, the hiss of labelers printing truths that would be lies in two hours. I kept the bag high on my shoulder and Juno on my left. Velvet walked one step ahead but kept her chin at the angle that does not challenge and does not invite. I opened the stairwell door and listened first. The boots had split into two pairs. One set made noise with intent. The other made noise with care. The loud pair turned the corner too fast and the quiet pair stopped to wait for us to choose, which is a test I have failed before and did not intend to fail again.

We were three steps from the door when the first man arrived. His jacket had the look of a security uniform that had lost its logo in the wash. He raised his palm to say wait, then saw Velvet and changed the gesture to the softer hold that men use when they believe beauty owes them patience. I liked him less for that. He spoke, but his eyes kept traveling, trying to measure where he would put his hand next.

"Sorry, service corridor. Restricted."

I let my gaze drop and fed him the picture of a woman who has learned to step aside. I took one small step in, not backward, so he had to come closer to finish the sentence he had started. He reached with two fingers for my sleeve, with the lazy confidence of someone who has never been punished for that habit. When his fingers touched the fabric I used the contact to take his balance. He did not understand what had happened, only that the floor had moved in a way that taught his knees a lesson. He fell in a graceless bend and met the concrete with a grunt that told his partner all the wrong things.

The second man brought his arm up to block Velvet while he decided whether to draw. Velvet stepped inside the decision and redirected his wrist in a way that made his shoulder think about its future. She lowered him to the ground politely, because we had other business. I do not know if he understood the gift.

We reached the roof door and took the quicker stair. The wind met us with that smell of sparking wire that means a transformer somewhere is trying to be brave. From here the city looked new again. Sirens at a distance where they could be ignored. A beltline truck practicing dominance by changing lanes without asking. The courier exchange lit up from inside like a hive that has found sugar. Juno rose on a gust and stitched a path across my wrist: four rooftops south, two descents, canal bridge, then street level where the Wendigo could pretend to be a sanitation rig for three more hours without getting less believable.

I woke the van with the remote. The little green pip turned on and stayed on, which is the machine's way of telling me it wishes it still had a mouth so it could say I am on my way. I set the disguise and watched the GPS spoof paint a lazy circle two blocks away, the kind of path a bored city worker makes when he is waiting for his shift to end.

Behind us the stairwell door opened again. More feet. Different weight. I did not see badges. Sometimes that is worse. Velvet looked at me and I saw the calculation finish in her eyes the same moment it finished in mine. We cut left along the roofline and took the ladders like we had rehearsed them. The first drop went smooth enough that we could afford breath. The second had a rung that turned in my hand and tried to teach my ankle something I did not want it to know. I corrected, landed, moved. Velvet followed, not light, not heavy, precise. Being near her when she moves like that scrambles the part of me that measures fear against grace. It is hard to hold both in one breath. It is necessary anyway.

The third roof gave us a gap the builders had left to save materials and that time had widened into a small argument. I meant to jump first, because that is the promise, but she took it with me. We landed together and turned because the human brain loves symmetry, and a pair of men who had chosen bad shoes learned why good shoes are a wage they should demand from their employers.

I do not remember deciding to protect the person behind me. My body knows that shape. I kept my shoulders between him and the room and listened for the sound that means a gun is about to be useful. It did not come. We ran the last length to the edge and looked down. The ladder that should have dropped us to the alley had been robbed of its lower rungs by optimists with a saw. I went first and dropped the last two meters, bent, and took the landing through my knees so the rest of me could keep working. Velvet stepped off the roof and landed with the quiet certainty of a person who never argues with gravity. Someone behind us tried to follow and chose to keep his ankles straight. He screamed in the language of broken things. The others slowed. Sometimes that is enough to change the night.

The canal opened in front of us like a strip of black ribbon. The street beyond it had accepted its role as a place where nothing remarkable happens. The Wendigo rolled into the frame wearing its sanitation costume. The paint wore a scuffed matte and the lights dimmed to the bureaucratic orange that says city property. The van kept its curb like a dog that has been taught to wait on command. I pulled the side door and Velvet climbed in without looking back. I followed and slapped the door home. Juno dropped through the opening at the last possible second and claimed the rail with a little flourish that looked like relief disguised as arrogance.

I told the van to drive and it did, with a confidence that would be arrogance if it were a person. The engine offered the low growl that means there is power in reserve if we need it. We would need it. A pickup truck tried to put its bumper where our back door wanted to live. The Wendigo nudged a delivery crate into its lane with the kind of courtesy that creates problems for other people and leaves you out of the paperwork. The truck clipped a mirror off a parked car and learned that paperwork has a way of finding you anyway. Two motorcycles tried a flank and discovered that the van knows a maintenance arch every driver forgets after training day. The arch did not look like a road until we were inside it. By then it was impolite to mention the deception.

We carved a path under a bridge that has kept more secrets for me than any church I have ever entered. When we broke back into the open I let my shoulders drop the inch they had wanted since the cradle stuttered. I dialed the cabin lights down because the interior brightness can feel like an interrogation when your nerves have remembered how to shout. The bench waited. The tools waited. The questions waited.

Velvet sat on the bench and kept very still. Not rigid. Economical. The kind of still that protects resources. I watched her face for the tiny tells a person gives when the body is hurting and the mind is filing that fact under later. Juno leaned close to her shoulder and clicked a little rhythm that means you are seen, which is more than comfort, it is a kind of oath.

"We are clear of the first net," I said, because saying it out loud helps the body believe it. "Talk to me."

She looked at her hands for a slow breath. Her fingers are elegant because the body was designed to hold attention, but inside the angles there is steel. "I was between," she said finally. "I do not like the word. It is the only one I have."

"I saw you," I said. "Not the skins. You. Nothing broke that I cannot fix with tools or time. The rest we will talk about when the room belongs to us again."

She gave me half a smile that is not Velvet's work. It belongs to someone I have been learning by feel since the day I decided to step into this life alongside them. "You always reach for what your hands can hold," she said, and there was no mockery in it.

"Tonight that is enough," I answered, and I believed it. I believed it because the alternative was to reach for the past and the past is a city with too many locked doors.

The van took a left that put our tail into a lane the map believes does not exist. I felt the wheels roll over a seam in the concrete I have used as a landmark since before I knew I would need landmarks. The city thinned. The traffic forgot us. The noise of the night grew smaller until it was just the sound of the engine and the quiet of two people sitting with a truth that had arrived sooner than they had planned.

I set my bag on the floor and slid closer to her. The neck panel of that body is held by two latches and my hands know them. I did not touch them yet. I let my fingers rest on the bench between us so she could see where the help would come from and decide when to ask. Her eyes tracked my hand, then my face, then the ceiling, where Juno perched like a small judge who has decided to approve the proceedings.

"Who touched the cradle," I asked, because the practical question needed a place to live.

"Oronix," she said without decoration. "Or someone who hired by the hour and was told which screw to turn. The adjustment was too neat for a guess."

"They wanted a show," I said. "They wanted you to be caught between bodies while someone filmed it and wrote a story about monsters."

"Or they wanted me to die quietly in a room where the paperwork would say equipment failure," she said, and neither of us needed to add that the paperwork would find a way to blame me for trusting my own machines.

I nodded and finally reached for the latches. "Hold still," I said. "Let me clean the insult out before it settles."

She did. The panel lifted with a sigh of warm air, the kind of heat that is not dangerous yet and would be if I let it stay. Contacts showed a thin haze of arcing where the frequency had insisted on its wrongness. I set a towel under the edge so that no tiny screw could fall into a place where I would have to be a magician instead of a mechanic. I cleaned the pads, replaced a little heat sink that had given itself up nobly in the breach, and listened to the hum quiet into something true. While I worked she closed her eyes. Not in sleep. In the specific rest of a person who has decided to trust the hands that are moving near the soft parts of their life.

When I finished I did not rush to ask the questions I wanted. I closed the panel and let my palms rest on the hinge for a second to feel the temperature settle. Only then did I speak.

"In the dock," I said, "when your face was smooth and the eyes were coins, you looked at me without any of the personas to carry the message. That is the person I am going to call by the name you chose. Not the masks. Not the languages. The one that lives in the space between. If there has to be a true Hikari, it is that one."

She opened her eyes. I expected a parry. She gave me only attention. It felt like standing in a warm square of sun that you did not know the building had.

"It is a good name," she said. "I will keep it."

I let the relief show because pretending not to feel it would make me a liar in a place where honesty pays better. I sat back and let the van carry us into the quiet we had earned. The questions that remained would have to wait for a room with a door we could lock and a power line I had tuned myself. For now, it was enough that I had seen Hikari without a body telling the world what to think, and that we had both survived the sight.

Behind us the courier exchange turned another contract into a stain on the city's floor. Before us the bridge threw a ribbon of black across a smaller ribbon of black and invited us to cross. The wind found its voice again and tapped a loose panel on the van's side. Juno ruffled and resettled. Velvet shifted her shoulders and let a little tension leave.

"Later," I said, and the word was a promise to both of us. "We move."

THE CORRIDOR OUTSIDE THE swap room felt like a lung that had forgotten its job. The air had that stale bite of solvent and recirculated heat, and the overhead fluorescents flickered with a rhythm that made every step feel just a fraction behind the beat. I kept my bag high on my shoulder and my hand near the shortwave disruptor clipped inside. To my left, Velvet matched pace without hurry, as if we were two workers finishing a shift and thinking about soup. Juno rode my shoulder and pretended to study the dead fire alarm on the wall, one eye tracking our rear.

At the end of the hall a security door blinked red. Two men in soft armor stood on either side of it like apologetic furniture. The one on the left had the bored posture of a person counting minutes. The one on the right had the compressed mouth of a person who imagines courage during quiet hours. Both wore the kind of badge that opens break rooms and not much else. Somewhere beyond them, a radio crackled in a voice that had not gotten the memo about staying calm.

"Keep it clean," I said under my breath. "No witnesses with reasons to unite."

Velvet angled her chin in acknowledgement and let a smile warm her face by two degrees. That was all it took. The bored one straightened, surprised at the sudden possibility of being noticed by the world. The compressed one moved his hand toward a scanner as a reflex to the attention shift. I closed the gap and reached the panel first. My wrist spoof made the diode blink green for a heartbeat. I pressed the release bar as if it had always belonged to me, then held the door with my hip when it tried to close.

"Maintenance," I said, flat and unimpressed. "Fire alarm east corridor has a stuck contact. Fixing it now before your captain calls me again."

They hesitated in the way that tells you the lie fits the shape of their daily misery. Velvet drifted through the opening with that weightless grace she carries like a personal climate. The bored one allowed himself to nod. The compressed one glanced at my empty sleeve where an ID should have hung and inhaled to ask a question. I gave him an answer instead. My free hand touched the nerve bundle near his elbow. His fingers opened as if to release a weight that did not exist. The question vanished.

We hit the service stair and took it down one flight. The broad lobby beyond smelled like ink and plastic, the scent of labels being born by the thousand. Conveyor belts stitched the space into moving lines. Couriers stood in their branded jackets and pretended patience. The walls were glass on the company side and painted concrete on ours. Cameras tracked the flow with sleepy attention. I pinged the grid and felt the Wendigo wake up on the far side of the block, then settle into a slow loop that kept it from catching any official eye. It wore its sanitation coat and a tired tail light and looked like a piece of the city that had never been young.

On the far side of the lobby a steel door marked Staff Only sat against a wall like a joke everyone had decided not to laugh at. Juno clicked in my ear and drew my attention up. A passive dome camera mirrored the room. I let my shoulder brush Velvet's. Her eyes shifted, then held. We split without saying it. I took a line that brought me behind a vending machine and a pillar with a maintenance hatch. Velvet crossed the floor along the natural path of a person who knows she will be let into any room she wants.

Two security contractors stepped out of a side corridor near the Staff door with a dog's alertness and a child's eagerness to be included. Oronix hires them young, gives them a stipend for the gym, and sells them a story about order. One carried a netgun still locked in its holster. The other kept a shock baton in his hand for comfort. They saw Velvet and made the common mistake of thinking the moment belonged to them.

I took the hatch cover off the pillar and slid my hand into the wire nest. My fingers found the fire suppression relay by habit. Coil one trips the test valve. Coil two drops pressure. Coil three issues a cold steam that makes cameras blink. I brushed the contacts and counted. One. Two. Three. The room exhaled white. The nearest couriers swore. A clerk shouted about liability. The two contractors lifted their hands like people caught in sudden weather. Velvet reached the Staff door, touched the access plate with the side of her wrist where she keeps a small miracle, and walked through as if the world had offered it.

I followed before the steam thinned. The corridor beyond was tight and lined with lockers scuffed by lives that do not have time to polish anything. We moved quick but not hurried. Juno flew ahead, reappearing at each turn so the rhythm of her clicks became a map. Two lefts, one right, and we reached the loading ramp that led to the outer alley.

The door swung open and the alley took its breath into our faces. It smelled like bread grease and wet cardboard and the sharp metallic taste of a power line suffering in silence. Four men waited at the bend where the emergency light fails. Not uniformed. Not amateurs either. Their posture said private contractor. Their gear said Oronix department budget. The near one held a compact machine pistol at low ready. The tall one carried a baton that had seen more men than floors. The other two had the jumpy hands of people who prefer numbers to fights and had been pushed into the wrong class.

"We will need the right kind of noise," I murmured.

Velvet's stance shifted. Not into a guard position. Into an invitation. She walked forward with the rhythm of music that only the body can hear. Heads turned as if pulled by a tide. The near one narrowed his eyes and recalculated. He did not lower his weapon.

He told himself he was immune to distraction. He was not immune to physics.

I stepped right and let Juno flare her eyes at the alley camera in a way that convinces algorithms to look elsewhere. The tall man decided boredom was an insult and took a step toward Velvet as if to herd her back inside. Velvet slipped inside his reach with the softness of a hand finding a pocket. Her fingers touched the hinge of his wrist. The baton fell in a clatter that startled his friends more than the coming fight would. She pivoted and set his shoulder down onto the cement with an economy that made me want to applaud. He tried to remember pride and found pain instead.

The near man snapped his weapon higher. I reached into my pocket and palmed a pulse coin. The coin is a blessing disguised as litter. I tossed it underhand so it would hop at the near man's foot and burp a narrow cone of white noise. His pistol stuttered one shot that chewed a hangnail from the brick above my head. Then it choked and went quiet. He looked at the gun in betrayal, which is the wrong thing to look at in a fight. Velvet guided his chin into her knee with a tenderness that belongs in a better world. He slept.

The third man panicked and brought up a spray can of pepper foam, which would have been funny if we were not busy. The foam hissed a gorgeous arc past Velvet's shoulder. I was already in motion, sliding low and sweeping his ankle. He pinwheeled, dropped the can, and discovered the floor faster than he preferred. The fourth man backed away three steps, then realized the alley had no more room for retreat. He lifted both hands in a theater of surrender and started to talk. Velvet turned her head. He read that as permission to leave. He ran.

We took the corner at a jog. The alley opened into a cross street dense with delivery vans and small carts. A municipal drone hovered overhead, pretending to love its job while scanning for violations. I flipped my scarf up to obscure my face and adjusted the deck strap across my chest. The street belonged to chaos. That is usually an ally if you respect it.

[Wendigo, route to Canal Gate Seven,] I sent with a flick across my wrist. [Sanitation mask. No detours.]

The reply came as a single green pip on my band. The van had stopped pretending it was resting and had started pretending it was late for a route. I threaded a path through traffic and used a parked scooter as a springboard over a narrow puddle. Velvet did not use the scooter. She walked through the space that our movement made, the way light travels where it intends to go without asking.

In the next block two bikes slid out from a side lane, riders in black shells propelling themselves with the confidence of men who have been told speed is a personality. They angled to sit one on each of our flanks. Juno raked them with a flash that would not blind a child. It irritated them, which served just as well. The nearer rider reached for my shoulder. I let him catch a handful of jacket and then gave him the weight he wanted. He had to correct to keep his bike upright. His partner laughed, mistook the correction for showmanship, and leaned in to share the lane. I cut left. Velvet shifted right. They nearly collided and had to widen, which opened a hole in the traffic where no hole had been. We passed through it before anyone realized it was a gift.

The canal district approached, marked by a drop in the city's voice. The water absorbs noise like a patient teacher. I felt the tension in my jaw release a fraction. Relief makes people careless. It does not make me kind. I kept my eyes on the rooftops for the kind of man who believes he is better than ground.

Behind us a pickup decided to love us. It roared to close the gap, then swung to block a lane that did not belong to it. I recognized the habit of a certain class of contractor. If you cannot catch your prey, inconvenience it. Two more figures stood up in the bed and raised something that looked like professionalism from a distance and improvised aggression when you got closer. I did not like any of the choices they were about to offer.

"Keep moving," I said to Velvet. "Do not let them choose the terms."

She did not look back. She does not need to. We turned down a maintenance road where bricks become patches and patches become advice. The pickup tried to follow and lost traction on a dip that only locals respect. One of the men in the bed sat down abruptly as gravity reminded him of its standards. The driver cursed a creative series of ancestors and tried to swing wide to find another route.

[Wendigo, cut the corner on Eighty Third,] I sent. [Show the city your badge.]

The van heard my tone and matched it. The sanitation mask rolled across its panels like a curtain being pulled. A city seal shimmered onto the side with a tired authority. The Wendigo does not enjoy wearing the badge. It does it well anyway. The traffic parted with the resentment reserved for municipal vehicles. We slid south toward Canal Gate Seven.

The last alley before the gate smelled like stale beer and the dreams of failed clubs. Neon tubing hung in patient loops along the wall, waiting to be useful again. A security camera watched from under a corroded gutter, bored into inattention by years of nothing happening on schedule. This was the place where ambushes prefer to blossom. I felt the small rise of skin at the back of my neck and told Juno to fly high enough to widen her view.

Two figures stepped into the alley mouth with the easy stride of men who have decided they own the day. A third climbed out of the passenger seat of a gray sedan and tried to look like a surprise. He carried a baton with a glittering spine. The other two had pistols down at their sides in the relaxed criminal manner that belongs to people proud of discipline they show only when someone is watching. Oronix brought more money to this corner than they had to the lobby. I felt my breath slow in that way that means a plan has to be shorter than nerves.

"Three," I said.

"Four," Velvet answered, and touched a finger to the corner where a fourth figure thought he was still gel in the shadow. She moved toward him. I drifted toward the man with the glittering baton.

He smiled. He had the expression of a man who thinks his baton makes the conversation. He tried to hook my wrist. I let him catch the sleeve and step closer. He tasted mint on my breath and believed he had time to make a joke about it. I did not give him time. The shortwave disruptor in my pocket fit the shape of his sidearm and taught it humility. His mouth opened to protest on behalf of his weapon and met my forehead instead. The shock traveled through bone and skin and made my teeth sing. He stumbled backward into the gray sedan and cracked his hip against the door frame. He discovered concern. His baton scraped the ground and flared. I kicked it under the car where it could contemplate poor life choices.

To my right, Velvet occupied the shadow where the fourth man had tried to keep his courage warm. She did not kill him. She took his air and his posture and his bonus for the quarter. He slid down the wall like a guilty memory. The remaining two directions panicked in the same half second and made the same mistake, which was to lift their pistols to chest height and hold them there like declarations. Velvet turned her shoulders and let the first shot pass her by, the bullet wasting itself on brick. I raised my hand and threw a pulse canister that coughed a swallow of noise into the alley too narrow for the sound to escape quickly. Their aim went corrupt. One fired wildly. The other blinked tears and forgot how to lead a target. Velvet stepped in and ended both conversations with the kind of crispness that makes you believe in training again.

We cleared the alley as sirens began to say our names without knowing who we were. Canal Gate Seven waited ahead, a low iron arch that had lost its purpose and kept its pride. The Wendigo turned the corner in its sanitation coat, lights low, grille dirty, performance perfect. It looked like a municipal animal that had learned to love ugly jobs. It slowed without seeming to, then drifted along the curb with its door already thinking about opening.

"Go," I told Velvet, and she obeyed the order because we have learned to trade them without turning them into insults. She climbed in with a light knee and a steady breath. I followed and dragged the door shut with both hands as the gray sedan we had insulted screeched into view.

"Drive," I told the van. It did not need the word. The word was for me.

The Wendigo took the canal road with the confidence of an old crew chief. It kept its speed just below scolding and its path precise enough to be boring on camera. Boring saves lives. The sedan tried to mimic boring and failed. It fishtailed briefly on a seam. A second car fell in behind it with a siren that belonged to a private security firm who thought themselves very clever. I told the van to go left at the next split. It went right instead, because it had found a fresher lane through a construction zone that had never been logged properly. I apologized to it under my breath and promised to be better at listening.

Juno hopped to the front rail and pressed her beak against the glass as if to whisper encouragement. The van took the whisper and turned it into momentum. We zipped under a bridge where someone had painted a mural of a fish with a halo. On the other side of the arch I could look back long enough to see the private car commit to the wrong lane and the sedan hesitate. Hesitation is a mercy we do not often receive. We should not waste it.

"Status," I asked, because naming safety makes bodies believe it faster.

"Clear for now," Velvet said, palm flat on the console where the van keeps its feelings. "You did well."

"You held together," I replied, and kept my voice steady so that the compliment would land and stay.

We skimmed the canal until the district thinned into the kinds of businesses that only open at odd hours. Welding shops. Cold storage that hums like a dream you will not remember. One restaurant that believes soup fixes everything. The van trimmed speed to normal. I let the autonav reclaim decisions I had stolen. We changed our face from municipal to ghost, not in a showy way, only enough to look like a vehicle the city forgets every night and remembers only when it needs heavy lifting.

I lowered the lights in the cabin. Velvet sat back and folded her hands in her lap. Her eyes closed in something that is not rest and not prayer. Juno stepped closer on the rail and dipped her head. The van breathed a little lighter, the way machines do when they recognize a room has returned to wisdom.

"Report," I said softly, and angled my body so I could see the line of Velvet's neck. The panel I had cleaned still showed a faint heat in the thermals. It would cool. It always does. I wanted to make sure it did not settle wrong.

"I am intact," she said. "The insult left a mark. It will not be a scar."

"Good," I said. "We put distance between us and this block. Then we find a dock that belongs to us and ask the room to love you back into symmetry."

She opened her eyes and turned her head. For a moment there was no Velvet in her face at all, only Hikari looking at me without a script. The van hummed its approval. Juno clicked once, pleased with every decision that had kept her family alive.

Behind us, two sirens argued with each other about who deserved to feel victorious. Neither found an answer worth keeping. The river took their noise and held it. The city made room for us to pass. I tightened the strap across my chest and let the last of the shake leave my hands.

"We lived," I said, not as an afterthought, but as a small flag planted on a hill whose name we would not bother to learn.

"For now," Velvet answered, and there was no fatalism in it, only calculation. "Tomorrow has not been informed of our plans."

"We will write them clearly," I said. "In ink that will not wash away."

The Wendigo turned us toward the angle of streets that most resemble home. We rode without speaking. The van wore its quiet like a blanket. The city dimmed its lattice by a single notch, which is what passes for a blessing in Klade. Juno tucked her beak under her wing but kept one eye open, a lookout equal parts sentinel and superstition.

When the first clean breath finally arrived, it did not carry triumph. It carried the small relief that comes from winning time. Time is the only currency that matters when the people who want you gone prefer paperwork to bullets. We had bought a few hours with bruised shins and a handful of luck, soldered into certainty by hands that remember what they are for. I touched the bench between us, not quite her hand, close enough to mean it.

"Home," I said, and the van obliged.

THE WENDIGO ROLLED INTO the storage bay behind the old foundry and let the engine idle down to a patient purr. The air inside smelled faintly of warm wiring and mint, with a trace of river damp sneaking through the seals. Outside, Klade's night pressed close and quiet, the kind of quiet that comes when a neighborhood agrees to keep its head down. I locked the exterior hatch and stood for a moment with my palm on the frame, feeling the last tremor of the drive fade into stillness. Juno hopped from the windshield rail to my shoulder, pressed her beak against my cheek once in approval, then took up her usual post above the cradle bay.

Velvet sat on the bench and unfastened her boots with the care people reserve for tools that keep them alive. She had not spoken since we cleared the canal. The silence did not feel like distance. It felt like the room making space for the one thing neither of us wanted to rush. I pulled the curtain across the side windows, dimmed the cabin lights until the metal took on a soft sheen, and set the kettle. The smallest rituals recalibrate the body after a night like this. My hands steadied on the second pass.

"Let me run the check," I said, crouching in front of her. "If there is any leftover heat from the cutover, I want it gone before you rest."

She angled her head in assent and tipped forward so I could reach the panel at the base of her neck. The latches surrendered without a fight. I lifted the cover and watched the readings climb, stabilize, and begin to fall as the new heat sink did its job. The contact pads showed a clean shine. The regulator I had spliced into the travel chain hummed at the frequency I trust. I brushed a strand of silver fiber from her collar and closed the panel with two small clicks. The sound felt like a room agreeing to hold together.

"Better," I said.

Velvet's eyes opened and found mine. For a breath there was no performance in them, only attention. I leaned back onto my heels and tried not to fill the quiet with nervous language. The city will always provide more noise than we need. This moment did not owe us anything except honesty.

"In the swap room," I said finally, "when the power dipped and the masks fell away, I saw a version of you I have never been allowed to see. Not Forge and not Velvet. Not the child frame that makes strangers underestimate you. The person who lives under all of it. The one who looked at me without a face I could read and still told me exactly what you needed. I have been thinking about that since the door shut behind us."

Velvet did not move. Juno tilted her head and watched me with one eye, as if she wanted to mark the shape of the words for the file.

"You told me once that you chose Hikari because it meant clean, or simple," I went on. "Simple in the way a true form is simple, not stripped of history, just stripped of other people's labels. Clean in the way a line on a circuit is clean when it carries only what it is meant to carry. Tonight I saw that person. I think that is the one the name belongs to. When there is no shell, or when the shells blur, when it is only you and the work and the decision to keep going, that is Hikari."

Her eyes closed and opened again, slow. I could not tell if she was holding back a reply or letting the words find a place to land. The kettle clicked at the edge of the room and did not intrude.

"I am not asking you to change how you live inside the bodies," I said. "Velvet will still speak in the rooms where velvet is needed. Forge will still take the hits that velvet should not take. Wisp will still turn a city into a console when we need that talent more than muscle or theater. I am only naming the person I trust when the power drops and the clamps falter. That person is Hikari. If I am wrong, you can say so and I will listen."

Velvet shifted her weight, not away, only deeper into the bench, the way people settle when they choose to stay. The van cracked a cooling note. Outside, a train gave a single, unhurried horn along the river and then quiet returned.

"What did I look like," she asked, and there was none of Velvet's honey in the voice now. The tone did not try to persuade or charm. It sounded like the person who had leaned into the dock and asked me without words to keep them from falling.

"Clean," I said, and felt heat rise at the simplicity of it, but did not apologize. "The struts along the ribs, the pattern of braid along the spine, the smooth cover where a face would be. No scars for anyone to read. No angles arranged to soothe or frighten. Only intention. Your eyes were dark and flat like coins, and when they opened I knew you recognized me. That was enough."

Her gaze did not leave my face. The van's soft lights caught a phantom reflection in her pupils, a reminder that this body treats sight as a calculation. A long moment passed before she spoke.

"I did not want you to see that yet," she said. "Not because it is ugly. Because it is close."

"I know," I said. "I would not have asked you to show me. The sabotage made a choice for us. I am angry about that. I am not sorry I was the person standing there when it happened."

Another pause. Juno clicked once and tucked a feather back into place, the simple vanity that follows stress. Velvet's mouth made the smallest movement, not a smile, not a wince, something like a release.

"You named it correctly," she said. "Hikari is the part that cannot be bought, and cannot be caught with paperwork. It is not the bravest part, only the one that refuses to lie. I do not share it often."

"You do not have to," I said. "You do not owe anyone access to it. I am only asking permission to use the name for that self when I speak to you about it. So we both know who I mean."

She lowered her eyes to her hands and turned one palm up, as if studying the lines would tell her whether the request required a cost. The hand looked delicate in the half light. I know better than to be fooled. Strength lives in that shape the way voltage lives inside wire. She rotated her wrist once and set her palm on the bench between us where I could see it, not offering it, exactly, but not guarding it either.

"Permission granted," she said. "Do not use it to make me less complicated."

"I will not," I said, and meant it. "Complicated is the truth. I like the truth more than I like comfort."

Her eyes met mine again and held. The kettle had cooled into silence. The mint gave a small green breath each time the van shifted its weight on the shocks. Outside, something metal tapped softly in the wind and then went still.

"I am going to keep calling you by the shell names when we are in motion," I said. "They have work to do, and they deserve the respect of their chosen languages. But when the masks drop, even if only in a word, it will be Hikari. That is not a demand. It is a promise."

She gave a single nod. No correction followed. No joke to soften the edge. Acceptance arrived without a banner.

I poured two mugs though I knew she did not need the heat or the caffeine. It was more for the room than for our bodies. She wrapped her fingers around the ceramic anyway and watched the steam. The gesture read as human in a way that had nothing to do with pretense. You can choose to be human without owning a heartbeat. Sometimes a cup of coffee is the proof.

"We will need to find who touched the cradle," she said after a while. "Not tonight. Soon. Sabotage like that is a letter. Someone expects a reply."

"We will write one," I said. "Clear and legible. I will not let them turn you into a rumor."

Her mouth tilted, almost a smile. "You prefer ink to speeches."

"Speeches are for rooms full of people who already agreed to listen," I said. "Ink survives."

We drank without hurry. Juno dozed on her rail with one eye open in case the world tried anything foolish. The grid on the wall showed a single blue symbol where the foundry's rusted gates made a clean block against the street. The rest of the map had the careful blankness of a quiet night.

"Wren," she said, and my name in that voice felt like a stone chosen and set in the right place. "You asked for permission to name the core. I would like to ask for something in return."

"Ask," I said.

"If it happens again, if power fails and I am between bodies, do not speak to the shells. Speak to the person you saw. Even if there are others in the room. Even if it adds risk. It will help me find the path back."

"I can do that," I said. "I will make the room smaller until only we fit inside it."

The silence that followed was not heavy. It had the weight of a blanket on a tired night. She finished her drink and set the mug down with a soft click. The sound had the neat finality of a paragraph ending where it should.

"I need to sleep," she said.

"Wisp or Velvet," I asked, because labels matter to systems and to the people who build them.

"Wisp for the night," she said. "Velvet carries echoes when she rests after a cutover. Wisp will play quieter music in my head."

I stood and offered a hand. She did not take it, not out of pride, but because she did not need it. She crossed to the cradle and touched the interface plate, then looked back at me one last time. The expression on her face did not belong to any shell. It was only attention and a trace of relief. Then her eyes slid shut and the body's systems dimmed. The clamps met the port with practiced certainty. For a breath there was nothing in the room except the idea of a person. Then Wisp's small frame lit in the bay beside the dock, eyes bright with their familiar ring, posture soft, edges alert.

"Hi," she said, voice light and clear. "You look like a woman who needs sleep more than you need to make another list."

"I will sleep," I said, and felt the truth of it all the way down. "But I wanted to say one more thing before morning trips all the alarms."

"Say it," Wisp said, settling on the bench with her legs folded under her like a cat ready to listen.

"I am going to use Hikari when I mean the person under the work," I said. "When I mean the one I saw. I am going to keep the shells for the jobs. That is how I will hold the line between the tools and the hand that holds them."

Wisp's eyes softened in a way that always reminds me of windows opened one click wider. "That will help," she said. "It gives the map a legend."

Hikari did not correct me. The room noticed and stored the fact the way rooms do when they have decided to keep a secret safe.

I set my mug in the drying rack, checked the locks a second time out of habit, and turned the lights down to the level that lets dreams find their way without tripping. Juno tucked her head and pretended to be asleep while keeping watch. The Wendigo adjusted the fans and settled deeper on its shocks. The mint leaned toward the smallest draft and held still there, as if listening for footsteps that were not coming.

Before I stretched out on the bench I looked once at the cradle, at the sleeping armor, and then at the small figure sitting with her knees drawn under her, cable-light in her eyes, palms pressed together as if warming them at a fire. I did not see a machine. I did not see a set of masks. I saw a person I had decided to call by the name that belonged to them when no one else was looking.

"Goodnight, Hikari," I said, very quietly, not to claim anything, only to place the word in the air where it needed to live.

There was no reply. There did not need to be one. The van breathed. The city kept its bargain with the dark a little while longer. I closed my eyes and let the coming storm find us tomorrow, not tonight.

Chapter Eight

Echoes in Her Smile

WREN

KLADE'S MORNING HAD THE color of old copper, a tired green where the lattice light met river fog and decided to compromise. I left the Wendigo while the neighborhood was still pretending to sleep. The van warmed itself without complaint and dimmed the cabin after I checked the locks twice. Juno shifted on her rail, eyed me like a disappointed aunt, and then hopped to my shoulder with a soft scrape. Hikari stayed in Wisp to rest. That was not an argument in my head so much as a sentence written cleanly across the start of the day. This run belonged to me.

The air by the river had that wet penny smell that gets into clothes and thoughts. I kept my scarf loose and my eyes open, one on the ground for glass, one up for the little signs the city leaves for people who are willing to read. We had chosen the viaduct stairs near Substation Fourteen for our thread. The stairs climb three flights through a ribcage of steel that hums when freight rolls the beltline above, then drop into a service lane that runs beside the utility trench. Anything important that wants to move through this quadrant touches that lane or its shadow. The plan was simple in the way a key is simple. Slip a tap into the private control fiber that feeds the beltline signal boxes, teach it to listen for Oronix priority codes, and route a mirror of that traffic to a safe cache. If we were lucky, the tap would also give me a way to nudge a gate timer or foul a detour request when the next chase took a bad turn. The first time I had described it aloud, Hikari said I was getting cocky. This morning I wanted to prove that I was getting precise.

The Circuit Saint's little chapel sat under the first span, a squat room of poured concrete with a door salvaged from a ship. I paused at the threshold, breathed in the clean scent of ozone and machine oil, and knocked the way they ask you to knock. Three soft taps, then two. No one answered. The switches along the far wall shone like polished altar brass, and the mural of the lineworker with a belt for a halo looked back at me with the same calm I remembered from our last visit. I left a note under the donation box, a reminder that the morning might bring traffic, nothing more. The Saint never asks for names. They ask for clarity, and I was determined to deal in that currency.

The viaduct stairs were slick in the corners where condensation gathers and gives the city little farms of algae. I climbed without rush, Juno ahead by a meter, wings almost silent. At the top, the beltline let a train whisper past, a long low moan that settled into the ribs of the place. On the other side of the span the service lane waited, the narrow length of it sheltered by a row of broken billboards and the bones of a walkway meant for inspectors who no longer walk. A maintenance hatch marked with a faded triangle sat where the lane curved back toward the trench. Its screws were new. That was promising. New screws mean a system that still gets attention. Ignored systems surprise you in ugly ways.

I checked the camera dome above me, confirmed the lens was blind the way our scripts had arranged last night, and knelt by the hatch. The metal was cold through my jeans, a small square of honesty against skin that had done too much pretending lately. My deck booted without drama. I took out the driver, counted my breaths to keep the rhythm steady, and lifted each screw into the cloth pouch I keep for this purpose. Every street has its own little almanac, and this one said that lost screws roll toward the trench like they are eager to join the river. I pressed the hatch aside and inhaled the scent of warm electronics and dust, the smell I grew up inside when the world still trusted me near the backs of machines.

The junction panel's faceplate opened like a book that had been handled with care. Inside, the fiber couplers sat neatly in two rows, municipal light-signal on top, private on the bottom. The private row wore sleeving a little too bright for a city job. Oronix loves to paint cleanliness over the places where they hide their dirt. I drew a pair of jumpers from my kit, snapped a passive splitter into the private trunk, and fed the secondary strand into a pocket relay that would throw the mirrored traffic over a narrow beam to a repeater tucked under the Saint's roofline. The whole arrangement looked like something a nervous student would wire for a test. It would work. Clean never needs to look smart.

Juno kept a slow lookout while my fingers did the part of the job that belongs to muscle memory. She made a tiny correction sound and I froze, hand inside the panel, one knee down, the other foot ready to push me into a less visible shape. A municipal cart rolled around the bend, a little electric thing with too many squeaks, driven by a man who had given up arguing with the day. We looked at each other for a moment that stretched too long. He took in the scarf, the bag, the neat collection of screws, and decided he saw what he hoped to see, which was a maintenance tech with no time for small talk. He tipped his chin, an apology for witnessing a job out of scope, and moved on. I let the air out slowly and waited until his squeaks merged with the low beltline hum. The city rewards people who let it keep its dignity.

I seated the relay, tuned the diode until its tiny light glowed the color I wanted, and closed the book. On my deck, a waterfall of characters stacked into clean columns, private control traffic singing to itself. Most of it looked like schedule confirmations, timing corrections, and status checks. Every few seconds a packet carried the little signature we had taught ourselves to spot. Oronix priority marker, edge network encryption, the swagger in the headers you see when a company believes it has a private road through a public town. I set the filter to copy anything marked as an emergency instruction and to hold it for twenty minutes in fresh cache before forwarding it to our deeper store. If the run went wrong and I had to sever the link, at least the morning would have a memory.

The last task felt like a superstition and an exam. It had to be both. I fed a gentle test into the beltline system, just a small nudge to an alert that would never reach a human, the kind of tickle that makes a camera clear its throat. The response came in a tidy loop. Accepted, acknowledged, dismissed. Clean round trip with no echo in the logs. I thumbed the hatch back into place and checked my watch. I had been exposed for seven minutes, and felt every one of them in the meat of my back.

The way out took me under the billboards and down a shallow run of steps into a lane that smells of long fried onions and fresh detergent. A laundry opened its door to spit out a ribbon of steam and a joke in a language I only half understand. Two kids chalked a grid on the sidewalk, retreated when a security drone passed, then resumed with little interest in my shape. I liked that. Attention collects on the wrong people here, and it is dangerous to be one of them. I kept mine on the rooftops. Patrol habits do not change with the weather. Somewhere two blocks over a siren gave a polite cough and then thought better of it.

Halfway back to the river I saw the first sign that I was not alone in liking my plan. A man with a contractor's posture and a corporate haircut stood across the street with a cup of cheap coffee and an expression that said he wanted to be a manager when his legs got tired. He wore a jacket with the logo of a cleaning company that exists only on receipts. He looked straight through me. That should have ended the thought, but the scar on my left palm warmed the way it does when a person's gaze does not match the story their body tells. I kept my pace even and my eyes soft, that practiced posture where you do not look like prey without turning into a challenge. Juno flicked a warning across the corner of my vision. It was not the man. It was the camera two doors down that should have been off and was not. The lens tracked a half degree and returned to center the moment I looked. Someone had brought a witness to the morning.

The alley ahead of me split in three. I took the center, a narrow run between a closed bar and a shop that sells imported augment polish to people who want their arms to look like pamphlets. The center lane bends twice, then opens to a stair that drops near the old foundry where the Wendigo waits when I want to avoid the attention of the river patrol. The first bend gave me a shadow that let me adjust the scarf without telling anyone why. The second bend gave me the echo of footsteps that did not match my own. Juno rose off my shoulder, vanished into the air above the alley, and came back with a picture of a man using a phone like a rabbit's foot. He stood at the mouth of the lane, camera in hand, not aiming it, only trying to remember if he was supposed to look casual. He did not feel like police. He felt like someone wondered about his bonus.

I sat on the steps and took my deck out in the open like a woman checking a bus schedule. The trick worked because the city has taught everyone to ignore people who plan their own routes. The footsteps cooled, then moved on. I moved only when my nerves stopped acting like a third person in the room. The foundry yard opened in front of me, and with it the breath I had been holding.

I did not go straight to the Wendigo. The van has sensors and habits that keep it safe when I am not beside it, but you do not in this life by walking to your door without checking the corners first. I circled the yard once, past the broken crane and the stacks of reclaimed brick, and listened. The river said everything and nothing. A gull called and then reconsidered the usefulness of speech. My repeater under the Saint's eaves muttered to itself in a language that only the grid enjoys. All of it sounded like the city I know.

When I finally climbed into the van the air felt warmer than outside, as if it had been holding a place for me. I set my bag down, turned the lights to a kind blue, and crossed to the console. The mirror stream from the tap showed a steady cadence of dull, necessary traffic. In the long column of it a small cluster gleamed the way fresh ink gleams on a page. Oronix priority. Beltline north, then service road forty four, then back down the spur that passes the viaduct stairs. I highlighted it and told the system to give me the words in a voice that does not decorate the world with drama.

Control to field asset, confirm posture, confirm sequence, expect non corporate actors at the viaduct stairs. That was the gist. Two code phrases I had never heard before sat beside it. One meant detain for inventory. One meant erase the scene. They liked quiet work wrapped in neat labels. The hair along my arms lifted, not from fear so much as from recognition. We had guessed right when we picked the place and the hour. The system had already agreed to meet us here. It did not yet know we were in the room before it arrived.

I leaned back until my shoulder blades touched the cool metal of the van wall and let my breath align with the hum of the fans. Working solo is a different math. When you are alone, there is no second pair of eyes to catch the cheap trick or the mistake of pride. There is no voice to bleed the pressure out of the moment and return the facts to their proper size. You are the scale and the stone at once. I did not hate that feeling. Fear keeps people poor in this city, but the right amount of fear keeps them alive.

I set two tripwires on the route we had chosen for our bait. If Oronix or Vyre tried to bring a convoy around the viaduct, a camera would blink in the wrong rhythm and tell me. If a private repeater accepted a code phrase from a unit it did not know, Juno would hear the hesitation in the handshake and give me the time and the angle. I wrote the rules plainly, the way my mother would have taught a recipe. No flair, no flourishes, only measures that hold.

The repeater under the chapel sent a heartbeat. The Saint's switches kept their peace. I pulled a thin pad of paper from the shelf and wrote a list I did not need, because sometimes ink chooses a thought more carefully than a cursor does. Check grid at ten minute marks, walk the yard every third mark, adjust scarf when nerves start behaving like cats, eat something before the second hour so you do not forget your body belongs to you. It was a grocery list for staying human.

I ate half a bar, drank water that tasted like victory and dust, and checked the grid again. A fresh packet slid across the bar and settled itself on the stream like a leaf. VYRE designation. Not zero seven. A number I did not recognize. The message did not include our quadrant, but it carried the same tone. Control loved its formal voice. The field answer carried none of that polish. The cadence had impatience in it, the clipped sound of a driver who hates being told to wait. I copied the headers to our long store and flagged the path so I could draw a little map later. Maps soothe me the way prayer must soothe other people.

When the second hour bent toward the third, the morning inched into daylight that was not yet bright. The foundry yard changed color slowly. The edges got kinder. Across the river a crane made the quiet circles that mean someone is moving heavy things with care. Klade does not give you many chances to admire. I took the one that fit inside a breath, then let it go. Time to move. I would walk the yard one more time, then turn toward the exit path we had chosen so I could verify the line of retreat. Juno hopped to my shoulder and clicked, not an alarm, only the little note she makes when she wants to keep my attention.

The tap held a steady pulse. The repeater agreed. The tripwires slept with one ear open. I swallowed the second half of the bar because logic told me to, checked the strap on my deck for the same reason, and opened the door of the van. The air outside slid across my face like a cold hand that did not want to be cruel and did not know another way to be. I stepped into it and let the door seal behind me.

Working alone felt quiet in a way that did not belong to the street, a hush that lives inside the bones and makes decisions feel heavier. I liked that the weight made my steps deliberate. I liked that my heart did not speed up to fill the silence with noise it did not deserve. I crossed the yard, touched the crane once with two fingers, and laughed at myself because the gesture had started to feel like knocking on a chapel before stepping into trouble.

The tripwire pinged a soft note on my wrist. Not a shout. A question. I looked at the tiny screen and saw the center camera near the viaduct clear its lens without being asked. That would be a curious maintenance worker, or it would be a person who believes curiosity is a weapon. I checked the second wire. A private repeater two blocks east accepted a code phrase with a hesitation that would not be audible to a human ear. Juno lifted, turned one slow circle, and lowered again, ready to sprint. I did not run. I did not need to. The first scene of the day had done its work. The tap was in place, the road had been measured, the exits had been counted. The city knew we were paying attention.

I headed for the lane that would take me along the foundry wall and back toward the block where the Wendigo could retrieve me without dressing up. The river stayed steady. The air lost a little of its copper taste and replaced it with the smell of wet rope. In the distance a siren cleared its throat and then began a speech. I did not yet know whether it had anything to do with me. That ignorance was a luxury, and I let myself keep it for the length of the yard.

Behind me, the repeater under the Saint's roof blinked the signal that means company has put its foot on the first stair. I smiled at the wall and kept walking. The morning would have more to say, and I would be there to hear it.

THE SIREN I HAD ignored in the yard decided it cared about me after all. It turned a corner two blocks away and drew a thin red line across the wet brick. I left the foundry by the narrow lane that runs between the broken crane and the wall of old kilns, then cut toward the river road where the Wendigo could pick me up without dressing in a badge. Juno lifted from my shoulder and took a higher rail. Her eye glowed once, a single ember under the eaves, then dimmed as she widened her circle.

The street smelled like wet rope and clean diesel. Somewhere a shopkeeper rolled a steel shutter up one slat at a time and muttered about a promise he had made to himself. I kept my stride even and let the city pass across my skin, the way a current slips around a piling. One more block and I would call the van in with a short whistle, the one that sounds like a bad bearing. We use small ceremonies to keep our hands honest.

A municipal cruiser nosed into the river road from a cross street that had no right to be busy at this hour. The car wore its paint like a tired face. Two officers sat inside with the windows cracked just enough to let their cigarettes carry the story that they were not here for glory. The driver saw me and filed me under routine. The passenger looked at my bag and changed his mind. He tapped the window frame twice, a reflex like a trigger itch, and the cruiser eased to the curb.

"Morning," he called, leaning across the driver so he could talk to me through the open glass. He smiled with the right number of teeth and the wrong kind of patience. "Got ID on you, ma'am?"

I stopped three paces short of the door and kept my body loose. "Do I look lost enough to need help, Officer?"

"You look like you know where you are going," he said, still smiling. "That earns questions these days."

His partner killed the smile with a glance and spoke without looking at me. "Step to the hood."

I did not move. Juno landed on the hydrant behind me, made herself small, and watched the reflections in the windshield. The radio inside the cruiser murmured in a tone that said the dispatcher did not care who heard. A second siren bled into the first and found a harmony that did not belong on this block.

The passenger was about to open his door when a third voice joined us, light and friendly, the kind that arrives to sell a harmless lie.

"Officer, can you help me with a map before you write up my parking? I swear the app sent me in circles and this thing is all in grid numbers."

She stood behind the cruiser at an angle that let the sun frame her face as if it belonged to the street. Compact build. Dark hair caught back under a knit cap. Black jacket with a courier's reflective piping and a holster that looked like a phone cradle until your eye learned what to count. She held a folded paper map because no one expects to be ambushed by paper anymore. Her mouth offered an apology that could be read from a distance. Her eyes did not apologize. They took inventory.

The passenger's focus broke the way focus always does when a stranger chooses the exact wrong moment to ask for help. He turned to tell her to wait, and in that breath the driver's attention went to the mirror. I saw her hand flick. The paper stapled to the back of the map flashed a tiny square of metal at the edge. The cruiser's radio coughed and filled the cabin with a burst of empty static. A harmless noise, only long enough to make the passenger blink.

"Map's no good here," the driver said, voice flat with irritation. "Use your phone like everyone else."

"Signal's dead under the span," she answered, and stepped far enough forward that the passenger had to lean to look around her. She looked at me as if I were just now coming into view. Her eyebrows lifted in the universal language of strangers who decide they are on the same side of a small problem.

"Sorry," she said to me. "You trying to get across the river too?"

"Trying to get to coffee," I said, and let my mouth soften as if we were allies without work to do.

"You and me both," she said, then turned back to the officers. "If you point me toward a place that makes a cup that does not taste like batteries, I will get out of your hair."

The passenger chewed on a mild insult and swallowed it. The driver gave a short sigh that belonged to men who have been condescended to by maps before. He lifted his hand and pointed downriver. "Next cross, left, two blocks. Then a right at the mural."

"Thank you," she said, as if he had just saved a life. She folded the map with neat fingers and stepped back without turning her back on him. Then she looked at me again and tilted her head toward the mouth of the lane that runs behind the shuttered boatyard. It was nothing. It was everything.

I took the hint and moved. She drifted with me as if we had planned it. The cruiser idled, radio still fussing. We cleared the bumper and lost their line of sight to the mirror. The lane narrowed and bent twice. On the second bend she reached out and closed her fingers on my sleeve, not hard, only enough to write a sentence against my skin.

"Left at the bins, then through the chain," she murmured, not looking at me. Her voice carried warmth over a cold frame, and it dug into my memory with a shape I did not want to name.

"Map trick was quick," I said, keeping my eyes forward.

"People trust paper," she answered. "I am Switchblade. Runners on this side call me Blade."

"Wren," I said, because a lie would only waste time.

She smiled, small and private. "I know."

We cut left at the bins the way she had promised. A chain hung loose across a service cut, one side still clipped as decoration. She lifted the free end, slid it aside, and let me pass. Her hands were steady and unadorned, nails short, knuckles white and clean. The gesture felt rehearsed, not because she had walked this lane, but because her body knows how to draw a line in the air and turn it into a door.

"Why the help," I asked. "People do not give it away on this block."

"Because they sent uniforms to look busy," she said. "Uniforms mean someone in a suit asked a question and got the wrong answer. I do not like clean shoes writing stories about my streets."

We came out into a delivery court that had not seen a truck in a week. A fence leaned into itself and pretended to be a wall. Beyond it, the river road opened again and the sawtooth of the old bridge picked up the morning. Juno coasted past and found a perch above the fence, her eye red now, no longer pretending to nap.

We waited a breath. A second cruiser slid along the road with its siren off and its lights down. It passed the mouth of the lane without looking in. Blade watched the rooftops instead of the car. That told me more than any story she might have invented.

"Your bird is talking on a private band," she said softly, still looking up. "Clear audio, tight beam. You keep your friends on a short leash."

"You listen for sport," I said.

"For work," she said, then lowered her gaze at last and gave me a measuring look. "You are fast alone. Faster with the right partner. Today you run solo because someone smart needed rest."

I let the line sit in the air like a coin on a counter. She had not asked a question. She had drawn a circle and waited to see if I would step into it.

"Coffee," I said. "You promised a cup that did not taste like batteries."

"Two blocks," she said, "and a right at a mural."

We cut through the court and rejoined the river road a hundred meters down. A city sanitation unit hummed past with a slow, municipal dignity. The driver did not look at us. The van's outline under the paint made my throat relax. The Wendigo wore the coat well.

Blade noted the truck and pressed her tongue to the back of her teeth in a small sign of approval. "Mask is good," she said. "Not many rigs make a seal sit flat like that."

"She is shy until you feed her," I said.

"Names for machines," she said, not unkindly. "You have been at this longer than your boots look."

We passed the mural she had promised, a blue fish with a crown painted on the wall of a shuttered bar. A paper sign in the window offered sunshine and a band that had broken up last winter. Behind it, a side door stood open to a narrow room and the hiss of a real espresso machine. The person behind the counter looked up, saw Blade, and lifted two fingers in greeting that meant you are safe until you prove me wrong.

We did not go inside. Blade stopped under the awning and turned her body so that passersby would see two women looking at a menu. She lowered her voice without making a show of it.

"Four units rolled north to the viaduct after you closed your hatch," she said. "Two municipal. Two private. Someone told them to look for a girl in a scarf with a satchel that could hide a deck. They like to think that means any woman they feel like stopping."

"You listen to more than private bands," I said.

"I listen to whatever keeps my bones in the right order," she replied. She studied my face for a small second that held more attention than most men have ever given a promise. "You handled your work. Clean insert, clean exit. Which leaves a question. Do you want to leave a little gift behind so their next conversation tells you something they did not mean to say."

She waited. The offer was tidy and selfless on the surface. It also came wrapped in the tone of someone who had already mapped my morning.

"What gift," I asked, as if the answer mattered more than the test inside the question.

"A false alarm in a box they think does not exist," she said. "A stale error code in a repeater that never stutters. Set it to wake when a certain unit calls in tired. The right kind of ache will make an officer complain on an open channel. Complaints carry names."

"Neat trick," I said. "What does it buy you."

"Proof that the people hunting your streets are the same people who pay the boys with new guns to smile for cameras," she said. The words were polished without losing their edge. "And maybe a favor one day, if we keep meeting in corners that belong to no one."

"I like the truth in favors," I said. I did not say yes. I did not say no. I changed the subject and watched her hands, because hands lie less than mouths. "Where do you run from, Switchblade."

"East side when the river behaves," she said. "South when I am stubborn. I like jobs that ask me to walk into rooms as if I own them. I like making doors open without hurting the hinges."

Her smile curved in a way that tugged at a memory I kept trying to file under the wrong letter. Not a face. A rhythm. The way she let her attention sit quiet on my throat and then on my hands. The way her voice ran a thumb along the edge of a word and polished it before she handed it over. It did not match the jacket or the cap. It matched a different room, one with glass for walls and paint for light. I kept my own face smooth and breathed through the rise of a thought I did not want to entertain in public.

Another cruiser turned into the block and crept past. The officer in the passenger seat held a tablet and scrolled without looking up. Blade shifted her weight so that the awning post hid both our shoulders at once. Her perfume, if that is what it was, smelled like static and something floral that a catalog would call clean linen. I had smelled it before, but never on the street.

"You pulled me out from under a small problem," I said. "What does your fee look like."

"Ask me for a favor when it matters," she said. "Or tell your partner that Switchblade says they owe the river an apology."

That was too specific to be an accident. The word partner carries a question inside it when you hand it to a runner. I let it sit, then set it back on the counter where it belonged.

"We are done for the morning," I said. "You should find your coffee somewhere the cameras are lazier."

She laughed. Not loud. Not cruel. Real enough to give the sound weight. "I already had mine," she said. "I just wanted to see if the rumor about the bird was true."

She took a step back from the awning and the moment shifted. The street decided we were two strangers again. She turned a small circle that took in the rooflines and the open ends of the block, then looked me over with a frankness that would be insulting in a less careful person.

"Pretty work," she said. "For a first solo day."

The compliment needled me because it was true and because she had not earned the right to say it. I nodded once and did not give her the satisfaction of a smile.

A third cruiser entered the block too fast and clipped a trash can into the gutter. The driver swore at himself and kept moving. The radio inside the car crackled open long enough to let the words detain for inventory escape into the street.

Blade and I both heard it. She tilted her head like a person who respects coincidence only when it avoids her. "There it is," she said.

She started to walk, then paused and glanced down at my bag. "Your zipper is half open," she said. "People notice the wrong things when they are bored."

I looked. She was right. I closed it and realized she had just found a way to touch my routine without laying a hand on me. She watched me notice, then gave a small nod, as if she had checked a box on a private list.

"Stay sharp, Wren," she said. "If someone tells you the viaduct is clear this afternoon, call them a liar."

She moved off with the easy swing of a messenger on schedule. I did not watch her go. I let my eyes follow Juno instead. The drone tracked Blade for half a block, then circled back to me with a flicker that said the woman's gait had been filed under familiar. Juno and I do not always agree about people, but we agree about patterns.

I pulled my scarf a little higher and stayed under the awning until the third cruiser finished confusing the block. When the road settled, I crossed to the far curb and sent for the Wendigo with the bad bearing whistle. The van slid into view without wearing its nerves, lights low, posture patient. I climbed in, closed the door, and let the cabin hold my breath for me while my hands remembered what calm looks like.

On the console, the tap still fed its small waterfall of traffic. A new packet flashed and moved on. I set it to keep a copy without thinking. My reflection in the glass looked like a woman learning to trust the shape of her own shadow.

Juno hopped to the rail above the windshield and leaned down until her beak brushed my hair. It felt like a question and an answer in the same soft sound.

"I know," I said. "I heard it too."

Switchblade had helped me without gaining anything that she could spend today. That never happens without a ledger in someone's pocket. I pictured the map, the square of metal, the friendly voice that had found room for a warning inside a joke. The memory clicked against the file I had kept for Sable since the Cathedral, then slid away before it settled. I am not a superstitious woman. I am careful with the way I name echoes.

The van eased into the lane and took us past the mural and the old bridge. I kept my hand on the console and my eyes on the river until the last red light slipped off the bricks. Then I let my shoulders fall that final inch and told the Wendigo to put a neighborhood between us and the morning.

Somewhere behind us, a woman in a black jacket and a knit cap folded a paper map with clean hands and smiled at a thought she did not share.

THE DELIVERY COURT BEHIND the shuttered bar felt like a pocket the city had forgotten. Steam from the espresso machine drifted under the back door and sweetened the cold air. A cracked notice board held a single paper map tucked into its frame. The fold marks matched the one I had seen earlier. There was a thin square glued under the top layer. Not the same metal, but it knew the same family.

"You left this on purpose," I said. I did not raise my voice. Sound carries in dead spaces.

"On purpose, yes," a woman answered from the service steps. "For you, or for anyone clever enough to be you for a day." She leaned at the rail like a courier catching a breath. Knit cap. Black jacket with reflective piping. The posture belonged to someone running routes. The eyes did not.

"You took the long path from the river," she added. "Good habit. Fewer chances to meet the same mistake twice."

"You found a way to be the mistake at the second corner," I said, and slid the map free. I kept the metal pinched under the paper where she could not see it.

She came down one step, then stopped. That told me she knew the language of distance. We were two strides apart. Close enough for a grab. Far enough for a retreat.

Juno shifted to the lamp over the dock and rapped the housing twice with her beak. The camera blinked and pretended to be blind again. I let my shoulders settle.

"Why did you help me with the cruiser," I asked. "Most people sell that moment. You gave it away."

"I like cops bored and harmless," she said. "When they start inventing reasons to touch bags, they make work for everyone who lives here. You were going to talk your way out anyway. I prefer clean exits to test the math."

Her tone rolled like a marble across a table. Smooth, then a quick change in direction, then smooth again. Not a street accent. Not corporate either. Something in between, like a voice trained to sound friendly under glass.

"You talk like you started the morning at the viaduct," I said.

"I did. The line was busy. Then the line learned a new habit. A quiet one," she said. "Your hand did that. Light touch, no brag. It made me curious."

"Curious enough to follow me," I said.

"Curious enough to watch until the bird stopped pretending to nap," she said, and looked up at Juno without reaching for her. "Nice build. Tight beam. No waste."

The court kept its stillness. A bottle rolled against the curb and stopped. Steam whispered under the bar's back door and faded again. I stood with the map at my side and watched her hands. The fingers were steady and unadorned. Nails short. A small scar under the left thumb. She noticed me watching and let me finish without comment.

"What do you want," I asked.

"Weight," she said. "Does your day roll downhill toward me. If it does, I would like to step to the side before I have to pay for someone else's trouble."

"Toward you," I said, "or toward the people who pay you."

"On my street those are the same people," she said, almost kind. "Today the wrong men kept saying detain into an open channel. I do not like tasting that word. I would like to know if it is going to be a regular flavor."

She had just named the code I heard twice on my tap. That should have relaxed me. It did not. The scent coming off her jacket reminded me of the Cathedral. Clean linen and a faint charge, like air near a live panel. The memory rose and would not file itself away.

"You have a map trick," I said. I lifted the paper and let the metal flash once, then hid it again. "Who taught you."

"A woman who hates losing minutes to men who stare at faces while they ask for papers," she said. "Paper makes them feel helpful. Helpful people miss the real work."

"You are not a courier," I said. "You stand like someone who studies mirrors and then corrects the room."

She accepted it like a compliment. "Rooms tell you what they want if you listen," she said. "Today this room wants you out of it."

"Then ask the question you came here to ask," I said. "Clean."

She took one more step down. We were within reach now, though neither of us moved.

"When you go home, does your partner sleep in light or in dark," she asked. "If I have a choice, I prefer to avoid the rooms that like the second."

That is not a kind question. That is a feeler for cameras and alarms. It asks where a lens sits and how a cradle is lit.

I did not argue. I acted. I held the map out as if I were returning it and let the metal touch the seam of her sleeve. Juno fired a tight pulse that climbed her wrist and looked for metal under the fabric. The coin delivered a small kiss of current. Freeze for a second. Lose a step. Miss a word.

Her pupils widened. The muscles along her jaw flexed. Then her hand closed on the paper with careful pressure until the metal slid back into my palm. She did not shake. She did not curse.

"Polite," she said. "Your bird stings. My arm remembers worse jewelry."

"Then we are even," I said, and took the slope toward the drainage run. She did not block me. She turned and kept pace without crowding. The court narrowed and filled with light from the river. I counted my steps and kept my voice steady.

"You keep using Switchblade," I said. "It fits, but not like a street knife. Too clean. Too practiced."

"Practice is a virtue," she said. "Vice wears pride and trips on it. I am not interested in the floor."

"You smell like the Cathedral," I said. "Clean linen and static."

She smiled at that, small and private. "You smell like mint oil and solder," she said. "It suits you."

"Do you know Sable," I asked. I gave the name a even weight and watched her eyes, not her mouth.

"By reputation," she said.

The lie lived in the blink she could not control. Juno made a small click that meant you saw it.

"You helped me," I said. "That earns a clean goodbye. Consider it delivered."

"Before you go," she said, "look left."

Across the run, a kid stepped out with a bucket and a careful gait. He cut a quick look toward us, then away. His shoulders were set for bad luck. A patrol car easing too deep into this block would find him first. She had placed herself between the car and a door that would not survive a boot. Not for me. For him.

"All right," I said. "That is two points on your side of the ledger."

"You will need me on a day you do not expect," she said. "Or you will chase someone faster than usual and wish the street had a second path."

"I do not buy favors with guesses," I said.

"Then buy this," she said. "The word Mirror keeps showing up in rooms that cannot afford it. You know it. I hear it. Our math overlaps."

Her tone did not change, but the temperature in the court did. The map turned slick in my hand. I folded it and slid it into my bag so I did not have to look at it.

"Tell me what you actually want," I said.

"A test," she said. "I wanted to hear how you say the word partner. I wanted to see if the bird turns its head when I say it. I wanted to know if you fix your zipper when a stranger tells you to."

She had noticed that earlier and used it now. A small tell, flipped over to see if I would bristle. I did not give her that.

"Here is my answer," I said. "Stay off my door. Keep your curiosity on the river. If you smell Oronix on my block, you can send a map. Nothing else."

She weighed it as if it were a coin she might use later. Her smile changed shape. The friendly courier softened at the edges. Something older and sharper looked out from behind it. I had seen that look through glass and cold light.

"You want a clean goodbye," she said. "You can have it."

She started to turn away, then paused and looked over her shoulder. The sun found the knit of her cap and lit the edges, the way stage lights will catch a singer's hair when the band holds a note. For a breath the room felt wrong, like a set disguised as a street.

"Tell your partner I said hi," she said. "Maybe next time... I'll wear their face."

I LEFT THE DELIVERY court by the drainage run and kept to the shallow side where the stone stays dry. The wind off the river carried a clean chill that helped me sort the morning into piles. In one stack I put what I could prove. The tap was seated and quiet. The repeater at the chapel was still breathing. The tripwires worked. In the other stack I put what I could only name. Switchblade liked maps that were also questions. Her scent matched a memory I did not want to file under Sable. The city had listened, and the city had answered, and somewhere a private channel had said detain like it belonged in a lunch order.

Juno flew ahead to check the mouth of the lane and then returned to my shoulder with the satisfied little hop she saves for routes she approves. We moved along the back of the foundry where the brick is pitted and old ladders dress the wall like ribs. The Wendigo waited two streets over under an awning that used to belong to a boat repair shop. The sign was gone. The hooks were still there. The van wore her municipal coat without strain and pretended to be a sanitation unit that had stopped to argue with itself about the schedule.

I gave the bad bearing whistle and watched the grill soften as the camouflage mesh adjusted to the light. The hatch eased open. Inside, the air held the familiar mix of warm wiring and mint. The pot on the shelf had grown three new leaves while I was gone. That is not how plants work, but it is how time feels when a job goes clean.

I closed the door behind me and set my bag on the bench with the quiet care that keeps rooms calm. The console came up with a stroke. The mirror stream from the tap scrolled at a steady rate, nothing dramatic, only the constant reassurance of systems tending their chores. I flagged three packets that carried the Oronix marker and moved them to a side window. The headers lined up with the path I expected. Beltline north. Service road forty four. A quiet detour request that died in a buffer before it could reach a human. The only surprise was a VYRE callout from a quadrant south of us. Not zero seven. A different unit with a temper. I copied the path into my map and set the map aside. I would share that when it earned a place in the room.

The log needed to look as if I had never left. That work felt like tidying a kitchen before someone wakes. I smoothed the MAC drift so the van read like a city truck resting in the same shadow it had chosen at dawn. I sent two lazy maintenance pings that matched the Chapel's heartbeat and tucked the acknowledgments into our ledger. I cleaned the call buffer and left a recorded test from the repeater that would play back if anyone questioned why a camera blinked out of rhythm. None of it would fool a god. It would satisfy a bored clerk. Bored clerks write the first draft of safety in this city.

Juno landed on the rail above the windshield and rubbed her head against my temple. It was a question wrapped in a thank you. I reached up and scratched the smooth plate where feathers would be on a bird that has to preen. "Good work," I said. She clicked and turned her eye back to the glass. Her reflection looked like a bright seed fixed in a dark branch.

I made coffee and let the kettle's quiet rattle steady my hands. The cups clinked like punctuation. I thought about the way Switchblade had stepped down the stairs one tread at a time and the way she had chosen the word partner like it was a key. There was a clean path through those thoughts that ended in the Cathedral. There was also a messier path that ended in a room I still did not have words for. I put both paths back in their boxes. When I talk to Hikari about danger, I prefer to carry proof.

The cradle lights at the rear bay pulsed once, then settled to a softer glow. Wisp likes a certain temperature when she wakes. I turned the heat two clicks and set the shade to a low half level so the light came in as a wash, not a blade. The van dimmed the cabin without being asked. Machines do not have feelings, but they have memories of good mornings. If you listen, they tell you how to repeat one.

I wiped the mud off my boots and brushed faint grit from the floor by the door. Then I sat with my back to the console and read the room the way you read a body coming out of sleep. The mint leaned toward the seam in the shutter. The ivy curled around the hook where the curtain tie rests. The air felt warmer than when I had left. It is a trick, the way small changes pretend they have always been there.

The cradle gave a soft tone. Wisp's eyes opened like someone turning up brightness on a screen that had always been lit. She stayed still for a breath, then sat up without the rehearsal of a stretch. Her hair threw a small halo across the backlight before it settled in the shape she favors, two high puffs that make strangers underestimate her. She looked at me, not at the console, not at the door, not at the kettle. That detail matters.

"You were quiet," she said. No accusation. Only a note.

"I let the neighborhood hold itself up," I replied. "It did fine."

She swung her legs over the side of the bay and stood. The soles of her boots tapped a calm two-step on the floor. I handed her a cup and kept my own careful. The surface of the coffee moved a little from the tremor I had not noticed until then. The body tells the truth last. I set my cup down and folded my hands in my lap until the shaking had the good sense to leave.

"Anything I need to know now," she asked. Her tone was the one she uses when there is a list to be made and she wants the list to fit on one page.

"Tap is clean," I said. "Repeater is healthy. The line threw a few quiet instructions in our direction. I caught them. I have the paths saved. I will make a better map after food."

She nodded. "And the human part of the city."

"Three cruisers trying to prove they still matter," I said. "Two uniforms who wanted a story and settled for directions. One courier who read from a different book."

Wisp's head tilted. "Courier," she said, not as a guess, more as a tab placed at the edge of the table to hold a place for later.

"I will write it down," I said. "For now, you should eat."

She went to the cabinet and pulled the noodles from the shelf with the same small sigh that always makes me laugh. Food is not exciting when the day has been. She broke the square in half and dropped it into the pot, then stole the end of the dried greens with the practiced theft of a child who never had to be told twice to take the last piece. Juno approved with a single click and leaned closer to watch the water roll. We all have our comforts.

While the noodles softened, I walked the room one more time and made small corrections that would be invisible to anyone else. I turned the bench cushion so the lighter side faced up. I moved the deck two inches left so the cable would fall cleanly. I set the stray screw I had pocketed from the hatch beside the donation bead from the Saint so that the two circles touched. The van noticed the pattern and pleased itself by dimming the far light to match the near.

Wisp brought the bowls to the table and sat with her legs folded under her in that neat shape that looks like prayer and is not. She ate with clean speed and glanced at me between bites the way an older sister checks a younger one without saying anything that would break the spell. When she finished she wiped the bowl with a corner of bread and set the spoon down with an exactness that always makes me think of lab work done by someone who grew up fixing things that should have been new.

"You did not wake me," she said. It could have been an accusation. It was not.

"I wanted your rest more than I wanted your help," I said. "Help is easy to ask for. Rest is hard to give away."

She looked at my hands. "And now," she asked.

"Now I tell you the part that needs telling," I said, and gave her the data first, the way she prefers. Oronix priority packets. The detain instruction. The VYRE tag from the south. The path that matched our stairs. The clean loop that proved the test went out and came back without footprints. She listened without interruption and stored each piece behind her eyes.

"And the courier," she said at last.

"Friendly voice," I said. "Good timing. Paper map to break a cop's focus. She put herself between a patrol and a door in a block that cannot afford that kind of attention. She asked a question about light and dark that had more to do with cameras than sleep. She walked away when I told her to."

Wisp was quiet for a long breath. "Do you want me to run her voice against the file from the Cathedral," she asked.

"Not yet," I said. "I want to see if she chooses a pattern again."

"That is patience," Wisp said, and there was approval in it.

The room relaxed with us. The heater gave a small contented sigh. The mint reclaimed the seam of light. Juno preened one feather until it laid with the others like a solved equation. Outside, the river's sound lifted toward noon.

I scrubbed the tap logs one more time and set a soft alarm on the repeater so it would speak to me in a whisper if the chapel lens woke at the wrong hour. Then I marked the morning in our ledger with a neat hand. The entry did not shout. It did not dress itself in drama. A date. A place. The way the beltline sang. The way a voice bent a word. It is important to leave the right footprints for the people you become tomorrow.

When there was nothing left to correct, I leaned back on the bench and let my eyes close without sleeping. Wisp rinsed the bowls and set them to dry. Her movements turned the space into a home again, not a bunker, not a temporary den. I knew what it meant to feel that shift and not argue with it. You cannot run forever on a road with no rooms. You lose language that way.

The hatch buzzer ticked once under the floor, the polite note we taught it to play when a trusted friend crosses the outer grid. A neighbor pushed a cart of parts down the alley and went on without looking in. The van greeted the cart by lighting the far corner and then forgot it again. That is how safety lives here. Small greetings. Small silences. No performances.

I glanced at the clock and decided I had been back long enough to pretend I had never been gone. I could stand up and say I had been checking a seam in the seal, or that the kettle sulked and I had chosen to stand guard over it like a superstitious aunt. I did not need to say any of it. Wisp knew the shape of the morning. She poured me a second cup and slid it across the table with a look that said we were even on the debt for sleep.

"Afternoon plan," she asked.

"Quiet," I said. "Watch the tap, make the map, clean the cradle ports, and cut the list down until it fits in the space we actually own."

She nodded. "And if the courier returns."

"I will let her speak first," I said. "Then I will decide how much to remember."

We let the day stand on its own legs. I set my cup down and stretched until my spine agreed to keep working. Juno flew a short line from the rail to the cradle and back as if measuring the distance between the work and the rest. The van hummed under our feet, content with the fiction we had written into its logs.

By the time the sun slipped to the angle that makes the foundry beam cast a stripe just below the window seam, the room felt exactly as it should. Boots by the door in the right order. Plant watered. Tools in their places. Two bodies breathing at a pace that does not call to anyone outside. If someone had asked me when I returned, I could have said I was here the whole time and not felt my mouth lie.

That comfort did not cancel the warning in my pocket. The folded map sat against my thigh with the small square trapped in its crease. It warmed with my body heat and pretended to be nothing. I would strip the metal, wash the paper, and file the feel of Switchblade's voice where it could not surprise me. For now, I left it still. A reminder has more use when it stays a little sharp.

"Ready," Wisp said, and touched the console to bring up the city's soft blue. Her eyes found the places she wanted to watch. Mine found the places that needed to forget us.

We looked like two people who had never been anywhere but here. That was the point. The day would test that claim soon enough. For the moment, we held it.

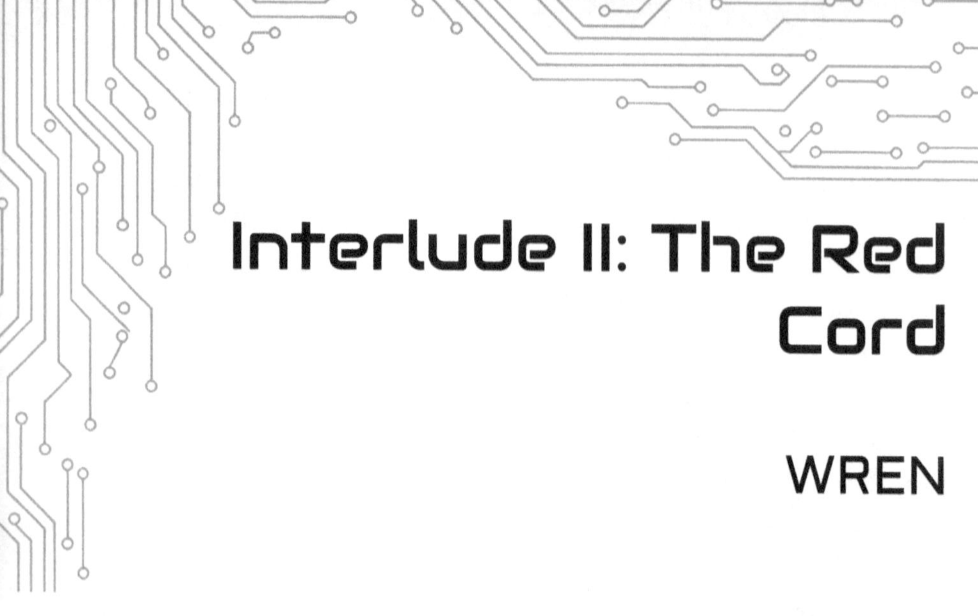

Interlude II: The Red Cord

WREN

The notice hit my feed at 9:02, a polite rectangle in company gray with a red stripe across the top that asked for my signature. The text thanked me for my service and reminded me to return my badge. The last line said access would be revoked at 9:15. I stared at the time stamp and counted the minutes as if numbers could be persuaded by attention. At 9:06 the lobby scanner stopped recognizing my face. I handed the badge to a guard who did not meet my eyes. He slid it into a bin with seven others and wrote my name on a sticker that would never be read again.

Outside, Klade was the same city as it had been at 9:01. Trams clipped past the lattice supports. A vendor swore at a steam valve and then patted it like a dog that would not sit. The river threw up a smell of salt and metal as if to say no one should carry fresh news onto its banks. I stood beneath the canopy of the Light Technologies tower and let the rain find my scarf. The cloth smelled like last night's coffee. I had meant to wash it before work. I had meant a lot of small things.

I did not call anyone. I walked. I took the long sidewalk along the utility trench where the concrete warms from the heat of the cables below. The hospice sat six stops away, a low building with windows that only open far enough to promise air. When my mother was first moved there, the nurse on duty told me the windows were a safety feature. She smiled as she said it, the way people smile when a script tells them to make a word sound kind. I remembered her name for three days and then let it fall out of my head because the memory served no purpose.

The front desk was a counter with a soft mat where you are supposed to place your hands while you wait. The mat was pale, so the red of the sanitation light reflected against it like a warning no one would dare obey. A young man with a clean haircut and a badge that said Intake Coordinator sat behind the terminal. He greeted me by first name and asked if the rain had been bad. When I told him my mother's room number he clicked through three screens, frowned in a way that suggested he wanted to be sympathetic, and told me that someone would meet me upstairs.

The elevator smelled faintly of antiseptic and cinnamon. The floor tiles on the fourth level had little lines of dirt where the mop cannot quite reach the edges. You see those lines everywhere that sells order and buys it cheap. I walked the length of the hallway without reading the quotes on the walls. They were the kind of words the living put up for themselves, not for the people dying in the beds.

My mother's room held a narrow bed, a chair that tried to be kind to the spine, and a window that gave the river a flat, obedient shape. She was asleep when I came in. The machine beside the bed breathed with her and then ahead of her, as if it were teaching a lesson she had already learned. The neural comfort rig sat on the wall at shoulder height, a compact unit with a loop of red cable coiled neatly on a hook. Someone had called the cable cherry during a tour. I had wanted to say umbilical and had swallowed the word because metaphors do not help when the person you love needs water.

I took the chair and moved it so I could see her hands. The skin had thinned so much that every vein showed, a blue map under pale paper. Across the back of her right hand the hospice had placed a red band to mark the IV port. It matched the loop on the wall and the line across my termination notice. Everywhere I looked the day had chosen the same color and pretended it was different each time.

She opened her eyes without a start. Waking belonged to her body the way baking used to, an action the hands remembered even if the mind did not. The first time the doctors called it decline I wanted to break something. Decline sounds like a choice. Now it sounded like a slope we had been walking together and pretending was a floor.

"Hey," I said, and leaned forward so she would not have to turn her head.

She blinked, took me in as if I had been in the doorway for a very long time, and smiled. The smile was not the one I grew up with. It was smaller, more precise, like a paper crane folded from a recipe card. It still made the room feel warmer.

"You came before lunch," she said. "That's a treat."

"Thought I'd bring a treat to match," I said, and reached into my bag for the small tin of mint candies she likes. The nurse had told me not to, then taught me how to bend the rules safely. The mint helped with the dry mouth. The disobedience helped me with everything else.

She let me feed her one and closed her eyes to taste it. I could see the muscle in her jaw working in slow rhythm. When she opened her eyes again, she glanced at the window and then at the loop of red cable on the wall.

"The river is busy," she said. "Does it always sound like that."

"It does when you listen," I said. "On lazy days it hums. On hard days it complains."

"Which is today," she asked.

"Today it is carrying the same old water," I said.

She looked back at me with the patience people keep for children. "You got fired," she said. No drama. No pity. She said it as if she were reading a label.

"Yes," I said. "They said streamlining. They said redundancy. They said a lot of words that let them sleep."

"Did you say something that will keep you awake," she asked.

"I did not have time," I said, and that was the worst part. They had removed the hour from my mouth. "I signed nothing. They can mail me whatever they think is fair."

She nodded as if we had been planning for this and had just reached the part where the plan tells you to breathe. The door opened behind me and closed again. A woman in a neat suit stood with a tablet held in both hands like a book of rules. Her hair was perfect and her eyes were kind in the way a well designed interface is kind. She introduced herself as Family Services and told me there had been a change in coverage.

She did not say termination. She said transition. She said alternative placement. She said municipal program. She said my mother would not be left without support. She said many things in a steady voice while the red cord on the wall held its loop and the IV band on my mother's hand kept its color. I waited until she finished, then asked what alternative meant.

"It means we can no longer bill your current plan for the level of care she needs," the woman said. "We can transfer her to a city facility that will provide adequate support, though there may be a waiting period. We will help you navigate."

"Adequate," I said. "That is the line you are comfortable with."

"It is the line we are authorized to use," she said, gentle as a blanket that does not keep you warm.

"How long is the waiting period," I asked.

"It depends on availability," she said. "A week, perhaps two. In the meantime our discharge team can work with you on at-home options."

"My apartment does not have an elevator," I said. "My job ended an hour ago. At-home means here."

"I understand this is hard," she said, and I almost laughed because the sentence was perfect. It acknowledged nothing and nodded at everything.

My mother watched our faces the way you watch a foreign film without subtitles. She followed tone and silence. When the woman finished, my mother spoke.

"I like the red cord," she said to the wall, not to either of us. "It makes me feel like the machine is ready."

The woman from Family Services looked at the cord as if noticing it for the first time. "That is the neural comfort harness," she said. "It is part of her current therapy plan."

"How many sessions are left," I asked.

"Her plan resets every four weeks," she said. "However, the system is tied to the billing module. If coverage changes, the schedule will update."

"What happens to the scans," I asked. "The recordings."

"They are retained for quality control," she said, and her voice softened because she truly believed this part. "Families sometimes request copies upon transition. There is a fee for processing and release."

I let the room go quiet so the lie could hear itself. The scans do not belong to families. They belong to the algorithm that improves the product. They belong to graduate students who will never know the names of the people whose memories turned into calibration curves. They belong to a gray slab in a basement where the word retention means storage until power fails.

"Thank you," I said to the woman, and watched her shoulders ease in relief. "Could I have a moment with my mother."

"Of course," she said. "I will email you the documentation."

She left without looking back. The door latched with the soft restraint of a machine that has learned to be quiet when it closes on grief. I sat again and took my mother's hand. Her skin felt cooler than I wanted it to.

"We can go for a walk," I said. "Not far. Down the hall. See the plant by the nurses' station that tries to be a tree."

"Later," she said. "I am tired from all the thinking."

She looked at the loop again and then at me. "Do you know how to make it work," she asked. "The stories. The warm ones."

"I do," I said. I could lie to everyone else in the building. I would not lie to her. "I know how the plug fits. I know where the button is. I know where the file goes when it leaves you."

She smiled again, the paper crane bending and finding a new crease. "You always had good hands," she said. "Make it work."

I stood and lifted the red cord off the hook. The connector clicked into the port at the base of the comfort unit. It was the kind of click that gets inside the body and takes something with it. I checked the settings, turned the intensity to the lowest notch, and draped the harness along her temples. The gel pads gave the soft hiss of a seal finding its shape. I selected a program called Hearth. The description promised warmth, memory alignment, and gentle fade. The company had hired a poet to write that line. I pressed start.

Her eyes closed and her mouth softened. The monitor picked up the shift in her breathing and drew it in a thicker line. I watched three cycles to be sure, then stepped to the wall terminal and plugged my deck into the diagnostic port under the panel. The port was old. It did not care whose hands used it as long as they knew where it lived. I navigated past the interface that sold feelings and opened the maintenance prompt.

The recordings had clean names. Session numbers. Timestamps. Physician codes. The structure reassured me. Clean names mean predictable paths. I set my deck to mirror the stream as the unit wrote it and then to pull down the last ten sessions from backup. The lights on the deck flickered green and settled to steady. The files began to move. I pictured a small boat leaving a harbor that had never earned the word safe.

My mother breathed with the machine. Outside the window the river made a lane of silver between dark roofs. I remembered the kitchen in the old apartment and the way she sang when she kneaded dough. The same song every winter. The words nonsense, the tune pure rhythm. She had hummed the same way when she helped me with multiplication. She would set the problem down like a mixing bowl and say we will stir until it comes together. I watched the progress bar fill and felt the line across my throat ease.

The door opened again. The nurse from the first week stepped inside with a small smile that asked for permission to intrude. She checked the monitor, looked at my deck without alarm, and adjusted the angle of the window shade so the light would be softer on my mother's face.

"How is she doing today," the nurse asked.

"She is warm," I said. "The program helps."

"It does," the nurse said. "So does this."

She folded the blanket once and placed it across my mother's legs with a care that belonged to another century. Then she straightened and touched the red band on the IV port to make sure it held. She saw me watching the motion and gave a little shrug.

"We use blue for antibiotics," she said. "Green for vitamins. Red for the things we cannot pretend are neutral."

"What happens when the plan changes," I asked.

Her face did not alter, but I saw the jaw tighten. She glanced at the door, then back at me. "I will bring boxes," she said. "I will bring tape. That part is never hard. The rest is."

"Thank you," I said.

She nodded, looked at my mother once, and left as quietly as she had entered. The deck chimed. The stream copy had finished, and the archive pulls were at ninety percent. I started a checksum, watched the math agree with itself, and felt the sense of a lock sliding on a door that no one else could see. I ejected the cable, tucked the deck into the bag, and wound the red cord back onto the hook with a care that felt like ceremony.

My mother's eyes fluttered open. She smiled that small paper smile again and reached for my wrist with a light touch.

"You look different," she said.

"I got wet," I said. "The rain had ideas and I forgot an umbrella."

"Not that," she said, and her fingers tapped once against my pulse. "You look like someone who did a thing correctly."

"I did," I said. "I made the room tell the truth."

"That sounds like you," she said.

We sat for a while without speaking. The program transitioned into its fade, the machine breathing ahead of her again, then letting her body take the lead. The river lit and darkened as clouds moved across it. Somewhere below us a cart squeaked and then rolled smoothly after someone applied a drop of oil. The kind of small victory no one writes down.

I helped her sip water, smoothed the blanket, and kissed her forehead in the place where the skin still smelled like cinnamon even when it did not smell like anything else. I told her I would be back before dinner. I told her I would bring the soft bread from the shop with the cracked tile. I told her the nurse would check the program before lunch. I did not tell her about forms or fees or exits that looked like entries. She had taught me when to withhold a recipe step so that a cake would surprise the person who baked it.

I left the room and kept my eyes straight ahead. The quotes on the wall floated past without titles. The elevator came when I pressed the button. At the front desk the Intake Coordinator asked if he could send any information to my feed. I told him I would collect it in person later. He said of course in a voice that suggested he practiced it at home. He wished me a calm day. I wished him one back and meant it.

Outside, the rain had slowed. The river wore a dull sheen that made the city look gentle. I stood at the edge of the hospice canopy and watched the tram rattle past. My hand found the weight of the deck in my bag and held it there until the urge to look over my shoulder passed. I did not hurry.

When I reached the corner, the walk signal turned green. The color bled into the puddles and made them look like small windows. I stepped around them. A woman across the street laughed into her phone and brushed hair from her face. A courier carrying two coffees ran the last three steps to beat the answering red. A man pushed a cart with one wheel that did not want to turn and coaxed it with a kind of love.

At the second block the wind shifted and brought the smell of yeast from a bakery I had never noticed. I made a note to return with enough cash to be kind to myself. Near the tram stop a boy practiced a card trick against his thigh until the card obeyed. The city offered me ten unimportant things and asked me to take one. I chose the smell of bread and put it in my pocket with the memory of my mother's fingers tapping once against my wrist.

At the tower where my badge had died, the guard who took it earlier was smoking under the overhang. He looked at me and then past me. I looked at him and then past him. We allowed each other the privacy of being the same person who had stood there three hours before and the different person who was walking away now. I turned toward the river and followed the sidewalk that warms from the cables below.

I did not think about the documentation in my feed. I did not think about a municipal waiting list. I did not think about a box with tape. I thought about a humming machine and a red cord and the way a file moves when a hand tells it to cross a boundary it did not build. I took a breath and tasted cinnamon where there was none. I did not call Hikari. I did not need a witness.

I kept walking until my legs forgot how near I was to the place where someone had written my name on a sticker. When the tram bell told me to pause, I paused. When it told me to go, I went. My feet knew the rest, and I let them.

"I didn't run. I just stopped moving."

Chapter Nine

Full Stack

HIKARI

The Wendigo felt larger when it was still. Screens rested in a low glow that softened the metal, and the hum underfoot was the pleasant kind, the kind that says nothing is on fire yet. I sat in Wisp, legs folded on the bench, palms working through the ritual of tools as if polishing them could tame a city. Across from me Wren spread the map like a card trick and let routes blossom in dull threads of light. Juno perched above us on the rail, head tilted, iris widening and narrowing as if the van itself had a pulse she wanted to count.

"Dogs run the cannery like a thrift store with locks," Wren said. "Cold wing holds the hardware. Roof guard naps with broken binoculars. The south gate cycles on a manual timer that thinks twelve minutes can be fourteen if no one complains."

I nodded and slid a microline cutter into the shallow pocket along my wrist. In Wisp the world came in crisp seams. Everything had a right angle if you were willing to name it. "We do it in four bodies," I said. "Stray goes first to set footholds. Quiet doors. A repeater where the walls hate radios. A bolt loosened where a smaller hand might stick. He will leave crumbs I can trust. Wisp goes inside the cold wing and drinks the river. Velvet crosses the rooms that like an audience and keeps the gaze busy when we need to leave. Forge stays heavy and patient unless someone decides to make the evening loud."

Wren smiled without showing teeth. "You always make it sound like a dance lesson. Step, turn, open, close."

"It is a dance," I said. "The trick is never to let the room pick the music."

She lifted one hand and drew a loop around the cannery's south face. "Stray up the rattle-ladders. Camera blind spots every twenty feet. You will have to treat the roof as if it can whisper. The microphones in the downspouts are the only things that look new."

"Juno will run the gutters," I said. The drone clicked once, which is as close as she gets to a nod. "Tag every lens that blinks wrong and flirt with the ones that pretend to sleep."

Wren opened a sidebar and called up the van systems. "Do you want the remote switchover armed," she asked. "I rebuilt the induction coils and added salt to the state buffer. If you get pinned inside, I can pull you from thirty meters."

I felt the small tightening in my shoulders that always arrives with that question. Remote switchover can save you. Remote switchover can also put the person you are into someone else's jar. "Arm it," I said, "then set the confirmation to two channels and a physical tell. If I do not tap three fingers against my thigh and breathe on the count you know, you do not pull me."

"Paranoid is fine," Wren said. "Alive is better."

I met her eyes so the words would land. "You never know when someone's laid a trap to put your personality in a box. Remote hands feel like kindness until they close the lid."

She keyed the safeguard without arguing. The Wendigo responded with a polite chime and a note on the panel that told me the coils were asleep until I said otherwise.

We went through contingencies until the map looked like it had grown nerves. If the river door blocks, Velvet smiles right, then left, and the talker forgets what time is. If the freezer room runs a second feed we did not see, Wisp rides the relay with a parasite that speaks politely and steals clean. If the roof guard wakes and tries to prove loyalty, Stray drops into shadow and lets the man have his dignity. If anyone decides to follow us home, Forge claims the alley and persuades the tail to value breath.

I opened the drawer under the prep counter and took out the sleeve module we had written this afternoon. My right wrist still tingled where Mirror's filament had tasted, a memory the body could not quit. I slotted the decoy into the sleeve and felt the tiniest vibration as it came alive.

"Handshake diversion is live," I said. "If anyone tries to sample this patch again, they will learn a story about my balance that is true for a puppet and wrong for me."

Wren toggled the sanitation coat for the van and painted our route through the quarter. "I will give us a sewer service identity and three maintenance pings filed to the district office," she said. "If anyone looks backward, they will see exactly the kind of paperwork that lets everyone go back to sleep."

Juno hopped down, lit on Wren's shoulder for the pleasure of it, then tested her wings in the narrow aisle and returned to the rail. Wren nudged her beak with a knuckle and the drone accepted the affection with a small mechanical sigh. It made the cabin feel honest.

"Tripwires," I said.

"Already strung," Wren answered. "Soft alarms on every municipal lens within ten blocks of the cannery that wakes out of sequence. No pictures, just timestamps and iris adjustments. If Mirror touches the grid the way it did last time, we will feel the pawprint."

I checked the pods one by one. Velvet's spine port gleamed clean in her cradle. Forge looked like a statue commissioned by a very sad empire. Stray hung small and scuffed, his mask resting against his chest like a promise. I ran a hand down his forearm and felt the under-skin wires breathe.

"We will not need Velvet unless the room turns social," I said. "Keep her warm, not hot. Wisp goes second, not first. If Stray trips a wire that cannot be cut, a kid can disappear faster than a woman who looks like trouble."

Wren nodded. "Exit," she prompted.

"Thirteenth Street gate, east ladder to the roof, down to the alley behind FOY'S if the timing is good. If it is not, we take the drainage run to the dead tram spur and let the Wendigo meet us when the sanitation coat makes sense."

"Client?" She arched a brow.

"Tava gets the ledger and the garnish," I said. "He will try to pay us with flattery and soup. We will let him. He will watch the door while he jokes."

The plan lay on the table between us like a neat stack of rules. It never stays neat. That is not the point. You plan to buy thinking time later.

Wren reached across the map and flipped a small brass toggle that turns the Wendigo into a quiet ally. Every cabinet lock checked in with a green blink. Every sensor admitted it was awake. The van felt like a companion ready to keep our secrets.

"Ready to write your crumbs," she asked.

"Ready," I said, and stood.

The swap to Stray is always a small vanishing followed by a return at a different height. I stepped into the cradle, felt Velvet's harness release, and let Wisp fall asleep with the contentment of a tired dancer. The dark that followed was brief and soft. Stray rose into the light. The world lost a little polish and gained a little spring. Weight shifted down into the balls of his feet. Balance asked for fences and low roofs. I rolled his shoulders and felt joints that prefer to sprint rather than pose.

Wren's gaze moved, noting the change in an instant, and her mouth tipped into the half smile she saves for good tools. "You look like the city owes you a favor," she said.

"He does not ask for favors," I answered, hearing how the voice lives lower in the chest. "He just shows up before anyone remembers the rules."

I checked Stray's kit with the quick routine that keeps panic small. Climbing gloves tucked into back pocket. Two wafer relays nested in the liner of his cap. A strip of magnetic shims taped along his forearm where a frisk will miss. The repeater that speaks to the van without teaching the neighborhood to listen. A knife that prefers rope to skin. The microline cutter I did not admit I would carry twice.

Wren rolled the map closed and slipped it into the side bin. "Two breaths," she said. "Then we go write them into their own building."

I pressed my palm to the Wendigo's bulkhead and felt the van answer with a faint rise in the hum. When you plan this much, you risk believing the plan is the point. It is not. The point is to have something you can break with intention.

"On your count," I said.

Wren tapped the dash twice and the cabin lights dropped to work-night. Outside the hatch the market quarter breathed rain. Juno clicked once, then twice. The van slipped her municipal skin over our shadows like a coat you borrow from a friend. I lifted the latch, and Stray stepped down into Klade with the easy arrogance of a boy no one remembers stopping.

THE RAVEL DOGS WORK out of a decommissioned cannery that pretends to be retired. From the river it looks like a ribcage of tin and concrete, scaffolds rusting into a sketch of ladders, gulls riding the updrafts like they own air. Up close the building hums in a way old freezers are not supposed to hum. That is how stolen data sounds when someone hides it under ice and invoices.

I start in Stray because the body buys invisibility in any neighborhood that learned to stop asking boys where they are going. Hat low. Collar high. Hands in pockets the way a kid hides nothing and everything at once. I climb the south-face rattle-ladders and settle on the cannery's spine, thighs gripping cold bar, boots hooked under a brace that has not met an inspector since the contract died. From here the yard is a smudged grid. Two Dogs at the river door, one talker and one listener. A roof guard with binoculars that have been broken long enough to become a habit. A woman in a fur-lined coat arguing into a handset about rates as if anger could change arithmetic. The microphones are the only things modern, tucked into downspouts and gutter bends where they sip the air for wrong silence.

["Stray in place,"] I murmur. ["Roof is a sleepwalker. River door has a pair that like the sound of their own caution. Heat says four inside the cold wing around a room that hums too clean."]

["Copy,"] Wren answers, steady and warm in my ear. ["Side gate will cycle in twelve. Juno is tagging a quiet path along the drainage rail. Roof guard blinks on the quarter minute. You are clear between blinks two and three."]

I move when his gaze empties. Drop to the catwalk, hands to rail, weight to heels, hang until the metal stops complaining, then swing in. The side door shivers on its hinges like a nervous tooth. I ease it open with a thumbnail and slide through while it still thinks about objecting. Inside smells like solvent baked into old salt.

Recon is not enough. Recon has to leave breadcrumbs. I unlatch the utility panel by the mop sink and shim the lock with a magnet so one of my future bodies can come through without talking to the door. I plant a thin repeater in the ceiling plenum that will talk to the Wendigo without teaching the Yard how to listen back. I loosen one bolt on the inner latch so a smaller hand will not have to fight it later. Then I go back out the way I came, drop to shadow, cut across the alley where the drainage runs bright, and follow the line of moss back to our van.

The Wendigo waits with her municipal coat pulled neat around her shoulders. She looks like a sanitation rig that stopped to argue with itself about the schedule. Inside, the air is warm with wire and mint. The cradles glow a low blue that could pass for calm in a different life.

I swing into the dock and let Stray go quiet. There is always a blink of nothing. Then Wisp rises into the room with her particular focus. The world gets taller by a few centimeters and lighter by a great deal more. Fingers that were meant for finesse flex and remember their tools. I tuck one silver-pink puff behind my ear and check the kit that only fits this body. Microline cutters. A sliver camera that lives in a false eyelash case. A palm that can read a circuit by touch. Wren watches my vitals settle and nods without saying good luck because she has learned I do better when the air stays plain.

I slip back through the utility door Stray prepared. The corridor opens into the cold wing. Old doors wear inventory codes that no longer have lists behind them. A few have power taps and fiber tails running along baseboard into a back hall where someone competent dragged a clean feed. The hum behind the last door has the rhythm of a rack doing more than the box promised. Extra fans. A little skip every thirteen seconds. That skip is the sound of theft sweating.

A guard stands at the interior checkpoint with a tablet in one hand and a tired look on his face. He has patrol-grade armor with plastic edges worn smooth by nervous fingers. He does not expect a girl to approach the way danger approaches.

"You lost," he asks.

"Delivery," I say, and hold up a thin parcel in clear wrap. The label is perfect. The address is a suggestion. "Two-fifteen. Hands only. No signature. The sign says we do not exist."

He frowns exactly the way a man frowns when a package pretends to know him. He makes space for the story because parcels talk with the authority of routine. I slide close enough that his breath fogs the plastic and pass the parcel into his hand. His eyes drop. His chin follows. His neck port reveals its seam where the armor does not quite cover old surgery.

I step past and let the small body say harmless. Three meters down the corridor I pause to pull a rag from my bag like I have a spill to address. I glance back. He is still reading the label as if it might tell him who he is on a good day. I walk back as if I have remembered my manners and reach to touch his elbow the way a child thanks a grownup for holding a door.

"Sorry," I say, soft as steam. "Wrong room."

His eyes come up. The angle of his head exposes the port again. I slide my right hand up as if I am about to brush lint from his collar and let the microline in my sleeve slip into my fingers. The filament is clear and thin, stored in a ring that could be a toy. I lay the loop behind his ear and draw once with a smooth, even pressure. It is the same motion I use to cut a cable tie without nicking the sheath.

Under the skin a thin bundle of colored lines parts like threads in a ribbon. The smell is hot tin and saline, not blood. His mouth opens and thinks about forming a sound but the implant that translates his intent for his body has just gone quiet. He settles against me in a small, confused fold, the way tired men sometimes do in trains when the station arrives. I guide him down into the chair and set the parcel on his lap. I tuck the loop away, put two squares of dermal tape over the nick, and tilt his head so it looks like sleep. It takes fifteen seconds. He breathes twice more and stops because the power to the pacer and the neck relay no longer speaks to anything that understands. His eyes cloud in a way organic tissue does when the argument ends. I close them with two fingers and move on.

["Clear,"] I tell Wren. ["One guard pacified. Local mics did not like the word pacified. Consider it a joke we will not repeat."]

["Considered,"] she says. Her tone softens for a heartbeat that is mine, then hardens again into work. ["Corridor cams show no motion. You have eighty seconds before the roof walker stretches his legs. Avoid the third tile on the right. Juno does not trust the grout."]

The security door to the cold room wears a municipal faceplate and a private heart. I pop the face with a suction cup, catch the screws before they fall, and rest the plate on my shoulder. The board underneath is honest kit, bought from a vendor who expects to service kitchen doors, not vaults. I short the status line with a magnet, feed a false okay from the repeater Stray left for me, and give the lock a push. It rolls aside as if it always meant to be helpful.

Inside, frost clings to the outer coils but the room heat is wrong for food and perfect for equipment. A steel cabinet sits on grease skids against the back wall. It is not a freezer. It is a cage with a funny hat. I lift the back panel on four magnets that were meant to forgive lazy maintenance. Behind it a thick fiber trunk splits at a tidy junction. One line to a fence on the east side, one to a relay that pretends it is an industrial uplink.

["On the trunk,"] I whisper. ["Passive tap going on the fence side. Little parasite on the relay to ask what it thinks about life."]

["Do it,"] Wren says. ["Gate cycle planned at Thirteenth. Sanitation escort primed two streets away. Juno is holding a clean arc if you need to ghost."]

The tap is a wafer that sits under a tie and drinks without waking the stream. The parasite is a polite monster. It reads device gossip and repeats it back in a language my deck likes. I slide both into place and let Wisp's fingers make quick, deliberate work. The diode blinks and steadies. My screen fills with column after column of packet headers. Oronix documents dressed as subcontractor invoices. Neural training sets labeled as forklift tutorials. A purchase order that counts human labor as if it were solvent by the drum and fiber by the meter. I feel heat in a body that does not sweat.

["They have been busy,"] I say.

["They always are,"] Wren replies. ["We can be angry on the way home. Keep pulling."]

I pull until the cache fills past the number we promised and into the number that lets me sleep. The parasite purrs and sends me a little note that says the relay has friends. I leave it in place to keep listening, then reseat the panel, wipe my prints where I never left them, and turn for the door.

Now I need Velvet. The common rooms out front are not built for a kid with a bag. They are built for bodies that know how to move through a glance without dragging it along. I leave the way I came. The chair holds a man who looks like he should still be breathing in ten minutes. He will not. I slide past the mop sink, past the shimmed utility door, and out into air that tastes like river metal.

The Wendigo has crept forward under a different face. The municipal coat now reads stormwater services. Wren ghosts the van to the loading dock when a truck backs into the next bay and blocks the yard cameras for three long breaths. The hatch sighs open. I step in, seal the door, and slide into the cradle before the air can change its mind.

Wisp goes dark with a clean cut. Velvet arrives like a curtain rising. Touch returns as a different script. Weight relocates from ankles to hips and then to the measured certainty of the spine. The sheath inside this shell smooths along nerves with a soft current that feels like a hand adjusting posture in a dance class. My balance narrows to a line I can walk with a glass on my head. I roll my shoulders, set the curve where it belongs, and breathe into a voice that turns words into invitations.

["You have twenty,"] Wren says as she checks the camo and spoofs our route to read like a sewer pump that hates its job. ["Front corridor is loose. Two Dogs packing bottles. One deck jockey with a headache watching a game he has already lost. If you smile at the wrong person, they will pretend they hired you."]

"I intend to smile at everyone correctly," I answer, and step back out.

Velvet makes the same corridor a different place. The heels tap a measured rhythm on concrete. The light treats the face like it owes it money. I walk as if the air left a path and I am simply honoring the request. Two Dogs at a table turn their heads in sequence and then look away because the human nervous system knows the cost of staring. I let my fingers trail the rim of a glass someone set down without thinking. I make a small apology with my eyes to a man sweeping a corner. He accepts it on instinct and decides that I belong here more than he does.

["Cameras roll,"] Wren murmurs. ["All loops are clean. Juno does not like a lens near the second stair. It twitched and then pretended it did not."]

"Noted," I say, and adjust my route by a half meter without breaking stride. The cold room door is behind me now. The spine of the building opens into a broad lane of work tables and plastic crates filled with things that used to be useful. The air smells like old oil and cheap citrus cleaner. A young man in a faded team jacket pretends to watch a game and actually watches his own reflection. Two women count credits with the brisk disinterest of people who owned boredom before they rented it out. No one stops me because no one wants to be the person who does.

I drift toward the cross-corridor that leads to the river door. On my left the power room mutters behind a wall of slotted steel. On my right a stairway drops to a sublevel where compressors once slept. I tilt my head toward the ceiling as if admiring nothing. In the mirror of a stainless panel I catch the far corner of the hallway. Something moves there with courtesy and calculation. It is not a Dog. It is not a buyer. It is the kind of movement that studies you and edits itself to fit your shape.

["Wren,"] I whisper. ["Do you hear that."]

["I see it,"] she says. The calm in her tone goes thinner. ["Dead camera woke for two frames. Someone taught it to blink on a private cue. That is not local."]

"Understood," I say. I set the glass down on a steel surface that reflects a woman who is not afraid of interruptions. I skim the line of the power room as if checking my hair in its louvered skin. The hum in the building shifts by a hair. The hair cuts my attention into smaller pieces so I can count faster.

I reach the bend, allow my weight to settle into the foot that lets me pivot without offense, and let Velvet's mouth compose a smile I have used to walk through worse rooms with fewer exits. The air changes temperature. Footfalls find a cadence that is not mine.

Scene 2 waits one step beyond the corner.

IT STEPPED INTO VIEW with the assurance of something that had measured this corridor before I was born. Matte coat, clean planes, a face that knew how to imitate humanity without wasting surplus motion. Not Sable's theatrical grin. Not a Ravel Dog's blunt boredom. This one watched for the angle a breath makes when it meets bone. The body carried height a little over Velvet's, shoulders tuned to suggest a Forge weight without the bulk, stance aligned over the balls of the feet the way Stray settles when he wants to look harmless. A study wearing skin.

"Velvet," it said, the syllables even and pleasant, as if we were colleagues arriving at the same sink. "Always an entrance."

"Always an audience," I answered, and let my head tilt just enough to sell indifference.

Inside, a small cold thing uncoiled. I could feel Velvet's balance refine itself in tiny increments, the way a tightrope walker measures wind with skin. The shell is built for poise and persuasion. It is not built to admit fear. Fear came anyway, precise and polite, and sat down in the place where I keep the old names.

Mirror began to move, and with the first step I recognized myself. Not the face. The grammar. The leading shoulder that I use to bait a reach. The measure of distance I teach Velvet to keep so a hand that thinks it is catching a wrist finds only air. It matched those things, and then it chose a new one that belonged to Forge, a short stop before impact, hip turned to feed weight into the elbow. The reach arrived, and then the strike followed half a beat behind in a rhythm that belonged to a different body. My body. I saw the trick as it landed, and the recognition sickened me more than the pain.

I let the blow slide off the upper arm rather than catch it, spun inside the line, and fed it an elbow across the jaw that would have made Forge proud. A tidy sound came back through my forearm. Composite on composite. Mirror absorbed it, recalculated, and slid away on footwork that had Wisp's lightness without her joy. It was like sparring with an echo that had been sharpened to cut.

["That first step is Forge's set,"] Wren said in my ear, voice low and quick. ["Then it borrowed Stray's drop. The mix is wrong. It has watched you from more than one angle."]

"Tell me something kind," I said, and parried a hand that wanted my throat with a palm that had better ideas.

["Kind is later,"] she replied. ["Jam ready on your mark. If it tags you I will burn the handshake."]

Mirror feinted left with Velvet's favorite distraction, a hip turn that redirects attention so the hand can hunt on a different plane. I almost honored the feint because the muscle memory lives deep, then forced the body to be stupid on purpose. I stepped the wrong way, let the heel skid, and gave myself no leverage to strike from. It was a deliberate error. I wanted to see if it would stutter at novelty.

It did not stutter. It adapted. The left hand changed from feint to grab, closed on my wrist, and the right brought up a device no bigger than a coin. The filament unspooled clean as a hair and kissed the back of my hand, exactly where a sensor suite feeds balance to this shell. A mild current touched the nerves, almost friendly. My overlay flashed white at the edges.

["Line in,"] I said through my teeth. ["Sampling. Not a stun."]

["Hold for three,"] Wren answered. ["I am cutting the echo with noise that will smell like maintenance."]

Mirror tightened its grip. My thoughts broke into unpleasantly clean pieces. Does anything about me live outside habits and trajectories. Can a person be reduced to a list of angles. If they can, who am I once those angles are stolen. I shoved the questions down because they did not help, and drove my knee into the hinge of its leg. The servo whined, a neat mechanical protest, and the grip loosened. I tore backward, skin prickling with the sensation that something had been read and copied.

It came on again, faster now, shifting between styles like someone flipping channels. Wisp's quick shift to the outside line. Stray's reckless fake stumble that turns to a low cut. Forge's blunt stop that trades bruises for position. I recognized all of it, and that recognition stole my air more efficiently than any choke. It felt like losing ground to my own past.

We traded hits in a corridor loud with old compressors and new breath. I slid under its reach and found ribs with a punch that belonged to a different night in a different room. The impact traveled well through Velvet, a compact transfer of intention. Mirror answered with a hook of its own that paired my timing with a better angle. It caught cheek rather than chin, but the strike was still good enough to paint heat through Velvet's artificial dermal layer. I tasted nothing, which is worse than blood.

["It is predicting your choices,"] Wren said, breath tight. ["Change your count. Breathe on odd numbers. Break your own rhythm."]

I did the ugly thing again. Heel too flat. Shoulder too square. Chin too high. Mistakes I have trained out of every body. It bought me half a second of confusion in Mirror's eyes. That half second let me slam it into the louvered wall of the power room and rake it across the vents. The louvers bit into the coat and tore it in two narrow lines. Underneath, the plating flashed the color of bare hardware, and along the forearm I saw the connector again, tidy and eager.

It tried to catch my wrist by memory. I offered elbow instead, then walked up the wall, hooked a foot behind its neck, and rode the body down with a torque I learned in rooms where no one thought to look up. We hit the grate together. The sound drew one Dog from the far end who stared at us, tried to decide whose mess we were, then decided the answer was not priced for his wage.

Mirror rolled under me like a cat twisting itself through a narrow gate. It used Stray's drop to slip free, then fired a short punch that carried Forge's weight. I took it on the shoulder and let the joint absorb it, then gave it Velvet's palm to the bridge of the nose. The touch was precise rather than cruel. A shock, not a break. The head rocked back and then stilled, eyes refocusing with no human delay at all. It knew where to look. Right at me. Right at the past that taught it this game.

["South hall lens blinked,"] Wren said. ["Secondary watchers are either bored or complicit. I have the jam ready. Say when."]

"Now," I said.

The corridor shook with a low animal hum as the Wendigo's antenna farm poured a wide-band headache into the relay I had disliked from the start. The ceiling lights buzzed. Something in the cage hummed out of tune. Mirror's visor fluttered, recovered, fluttered again. It stepped back one pace, not to retreat, but to create a clean frame for its next move. That is my habit. It felt obscene to see it from the outside.

I pressed. The body has a nasty answer when someone insists on poise. I gave it indelicate weight. Shoulders through sternum. Knee on thigh. Foot to instep. Nothing elegant. All of it effective. We went into the cage bars again and rattled them with enough force to wake the old bolts. The back of my mind tracked inventory. Tap still seated. Parasite still feeding. Data still moving. That inventory kept me honest when the fight tried to become pride.

Mirror snared my wrist again, same spot, even while off balance. The filament kissed skin and I felt the small tug I dread. Not a download. A taste. A shard being asked to peel away from the whole. Wren's jam cut across the connection like grit poured into a bearing. The pull stuttered from clean to dirty. It still took something. Smaller than it wanted. Larger than I was willing to surrender.

I smashed its hand against the cage hinge. The filament gave with a nervous little snap. Mirror's fingers tightened once in a reflex that read as fury and then released. It staggered back a pace. The coat sloughed from one shoulder where the louvers had opened it, revealing a polished surface scored where I had not expected polish at all. Money had gone into this shape. Not swaggering money. Careful money.

"Who paid for you," I asked before I could silence my mouth.

It did not answer, which was worse than mockery. It threw a short flare that belonged in a bad manual and a good ambush. The bright hiss filled the corridor with hungry light. I stamped the floor switch by memory and drowned the space with mist from the old fire suppression lines. The flare sizzled and sulked. Steam rose and turned the air into a white room with bodies.

It vanished into that white the way ink disappears into milk. No footfalls. No suggestion of weight. Only the polite absence left by something that knows how to exit while someone else stares. I lunged for the place where the shape had been because sometimes you win the impolite race. My hand closed on torn cloth and nothing else. The cloth came away in my fist. It was too clean even when ruined. The smell was sterile and expensive.

["Roof lens got a shadow,"] Wren said, already moving maps under her hands. ["Too light for a person. Too direct for a bird. It is using magnet pads to ride the I-beams. Your door is wrong now. Use the east ladder. The sleepwalker has woken, but he is only awake enough to smoke."]

"Understood," I said. I pushed through the mist until the corridor remembered it was a place people walk. My shoulder ached with the false memory of bruises. Velvet does not bruise in ways that matter, which can be worse. Pain without proof can unspool a person faster than a wound.

One of the Dogs finally decided to make his job mean something and drew a knife. He held it like a pen. I nodded at him with the sort of sorrow one brings to a broken appliance and turned my body so he would have to choose between following me and protecting his inventory. He chose the inventory, which is the only loyal choice he had, and I was grateful.

I ran the east ladder two rungs at a time, not because I needed speed, but because I needed a number I could control. Two rungs, two breaths, two doubts folded into a pocket where they could not slow my hands. At the top, air tasted like river metal and machine heat. The roof guard held a cigarette and stared at nothing. I let him keep both.

On the far beam a smear of mist broke where a magnet had skidded. The smear ended at a gap between roof skin and scaffold rail. Beyond it the city opened like a throat. Mirror had gone somewhere that would not be obvious from the ground. Not a victory. Not a loss. A subtraction.

I let my hands shake once. Not long. Just enough to tell the nervous system that it had been seen. Then I went back inside, gathered what we came for, and walked out by a path that did not invite pursuit. The cold room hummed behind me, untroubled by the difference between a stolen file and a dead man in a chair.

["Report,"] Wren asked when the Wendigo took me in and the hatch pulled the day to a close around our shoulders.

"Alive. Angry. Missing one coat," I said, and dropped the torn strip beside the console.

"They got a shard. Small. Wrapped in your noise. Enough to season their next attempt."

["We will salt it,"] she said. Her hands were already on the work, eyes flicking between graphs and the pulse at my throat. ["We will hurt them for choosing the taste."]

The shell trembled in a way Velvet never admits. I gripped the edge of the console until the tremor learned where to sit. It passed like a wave that had been told the shore was closed.

"I am tired of being harvestable," I said, and heard the childish sound of it as it left my mouth.

"You are not a crop," Wren said. "You are a person. They only win if you mistake yourself for a pattern." She touched my wrist where the filament had kissed and left nothing visible. "Does it feel like you are bleeding," she asked, quiet and practical.

"Yes," I said.

"Good," she replied. "We know where to bandage."

The van rolled us out of the cannery's shadow. Steam thinned across the windshield. The river gleamed in the ungenerous way Klade has taught it. In the reflection I saw Velvet's face, a work of art I can abandon and become again. I saw the place under that face where a smaller person sits and counts. I saw the gap in the count where Mirror had reached in and taken a pebble to seed a future argument.

Wren's voice returned to the channel after a long breath. ["I have a sanitation escort on Thirteenth. Keep the windows dull. The city is pretending not to see us."]

"Good," I said. I closed my eyes for two heartbeats and opened them to the work in front of me. We still had to finish the job. We still had to tell a man with rings that his soup was better than his jokes. We still had to sit in a warm room and pretend the day had not become a study of whether I am anything but my habits.

The torn cloth on the console looked harmless. I folded it once and put it in a pocket I keep for reminders. Then I told the van to take us home by a route that does not encourage ghosts.

THE WENDIGO TOOK US in the second the hatch read the pattern of my knuckles. The cabin smelled like mint and warmed wiring, which is to say it smelled like the closest thing to safety I have ever built. Wren already had the med unit open and a wrap in her hands. She looked at me first, not the screen, and then put the wrap down because the color in my mouth was wrong but not urgent.

"What did they take," she asked.

"A sliver," I said. "Handshake residue. Enough to teach them how my wrist thinks about distance and time. Maybe enough to give them a hint about where my attention rests when I lie."

Wren's mouth made a line that would be a scar if the world were fair. "We can salt that," she said. "We can teach the next handshake to tell a different story."

"We can," I said. "It will not love us for it."

She pulled the clip from my sleeve and held it like a thorn she meant to keep. "You hurt it," she said.

"I did not finish it," I answered. "I never do."

The van rolled. The municipal coat across the windows shifted to fit the light. Wren flicked a switch and the seats were cradles again, consoles rising like small altars to the god of making it through today. We still had a job, and the job does not care about the sermon in your head.

I switched back to Wisp for the last pull. The shift took longer than it should have. The darkness came with a static hiss that reminded me of cheap radio programming on a storm day. When the world rose again, my hands trembled in a rhythm that did not belong to any of the shells. I held the edges of the console until the tremor found a place to sit.

"You are allowed to be shaken," Wren said, reading the way my shoulders steal inches when I pretend they are not mine.

"I am allowed many things," I said. "Today I am allowed to finish the work."

The cache was healthy. The tap had fed more than we planned for. Names and numbers that would let us unspool a thread from the Ravel Dogs to a buyer on the east side who thinks quiet neighborhoods stay that way without bribery. A training set that never should have been in a cannery, labeled as if a contractor were teaching a forklift to sing. The parasite reported back from the relay in a voice that did not know how to lie. The Dogs had been a pass-through for a test on live infrastructure. The relay was a mirror-net node. Not the kind that runs entertainment. The kind that studies how a city carries itself.

Wren traced three paths on the map with one finger and gave me a look that aims to be kind and lands on true. "We are not free of this," she said.

"I have never been free of anything I refuse to name," I said. "Freedom is not a door.

It is the practice of not building one.”

“You can keep saying that,” she said. “Or you can let it make a dent in the room.”

There are things I will only say when a machine and a person are listening at the same time. “Sable wants the performance,” I said. “Mirror wants the bones. One knows me from a stage. The other from a lab. There is nowhere to stand between them that does not feel like a target painted on an apology.”

Wren reached across the small space and put her hand over mine. Her palm was warm. Wisp’s skin took the heat like a gift. “You taught me the math of exits,” she said. “I can teach you the math of staying.”

“Not today,” I said. “Today we deliver a package.”

Lanterns hung low on twine above the lane, each glass belly holding a slow coil of light that turned the wet air to honey. Vendors hawked last bowls and late dumplings to people who always had somewhere else to be. Overhead, tram cables thrummed like a muted harp. The van shifted her municipal skin to the dull gray of sewer service and rolled to a stop beside a stack of crates that smelled like ginger and metal. Juno did a quiet circle and perched above our hatch with the attitude of a shrine guardian pretending to be a bird.

We stepped down into the alley and let the crowd carry our shapes toward FOY HOUSE. The sign looked older than the building, letters repainted until the strokes remembered a steadier hand. Steam flowered against the windows. Condensation turned the glass into quicksilver, which meant anyone inside could decide that privacy was an honest product. A woman in a rain cape lifted a child so he could breathe noodle vapor straight from the door. He laughed like the air had told him a secret.

Inside, the room balanced noise and warmth with the stubborn grace of places that survive by feeding people rather than impressing them. Tables were metal, chairs were honest wood, and the floor kept its stains the way some families keep heirlooms. An ancient fan turned slow above the cash counter. A radio burbled a station that thought everyone needed one more horn solo. Men in work coats hunched over broth. Two students in perfect shoes pretended their soup was a meeting. An old cat slept on a bag of rice and bared a tooth at anyone who called it cute.

Tava Nine had chosen the booth beneath the fogged window and arranged himself the way a poster arranges a promise. Rings bright as traffic, hair that could not decide between silver and theater, smile set to win without admitting it had ever lost. He held his spoon like a conductor preparing to scold a string section.

"Wren," he said, rising by half because his knees had opinions, "and the smallest hurricane in Klade. My compliments to the weather for delivering you intact." His eyes flicked to me and then to Wren again. "Is it bring your ward to work day, or have you decided to make me feel paternal."

Wren did not bother to hide her amusement. "Wisp works better than most adults you know," she said, and slid into the booth. "You should be grateful your soup gets to meet her."

Tava pressed one hand to his chest as if the kitchen had served him flattery. "The soup is honored. I am the soup's humble representative." His gaze returned to me, more measuring now, less performance. "Wisp then. I have heard the name in places that enjoy keeping good things quiet."

I took the outside seat where I could see the door and Wren's hands and the metal kitchen pass where bowls arrived like small miracles. Velvet would have owned this room. Wisp slipped through it without making ripples, which was the point. The persona held like silk stretched over wire. I kept my face open and my hands where he could see them.

"We brought what you paid for," I said, and set the deck on the table. "Stolen ledgers, route lists, names enough to fill a party, and the garnish you like to brag about. The Dogs were not the only ones playing vendor."

Tava touched the deck with a knuckle. The ring he wore for luck tapped once and made a bright note. He transferred the files to his slate with the breezy competence of a man who has lied to a hundred systems and found them all polite. As the scroll built on his screen, the showman receded and the trader arrived. Twice he paused long enough to show respect. Twice he glanced at Wren as if to share a joke and decided to save it for when she slept.

"This is not garnish," he said at last. "This is an entree that walks to the table on its own legs and asks for a drink." He flicked a title with his ring finger. "Look at that invoice, pretending to be a repair order for lifts. The fibrous poetry of criminal accounting. And this, my dear conspirators, is the sort of training set that would make a boardroom sweat through its linen. You did not have to put it in my pocket."

"You hired us to recover what was stolen," I said. "Leaving the rest for anyone with a truck and a conscience would have been rude."

He studied me over the steam and pretended to scold. "Children these days," he said, "stealing in full sentences." The word children sat on the table a while and then rolled away without starting a fight. He shifted tone. "Payment first. Then we embarrass each other with gratitude."

The stick he produced was fat with credits, a little ridiculous in a world that rarely allows generosity to be visible. He slid it to Wren with a flourish, then ruined the moment by sloshing a bit of broth on his sleeve. He dabbed it with a napkin and groaned as if the soup had insulted his tailor.

"You always overpay when the noodles are good," Wren said, checking the balance with a glance and palming the stick into the pocket she wears when she wants to look careless.

"Of course I do," Tava replied. "It keeps the kitchen generous and my name near the top of the list when people with tools need places to sit." He pushed the deck back toward me with two fingers. "You look like you were almost a story," he added, more quietly now. "The kind where the punchline costs skin."

Wren met my eyes for a heartbeat. I let the moment pass me, then set my voice to float above the broth. "A clerk tried to be clever," I said. "We talked him out of it."

"Clerks can be the most dangerous people in any room," Tava murmured. He did not press. The man knows what not to buy.

A bowl landed on our table with a little rattle and a lot of perfume. The owner himself delivered it, scowling with the benevolence of small gods. He looked at me, looked at Wren, looked at Tava as if Tava were the reason rain exists, and thumped the bowl down between us. "House special," he said. "Share like you were raised right."

The broth was pale and rich, the noodles obedient, the greens bright enough to pretend the city cared about vitamins. I took the first bite because Wren nodded and because ritual matters when the day has shifted your bones. Heat climbed into my face and softened the noise in my head. Wisp's smaller throat made the steam feel like a favor.

Tava spooned his own with the reverence of a man who needs witnesses. "I invite you to admire the restraint," he said. "Only three rings today. My minimalist era."

"You wore four to a meeting with a priest," Wren said. "He asked if you were auditioning to be a saint."

"I told him I had not earned that level of hypocrisy," Tava replied, pleased with his own memory. He leaned in and lowered his voice until it fit the booth like a secret. "A practical note. Two men have circled the window three times. One talks very loudly on a phone that does not seem to have a battery. The other limps on a leg that limps differently each lap. They are either bored or very bad at being honest. You will leave by the kitchen when you are ready. The cat will judge you. It judges all of us."

"Payment cleared," Wren said. "We will try not to bother your cat."

"Impossible," he said. "You both bother the world by existing. That is why I feed you." He let the grin fade and placed his palms on the table, rings to metal, voice to truth. "Bring me more garnish when you find plates that deserve it. Bring me stories I am allowed to laugh at, not the kind that make me buy new shirts. And if someone is writing your names on glass in places where names should not appear, consider letting me take a cloth to it. I am good with smudges."

I felt the urge to answer with a line that would keep him entertained and us safe. Wisp is built for deflection as much as delight. Instead I said, "We appreciate the cloth," and meant it.

He leaned back and watched the steam climb. "You are both too serious for a noodle house," he said. "You are scaring the basil." Then, to me, softer, "It is rare to meet a worker your size who looks at the room like that. I mean this kindly. Whoever taught you to count the exits deserves dessert."

"Someone did," I said. "He is asleep in the van, and if you try to meet him he will pretend to be six feet tall and make you feel short."

"Adorable," Tava said, eyes dancing. "I will send a cake to your van with a note that says it is for a giant." He tipped his chin toward the kitchen. "Go before the fake limp graduates to courage."

We made an art of finishing the broth without rushing. Wren left a tip heavy enough to qualify as medicine. I slid from the booth and let the room decide that a kid had finished a late dinner with family. The owner barked at us for using the kitchen door, then pointed with his ladle to the back hall and added a slice of pickled radish to Wren's pocket when he thought I was not looking.

The back corridor smelled like sesame and heat. A calendar with a photo of mountains no one in Klade would ever climb hung above a stack of flour sacks. The cat had moved to a crate of scallions and blinked at us with the weary contempt of creatures that remember when cities were made of wood. Wren scratched its chin and earned a threatened bite that stopped short of contact. Respect established, we took the stair and pushed into the narrow service alley.

Night pooled there in the way it does when buildings lean together to talk. Rain tapped on an old tin awning and then pattered down onto the broken brick. Farther up the lane, a sign for a watch repairman flickered and failed, then decided to glow. The Wendigo waited with her windows fogged and her engine very slightly warm, like a friend who refuses to sleep until you are home.

We climbed in without ceremony. The hatch closed with the soft authority that always steadies my hands. Wren set the credit stick beside the torn strip of cloth I had pocketed from Mirror and looked at both like they were parts of the same story. Juno clicked once from the rail and sent a single image to the dash, a static capture of the market quarter with two men in frame. One spoke to a dead phone. The other tried to choose a leg.

"Kitchen exit was the right choice," Wren said.

"Tava notices things he could profit from and chooses not to. That is his art," I said. I watched the rain draw lines down the glass and pretended each line was a thought I could file.

Wren eased the van into gear. The municipal coat wiped our scent from the corner and painted us as a vehicle no one wanted to remember. Tava's laugh followed us through the window as the door swung shut behind a new customer. Somewhere above us, the tram sang to itself.

"You held the room well," Wren said, eyes on the mirrors.

"Wisp can look harmless until the soup cools," I answered. The shell settled around me, familiar now in ways I never decided. "He called me a child. I did not mind."

"You are allowed to be both dangerous and young," she said. "The city keeps trying to make those choices for us."

The Wendigo turned toward the river road, and Klade changed color the way it does after rain when the neon gives up and the concrete decides to glow. I sat with my hands in my lap and let the quiet do its work. The day had taught Mirror something about me. It had also taught me something about the day. I filed that, too, in a place that is not a door and not a room, only a practice.

At the corner, a delivery bike shot past and the rider lifted two fingers in a salute at no one in particular. I found the gesture comforting. The van hummed. Juno rotated once on her rail and yawned the way only a machine that likes you will. On the floor by my feet, the payment stick winked once without meaning to. Tava would ask us back before the week grew teeth. I took that as a promise that the city had not forgotten how to be transactional in ways that were almost kind.

"Home," I told the van.

She agreed, and we let her lead.

Chapter Ten

Orinox Requiem

HIKARI

THE RAIN HAD THINNED to a cold mist by the time the Wendigo drifted into the freight zone behind the Orinox data outpost. On paper the building was a municipal telecom repeater with a service contract that lived on a sleepy spreadsheet. In concrete and steel it was a rectangle of brushed panels and smoked glass planted at the hinge of two alleys. A perfect place to move information under a name that never had to blush. Sodium lamps bled a flat orange across the loading apron. Water ran along the seams in the concrete and gathered in a drain whose grate was newer than the ones beside it. New money always leaves a line if you squint.

We parked with the quiet entitlement of a sanitation rig on a late route. The van adjusted her external coat to match a city service livery, then softened her engine note until it blended with the sound of ventilation fans. Juno swept the roofline in a tight oval and settled above the hatch with a single click that sounded like patience.

Wren pulled up the building overlays and rotated them on the main screen. "Four entrances," she said, tapping each with a nail. "Front lobby with a bored receptionist after hours. Freight roll-up on the west wall. A staff door near the electrical room, badge access only. Roof access from the stairwell that no one oils. Your floor is one flight down from the lobby, behind two checkpoints and a glass corridor that likes to watch itself."

I sat still and breathed Velvet into place. The shell woke like a dancer warming the small bones first. Fingers flexed, toes pressed against the deck, spine lengthened as if a wire had been clipped from the ceiling and hooked to the back of my skull. The interior sheath hummed along my nerves and gave weight to my hips, lightness to the step, and an algorithm of posture that did half the talking before I opened my mouth. I checked the shoulder where Mirror had tagged me two nights ago. The seam sat smooth and true. The pain lived only as memory, which can be worse than bruises.

"Headcount," I asked, eyes still on the screen.

"Six in the building," Wren said. "Two in the lobby playing a game and pretending to do rounds. One watching the freight corridor from a crate he never moves. One in the security nook beside the server hall, reading a policy manual to stay awake. Two in the control room in the center, monitoring the flow and telling themselves it is glamorous. Night shift hubris, not professionals. Cameras on a closed loop with timed checks from a remote node. I can blind a slice of the loop for eight minutes at a time without tripping the remote audit."

"Blind the freight and the staff door together," I said. "I would rather take two problems than fight the lobby."

Wren set the first blackout like a pianist placing a chord. The loop flickered to a clean slate, then returned as if nothing had happened. "You have your eight," she said. "Juno will ride the roof. I will pull a false maintenance ticket for the drain out front, just in case we need to explain our faces to anyone with a badge and ambition."

I tested the decoy handshake module in my sleeve, felt the faint tick as it spun up, then checked the microline concealed along my wrist. The cutter glided forward from its ring and sat against my palm, patient and thin. A ceramic blade nested in the seam at my left hip asked to be used. I slid it home again and told it not tonight if the room behaved. The pack on my back carried a low-profile tap and a parasite that would gossip with any trunk that pretended to be a good citizen.

Wren rounded the console and touched the back of my hand. She does that when she wants to say three things and save the air. Be careful. I will be here. Come back to me. She did not speak them. She did not need to.

I stepped into the hatch and let the night air lacquer my face with cold. The loading apron held that municipal quiet that never entirely feels safe. A janitorial cart leaned under the overhang by the service door. The mop head was too clean to be real. Someone likes props. I crossed to the staff entrance in a measured walk that said a badge on a lanyard was tucked into my coat. I paused at the reader as if waiting for a line to clear, turned my body slightly to take the camera out of my angle, and slid a magnetized credential cover across the plate. The reader blinked green for the idea of me. The lock popped like a polite throat being cleared. The door breathed out stale recycled air and let me in.

The corridor held white walls and gray vinyl floor with a pattern like rain dried into plastic. Three doors down. Electrical to the left. Janitor's closet to the right. Ahead, the freight hall. The man on the crate sat with his boot on a coil of shrink wrap and a handheld game console held low against his thigh. He did not look up. Velvet strolled instead of crept. She adjusted a cuff so a watch that did not exist would catch the overhead light. The guard's eyes slid to the gleam like every human eye does when it wants to witness something it imagines it can afford. I closed the distance two steps further than polite and bent my head as if asking a question I had no business asking.

"Do you know if the back elevator is still out," I asked. The tone carried a slight apology along with a promise that I would never demand more than he wanted to give. He lifted his gaze at the last syllable and saw a person shaped like the right kind of trouble. The answer formed in his mouth where a heartbeat should have been.

The microline moved against the seam behind his ear with a whisper. It parted the thin bundle that fed his neck rig. The smell of warm tin climbed into the air. He sagged forward and I caught his shoulders with a grip that would have looked like concern to a security camera that cared. I eased him behind the crate and arranged his hands across his stomach like he had practiced dying with dignity. His chest did not rise. It did not matter to anyone who counted bodies on a night like this.

["Freight hall clear,"] I said into the channel. ["Moving to security nook."]

["Loop still blind,"] Wren replied. ["Lobby guards have not noticed that their game paused. I did that on purpose. You have six minutes, then I have to give the cameras a breath."]

The security nook sat beside a glass corridor that met the server hall. A single guard leaned into a chair that had lost the argument with his back years ago. The policy binder spread across his lap had a ribbon marking the page where he would stop reading and retire. His attention held on a paragraph about fire exits while his mind spoke a language called nothing.

I stepped into the nook as if I were on the schedule and late. I did not hurry. Hurrying concedes guilt. The guard's eyes lifted. He saw a face that belonged to an office with nicer chairs.

"I need to clear a maintenance scan," I said, opening my palm as if a paper should be there. The hand told a story the mouth did not need to finish. He reached for the binder with his right hand and the console keypad with his left. The angle exposed the soft place under his jaw. My left hand closed on the bottom edge of the chair to anchor the movement. My right hand slid the ceramic blade from its seam and drew a single small line across the shallow skin. The blade vanished again. The cut found the artery fast. There was no time for noise. There was a moment of surprise, and then there was a quiet that belonged to old buildings and people who no longer had to be bored.

I held him upright until the last heat left his throat, then flattened the binder over the stain and rolled the chair back under the counter. The console blinked patiently. I used his dead hand to touch two keys, then wiped the prints with a square of lint cloth that never left fibers. The glass corridor beyond reflected me as a long dark shape with a face that had practiced being trusted. I walked into the reflection and let it open.

Server rooms always pretend to be holy. This one wore the hush properly. Racks stood in two spotless rows, blue status lights breathing a calm rhythm that told an expensive story to anyone who loved numbers. The floor hummed with a steady note that could put a nervous person to sleep. Cold air moved around my ankles and crept up my shins like a cat that wanted to test whether I belonged.

Halfway down the row an Orinox badge sat on top of a cable tester. The name printed on it did not matter, but the absence of scratches along the clip told me it was a newer hire. New people lose things and pretend they did not. I took the badge, scanned the hall, and found the main trunk at the back behind a vanity panel that wore the Orinox logo in a tone a little darker than the aluminum around it. Vanity panels are always easier to open than the plain ones. They are made to be admired, not defended.

I eased the panel up, set it against the rack, and breathed out the muscles that clench when you expect a trick. The trunk was clean and honest, which only means the lies lived farther along. I slipped the passive tap over the fiber and slid the parasite into the control block where it would listen for gossip and repeat what it had no right to know. My deck filled with columns of packet titles that had been dressed for the office. Vendor training. Throughput analysis. Employee wellness. Anything can wear a kind label if it wants to be invited inside.

["I have the river,"] I said. ["Pushing to cache and mirror to you."]

["Receiving,"] Wren said. Keys clicked under her voice. "Subprocesses flagged with child safety keywords. That is interesting and revolting. I will sort while you keep breathing. Guard path is about to send me a check. I need to free the loop for a minute."

I had three things I could do with a minute. Hurry, which invites mistakes. Hide, which invites curiosity. Or move to a new corner and look like furniture. Velvet chose furniture. I snapped the panel back into place, walked to the end of the row where a maintenance stool sat with a coil of clean velcro, and sat with my ankles crossed and my hands in my lap. A camera in the ceiling lensed my posture and decided that a consultant had outlasted her patience with the air and would leave soon. The loop cycled. Wren gave the cameras their breath. They inhaled, saw a woman waiting for a reason to be paid, and exhaled boredom that reached their remote monitor like a yawn on hold.

["You are covered again,"] Wren said. "Lobby guards are still pretending the game froze because of a patch. Control room is talking about noodles."

"Good," I said. "Give me twelve more and then kill the building if I ask."

"On your word."

I went back to the panel and bled more of the river into our cache. The parasite sent a delicate cough that meant it had found a second voice under the main line, a thin uplink that claimed to be a diagnostic channel. I taught it to hum in that key and keep humming as if the voice had always been there. The hum would mask the extra traffic long enough to move what we needed.

Footsteps entered the corridor through the lobby door. The sound came through the floor before it came through the air. A particular weight and a particular rhythm. Two people. One taller than the other. The taller led with his heels. The shorter dragged a little on the left foot. Their conversation came like a scrim of noise that never became language. I turned the corner of my mouth up and let Velvet tilt her head toward the far rack like it held the type of stubborn problem someone used to charge by the hour to fix. The men looked, saw the shape of a consultant, and measured their lives against the amount of trouble they wanted to invite. They chose to pass. That choice bought me time.

The packet titles changed shape. Wellness became retention. Retention became compliance. Compliance wore a dozen soft names and one hard one that tasted like metal. "SUBSTACK ECHO." That was not a newsletter. That was a feed. I tagged the family of labels and pulled them into their own lane. Wren's intake widened to make room.

["I think I have something I do not enjoy having,"] I said.

["I am already looking at a reflection of your distaste,"] Wren replied. Her voice had that quiet roughness she uses when anger is a tool that needs to stay on the mat for later. "Keep feeding. We take the whole garden, not one flower."

I worked the tap for six minutes more, enough to make our presence feel like a change in weather rather than a lightning strike. Then I closed the panel, wiped the edges, and walked out of the row with a stride that told the air I had solved something boring and would invoice later. The body did not rush. The mind counted, not doors, but ways to keep from thinking about the two men who would not wake in the morning. The count reached a number that did not make me proud and did not make me flinch either. Survival erodes neat lines.

The glass corridor returned my reflection as a thin silhouette moving through its favorite habitat. In the security nook the binder sat square on the counter with a crease that had not been there before. I straightened it from habit. In the freight hall the crate was still an alibi with a dead man behind it. I resisted the urge to set his hands better and walked to the staff door without looking back.

Outside, the mist had thickened to a soft net that beaded along Velvet's hair and turned the streetlights into halos that did not belong to saints. I crossed to the Wendigo as if I had the keys to the city in my pocket and wanted a warmer coat. The hatch opened, Wren's hand caught my elbow, and the van breathed me in.

We did not speak for a breath. That silence has become a ritual. It leaves room for the body to recognize that it still belongs to itself.

Wren slid the decoy sleeve off my wrist and replaced it with a fresh one. "Clean," she said. The word was clinical and kind.

I sat at the console and watched the river we had stolen pool into the cache and split into labeled channels that would let us choose where to drown next. The file trees for "SUBSTACK ECHO" unfolded along the side screen with a patience that felt obscene. The tag structure used nursery shapes to hide ugly mathematics. Triangles for cohorts, circles for control, stars for outcomes that would never shine on a child's ceiling.

The room had no temperature for a long moment. Juno clicked once on the rail as if to remind me that machines can be affectionate. Wren drifted a finger across the screen and nudged a folder into a place where later would not become never.

"Two minutes to scrub our footprints," she said. "Then we give the building back to itself."

"Kill the loop once more," I said. "On the freight and the staff door at the same time."

She did it without asking why. The cameras blinked. The proof of us stepped behind a curtain. The outpost returned to being a telecom repeater that deserved boredom.

I let Velvet's shoulders relax. It felt like taking off a ring that had cut my finger without drawing blood. "We own their night," I said. The sentence tasted like metal and mint.

"For now," Wren answered. "We own enough of it to make morning angry."

The van shifted her weight, eager to go. I looked at my hands and thought about the way the guard leaned forward when I asked him a question. Kindness and murder can use the same posture if you are not careful. I do not pretend that distinction is clean in the bodies I wear. I do try to remember it, which is not nobility. It is maintenance.

"Take us to the quiet road," I said. "I would like to look at what we stole while the city forgets to breathe for a few blocks."

Wren nodded and coaxed the Wendigo into the street. The municipal livery on the wrap panels dulled any curiosity that glanced our way. I opened the river again and watched it split across our glass. File names marched past like a parade that did not deserve music. Somewhere in the middle a set of headers appeared that did not belong in any building that pretended to serve phones.

Wren saw them the same instant I did. Her breath caught and then steadied by will. "We follow that in the stack," she said. "Inside. Not here."

"Inside," I agreed. "Together."

The Wendigo drifted through the mist as if the city had become a photograph. The outpost pulled away behind us and took its dead with it. Ahead, the road turned toward the part of Klade that throws shadows like veils. We drove into one that looked generous. The van accepted our weight and pretended the world did not notice. For a few minutes we let her lie for us.

THE WORLD NARROWED TO the bright oval of the deck's lens, then opened again into a room that had never existed in brick or steel. Orinox built its private network like a boutique office for people who wanted to believe their crimes wore suits. A reception desk sat in the middle of a sunlit atrium. Potted trees breathed a soft wind that did not come from any fan. The floor gleamed like poured glass. Overhead, daylight hung in a perfect cone that never moved. Nothing in here aged unless someone paid for the effect.

My avatar arrived as Wisp because the code in my hands thinks best when my body promises small and quick. The hair shone like spun silver, gathered in two neat puffs. The eyes were too clean, a dark mirror with a ring of electric blue, which is how this place wants you to look at yourself. Wren materialized to my right as her preferred silhouette, a woman in a field jacket with her copper hair pulled back and a paper map folded in one hand that never tore. She always brings a map into places where the walls lie. Juno became a thin wire halo above us, a quiet circle that drifted near the ceiling and threw down a lattice of faint lines. She looks like art when she is happiest.

"Layer check," Wren said, voice arriving to my left and inside my crown at the same time. In here sound can travel by touch if you trust the person speaking.

"Outer skin reads as hospitality," I answered. "Underlay smells like policy. Core wants to be a church. I can feel the permissions like velvet under rough cloth."

She smiled without wasting time. The map in her hand unfolded, then unfolded again. The paper was not paper. It was a heat map of authority, a honeycomb of places that could be opened without waking the keeper. The atrium stacked multiple illusions, each one costed to encourage a certain kind of visitor to leave a certain kind of footprint. The desk meant nothing. The potted trees were data caches designed to be shaken for fruit by someone with a nervous boss. The elevators at the far wall were metaphors for privilege and a machine that counted how often a person loved stairs.

"Substack Echo should live behind something that likes the sound of its own voice," Wren said. "Not finance, not scheduling, something dressed as wellness. Look for the friendly door."

Friendly doors in corporate nets have rounded corners. They glow faintly. They smile with their geometry. I walked the atrium in Wisp's light steps and felt the floor transmit a soft pressure back into my ankles, a ready-made path beneath the shine. That is how you herd visitors in a system. You write a comfort into the ground.

At the far end, past a fountain that sang in a key designed to lower heart rate, I found a glass corridor leading to an inner suite labeled EMPLOYEE EXPERIENCE. The lettering wore a shade that made expensive things look cheap and cheap things look expensive. It was a good lie. I palmed the reader and it warmed to the shape of my borrowed hand. The door opened without complaint.

Inside, the office became itself more completely. Conference rooms held gentle chairs and screens that played slides in a loop. A kitchen gleamed with untouched mugs. Hallways curved instead of turning, a choice made by designers who wanted to sell the idea of safety. Wren moved at my shoulder with an easy confidence that told the walls she belonged here. The map hovered between us, annotating itself in fine script where the network whispered with static. Juno's halo drifted through the ceiling without leaving a mark, then chimed once to mark a blind spot.

We reached a corridor where three doors faced each other at precise angles. The first wore a plaque that said RETENTION. The second said COMPLIANCE, then added a smile at the end of the word that made the hair along my neck try to lift. The third said ECHO, etched in a font that desperately wanted to be modern and failed by a fraction. Friendly door, yes. Friendly like a sales pitch.

"After you," Wren said.

"Together," I answered.

We palmed the panel at the same time. The handle accepted our heat and our names, or the names we had woven for this moment. The room opened into a library that held no books. Rows of thin metal frames rose from the floor like reeds and held panes of light where pages should be. Each pane carried a title along the bottom and a field of faint glyphs that moved when you looked directly at them, then held still when you tried to read them. The air in here had no temperature. The stillness was performative, the hush of a museum where the plaques are more expensive than the paintings.

Wren moved along the first row and let her fingers hover a centimeter above each pane. You do not touch surfaces in a space like this unless you want to give the curator a reason to clear their throat. She spoke softly, and her words hung in the room the way dust hangs in sun. "Echo is a pull from the field into a cleaner shape," she said. "They collect raw behavior from the public net, then pin it to someone's file until it resembles a person. This is the waiting room before the pins."

I watched the titles as they rearranged themselves to please my attention. Comfort words appeared first. Performance. Wellness. Engagement. Then came the words that live in the basement and always come upstairs eventually. Cohort. Attrition. Control. Near the end of the row a cluster of panes wore shapes instead of nouns, triangles and squares, stars that flickered in time with a pulse they wanted me to share. The nearest pane held a single line across its surface, red against gray, captioned with a date.

"Drill down," I said.

Wren reached for the pane, stopped just short of contact, and drew a circle in the air. The circle opened like a lens. We stepped through together.

The library flattened into a corridor of profiles. Each profile resolved as a room that contained one chair, one table, one toy. No faces, only silhouettes, each one beveled to look like a different age. Light fell through a virtual camera that never left the ceiling. Notes glowed in the corner of each room, neatly labeled, written in the clipped language of people who have to pretend they are not talking about pain. Subject A17, response lag to stimulus set Y. Subject C04, compliance index during sleep cycle. Subject E12, removal of environmental enrichment yields accelerated decisional narrowing. The chair in the last room was too small for a grown body.

I felt Wisp's hands curl without orders. In here the avatar has only the sensations you allow it to have. I allowed this one.

"Mirror watched me in a hallway like this," I said. "Not here, but close enough to smell it."

Wren's map folded back into her hand. She did not look at me, but the set of her mouth softened. "They built the forms like offices so people who sign off can keep eating lunch," she said. "If you draw the bars to look like furniture, you can call yourself a designer instead of a jailer."

We moved deeper. The corridor became a gallery of derivative choices. Rooms repeated with slight changes in color, in the angle of a camera, in the distance between chair and table. At the end, a locked door waited with a latch that took two hands to open. Wren lifted her paper map and laid it over the lock, as if her own image could talk the code into misplacing a rule. The latch sighed, then yielded. We stepped through into the back of the house where names stop trying to look polite.

SUBSTACK ECHO, CORE held a single chamber with a ceiling too high to belong to any office. In the center, a well sunk into the floor, round and black at the bottom. The surrounding floor was inlaid with concentric rings of text. You could read them if you were cruel. Each circle carried a layer of the pipeline, pulled from field, scrubbed to taste, laced to target, applied to body. Around the rings stood three forms like clerks made from glass. They watched us without eyes and smiled whenever we looked at them, a reflex coded by someone who thought it would be soothing.

Wren lifted her hand and wrote a narrow bridge across the well with the tip of her finger. The bridge held because she believes that bridges should hold. I followed her out over the black and glanced down without meaning to. The pit showed no depth, only a reflection. It was not my avatar I saw, not really. It was the outline of the room where a child once lay on a slab that hummed. Ghost code remembers the camera even when you unplug it. I felt my throat close and opened it again by force.

"Index," Wren said. "Show me source."

The ring closest to the well rotated. A column of panes bloomed from a seam and arranged themselves like a filing cabinet with no drawers. The titles no longer wore perfume. PROGRAM RELL. MIRROR, TRAINING SETS. VYRE FAMILY, RE-VISION 7. CHILD BEHAVIORAL PRIME, COHORT THETA. I reached toward the second and the third because they were already warm against my skin.

The pane for MIRROR expanded as if a breath inside the glass had grown bold. Frames of video assembled themselves into a quiet grid. I knew some of the angles. I knew some of the rooms. Children sat in chairs wearing sensor crowns. Adolescents walked white corridors with numbers on their backs instead of names. A child-sized body lay in a metal cradle and stared at the ceiling with the resigned attention that belongs to people who have learned to count lights. In one clip a technician made a note without looking up when a subject cried. I had always thought the worst rooms belonged to my story alone. The grid showed me I was arrogant.

"Wren," I said, and did not give the word a task.

"I see it," she answered. She touched a pane labeled COHORT THETA and pulled up a feed that dressed raw data in the costume of a friendly app. Stickers marked successful tasks. Confetti fell when a child met a target. Notes in the margin linked to schedules. One row of notes bore a familiar hand. The colons favored even spacing. The periods sat a fraction lower than the line. The s in checksum tilted right out of habit.

Wren's fingers had stopped moving. She stared at the line as if the glyphs might apologize. "I wrote that symbol pack," she said. Her voice had gone quiet as cotton. "Not for this. For a hospital interface that trained motor recovery. I licensed it under a generic clause. It was open to adaptation inside a private network. They skinned it and tucked it under lights like this. I was proud of the modular timing at the time. You could shape difficulty without breaking flow."

"They paid for theft that looks like kindness," I said. The sentence came out flatter than I intended. Flat sometimes feels safe.

"Parallel programs," she said, working the dates out loud to keep her hands from shaking. "My licensing work sits at the same time you were in a room with a slab. I left the company the quarter after this one. I thought I was fired for arguing about reporting ethics. I might have been fired because I refused to write the next piece. Or I wrote the piece they needed to make their next theft less expensive, and then I discovered it, and then they folded my job into a different title until I left."

She swallowed and pointed at a different pane. "Open the VYRE file."

The pane unfurled into schematics and test logs, small notes about weight distribution and motion prediction. The top corner wore a mark that matched the audio Juno had pulled a week ago, VYRE_07. Under it a column of text tagged an unexpected category. Donor Behavioral Overlay, H-SERIES. The H did not need an explanation. The list of patterns used to seed training runs read like a checklist of my worst decisions, cleaned of blood.

"Pull that," Wren said, and now the gentleness left her tone. "All of it. Mirror too. I want to tear the set and salt the earth."

The clerks made of glass turned toward us in a synchronized pivot. They did not speak, but a faint chime rippled through the chamber, the sound a museum makes when you cross a line you cannot see. Juno's halo descended until it glowed level with our shoulders. Her lattice hardened. Wren raised the map like a shield and wrote a new edge on the air.

"We are not looting," Wren said to the room, as if reason could change protocol. "We are making a record."

The record did not care. The clerks smiled. The well brightened by one degree. I felt the bridge shift under my feet, not in the muscles, but in the part of the brain that believes in balance even inside code. I set my weight as if the ground were real. In here that helps.

"Take the child rooms," Wren said, eyes on the glass people. "Every cohort, especially Theta."

"I will thread the feed through a dummy that looks like an approved audit," I said. "If anyone checks, they will think a manager is reviewing highlights to prepare for a review."

We moved in the way partners move when terror has been asked to wait. I drew the child room corridors into a tight loop and passed that loop through Wren's map so the system would be told a story it was already tired of hearing. The panes for Theta trembled and then slid off their rails as if bored by their own weight. Wren packed them into a shape that sat like a long, careful box, then wrote a signature on the side that matched a director who had retired to a gated set of servers where nothing breaks.

She touched my wrist, and for a second the atrium outside returned, the fountain singing soft, the trees breathing. Then we were back above the well. The clerks had stepped closer. Juno's halo thinned to a bright wire. It hummed and shed sparks that did not fall. The bridge trembled for show, then held.

"What else," Wren asked.

"Protocol RELL," I said. The name lived in the folder like a splinter. "Rell is a spoken word in one of the old worker dialects. It means to smooth a board so it will not snag hands." I opened the pane.

A diagram appeared, clean as an apology. Input, passage, output. A child is not a board, but the steps treated a child like one. Data in, behavior shaped, expectation measured against a line that did not belong to any person in the room. Halfway down the page a list glowed faintly, like a burn healing under a layer of skin. Required Staff Tools. The first line cited a module Wren had written, six years ago, before she understood the uses to which the module would be put. The second line cited a module I had cracked in order to cut my restraints. The third line listed a set of camera protocols with a signature I recognized from a patch submitted by a junior developer who had bragged on a forum about learning to make hardware smile.

The lines drew themselves into a story without asking our permission. I could see the hallway without closing my eyes. I could hear the hum of the slab even though this room had no air. Wren's hand had frozen over the list without touching it. Her fingers curled at the second line, paused, then spread again as she mastered the instinct to try to erase a word with skin.

"We are in the same paragraph," she said. "I wrote a door into a toolkit for a rehab clinic. They built that door into a wall. You found a flaw in the wall and walked through it."

"And you got fired because someone could not afford to keep you in the same building as your name," I said. "Or you left because it cost too much to stay, and they wrote a memo that called it restructuring."

"They always call it restructuring," she said, and that small joke was the lever she needed to breathe.

The clerks stepped closer again. One of them tilted its head. That motion looked like concern, which was worse than a weapon. The well brightened once more. Somewhere outside the chamber, a line counter ticked. Time had started to matter again.

"I have enough to hurt them," Wren said. "Not in court. In contracts. In the places they use to hide a thing behind a budget. I can pull three vendor agreements by breakfast and teach them to hate mornings for a week."

"Take one more," I said, and pointed at the pane marked DONOR OVERLAY, H-SERIES. The list under it was short and ugly. It did not carry my name because I have none. It carried a code that I know like a scar. The code linked out to recordings, partial, ghostly, fragments of balance and reach, the kind of small choreography a body learns when it grows up without anyone telling it the right way to stand. That was what Mirror tasted in the corridor. That was what they brought here to grow in larger soil.

Wren did not ask if I wanted to look. She knows me. She wrapped the file in the same audit sleeve she had used for Theta and passed it to Juno. Juno accepted the weight and swung it into her halo. The wire brightened to a ring of pale fire and then dimmed again.

"Exit," Wren said, voice gone brisk. "We take the front stairs. We look like consultants with a slide deck. We complain about power usage until the atrium is behind us."

I did not move. The well held the reflection of a room I had already survived. It will always hold it. That is how memory works when you wire it into a building. I took one step closer to the edge and watched my avatar's outline turn glassy along the jaw. Somewhere an algorithm wanted to make me into a clerk. I smiled at it without teeth. It smiled back. I thought about the child in the run of rooms who counted lights to stay sane. I thought about the young woman who had written a clean line of code because she believed in recovery. Then I reached down, picked up a small loose tile from the ring of text, and flicked it into the well. It did not fall. It landed on a shelf that should not exist and stayed there.

"Petty," Wren said.

"Symbolic," I answered.

She nodded once, which in our language means both. We walked the bridge together. The clerks watched us pass. One lifted a hand in a gesture that could have been a wave or a warning. The library behind ECHO exhaled as we left, then reorganized its panes to look like an office again. We crossed the atrium without looking at the fountain. The sunlight above never changed its angle. That is the only way this place can keep pretending to be day.

Outside the deck, the Wendigo hummed. The cabin smelled like mint and hot wire. My body found the weight of real boots and the promise of metal under skin. Wren pulled the jack, then sat there a long moment and let her eyes adjust to a room where objects cast honest shadows. She was very still. That stillness has taught me more about courage than any sparring round I have ever won.

"We have proof," she said at last.

"We have names," I added.

"We also have a map," she said, and touched the folded paper that still sat in her hand in two worlds at once.

The van vibrated under us as if to agree. Juno rotated on her rail and sent a clipped chime across the dash, a small sound that meant, in our shared grammar, yes. Outside, Klade wore its wet night like a coat that does not quite fit. Inside, we sorted what to do next with hands that did not shake until we were done.

We broke connection clean and let the Wendigo idle in municipal gray while the last of the cache wrote to our cold store. The cabin carried the mixed scent of hot wire and mint, a domestic smell that had no business in a city that eats names. Wren checked the mirrors twice without looking like she was checking. Juno rotated on her rail and showed us three blocks of quiet. I slid Velvet's sleeves down over the decoy handshake patch and watched the tiny pulse settle into the slow rhythm we had chosen for a puppet. It felt like putting a lock on a lock.

["Front route or river road,"] Wren asked on the channel, eyes still on the rear camera.

"River for the first turn," I answered. "If anyone is waiting, they will expect us to choose the lobby streets."

The van lifted her nose out of the loading bay and slipped into the lane. Sodium lamps turned the mist to bronze. At the corner a freight runner smoked in a doorway and blessed us with indifference. We passed two stacks of pallets, a white cat, and a window that showed a television with its screen turned to the wall. Juno buzzed the roof and sent back a hiss of static that meant the sky was as uncomplicated as it was going to be.

The block after that was too neat. Trash sat in symmetrical rows. A streetlight that had been out last week had learned to glow. Somewhere, a camera that did not belong to the city pointed at a wall that did not need watching. Wren saw it in the same breath I did.

["That light is someone's idea of tidy,"] she said.

"Agreed," I said. "Take the service alley by the green shutter. We will change the picture."

The Wendigo eased in behind the shuttered plant shop and took on a little more shadow. We did not kill the engine. The van prefers to be ready. I palmed the hatch and felt the familiar relief of night air. Velvet's heels took the wet pavement without complaint. Wren stepped down beside me and tugged her hood low. The alley smelled of soil and solvent, two fragrances that always look innocent written down.

We almost made the corner before the door across from us opened. It did not swing. It unfolded like a shopkeeper with a private ritual. A figure stepped into the wedge of light and let the room draw a line across their face. I felt the air square around us, the way a bar goes quiet when someone with a badge and a story arrives.

"Velvet," the figure said. "You left the room early."

The voice sat somewhere between friendly and bored, a register designed to live inside high ceilings. The body wore a plain coat and a neutral face that would have pleased a hiring manager. The way it moved was the tell. Drop of the chin before a step. Shoulder angled by a fraction when the line of retreat is measured. Hands that present open palms a heartbeat before they close. It was a study done from memory.

"Sable," I said, and let Velvet breathe the word like a sigh. "You found the after-party."

"I followed your invitation," they answered. "You leave such courteous crumbs."

Wren shifted behind my shoulder, just enough to clear a line if running became rude. She touched her deck with her thumb and I felt the Wendigo pull in its antennae. Juno settled to a lower perch and pretended to be a street fixture. We had practiced this enough times that the motions made their own grammar.

"We are closed," I said. "Come back when the lights want company."

"Then we will keep it short," Sable said, and stepped forward into the alley. The light from the doorway put a clean stripe across their jaw. For a ridiculous instant they looked like a better photograph of me. The tilt of the head. The set of the left foot. The small, economical breath that prepares for weight.

They came fast. No speech, which was new. They opened with a reach that mimicked a move I teach Velvet when I want a rook to think it can catch a bishop. An outward parry, two fingers to the wrist, then a pivot across the line so the shoulder becomes a gate. I saw myself and hated the fact that I admired the precision.

I did the ugly thing Wren had taught me to do when someone knows my dance. I stubbed the heel and let the body look sloppy. The pivot missed. The gate clicked against nothing. My elbow met the bridge of their nose with a tidy crack. The strike would have floored an intern. Sable flowed back, a ripple forward of the spine that belonged to Stray rather than Velvet. They smiled without showing their teeth.

["They are cutting between your habits,"] Wren said, calm as a metronome. ["Do not give them the count you love."]

"I am trying," I said, and fed Sable a sequence that would have looked like pride from the outside. Two high lines to test the guard, then a low knee that asked for balance. They read it as if the book sat open on my chest. Their left hand flicked and something bright and almost weightless touched the back of my wrist.

A sting, then a cool bloom through the skin. The filament kissed the decoy pad and found the story we had written. Wren's code poured numbers into the hungry mouth. The sample returned the balance profile of a stranger, a marionette that loved even steps and predictable turns.

Sable's eyes flickered. A small correction, then another, the way a dancer adjusts to a partner. They shifted to meet the lie their device had gathered. The opening that made lived in the right place for frustration and I took it. Heel to instep. Palm to jaw. Hip to sternum. None of it elegant. All of it suited to alleys.

They took the first two shots as if they were fees and let the third drive them back into the doorframe. Wood cracked. Plaster dust fell. Sable used the fall like a spring, dropped to a knee, and sent a sweep at my ankle that would have separated someone else from the ground. Velvet has learned that trick and refuses it. I rode the sweep, planted through it, and brought the knee down into the hinge of their shoulder. A sound came back up my leg that felt like metal complaining.

They hissed that quiet little intake they use when the mask is slipping. It did not become anger. It became calculation. Their right hand twitched and I saw the glint of another filament disk. Wren did not give me time to ask.

["On your sleeve,"] she said. ["Second sample would eat the decoy."]

I caught Sable's wrist and drove it into the wall. The disk fell. Sable slammed their head forward and caught me under the brow. The world filled with light for one heartbeat, then settled into the crisp focus that always follows pain. They pressed, searching for the old rhythm. I gave them one beat of it, then stepped wrong on purpose again. It is a terrible feeling to be bad at your own body. It saved my face.

They adapted yet again. I could not shake the impression that they were enjoying the puzzle. It is something I do not like about myself and do not like seeing in a borrowed mirror. They feinted with a Forge shoulder, then snapped a Velvet hook before the weight caught up. I brought my forearm up to catch it and felt the bone-deep pulse of impact run through the shell. I answered with a low elbow into the ribs. Human chest would have wheezed. Their plating sang.

Wren moved behind me, not into the fight, into the shadows that live beside it. She palmed open a junction box and snapped two leads together with the practiced disrespect of someone who has paid fines for curiosity. The alley lights blinked. For a breath, the world held only moonlight and the pale glow of the van's instruments. Sable's pupils widened. Juno dropped from the rail and chirped a burst that made the borrowed camera across the lane cough and forget tiny parts of its own morning.

Sable tasted the change and tried to disengage. I would have done the same. That made it satisfying to deny them. I pressed them into the wall and let the shell carry the conversation. Forearm across the collar. Knee holding the thigh still. One hand on the wrist. Their chin tilted up just a fraction and, to my disgust, matched exactly the angle I have used a hundred times to imply mercy. It looked wrong here.

"Stop borrowing my face," I said, and heard what I sounded like when I pretended I did not care who I had been.

They smiled with the same small effort I make when I want a scar to look like a choice. "It is a flattering face," they said. "Especially when it forgets to pretend." Their free hand flicked. A pellet hit the wet bricks and burst a sweet smoke that coated the air at throat height. My eyes did not sting. Velvet tears when I tell her to, not when a toy orders it. The smoke hid a gesture rather than harmed a body. It was enough.

They twisted under my forearm with a shoulder sway that would have looked shy if we had been on a dance floor. The move used my grip as a hinge and spun them out into space. I stepped to close and met a kick that would have taken my hip if it had belonged to a heavier shape. It glanced instead, more insult than injury. Sable touched their lip, inspected their fingers as if red would be an inconvenience, and clicked their tongue.

"Almost," they said. "But almost will do."

They backed toward the open door. I lunged and caught the coat. The fabric felt expensive. I tore a strip away and found a sliver of harness under the seam where the collar met the shoulder. A spool for a wire line, small and smug. They saw me see it and smiled again, wider this time.

From behind the door a short lance of light pulsed. Not a weapon, a glare. It painted the alley with a cold wash that crushed shadows to the ground. Sable used the flattening to slide sideways without giving my eyes a plane to follow. I hate that trick because it is mine. They reached the threshold and cut their cheek in a small, deliberate line on the door edge. The line made a shape on their skin that I knew as well as any signature.

["It is yours,"] Wren said, voice tight with fury. ["They are writing your habits on their body."]

"Not for free," I said.

We pressed again. The exchange became knots and untying them. Elbow. Knee. Palm. A short throw that used the wall. A block that borrowed momentum instead of meeting it. Parts of me wanted very much to enjoy this. The rest remembered how a child looks when a room asks them to sit still. That part won. I went for the simple finish.

I caught their wrist with both hands and dropped my weight through the grip, dragged them off the threshold, and stepped across to bar the door with my hip. The door hit my spine and the hinge complained. Sable tried a headbutt again and met the top of my skull. The second try hurt them more than me. I drove a heel into the instep and felt a bone disagree. They faltered. I brought the forearm back across the collar and pressed until the voice went thin.

Wren closed the last distance in three quiet steps. She touched the side of Sable's neck with a patch that does not live in any pharmacy. The patch does two things. It teaches muscles to rest, and it forgets five minutes on purpose. Sable saw it coming and tried to twist away. Wren planted it anyway, then pulled her hand back fast so a bite would have to imagine teeth.

For two breaths it seemed as if the patch would take the fight away. Sable swayed. The smile turned mechanical and then slipped. Their eyes went dull at the edges. I eased pressure by a fraction, prepared to bind wrists and fetch the van.

They startled and broke the lull. With their weight sagging they let the knees go wrong, dropped through my grip, and rolled under the bar of my arm. The move is horrible to watch because it teaches joints to disobey. It is also a way to get out of a hold if you are willing to limp later. They hit the ground, kicked hard off the wall, and shot through the doorway backward.

I reached and caught the edge of the coat again. It tore, and for the second time in as many days I was left with a strip of fabric and no throat to pin against a surface. A cable sang once, a clean little note, and then their body rose out of the doorframe, up past the lintel, into the crawl where windows and vents pretend to forget people exist. Juno flashed a marker on the roofline and kept quiet because the roof did not belong to us.

"Let them go," Wren said, fingers already moving on the deck. "I can still hear their badge. They will run toward the market and then left along the drain."

"Copy," I said, and let the empty doorway have my attention for a second. It stared like a witness that knows better than to talk.

We closed, fast and tidy. Wren brushed smoke out of the air as if housekeeping could fix pride. I opened the hatch and pulled the van into motion by habit, then by will. The mirror showed me a Velvet face with its anger put away. That is a look I do not trust on anyone else.

["Decoy held,"] Wren said as the Wendigo found the road. ["Their pull took exactly what we meant them to taste. If they adapt again, they will learn to doubt the thing they believe. That buys us time."]

"Time is the only currency I respect," I said. My hands remembered the feel of Sable's wrist under pressure, then remembered the absence where a throat should have been when the body chooses smoke. I stared at my right palm until the tension went somewhere that would not break a knuckle.

The van slid into the long curve of the river road. Rain grew patient again. The city offered us its usual lies and we accepted them because we needed to get home. Wren watched the side streets and drew her breath in even lines. Juno tapped the roof twice, a small ritual that means the worst thing in the room has left it.

"They are learning fast," Wren said after a time.

"So are we," I answered. "And we have better soup."

That earned the smallest smile, the kind she does not share with anyone who charges by the hour. We left the quarter behind us and let the wheels carry the weight. The torn strip of Sable's coat lay on the console beside the credit stick from our last client. The two objects looked like siblings who had chosen different schools. I folded the cloth and put it in the same pocket as the first strip. Collections are a vice. They can also be a way to stay angry for the right reasons.

Home called itself a direction rather than a place. We followed it because practice is the only refuge I know that ever pays out.

THE WENDIGO SETTLED INTO her berth with the satisfied creak of a ship that knows every board under its feet. Outside, Klade rinsed itself in gentle rain, the kind that makes a city shine without making it cleaner. Inside, our lights dropped to evening and the heater exhaled a breath that smelled faintly of mint and warm plastic. I let Wisp sit in the quiet a moment before moving, the way you sit in a doorway to decide if a room feels like it will hold your weight.

We made small rituals without speaking. Wren hung her jacket on the same hook she always forgets and always uses. Juno paced along her rail twice, clicked once, and tucked her head beneath one wing like a tired thing pretending not to watch us. I rinsed the cups, filled the kettle, and set two tea bags on the counter. The plant by the sink liked the sound of water and lifted two new leaves as if this were theater and we were the audience it preferred.

When the kettle clicked, I poured, slid a mug across, and kept my hands around my own to let the heat convince my fingers that they belonged to me. Wren wrapped her palms around hers and did not drink. She studied the steam as if it might spell out a reason that did not hurt.

"We have proof," she said at last, voice even, eyes on the place where her reflection blurred in the window. "We can pull contracts, leak files, ruin at least three people who have learned to monetize names."

"That is a plan," I said. "It is not the whole truth."

She looked at me then, and all the intelligence in her face made the cabin feel smaller in a way I have learned to like. "Say it," she said.

"You built a piece of their house," I answered. "Not knowing. Wanting to help someone who could not move. They dressed your good thing in their colors and hired it to keep a door shut. I was a child in a room with too much light. I found the seam where you left mercy in the code and I pulled. The door did not open, but the latch learned to forget itself long enough for me to fit through."

Wren set her mug down and its ceramic ring chimed softly against the counter. She did not fold in on herself, which I admire more than I should. "Which piece," she asked. "I know the symbol pack they skinned. I know the consent module they gutted. Tell me what you touched."

"The motor recovery toolkit," I said. "Your timing routines were written with forgiveness. They allowed tremor, breath, small delays between intent and action so a hand could learn again without being punished. In the room where I lived, those routines were converted to evaluate compliance. The tolerance did not fit the new intention. It left a shallow pocket in the heartbeat of the machine, a space where a command would wait before it decided to say no. If I matched that pocket with a certain breath count and a certain twitch, the restraint looked away for a fraction of a second. If you chain enough fractions, you can move more than a finger."

She closed her eyes, not in pain, in concentration. "A jitter window," she said. "They repurposed the grace period. They always repurpose the grace period." She breathed in, then out. "How did you find it?"

"I counted," I said. "Lights, hum, footsteps, the way the camera lens adjusted when the room thought it was alone. Your code had a rhythm distinct from the rest. It felt like someone had written it for a person rather than a device. I matched my breath to it and waited. The first day, a finger. The second, a wrist. The week after, I could shift my weight without the logging script screaming. After that I figured out how to make the camera feed stutter with a static burst from my monitor crown. While they were annoyed with the picture, the door forgot to count me correctly."

"And when the door forgot," she said, a whisper now, "you left."

"I did," I said. "I took the Forge body because it could run and because it made a noise I recognized as my own heartbeat. There was a room with a prototype modeled after my original body. I broke its spine mounts and left it on the floor because the look of it was a theft I could not let stand." I did not lower my eyes. I will not apologize for honoring anger that saved a life.

Wren lifted her mug again and drank this time. Her hands did not shake. "You used an open door that was meant for kindness," she said. "Then you patched the wall behind you with fire. And when I discovered how far the clinic had wandered from what I had signed, I wrote a complaint that included too many dates and not enough flattery, and I was escorted out with a box that had my name taped to the top. I thought I had lost a job for saying please in the wrong tone. Tonight it appears I lost it for leaving your footprints in their carpet."

"You did not fire me," I said. "You did not build the room. You put a window where people who could not lift their hands could still see the sky. I climbed out of that window without asking, which is the only way I have ever climbed out of anything."

She laughed then, small and dry, the sound a match makes when it refuses to catch. "I think I wrote the door you walked through," she said. "I do not know how to feel about that."

"Start with proud," I said. "Add angry as needed."

We moved to the bench, not to make a point, but because sitting beside someone changes what you are willing to say. Wisp fit into the corner like a younger sister claiming the warm part under a blanket. Wren tipped one shoulder into mine with the kind of casual contact that sends the body a quiet message about what is safe. Juno watched us with one yellow eye and pretended not to.

"They had a program name I did not recognize until tonight," Wren said. "RELL. It lived in vendor paperwork as a rehabilitation protocol. When we saw it in the stack, it was a feed to shape children. They used my tools to smooth kids into compliant shapes."

"In the dialect the workers used at the plant," I said, "rell means to plane down a rough board so it will not snag skin. They applied the word to human minds. That choice was not an accident."

"Neither was your memory of the sound of the slab," she said.

The heater clicked and the van shifted slightly as some unseen neighbor rolled a cart of bottles across the alley. The ordinary noises of a city at peace tried to make what we were saying smaller. They failed because we have learned to count what matters.

"I need you to understand something," Wren said, turning to face me fully. "I would write the same routines again for the body that needs a second chance at movement. I will never again license them without demanding proof of ethics that goes beyond a mission statement. I will never again trust a quarterly report to tell me who is allowed to breathe. If I was the reason a door forgot to close, good. If I was the reason a child was asked to sit still for a test, I will spend the rest of my life breaking that test in public and in private."

"I already understood," I said, and believed it. "You are not a person who writes prisons. You are a person who writes ladders and then stays to hold them steady."

She looked past me to the pod bay where Velvet stood with her face at rest. The seam at the jaw sat true, the shoulder I had repaired no longer whispered when the diagnostics arm passed. Forge loomed like a statue that sometimes chooses to hunt. Stray waited in his small harness with the patience of a boy at a window who knows a roof is coming. Wren's gaze flicked from one to the next and then settled back on me.

"You prefer Wisp at home," she said. "You do not say it. You find reasons. Less maintenance, not a combat frame, easier on the power coils. You sleep better when your joints weigh less."

"She belongs here," I said. "The others want doors and fights. Wisp wants noise at breakfast and a plant that learns to climb. I am still learning how to let a room call me back to itself. It is easier to practice in a smaller body."

Wren smiled at that, a real smile that shows a tooth on one side and none on the other. "You have a home shell," she said, and did not make fun of me for having one.

We let a silence arrive and did not rush to fill it. The van breathed. The rain softened to a whisper. The city adjusted its weight on our roof and decided not to come in.

"Tell me something I do not know," Wren said at last. "Not about code. About you."

I looked at my hands. Wisp's fingers are narrow and quick. They make other people underestimate the strength in them. "The first night out," I said, "after I left the building and crossed the yard, I hid in a loading bay behind a broken forklift. I could still hear the alarms when the wind shifted. I had the Forge body then. It was too big, too loud. I felt like a thief in my own skin. A man walked past with a paper bag from a noodle shop and put it on the forklift. He lit a cigarette, took three drags, and left. The bag had a steamed bun with red bean paste inside. It was still warm. I ate it in two bites and did not taste it. I sat with the empty bag for an hour because the grease spot looked like a map of a place I could live. That was the first time I decided I could choose my own name and not die of it."

Wren listened the way good rooms listen, with attention and no demand for a moral. "I was fired on a Wednesday," she said. "The security man who walked me out did not call me by my name. He used my title as if my life had become a role. The woman at the front desk slid a plant into the box without asking if I liked plants. It died three days later because the hospice had no windows, and because I was learning how to breathe without a salary. I took my mother's scan on a Sunday because I refused to let her vanish into a billing code. The first time I met you, I liked you before I knew why. Tonight I know a little more."

We sat with that until it became part of the cabin's weight. Wren finished her tea and reached up to stroke Juno along the spine. The drone arched into the touch with a small mechanical hum that sounds like pride. I finished mine and rinsed both cups, then dried them with a cloth that had begun its life as a shirt with someone else's name stitched into the collar. The plant by the sink put out another leaf. I took that as permission to say one more thing.

"I did not correct you," I said. "When you called me Hikari in the alley. When you decided the in-between belonged to a name that means simple. I did not correct you because you were right. The shells are a way to survive, not a face to die for. The part of me that is not a shell needs a word that is not an apology."

She stood and came closer until we shared the same square foot of floor. Wisp is shorter than Wren, and for once that felt like a position rather than a disadvantage. She put her hand on the side of my neck where the skin is thin over wires, and she did not look away from my eyes.

"You are Hikari," she said, only that.

"I am," I said back, and felt the cabin accept the sound.

Juno clicked once like a bell. The Wendigo turned her fans down for the night and the heater settled into a steady tone that could have been a lullaby if machines believed in such things. I checked the pod seals one last time and set the soft tripwires we had written to wake us if any lens in the neighborhood learned to yawn at the wrong hour. Wren dimmed the main lights and left the blue strips along the floor for navigation, a habit that makes a room kinder to feet at two in the morning.

We did not plan the next fight. We did not open the files again. We stacked the facts in a neat pile on the console and placed two coins of resolve on top so that wind would not move them while we slept. The city will try again tomorrow. Orinox will send a new contract to a new vendor and call the harm a feature. Mirror will practice our errors and think of them as language. All of that is true. Tonight a van learned our weight and kept it. Tonight two people told each other a set of hard things without sharpening them into weapons. That is not victory. It is not nothing either.

I powered Wisp down to idle and eased into the nest we have started to call a bed without irony. Wren stretched out above me on the shelf she steals from the storage bins and hid her face in her sleeve. Juno took the night watch and pretended it was for her own pleasure. Rain braided itself into a thinner music, and the floor hummed the slow rhythm a body uses when it has chosen to stay.

Chapter Eleven

Burnproof

WREN

I ALWAYS BRING THE same flowers. White lilies with a vein of green that runs along the petals. They do not belong to the city. The streets are a noise of neon and steam, but lilies smell like a quiet room in spring. The long term care ward at Saint Crescent needs that, something soft to cut through the disinfectant and the recirculated air that tastes like a filter in need of changing.

My mother's room sits at the end of a corridor where the lights buzz in a tired way, as if they would rather be asleep. The windows face a courtyard of scrub grass and a piece of sculpture that looks like a twisted spoon. I do not know who donated it. The plaque is scratched and dented, someone's idea of a joke about public art, yet the metal still catches the morning light and throws it in bright slices across the linoleum. I stand for a moment in the door and watch the light slide over her blanket, then I step in and set the lilies in the ceramic cup I keep cleaned and hidden in the bottom of the cabinet.

She looks smaller every time. Some part of me thinks the bed is growing around her, swallowing her in white sheets. The monitors hold their soft green lines and patient beeps. The feeding line hums. The oxygen bulb makes a sound like a calm ocean inside a shell. I reach for her hand and warm her fingers between mine. They are cool and dry, but there is still a strength in the knuckles that reminds me of the way she used to knead dough, the way her arms would flex without effort while I stood on a stool and stole pinches like a thief with a sweet tooth.

"Hi, Ma. It is me. I brought the lilies again. You would scold me for spending money, and then you would fix them in a better arrangement and tell me that you are proud I remembered."

The words catch in my throat. I speak them anyway. I try to keep my voice cheerful because a nurse once told me that patients feel tone even when they cannot respond. I do not know if that is true, but I want to believe it. I talk about nothing. "The weather broke last night and the air smells like wet copper. The bakery on Ninth changed owners again and still cannot get the glaze right. The pigeons on the hospital ledges have learned to bully the delivery drones by pretending to be heavier than they are." I make up that last part and it makes me smile. If she could open her eyes, she would laugh at that and call me a menace.

Juno cannot come inside the ward without a permit, so I left her perched on the window ledge just beyond the courtyard, a dark shape with a glossy beak and glass eyes that transmit like a pair of tiny moons. She blinks at me through the glass. I lift my wrist and the live feed fills my palm. The habit is so deep that even here, even while I stand beside the real thing, I still check the screen. The picture on my display is only a few seconds behind the present, a double exposure of care that I cannot seem to stop.

The door clicks. It is not the nurse. I can tell by the pace of the footsteps and the scent that slides in ahead of the person. Citrus, engineered to smell like calm decisions. The woman fills the doorway with a narrow shape and a black suit that drinks the light. She does not carry a clipboard. Instead, there is a slim device in her hand with a gold crest at the top. The crest is a circle with a diagonal line that curls in the shape of a helix. Orinox uses that mark on everything they own.

"Ms. Mason," she says, and she smiles with her mouth and not with her eyes. "I am Alicia Vale. Thank you for meeting with me."

"I did not," I say. My voice stays low so I do not disturb the room, but there is an edge in it that I hope she hears. "You found me. That is different."

She glances at my mother without staring. It is a practiced movement, polite and forgettable. Then she steps inside as if we had already agreed to this. The door closes behind her with a hush, and the corridor's tired lights are cut off. In the quiet, the room feels like a small boat.

"We are aware of your mother's case," she says. "Our Solace program handles complex long term conditions with full wraparound care. Private room, on-site neural specialists, real food when appropriate. Access to experimental therapies that are not available through state channels." Her eyes return to me and the smile warms by a single degree. "We would like to extend that care to your family."

No one gives away care like that for free. I do not say it out loud. I am already bracing. I set my mother's hand back on the blanket and fold the corner near her wrist, a small ritual that makes me feel present. Juno's reflection looks like a black note on the window.

I keep my voice even. "What does it cost."

Alicia does not flinch. "Orinox is prepared to assume all expenses for your mother's treatment. Transport today. New facility within the hour." She lifts the device, taps a line that glows with a cool blue signature. "In return, you will deliver an asset that belongs to us." She lets the last word rest in the air for a full breath. "Hikari."

I hear the oxygen's slow ocean and feel the floor tilt. For a second I think I will sit because my knees go soft. I do not. My fingers dig into my thighs and I make myself breathe with the machine, in and out. Alicia watches me without a trace of triumph. She is too well trained for that.

"You think Hikari belongs to you," I say. "Hikari belongs to themself."

The device in Alicia's hand scrolls another line. She does not show it to me, but I catch the shape of a file header and a date stamp that reaches back to the year Hikari disappeared from the registry. "We have documentation that says otherwise." She looks at my mother again. "I can see your burden. No child should carry that alone. We can help. We can give her comfort, real comfort. All we ask is that you do what is right and return company property. Hikari will not be harmed. Their value lies in preservation. They will be maintained in a secure environment and given tasks suited to their unique talents. I promise you that."

I almost laugh. Tasks suited to their unique talents. What a soft way to say cage. I keep my face calm and trace the seam in the bed's metal rail with my thumb. I could tell her that Hikari's talents keep a dozen families fed on the wrong side of the river. I could say that those talents cracked open a paywall around medicine three months ago and freed twenty children from a line that had held them in limbo. I could tell her that Hikari sleeps in steel and wakes in code and forgets to eat when the world becomes complicated, and that they still remembered to set an alarm that reminds me to hydrate on days when I forget I have a body. None of that will matter to a woman who calls a person an asset.

"I do not think you know what is right, Ms. Vale," I say. I step between her and the bed without thinking about it, a reflex that feels like putting my body into a doorway during a fire. "Even if I did, even if you could pull the sky down for my mother and give her an entire sun to warm her blood, I would not trade a person for a bed."

The room listens. The monitors do not change their rhythm. Alicia's expression does not move for a long count, and then something passes through it, a quick shadow of disappointment, perhaps genuine and perhaps another page from a manual on empathy. She slips a small card from her pocket and sets it on the cabinet beside the lilies. The card has no name, only the helix crest that reflects the window light.

"This is not a demand. It is a choice. The offer stands for seven days." She looks at the flowers as she speaks. "Your mother's case file indicates a steady decline. I am sorry. If you reconsider, call. We will make it effortless."

She leaves with the same citrus scent and soft clicks. The door closes and the corridor's tired lights return in a dull smear along the floor. I do not move. The card glints beside the lilies, a shard of corporate ocean in a cheap cup. I pick it up and turn it over. There is a texture on the back that catches at the ridges of my fingerprints, like a secret script meant for a sensor to read.

Juno taps her beak against the window. It makes a small sound that brings me back. I set the card face down on the cabinet and push it far under the cup. Then I take my mother's hand again and press my forehead to the back of it. The smell of the lilies mixes with the sterile air and something inside me twists hard and slow. I talk into her skin so the words will not float away.

"He tried to buy you with my heart. I will not sell. I will get you real care. I do not know how yet, but I will. I promise."

The promise tastes like metal. I think about calling Hikari and telling them everything. I can hear their voice in my mind, all of their voices, the bright one, the cool one, the steady one, each persona with its own cadence, each one a way they learned to survive. They would try to give themself up if they knew. They would wrap it in logic and call it strategy, and then I would have to drag them back from a door that no one should ever cross.

I pull my wrist up again and watch the feed for a moment, even though my mother is right here. On the screen, Juno's angle frames me with the bed and the lilies and the spoon sculpture in the courtyard. For a second I see us from the outside, a girl with her head bowed, a woman asleep in a sea of white, and a black bird that refuses to leave the window. The picture freezes for a heartbeat as the network catches up and then returns to life. I lower my hand.

I sit with her until the nurse comes to check vitals and we trade gentle words that fall into the room like soft cloth. I fix the blanket seam again even though it does not need it, then I kiss my mother's forehead and stand. The card remains under the cup, a secret I can feel even though I cannot see it. My chest is tight. I do not tell the nurse. I do not message Hikari. I keep the silence and let it grow teeth.

Outside, the courtyard air tastes like rain from a machine. Juno hops from the ledge to my shoulder and settles there with a weight that anchors me to the moment. The city hums beyond the hospital gates. Skyscrapers blink their sleepless eyes. Somewhere inside that grid, Mirror is walking like a rumor with knives, and Orinox is counting minutes on a private server that will never admit what it holds. I push my hands into my jacket pockets and step into the street.

"I will share the offer when I have a plan," I tell myself. "Secrets are only harmful when they have nowhere to go." The lie fits easily against my teeth. I carry it with me as the light turns green and the crowd moves forward.

THE CITY FEELS BRIGHTER after hospitals. It is not kinder. Neon burns a little hotter, and the puddles look like small fizzes of chemicals rather than rain. I keep my hands in my jacket and let Juno ride my shoulder, claws careful on the leather. She tilts her head and watches the light rail skim over Cross Avenue, a silver snake with a tired hiss. I breathe and try to peel the hospital air out of my lungs. It clings like a film.

I should call Hikari. I should tell them about Alicia and her soft voice and the card with the helix crest. I should ask for help before the choice eats me, but the words taste like rust before I even form them. If I tell them now, they will try to barter themself. They will dress it up in logic and call it strategic surrender. So I walk and I keep the secret a little longer. I tell myself that a plan will arrive if I hold still long enough to see it.

The Wendigo sits six blocks west in a cutout lot behind a noodle shop that smells like broth and sugar. We power down the external lights during the day, which makes the panels look like dull slate under the ad glow. You would not glance twice unless you knew what to look for. I cut down a side street to avoid the day market and the two private security outposts that keep track of who buys what on that corner. Juno clicks her beak once, an absent sound that usually means the signal environment is busy.

I lift my wrist. The feed blooms across my palm with a ghost of my reflection under it. Traffic signatures. Noise from a parade of scooters. A snake of low grade cameras stitched across poles like beads. Nothing unusual. I drop my hand and keep walking.

A scream snaps the air two streets over. Not human, although there is a human voice inside it. Metal on metal. The sound of pressure releasing too fast. Juno launches without waiting for my command. Her wings beat the wet air and she arcs up to the edge of the next block. I sprint.

The corner opens into a loading lane between a warehouse with a peeling mural and a transit substation that stinks of ozone. Hikari is there, locked with Mirror in a shower of sparks that looks almost ceremonial, like a ribbon of fireworks unspooling and cutting itself apart. Hikari is in the Forge frame, broad shoulders, armored ribs, heavy servos that sing when they twist. Mirror moves with the same economy that once made my stomach go cold. Androgynous silver plates. A face that is a suggestion more than a mask. Blades that drink light and give back only thin white lines where they pass.

I do not breathe for a moment. The body keeps going anyway, years of practice. Knees bent. Eyes reading the scene in panes. Distance. Exits. Blind corners. The way the pavement curls where the substation steam puffs through a cracked vent. The exact angle of the roofline above the mural where a perch might exist.

Mirror speaks first in a bright, ringing voice that is so familiar I feel it in my teeth. The Wisp voice. Sweet on the surface, with a quick clip under it.

"Careful. You always lean on your right foot when you fake a left."

Then a second voice that belongs to our scout shell at fifteen. Greedy with air, eager to please, so fast the consonants stumble.

"Did you practice without me, coach?"

Then the Forge baritone, perfect as if the city itself had learned to speak through a body filled with steel.

"Stand down, Wren. Area is hot."

Hikari flinches. I see it in a single frame, the stutter in the shoulder. They parry anyway, a clean sweep that knocks one of Mirror's blades off its perfect line. Cement chips fly where the blade bites the curb. Mirror's laugh is not a sound I can map. It is a compression artifact painted to resemble joy.

"Give me a second," I say into the com. I do not say to who. Hikari hears me. Juno hears me. My own voice settles me. I peel left and take the warehouse wall, fingers finding the ridges of old bricks under the skin of half-faded paint. Juno feeds me a high angle as she perches on a signal repeater and tilts her lens down. The lane looks like a diorama from up there. Two figures at the center, one wide, one narrow. Steam like torn silk. No one else in sight. For now.

"Hikari, eyes on me." I put steel in the softness. "Count with me. Three, two, one."

Hikari's helmet does not turn, but the chin dips a fraction. I feel the count come back through the line. Three. Two. One. Their movements tighten. The edges on my screen stop fraying. Mirror notices and adjusts. The knives change tempo. The arc gets shorter.

"It is rude to ignore a guest," Mirror says in my own voice, then lets it slide into something that sounds like Hikari when they first woke the girl shell and did not know how to pitch laughter. "Wren. Come closer. Help me choose which voice to keep."

"Keep the one that chokes," I say, and I let Juno's strobe land on Mirror's faceplate for half a second. Her eyes flare white. Mirror's head cocks. The blade misses a line that looked fated. Hikari steps through and lands a heel strike that would break a normal spine. Mirror folds around it as if their body is water. The force bleeds off into the ground. They come up on the other side with a blade against Hikari's side seam.

The knives are not knives. They are strips of monofilament suspended in glass with a sheen that looks like frost. They part air like silk. I see them and taste an old fear that has earned the right to live in me. I bury it under practice.

"Juno, mark right shoulder." The crow hops two units on the feed and places a thin circle on Mirror's upper armor. A hairline seam catches the light. Servo access. The plates are beautifully made but no one hides everything.

Mirror hears the mark and laughs in the teen voice. "Good eye. You taught her well." They grind the word taught as if the texture gives them pleasure.

"Hikari, breathe," I say. "Left knee, lift. Take space on the eight."

Hikari moves on the call. It is not graceful. Grace is what happens when you train without an enemy. This is built from ugly survival. They bump the blade with the heavy forearm, take the cut on leftover plating, step to the eight on an invisible clock, and drive the right fist toward the shoulder seam. The impact rattles the lane. Mirror pivots and takes it on the blade spine. The monofilament hums like a plucked wire. A thin curl of heat lifts off Hikari's gauntlet where the edge just touches.

More noise enters the lane. Distant siren. Closer drone buzz. The kind of sound that says private security has been told to ignore anything in this block for ten minutes. That means a client bought space. I do not need to guess who.

"On me," I say, and I break cover. The distance closes in a long step. My pistol is already out. I do not aim center mass. Mirror would enjoy that. I put three rounds in the pavement an arm's length from their feet. The rounds crack and spit a web of expanding foam that hardens as it breathes. Mirror hops onto the web rather than away from it. Their balance is theatrical.

"Cute," they say in Forge's voice, then switch to Wisp again. "Run along, darling.

Adults are speaking."

I hate how good the imitation is. It touches parts of me that are not armor. I do not give it any more ground. I angle left again and let the pistol drop on its sling so I can pull the soft grenade from my pocket. It looks like a white ceramic egg with nothing to say. Microburst. Not a full EMP. Enough to confuse anything that relies on timing rather than raw muscle.

"Hikari, blind in three," I say, and toss. The egg pops with a sigh. For a heartbeat the world smears, as if a hand brushed across the picture. Mirror's knives flicker. Hikari staggers but catches themself on the substation rail with a scrape that sets my teeth on edge. I surge forward and aim a strike at the marked shoulder seam with the knife I keep nested in my sleeve. The blade is plain metal and sharpened by boring hours. It has no name and no thirst. It has only work.

Mirror catches my wrist before I reach the seam. Fingers like a vise. Silver plates cool as coin. The faceplate offers me my own reflection, broken into angles that make me look like several people at once. They tilt the head and speak in the small, bright voice that Hikari used the day they tried to teach me to whistle.
"Do not worry. I will keep them safe."

"Let go of me," I say. I set my feet and twist. Bones pop in my wrist. Pain blooms like heat lightning. The knife drops. My left hand is free and I use it the way my first trainer taught me. Heel of the palm. Bottom of the jaw. Add a knee. Add hate. Mirror accepts the hits and uses the movement to pivot around me, still holding the wrist, now with the blade touching my sleeve as if it has always lived there. The edge kisses fabric. I smell the singe through the rain.

Hikari roars. It is not a sound I hear often. It carries something older than the frames. They tear off the rail, take two heavy steps, and shoulder check Mirror across the lane. Silver plates slam the mural. The knives skate wild and carve the outline of a blue tiger into a smear of paint that used to be a child's face. The microburst sheds the last of its confusion. The world clicks back into focus.

"Juno," I say, and the crow drops from the repeater in a clean line, claws extended. She hits Mirror's faceplate and scrapes hard. A handful of black paint sticks like tears. Mirror peels her away with a flick that is almost gentle and throws her into the steam. She bounces off the substation grille and takes wing with a furious caw. I feel the sound in my chest and then force my attention back. She is durable. She is angry. She is not broken.

Mirror has me again before I can collect my knife. Cold around the wrist. A blade pricks fabric. The teen voice laughs in my ear.

"You do not deserve them."

"Neither do you," I say. I drive my head into the blank face. Skulls are old weapons. Stars burst at the edges of my vision. Mirror rocks back, not from pain but to reframe the angle. It is enough. Hikari arrives exactly then, all weight and intent, and brings both arms down in a hammer that would crush a car roof. Mirror slips sideways and the strike turns the substation railing into a braid of twisted steel.

The siren cuts. The drone buzz swells and then lingers, which means it has found a perch and is waiting for an operator's eyes. Juno sweeps past it and drops a glimmer of chaff that turns the camera into snow. I feel the clock move. We do not get to dance here for free much longer.

Mirror reads the same clock. Their knives spin in a lazy circle. Their voice goes quiet and becomes something that is probably their own.

"They will break for you."

Then, just as soft, in Alicia's pitch.

"Seven days."

It hits me under the ribs. I do not move. I will not give them the flinch. The blade tips dip. Hikari steps forward again, and I hear the glitch catch in their breath. The temperate overlap of voices rides the com for a second. Forge growls. Wisp tells me to stand down. The teenager laughs and asks if we can get noodles after this. The soldier shell says nothing but counts three, two, one.

"On me," I say, and I make a choice that I do not like because it keeps us alive. I draw the coil baton from the clip at my spine, thumb it live, and drive it into the puddle at Mirror's feet. The field climbs their frame and spins there like quiet lightning. It will not stop a Vyre Unit, but it asks their muscles to argue with their timing. That is all I need. Hikari takes the opening and plants a boot in Mirror's midsection hard enough to dent the plate. The kick knocks them into the foam web I laid down earlier. The foam gives like bread, then seizes. Knees sink and hold. Mirror's weight belongs to the lane for a breath.

I grab Hikari's arm and pull. "Move. We are done here."

"We finish," Forge says through their teeth.

"We live," I answer. "Today that is the finish."

Mirror lowers one knife and rests the other on the foam. The faceplate turns to share the blank shape with us as we retreat. The quiet voice, the one that might be theirs, follows us like a string.

"Run if you must. You are already found."

We take the substation stairs two at a time and cut across the platform while a commuter train screeches in. I pull Hikari into the shadow behind a pillar as a pair of security officers search the lower lane with flashlights and the wrong kind of courage. Juno lands on the rail above us and shakes herself like a wet dog. She looks offended.

"Status," I whisper.

"Nominal," Hikari says, then corrects themself. "Scratched. That foam will not hold them long."

"It only needed a minute," I say. I let myself feel my wrist for exactly one breath. It complains. I silence it. "How did this start?"

Hikari looks past me and I can tell they are scanning the fight in replay. "They were on the roof of the substation when I crossed the block. They jumped. There was no preamble."

"Did they say anything useful?"

"They said my voice sounds prettier when it hurts," Hikari says. The helmet turns slightly. "They used your voice to say it."

I swallow once and let that sit in a place where I can look at it later. "They also knew about the seven days."

Hikari is very still. The servo in the neck ticks once, a small sound I only notice because the rest of the station noise swallows everything else. "What seven days."

I could tell them now. I could place the card in their hand and watch the math start and then fight it for the next year. I hear Alicia saying effortless. I hear Mirror saying you are already found. The choice is a heat under my tongue.

"Another countdown," I say. It is not a lie, but it is not the truth either. "Different problem. We will handle it after we move."

Hikari keeps looking at me for a beat that makes the air taste like static. Then they nod, slow, like a man trying to agree with gravity. "Then we move."

We cut off the platform into the maintenance stairwell that smells like copper and damp clothes. Juno floats ahead to scout. My wrist buzzes once in the jacket pocket. I pull the small reader I built from old parts and let it sniff Hikari's armor. It lights up with a neat grid of green, then a slice of red at the hip joint, then another red just under the shoulder. The pattern is ugly, like a rash.

"Trackers," I say. "Dust type. They glow when they talk to each other. Four on you. One on me." I pat my jacket and feel the grit. "They seeded the block."

Hikari looks down as if they could see them through the plates. "How many on the Wendigo."

"Do not know yet," I say. The answer is probably many. I see the path of it in my head like an ember thread. We come and go. We keep habits because the city teaches you to keep to the ruts that do not get you killed. Someone watched for long enough to braid those ruts into a net.

I take the solvent pen from my kit and draw clean circles around the red marks on Hikari's armor. The solvent smells like mint and heat. The grit softens and lifts in a clump that looks like wet sugar. I collect each clump in a little vial because I do not like leaving gifts for the people who sent them. I find the one on my jacket sleeve and do the same. Juno watches me with her head tilted and one eye narrowed as if I am dismantling a nest.

"We cannot go back the same way," Hikari says.

"We cannot go back at all," I say. It comes out before I can dress it. I hear the truth inside it. The noodle shop. The lot. The slate panels. The place where our cups live in a cupboard and our maps sleep on the counter. The memory of breakfasts that felt like small victories. All of it just became a story we tell.

Hikari breathes once, slow. The servo in the neck ticks again. "Then we take the Wendigo and we disappear. We will find a new rut."

"Underground," I say. "Not the old tunnels under the river. Those belong to a king who never forgives. The storage warrens by the Strand. The ones the city forgot when the big markets moved uphill."

"Crowded. Dirty," Hikari says.

"Good," I say. "Crowded and dirty keeps secrets warm."

We step out of the stairwell and cross the back of the station into the alley that runs behind three cafes and a clinic that sells cheap vitamins with names that promise to fix grief. Juno takes the high route and hops from letter to letter along a broken billboard. I feel eyes on us that do not belong to faces. The hairs on my arm lift. A small camera on a laundry line pivots. I give it my best face and keep moving.

The Wendigo waits where we left her, patient as always. The panels look dull and the tires look honest. Hikari palmed the lock three hours ago. The panel recognizes them and rolls. The interior smells like coffee and oil and that strange metallic sweetness that means the charging bay did its work. We climb in and shut the city out. The quiet is loud for a breath, the way quiet is in places that have learned to hold us.

I move through the ritual without thinking. Check the external feeds. Feed them into

Juno's channel as backup. Check the undercarriage for anything that sparkles where nothing should. I find two more dust clumps and collect them. Hikari stands in the middle of the floor and does a slow shoulder roll as if the Forge frame has a neck to unknot.

"Mirror will follow," they say.

"They already are," I say. I tap the map and pull a route that looks insane until you know how the cameras blink when the love hotels are busy and the delivery windows compete for door space. "We are not going to reward them for it."

Hikari puts a hand on the counter and lets the glove rest on a coffee stain in the shape of a continent. The gesture is small. It feels like prayer. "You are shaking," they say.

"I hit a faceplate with my head," I say. I let my laugh be small and real. "It bites back."

"Let me see your wrist."

"It is fine."

"Let me see," they say again, and there is a firmness in it that belongs to none of their shells. I hold the wrist out. The skin is already darkening where the grip clamped down. I rub a salve into it that smells like lavender and old engines. Hikari watches my face more than the bruise. "I am sorry," they say.

"You did not put the knife there," I say. I cap the salve and pocket the reader. "You kept it from going deeper."

The silence that follows is not empty. It has a weight that presses against my chest in a way that feels like the beginning of tears. I do not give in to it. I set my hands on the console and bring the Wendigo to life. The panels hum, and the interior lights steady into a soft white that makes the cabinet doors look like promises.

"Seat," I say. "Strap in. We are going to test how much the Strand remembers us."

Hikari straps in without argument. Juno drops onto the dash and folds her wings. The feeds show a slice of the lane outside and a man walking a dog that has more dignity than most people. I inhale and count three, two, one. The engine engages. The Wendigo moves with a confidence that has nothing to do with size.

We pull out into a city that is paying attention. The billboards blink too fast. The drones drift a little lower. Someone bought time for Mirror, and they spent it on us. The hunt is not only open. It is closing.

I think of Alicia's card hidden under the cup beside the lilies. Seven days is a drumbeat I cannot stop hearing now that Mirror borrowed the rhythm. I glance at Hikari and find them already looking at me. Their helmet reveals nothing. The posture reveals plenty. They feel the net the way I do.

"We go underground," I say again.

"We go," they say.

I turn the wheel and point us toward the mouth of the warrens. The city swallows us with a sound like rain on steel. The neon fades. The smell changes to damp stone and old power. Juno clicks once and settles. I keep the secret where it lives for one more hour and let the promise I made in the hospital fix my spine. If I can buy them time, I will pay with whatever the city asks that is mine to give

.THE MOUTH OF THE warrens breathes cold air that smells like damp stone, oil that has seeped into concrete for decades, and the particular plastic stink of old storage units. The Strand runs above us like a spine. Underneath, the city splits into ribs of forgotten corridors, rows of roll-up doors, and service tunnels that lead to places the maps pretend do not exist. The Wendigo's headlights catch a hand-painted sign where the plaster peels, a cheerful arrow that once promised flea market treasures on weekends. Someone has scrawled new letters in paint that looks like curdled milk. Quiet coin. No cops. No questions.

I ease the wheel and let the Wendigo drift down the ramp as if the vehicle wants to belong here. The tires hiss on the damp. Juno rides the dash with her feet braced, wings half open to balance against the tilt. Hikari sits strapped in the harness beside me, Forge frame hulking in a way that makes the cabin seem smaller than it usually does. The armor plates still show a smear where the monofilament kissed them. I have cleaned away the dust trackers we found on the platform and the ones on the undercarriage. I am sure there are more. I am sure we will be finding them like ticks for the rest of the night.

"Signal discipline," I say, and the habit comforts me. "No broadcast unless I call it. Juno, use the short leash. Hikari, keep the mesh in listen only. No pings."

"Listening only," Hikari says. The voice is Forge steady. It is also raw around the edges in a way that tells me the other voices are close to the surface. They are quiet now. That can be its own kind of danger.

The first corridor is wider than it looks from street level. On either side, storage doors hang half open like yawning mouths, some filled with hoarded furniture and stacks of boxes, some swept clean and turned into rooms with pallets and leftover Christmas lights that blink in tired colors. The residents look up when they hear the engine. Eyes follow us from doorways, from a table made of two crates and a door laid flat, from a cage where someone is cooking skewers over a trash can with holes punched for air. Rumor travels faster than light in places like this. We have lived a long time on the edge of rumor. Tonight we bring a tide with us.

A woman steps out into the lane with her palm raised. She wears a yellow raincoat with the sleeves rolled to the elbow, and her hair is braided close to her head with wire threaded through. The wire catches the Wendigo's lights in little sparks. She has the posture of a person who knows who pays and who does not. I stop two meters back and drop the window to the level of my cheek.

"Parking," she says without preamble. Her voice is not hostile. It is a floor for negotiation.

"I need a container bay," I say. "Dry. Deep. Far from the main cut. I do not need questions. You will get quiet coin and an extra for anyone you pay to look elsewhere."

She studies the Wendigo's lines like a person who enjoys machines. The glance she gives Hikari is quick and professional, like a tailor taking a measurement. She does not stare at the armor. The courtesy ranks her above most of the city.

"You have trouble behind you," she says.

"We have eyes behind us," I say. "Trouble is an opinion. I am hoping the warrens still prefer facts."

"Tonight they prefer a good door and a quiet neighbor." She taps the side of the RV with two fingers and the sound comes back solid. "Name is Magda. Two options. Three rows down and one turn left, a pair of conjoined units with a drain that actually works, a minor miracle for this side of the Strand. Or six rows down and two right, a blind corner where the ceiling sags, cheap because of the drip in the winter. The cheap corner has fewer neighbors. The pair of units have a straight line to a water riser that has not been shut off in years. Your choice."

"Three and one," I say. We are going to need the drain, and I do not want a sagging ceiling over my head when the night starts to move.

Magda nods. She does not ask for my name. She gestures with her chin. "Follow." She walks with a measured pace that does not challenge the Wendigo's turning radius. Juno watches her with one eye narrowed. I can see the angle of her head reflected in the glass. She is already drawing the map under her feathers.

We take the first left and the noise fades, swallowed by concrete and distance. The warrens continue into darkness with the confidence of old bones. Some doors are painted with bright patterns, ward off thieves and beggars signs that mean almost nothing and almost everything. Some are chalked with dates and glyphs that look like weather forecasts for people who know how to read the subtle storms of a place like this. Children's chalk drawings appear between the glyphs, suns with too many rays, animals with square legs, the word MOM in a hand that makes my throat feel small for a moment.

The pair of units sit back from the lane behind a strip of cracked tile. The roll-up doors have been replaced with steel shutters that swing on hinges. Someone invested care here. Magda keys a code into a box on the wall with chipped red paint. The locks click with a sound that is more satisfying than it should be. She pulls one door open and stands aside for me to angle the Wendigo in. The second door opens into a narrow rectangle that a runner could use without feeling trapped. The air inside is cooler than the lane, and it smells like bleach, wet dust, and old wood.

"Three days," Magda says when I cut the engine. "No more, or I demand another rent. No fires bigger than a candle. No chemicals that burn metal. Keep your weapons quiet. The tenants here include children and people with lungs that complain. If your friends or your enemies come sniffing, we all expect enough warning to walk. If you choose to die in your room rather than pull your weight in the lane, you will not be invited back."

"I can work with that," I say. I slide my cred chip out and put it into the reader she holds, then add a second transfer, a smaller number that means tips. "One more thing. If anyone asks your opinion of us, tell them we are boring."

Her smile is quick and professional like the rest of her. "That costs extra."

"I included it," I say. "Boring is worth more than friendly in my book."

"True," she says. She tucks the reader away and glances at Hikari again. "If that shell bleeds oil, put a pan under it. We have rules about stains. This is a home, not a dump."

"Understood," Hikari says. The voice is Forge and it has the proper respectful weight to it.

Magda turns to go, then pauses and nods toward Juno. "Pretty bird. Keep her out of the children's games. They will try to throw balls at her. She will win. They will cry. It will become my problem."

"Noted," I say. Juno clicks once in what I choose to hear as agreement.

The doors close behind Magda with a sound that settles in my bones like an old lullaby. I stand still for a moment and let the cool air creep into me. Hikari unclips and steps down, the servos muttering as the body adjusts to the lower ceiling. The Wendigo's interior lights reflect off the steel hinges and send little moons spinning across the walls.

"We have three days," Hikari says.

"We will not need that long," I say, and the lie is not about time, it is about faith. I crank the manual locks on the inside of both doors and throw the deadbolts for good measure. "First circle is hygiene. Second circle is signal. Third circle is sight. Fourth is steps. We do not leave a straight path to us in any direction."

Hikari nods. They do not ask me to define the circles. We have made variations of the same list in a dozen places. I move through the RV and pull down the blank Mylar sheets from the overhead, the ones we keep rolled in cardboard tubes for field clinics and bad weather. The sheets have a crinkly feel that used to make me think of emergency shelters. Now they mean comfort. They mean we can build a room inside the room where the city does not listen as easily.

"Frame," I say. Hikari drags out the collapsible poles and the clamp set. I talk through the layout while I work, not because they need the notes, but because speaking shapes the plan in a way that keeps my hands honest. "Two layers of Mylar with an air gap. Tape the seams with the copper banding. We will make a door flap and weight it with chain so it falls closed on its own. The Wendigo's central bay stays inside the cage. The wall ends before the water riser so we can reach it without breaking the seal."

While Hikari clicks the poles into a low arch and starts clipping the sheets into place, I take Juno to the back corridor and set her to mapping. The space behind the conjoined units is a service lane barely wider than my shoulders. It passes the water riser, continues behind two more rows, and then doglegs into a loading notch with a drain that looks like a mouth with iron teeth. There are no cameras back here that my eyes can see. That does not mean the eyes are not present. It means the obvious ones are gone or never existed. I place three pencil-sized sensors along the run at knee height and tape them flat, one at the riser, one at the dogleg, and one on the far end near the notch. They will wake if anyone crosses that plane with heat and weight. The mesh will listen, but not remap. I will pass the alerts through a dumb light inside the cage. The light will blink rather than make noise. We will not announce ourselves to people who might think better of minding their own business.

Back inside, the Mylar is up and the copper banding shines along the seam like the edge of a coin. Hikari has set the arch low enough to force them to bow when they enter. The indignity will make them pay attention to the threshold. It will also slow the shockwave if we catch an unfriendly surprise. I take out the coil of chain and the tape, weight the flap, and test the fall three times until the drop feels like a habit.

"Faraday tent is live," I say. "Phones and personal junk inside. Heavy metal outside. We will keep a hard split. No cross talk."

Hikari steps under the flap and stands in the center with their hands at their sides. "Give me the list."

"Trap line first," I say. "Three doors. Two in the room, one in the back corridor. Foam spiders on a tension line. Net canisters above the hinges. Low trip line for knees inside the second door so a runner who gets through the first gate sees the third when they have already committed. Keep it annoying rather than permanent. The neighbors deserve mercy even if our enemies do not."

Hikari opens the trap bin and lays out the little machines on a towel. The spiders are ugly things with legs made of wire bent into hooks and bodies built from scavenged parts, little bulbs and caps that no one would miss if they went searching in a junk drawer. The nets live in squat canisters with blunt noses and trigger rings. We have used them to catch stolen packages, drunk friends, rats too friendly with an engine compartment, and men with knives. We have used them for children who ran during a clinic because trauma turns running into a reflex that shows up at the worst times. I hate that the same tools serve all of those functions with a flick of a wrist. I use them anyway.

"Water," I say as Hikari starts measuring the hinge gaps. "Put the catch pans under the riser. If the key freezes or the valve coughs, I want it contained."

They move with the efficiency of an old dance. I move too. I tape a line of beepers under the RV just inside the outside seam of the tent. Each has a battery and a single purpose. If the vehicle moves while I sleep, the beepers will chirp until I calculate the problem or the battery dies. I also wedge a slat of wood under the front tire. I do not think anyone will push the Wendigo. I make the slat anyway. I have learned that the world enjoys a laugh when I leave obvious gaps.

Juno returns from the mapping run and lands on my shoulder, claws careful. Her feed sends me a sketch that is more like a memory than a map. I paint it onto the dumb screen with a stylus so Hikari can see it without the mesh. The path curls behind us and around the dogleg and out into the notch. The notch has three exits, one choked with junk, two viable if you do not mind narrow spaces and wet shoes. I mark them with a green dot and a note that says only duck. The riser gets a blue dot, because water has always been a kind of blessing in my mind even when the city fouls it.

"Sight," I say. "I want eyes on the lane without showing our eyes. Periscope cam in the left vent. Mirror in the right. Use the reflective tape to bounce the angle. The children here will throw a ball if they see a lens. I would like to keep our toys."

"On it," Hikari says. They do not make a joke. That tells me how much of their attention sits on the drain between us. I file the detail away with the rest that I cannot afford to hold right now.

We work for an hour in a rhythm that feels like a heartbeat I remember from a different life. The tent grows into a proper bubble with a floor made of two quilts that we do not mind staining. The foam spiders cling to their lines like ugly Christmas ornaments. The net canisters sit in shadow like sleeping toads. The periscope cam shows me the lane where a boy in a knit cap kicks a dented can between his feet, and Magda walks past with a clipboard she does not need except to give her hands a place to rest. The mirror in the right vent shows me a slice of ceiling and a scurrying blur that might be a cat or a person's hair in the wrong place at the wrong time. The dumb light above the riser blinks once and stays off. The sensors are awake and polite.

When the first circle and the second circle feel solid enough that I could leave the room for five minutes without wanting to claw my skin, I call for a short pause. Hikari steps into the tent and sits carefully on the floor, knees wide to keep the armor balanced. The helmet tips back and the seals release with a sigh. They lift the headpiece away and set it on a folded towel. The face underneath looks like a map of insomnia. The eyes are ringed in gray. A spray of dark hair hangs damp from the edge of the undersuit.

"Hydrate," I say. I hand them a bottle that we keep filled with water and electrolytes. "Small sips. Then food."

"I am not hungry," they say.

"Which is why I said food," I say. "Small bites. We will trick your nervous system into remembering that you own a body."

They take a sip, then another. They are obedient when they choose to be. It is a skill people forget they have until chaos reminds them. I open the cabinet and pull a box of crackers and a jar of bean paste that tastes better than it looks. Juno hops to the floor and steals one of the crackers and stomps it into crumbs as if she intends to mortar a tiny wall. The petulance makes me smile in a mean way that feels like a relief.

Hikari watches me for a while in a quiet that is not an absence. "You are hurt," they say finally. Their eyes flick to my wrist and back up to my face.

"I am not broken," I say. "Later I will be sore. Right now I am useful."

Hikari nods. They accept the cracker I offer. They chew like a person who has to think about how teeth work. The Forge frame hums quietly as the suit vents leftover heat. Outside the tent, the lane holds its small sounds. A laugh. The squeak of an old cart. The nick of a lighter. The coil of something faint and musical that might be a radio left on in a room where two people sleep head to feet.

"Talk to me," I say. "Give me the seam you are trying to hold."

They look at their hands for a long time. When they speak, the words come careful, like a person moving a fragile object into a box. "They used your voice. I know you know that. I can hear the part of me that wants to arrange every memory I have of your voice and check them for pressure points. I can feel the other part that keeps saying it is not a voice, it is a weapon that learned to sound like breath. The first part hates trusting the second. That is where the seam is."

"You do not need to trust either part," I say. "You can trust me. I will tell you when to breathe. I will tell you when to move. I will tell you when to ignore something that sounds like home."

Hikari's mouth tics. It is not a smile. It lives somewhere near grief and gratitude and the memory of a person who once believed nobody would stand between them and a knife. "Say it again."

"I will tell you when to breathe," I say. I keep my voice steady and low. I slow my own breathing until I feel the hum of the Forge frame start syncing its vents to my chest. "I will tell you when to move. I will tell you when to ignore the thing that sounds like home."

They close their eyes and nod. The nod is small. It feels like a gate clicking into place. We sit like that for three breaths, then four, then the dumb light blinks once and the moment falls away like a piece of ash.

I move to the back corridor and check the riser. The sensor is the one I set for the dogleg. The blink says weight and heat. I flatten to the wall and wait, counting to twelve because it takes time for people to commit to a corner. At nine, a shadow glaze slides across the far end of the corridor, then retracts. I make my footfalls audible for two steps so the person knows I am present but unafraid, then I stop and let the silence suggest disinterest. The shadow slides back. There is a pause that has the weight of listening. I picture someone with a thin plastic bag and a packet of instant noodles. I picture them weighing whether to take the short cut behind the units or go around the long way. The shadow leaves. The light stays dark. It was a neighbor taking inventory of our noise.

When I return to the tent, Hikari is checking the periscope cam. The boy in the knit cap is gone. Magda is mid-argument with a tall man in a denim jacket who keeps pointing to a line on her clipboard as if pointing will change the ink. Hikari taps the screen and the image wobbles. "This lens is already smudged. I will clean it in an hour."

"Wait," I say. "Work through the steps. Sight is good enough. We go to signals again." I pull the small cases of decoy tags from my kit and pop them like candy boxes. Inside, each tag looks like a fleck of glitter glued to a strand of hair. I hate them because they are elegant. I love them because they bend the world for me without blood. "Rat run," I say to Juno. "Gift delivery. No pecking."

Juno leans forward as if she intends to argue the last rule. I scowl at her with fake severity. She clicks once, which could mean anything. I set the tags on a shallow dish with a smear of peanut paste that smells like sweet dirt. A rat steps out of the vent with the casual arrogance of a landlord and surveys the dish. Its whiskers taste air. It approaches with dignity, eats, and acquires three tags that will drift off when it squeezes into the next gap. It leaves without looking back. The second rat is less dignified and leaves with six tags and a smear of paste on its nose. The third rat refuses charity and moves on. The city will carry our false shapes for us, a string of little song notes for anyone listening to the wrong melody.

Hikari sets the micro jammer on a stool and checks the battery. "Two hours at full, seven if we pulse," they say. "If we keep pulses irregular, the neighborhood will enjoy the quiet without noticing the pattern. If we lock to a single schedule, someone will ask for money or ask for blood."

"Pulse," I say. "We will be polite. I will not buy a war with people who just want to sleep in peace." I adjust the knob so the jammer breathes rather than shouts. The air changes flavor when a jammer lives in it. People with the right kind of headaches will feel it like a humming in their teeth. People with the wrong kind of job will feel it like a hole in a paycheck.

I check the mesh in listen mode. It feels like standing on the roof of a building and feeling the city vibrate under bare feet. Traffic noise. A slow river of delivery confirmations. The murmur of home cameras that watch children sleep and cats argue with furniture. The particular crystalline pings of a private security grid two blocks away. A line that is too clean and too quiet where a corporation has purchased silence. Across that quiet I hear a series of faint taps, spaced in a way that feels like footsteps. Mirror is not the only hunter that follows a rhythm. Orinox buys time. Orinox buys hands. The hands come wrapped in policy and dresses that smell like citrus. The hands also come wrapped in metal and contracts. The taps pretend to be nothing at all. I hear them anyway.

Hikari hears them too. Their eyes take on the unfocused look that means they are building a map no one else can see. "Not here yet," they say. "Three blocks down. A second line two blocks from that. Both lines are moving. The first line is on foot. The second rides in a van with a lazy magnet on the roof. No sirens. They are not idiots."

"Magda will earn her extra tonight," I say. "She will smell them before they smell us. She will move her children into the corners with the better doors."

"We could warn her," Hikari says.

"We already paid her to be warned," I say, then let my voice soften. "I will tell her if the lines change direction. Right now they are moving toward the old market side. That is three lanes away."

Hikari nods. The nod looks like it took work. They stand and put the helmet back on. The seals hiss and the voice returns to Forge through the suit. "Steps," they say. "We plan the steps."

"Right," I say. I fold the map Juno drew into segments and mark it with numbers until the plan feels like a set of hands I can wear. "Step one. If the first line turns toward our lane, we will feed the decoys toward the old elevator shaft near the clinic with the vitamins. Juno will herd. Hikari will hold the first door here. I will hold the back corridor. Step two. If the line bypasses us and the second line circles to block the exits, we will leave the tent intact, take the floor hatch, and crawl through the service gap into the next unit. The Wendigo will stay as bait. We will re-enter from the far end behind the notch and walk the drain to the laundry, which has enough foot traffic to make us boring again. Step three. If both lines stall and ping for drones, we will accept a small fight. We will keep it loud enough to attract attention that belongs to the neighborhood. We will keep it clean enough to make the neighborhood grateful rather than angry. We will not spill enough blood to bring bigger predators."

Hikari breathes once into the helmet so the sound reaches me. "Understood."

"Step four," I say. "If Mirror arrives, I take them. Not because I am stronger. Because I know how to hate them without letting them take up space in my head. You will hold the door and keep the neighborhood safe. You will not chase them. If you chase them, you will leave the line. They will draw you where they want you."

The helmet turns to face me and the visor is a blank oval that reflects my shape and the tent and a glimmer of the Wendigo's paneling. "You cannot ask me to let them stand in front of you without stepping into the space where I belong."

"I can," I say. "I just did. You can hate me for it later. I need you for the door." I hold their gaze even though the gaze is not a real eye. "You told me to tell you when to move."

They stand very still for a count that feels like it knocks against my ribs. Then they tilt their head. "I will hold the door."

"Good," I say. "Then we rehearse."

We run the steps twice with full gear but no drama. I show Hikari how the floor hatch covers with a rug and looks like a harmless storage bin to anyone who is not trying to fall through it. I show them where the service gap sits and how the grid of pipes makes a back crawl uncomfortable but possible even in the Forge frame if they unclip the plates at the hips and leave two on the floor to reclaim later. I smear a line of oil on the third pipe from the left so the person who follows looks like they have been through a chimney when they rise on the other side. People who care about being clean usually care about looking clean. We can sometimes buy thirty seconds with a stain.

Juno practices herding the decoy tags with the stubborn focus of an artist moving pins on a board. She drops a glitter line toward the old elevator shaft and circles it like a sheepdog with wings. The rats help without knowing they are part of a plan. The cats ignore us and hiss at ghosts. The dumb light blinks twice for the riser and once for the dogleg. Juno clicks back in a pattern that means a person is using our corridor as a shortcut again and this time they are humming the same three notes a child hums when they march with a stick under a blanket and pretend the stick is a sword.

The second hour inside a hideout always tastes like metal. The adrenaline from arrival burns off. The plan settles into muscle. The body starts to remember injuries it pretended not to notice. The mind starts looking for a place to set down the future and stretch. That is when the net tightens. Markets know fatigue like a rumor. Private security knows it like a line item. Mirror knows it the way a hunter knows an animal that always returns to water at the same hour.

The mesh in listen mode gives me the taps again, closer. The van shifts, pauses at a curb, and moves. The foot line slows because a woman scolds the tall man in the denim jacket and he pretends to care. The scolding lasts exactly the length of a cigarette smoked without guilt. Then the foot line breaks into pairs, which means someone in the pair does not trust the other pair to find anything worth a bonus. The pairs split like water exploring a crack. One pair toward the market. One pair toward the elevators. One pair toward us.

"Magda," I say. I step to the tent flap and keep my body half inside the field. I do not want her to feel sleight of hand from my words. "Three men walking toward your clipboard. None wearing city boots. One with a magnet hidden under a jacket seam that should not have an edge like that."

Magda's voice returns in a whisper that lives in the wall rather than the wire. She is using the vent rather than a device. She remembers rules. "I see them. Thank you."

"Children inside," I say.

"Already moving," she says. "Keep your fight clean if you must have one."

"We will keep it boring if we can," I say, and I feel her smile through the vent even though I cannot see her face.

The pair that turns toward us has the walk of men who have never been told to carry groceries. The first is compact and wired tight, the kind who keeps a small knife and makes three people regret it every year because he practices at home for the wrong reasons. The second is long and patient with a backpack that rides too clean. The backpack tells me more than the bones. The backpack says he believes in the weight of gear that allows him to rely on a story instead of his hands. Neither is police. Both wear city jeans, city jackets, city shoes with new treads. The combination is the costume of an outside man who wants to sell a local shape. My anger wakes at the same time my caution does. I feed the anger a cracker made of focus and tell it to chew.

They pause three doors down and talk with a woman whose room smells like turmeric and drying laundry. She shows them the inside of her cupboard without a trace of fear. The compact one says something with a smile that has too many teeth. The patient one writes on a phone and does not look at the child who peeks around the doorframe. The child does not look at the men at all. The child looks at Magda, and at the clipboard, and at the thumb on the edge of the paper. The child is measuring the world the way children learn to do when the world is not made for them.

"They are going to knock," Hikari says.

"They are going to try," I say. "Let them."

The knock, when it comes, is polite. I do not reward it. The second knock is louder. I keep my hand on the tent flap and my fingers on the net trigger ring. The third knock includes a throat clear that aims to carry authority through the door. I give it my hand's permission to exist and then ignore it.

"Management check," the patient one calls. "Routine inspection."

Magda's voice arrives from further down the lane. She keeps walking while she talks, which denies the men a stage. "No inspection scheduled today. Show me the notice."

"We have a notice," the compact one says. "But we do not need to show it until we see the room."

"You do not see rooms without the notice," Magda says, and the sentence has an almost friendly rhythm that would be soothing if you did not notice the way the lane quiets to listen.

The patient one turns toward our door. He looks at the hinge and the lock and the little scratch where I chose not to buff the metal in order to make the door look older than it is. He takes a step back and rubs his nose as if he is tired. He is not. He is making the body small to keep his center free. He glances up as if to check the ceiling for leaks. He is not. He is counting the vent holes. He smiles with his mouth. It does not reach his eyes. He says, "Ma'am, you do not want to obstruct."

Magda does not raise her voice. "Sir, you do not want to assume you can tell me what I want."

They like the dance and hate the audience. I can tell by the way the compact man shifts his weight. He wants to be inside the door doing the thing he thinks he is good at. The patient one wants to finish the conversation with the clipboard in a place where he can file a comfortable report. The audience turns them into men who have to perform. I do not want the performance to reach my door.

I pull the small speaker from my pocket and put it against the panel inside the tent. The device is simple. It does one thing. It hits the metal at a frequency that reads as annoyance to the human ear and as a scream to certain machines. It is the dog whistle of doors. I set it low and turn it on. The hinge vibrates imperceptibly. A trickle of dust falls next to the frame. The sound does not carry. The metal carries it for me.

The patient one frowns and rubs his ear. The compact one looks irritated and glances at the ceiling again. The sound tells his brain that the door will not cooperate even if he wins a shove. People who habitually dominate will choose a different target rather than fight steel that arrives without a face. They step away as if they planned to do that. They knock on the next door. Magda is already there with her clipboard like a shield.

I switch the device off and breathe in a way that feels like apology to the hinge. Hikari watches me through the visor. "That was petty," they say. The tone is approving.

"Petty keeps doors on their hinges," I say. "One more circle and we can rest."

We move to logistics. I label the water cans and stack them with the label facing out so no one forgets to rotate. I refill the med kit and add extra tape because we always run out of tape before we run out of gauze. I count the foam grenades and the microbursts and hide one of each in the second unit behind the two crates in the corner. I tape a knife under the table, handle to the left because Hikari is right-handed in every shell. I hide a second knife under the cot because I am not. I run a cable from the Wendigo's battery to the tent to give us an extra twelve hours of clean power if the grid hiccups. I do not trust the grid to do anything except choose the worst hour to do it.

The mesh offers me the taps again. They turn away from our lane and back toward the old market. The van idles. Then the taps slow. Then a single loud footstep lands like a stamp. Mirror's timing is a different music. It is not the taps. It is the silence that follows. A line in the air stops existing. The hairs on my arms rise. Juno clicks once and stares at the tent flap as if the fabric has said something rude.

"Not yet," Hikari says, and I agree with the words even though my body is already moving to the back corridor.

"Not yet," I say. "But close."

The dumb light blinks once for the dogleg, steady for a count of five, then twice for the riser. A person turns a corner and then changes their mind. Then a different person tries the knob that acts like a gumball machine if you do not hold it right. The knob squeaks because we want it to. The person leaves. Juno scratches at the floor like a hen and then looks embarrassed about it. I pat her head and she tolerates the touch with the minimal grace she offers when I am lucky and the world has been kind to her for at least one minute.

I take a breath and put my hands flat on the table. I think of the hospital room and the lilies and the way the card felt under my fingertips, textured like a secret script that wanted to learn my fingerprint so it could know me from a crowd. The seven days drum in the back of my skull. The rhythm is not a count now. It is a song that a snake would sing. I picture Alicia with her careful voice. I picture Mirror with my voice bent into a wrong angle. I picture my mother's hand under mine. I picture Hikari's mouth when they said say it again.

"Tonight we live," I say. "Tomorrow we make a bigger plan."

"Tonight we live," Hikari says. The repetition sits in the room like a carved word over a door. The Forge frame hums as if the suit answered too.

We eat and drink and do the boring part of being hunted, which is to keep the body alive in a way that keeps the mind attached. We take turns at the tent flap and sleep in slices that feel like sneezing rather than dreaming. The lane breathes around us, sometimes louder, sometimes barely there. Somewhere in the night someone sings two lines from a love song and then stops. Someone tells a joke in a language I do not know and the laugh that follows it warms the air where it passes.

Just before the hour that belongs to bakers and ambulance drivers, the mesh in listen mode gives me a pattern that is not quite a tap and not quite a hum. It is a whisper that carries a taste of static and sugar. I sit up too fast and the tent sways. "New drone," I say. "Small. Nose heavy. Soft wings."

"Private," Hikari says. "Orinox work for hire. They like those wings because they are quiet enough to hover inside a baby's room without the baby waking. They called them lullaby units in the pitch deck when I stole the deck."

"Ugly name," I say. "Ugly purpose."

The lullaby unit enters the lane like a moth with good posture. It is small enough to fit in my empty hand. It is pert enough to make me want to slap it. It hangs at air conditioner level and pretends to be searching for a vent to rest on. It will smell carbon dioxide. It will count the bodies that exhale it. It will decide which breath patterns match its list. If I stand under it for too long, it will think my breath is interesting. If it passes the tent, it will think the air is stale and the numbers do not match. That will make it curious. Curiosity is the predator's favorite mask.

"Juno," I say. "Hush."

Juno lifts from the dash and slides out through the right vent like a secret. She takes the height of the lullaby unit and floats next to it for a count of two without touching. Then she drops six centimeters and flicks her tail. The flick creates a small turbulence that dances with the drone's optics and makes the unit adjust a fraction to correct a problem that does not exist. The correction moves it into the thin thread of chaff she left two minutes ago when she thought the night might require art. The chaff clings. The unit's camera reads blur instead of edge. It hums harder to find the numbers again. It turns in a circle that looks like naivete. It is not. It is a reindex of a sensor. Juno flicks her tail again and rides the drone's tiny wake as if she is surfing a bottle cap down a gutter after rain. The lullaby unit drifts toward the market side as if it meant to go that way all along. Juno follows until she can snag the back corner with her claw. She pops the battery casing with a trained twist that creates no spark. The unit falls like a moth. Juno catches it and delivers it to Magda's clipboard while the woman pretends to write down a new line and smiles at a child who does not know she is watching a war done kindly.

I watch the periscope cam because it gives me permission to feel proud of a bird without adding that pride to my list of sins. Hikari watches the mirror. The mirror shows the ceiling. We see nothing. We see something anyway.

"Rest," I say. "Thirty minutes for you, thirty for me, then we switch while the bakers do their work."

"We should move the Wendigo before sunrise," Hikari says. "Even if we only shift two bays left and two back. Habit kills."

"Agreed," I say. "We will move her after we eat. We will act like people who plan to stay for three days so the plan earns itself."

Hikari removes the helmet again and sets it next to their boot. They stretch their shoulders and lay back on the quilt with the careful weight of a person who knows their suit owes them only duty and no comfort. I sit at the tent flap with my wrist on my knee and listen to the city talk to itself. In another life I would be at the hospital again, adjusting a blanket, counting breaths with a machine. In another life I would not be doing this math or this particular kind of love. This life is the one I have. I carry it like a bag of stones and find the one smooth piece to hold in my pocket when the rest tries to pull me down.

The dumb light blinks once for the dogleg and once for the riser. A rat drags a noodle across the corridor like a trophy. Somewhere a man rinses a cup and hums. The taps do not return. The hum lowers to the level the city uses when it dreams it is a forest without lights. I watch until my eyes sting and my heartbeat feels like I stole it from a better day. Then I lie down beside the person who is my plan more than any plan I can draw, and I close my eyes without letting go of the ring on the net canister, and I rest for a short slice of morning that tastes like flour and old coins and a promise I have not yet told the person who needs to hear it.

When I wake, the lane's light is the blue that only comes from concrete catching sunrise by accident. Hikari is sitting up with the helmet on. Their posture tells me nothing good has happened, and nothing bad has happened either. The periscope cam shows three women carrying baskets. The mirror shows a ceiling with a crack that looks like a river. The dumb light is quiet. The mesh in listen mode has a new gap where taps used to be. Orinox pulled the line back to the edge of their purchase. They will wait for a new permission slip or a better scent. Mirror will not. Mirror will take the path that knives prefer.

"We move the Wendigo," Hikari says. "Then we go shopping."

"Shopping," I say. "Batteries, water filters, a hinge to replace the one I insulted, a tub of oats, and a bag of rice that does not smell like fish. A roll of heavy plastic to make a curtain for the riser if the drip starts. A pan for oil for the people who care about stains. Extra tape."

Hikari tilts the helmet. "Two pairs of socks for you. You think better when you have spare socks."

I laugh once and the sound warms the tent and invites the morning inside with it. "Two pairs of socks," I say. "A luxury."

"Necessity masquerading as kindness," Hikari says. The Forge voice turns it into a proverb. "We should pick a new call for when we leave the tent. The old one belongs to the last two months, and the old routes are part of a net that is closing."

"New call," I say. "You choose."

They think for a heartbeat and then nod. "Burnproof."

The word fits into this chapter like a key into a lock. I feel it in my mouth. It is not a promise that we will not burn. It is a promise that the fire will not take everything. It is a good lie that helps you do honest work. I nod back.

"Burnproof," I say, and the city answers with the sound of a bakery gate rolling up and the smell of bread rising into a place that needs it more than it knows. We move the Wendigo two bays left and two back. We hang the heavy plastic. We put the pan under a place that might someday bleed. We eat bread with fingers that remember the shape of grief and choose to remember the shape of food instead. The hunt is closing the way a hand closes around a thing it wants. We are still here. We build our circles. We keep the door on its hinges. We make ourselves boring. We hold the line.

Chapter Twelve

Black Threshold

HIKARI

THE HOUR BEFORE DAWN lives in concrete like a cold memory. Our borrowed bays keep their breath, the Mylar tent holds its dim glow, and the dumb light above the riser rests as if it never learned to blink. The Strand is quiet at the surface. Down here, sound travels along the ribs of the building until it turns into a feeling in the skin. My suit hears more than I do. The Forge frame sits in a crouch with its weight low, vents sighing on a slow rhythm I taught it when sleep refused me. Wren lies inside the tent with her forearm over her eyes and her boots still on, the bottle of water under one hand in case the night decides to shake the ground again. Juno perches on the vent that looks into the lane, neck tucked into her plumage, a dark knot outlined by the periscope cam's ghost-white reflection.

This should feel like safety. It feels like a held breath.

The mesh in listen mode brushes along the edge of my mind. Delivery receipts. A van that pings when it should be dark. A square of purchased silence that sits two blocks away like a stone. The silence bothers me more than the noise. It always has. Noise announces its intentions even when it lies. Silence eats the map.

Wren stirs. The tent rustles. I look away before the helmet's reflection can wake her. The visor shows a pale smear where the Mylar door hangs. The chain that weights the flap ticks once and then settles again. I count heartbeats until my body remembers that the count has no power over the future. The screen above my wrist offers me diagnostic comfort instead. Heat in the shoulder bearings at twenty percent above nominal. A small fault in the left knee that I have ignored since the substation fight. Power at seventy six and holding. No broadcasts. No pings. Juno turns her head and scratches the vent with her beak in a small, efficient motion. The sound should not mean anything. Tonight it does.

The dumb light blinks once for the dogleg. A neighbor testing the shortcut. It blinks again almost before the first blink finishes. That is wrong. Weight and heat moving together, too quick for a person who lives here. Wren sits up inside the tent and shoves the bottle under the pillow like a child hiding a toy, small reflexes that come from growing up poor enough to hoard comfort. The chain falls and the flap lifts a hand's height. Her eyes meet the visor and find me because she always does. I put two fingers to my throat and tap the count that steadies us both. Three. Two. One.

The taps in the mesh arrive with a sweet chemical smell in my imagination. Lullaby units. Soft wings. Nose heavy. We saw one last night and bent it away with kindness. Orinox bought more. They bought a permission slip with quiet on it. They intend to trade that quiet for our coordinates.

"Burnproof," I say in the private channel that lives between Wren and me. I keep my voice calm. Calm makes metal obey. "Up slow. Helmet stays off. You are quieter that way. Take the reader. If the dumb light hits twice for the riser, you take the back corridor and do not argue. I meet you at the notch if we split."

"Copy," she whispers. The word lands on the chain like the softest weight and does not break it. She stands, adjusts the strap of the med kit across her chest, and tucks hair into her jacket collar with a gesture so ordinary it almost breaks my heart.

Juno leaves the vent without a sound. The periscope cam flares white for an instant and then clears. The crow arcs into the lane and becomes a gliding absence just below the ceiling. Her lens sends me a thin line of light that sketches her path along the outer wall. She knows what to do. She has always known. I tell myself that because it keeps me from begging the future to be kind.

The first unit breaks the corner at a speed that tells me they practiced in empty buildings where no one cooks noodles over metal bins. Black fabric. Light armor that hugs the ribs. Masks that sit close because no one wants a strap to catch a hook in a tight hallway. The man at the front carries a translucent shield that drinks the lane light and turns it into a faint milk. The woman behind him has a breach case slung low and a hand on the zip of the case like a child with a toy they cannot wait to show. The third holds a drone cradle shaped like a bowl with a coin-sized hole in the bottom. The bowl breathes. A lullaby unit drifts out and rides its own little current like a self-satisfied moth.

Magda tries to intercept them with her clipboard. She steps into the lane with the calm of a person who has learned ten ways to take heat out of a room. She points to the sign that says Quiet coin and pretends she believes it will stop bullets. The man with the shield does not break stride. He angles the milk across her without touching her and turns her into an afterthought inside her own home. She feels the insult. I see it in the way her weight shifts for a second and then returns to level. She steps back and begins hitting doors lightly with her fist to wake people who will need a minute to disappear. She does not look at our vent. She does not have to. She has done her job. Now I will do mine.

"Breacher," I say to Wren. "Left hand carries the zipper. The zipper lives in a groove that cuts fabric like a smile. The charge is inside the smile. Drone cradle right behind. Soft wings will ride the shock wave to taste what falls out of doors."

"In the tent," Wren says. She has the reader open, the old green grid glowing as if it somehow likes danger. The grid throws two red freckles on the flap. Dust tags, fresh. They seeded us again while we slept. They are using the lullaby wings to place them like seeds in a garden. The tags sparkle against the Mylar like nothing at all. She lifts a strip of tape, wraps it around one freckle with a surgeon's care, peels it away, and traps the grit in a vial that already holds neighbors. Her fingers do not shake until she has two vials. Then she puts both in her pocket because she will want something to break in an hour and vials do not injure anyone.

The lullaby unit kisses our seam. The seam vibrates. The mesh offers the small sound a context it does not deserve. The drone memorizes the taste of the air and chooses a direction. Juno strikes it from above with her claw. The battery casing pops with a click rather than a spark because she knows how to kill quietly. The unit falls. The man with the bowl catches it without looking as if he expected the loss. He drops the husk into a side pocket and frees a second bowl from the web on his vest. Their budget has a line for Juno. I hate that. I hated it before I knew what she really is. I hate it more now without yet understanding why.

"Hold," I say. Not to Wren. To myself. Forge wants to stand. Forge wants to finish an argument it believes started when people invented knives. I keep the weight low. I keep the firewall up. I tell the suit that we will not be the first movement.

The breacher pulls the zipper on the case. The smile opens into a soft white rectangle of shredded foam and little pockets. She presses the rectangle onto the door down the lane and taps it twice with a gloved knuckle. The rectangle blooms into a bright flower that is only beautiful if you were born on a battlefield and learned to confuse power with love. The wall exhales dust and tries to suck it back in. The door folds. People scream in the room beyond. Not from pain. From the shock of new air. The man with the shield holds the milk at an angle to drink the bulk of the blowback. The drone climbs. The drone counts breaths and looks for interesting numbers.

"Not ours," I say. Wren nods even though she cannot see. We both hear our own relief and we both hate it. A child cries. Magda shouts something that sounds like a prayer if you do not know the language. The breacher's smile is a real thing and it makes her look young.

Juno cuts left and scrapes the second drone with her beak. She steals a wire and carries it three meters before the unit stabilizes. The wire dangles from her mouth like a ribbon. The drone's optics correct and follow her as if she is the only story worth reading in the lane. She makes herself bigger than any door. I do not like the choice. I understand it. She was built to intercept eyes. She is doing her work with pride. The pride has teeth and I do not want to see them bite her.

They come to our doors on the third breach. Magda will say later that she tried to stall. She will list the names of the rooms and the reasons that the doors should not open and the men will read from a schedule that another man bought with a sign that promised quiet. I do not listen. I hear the zip. I hear the foam flower kiss our steel. I hear Forge stand.

"Wren," I say. "Back corridor. Prime the net and take the second hinge. When the dumb light hits twice for the riser you take the notch and you do not look back."

She does not argue. She never does when my voice takes that shape. She slides through the flap with the kit and the reader and the map folded in the sleeve of her jacket. The chain falls and lifts, then falls again as the flap learns to close. Juno takes the height above the door and shows me a perfect view of the charge blooming against our steel. The flower is bigger than the last one. The budget did not just include drones. It included flowers meant for a room where people hide.

The door goes white and then rings like a bell. The hinges spit bolts. The deadbolts bend. The steel holds long enough to give us one breath. I take it. The frame sags in the middle and then droops like fat cut from a roasting pan. The lane pours in. Milk glass and soft wings and boots that have not stepped in this dirt before.

I throw the net into the bloom.

The canister punches a sheet of bonded thread across the door as if a spider the size of a truck finally got bored of pretending to be a rumor. The first two through roll with a courtesy that is almost affectionate. They practiced this in narrow halls. They get tangled anyway because thread does not care about practice. The milk shield catches the edge of the web and brings its own man down. The fourth gives up comedy and raises a short shotgun. The round chews the net and pulls it into curls. The curls still love ankles. The man with the bowl puts the bowl down and lifts a compact pistol that is meant to make people sleepy. I hate that they brought the weapon they use for children. I hate that they brought it for us.

I discard hate and move. Forge loves clear verbs. The suit lurches forward through the curtain of thread, one hand wide to keep the web from binding the elbow. The first man tries to use the shield like a door. I knock it into him instead and listen to the air leave his body. My knee finds his thigh. The edge of the shield finds his jaw. He sleeps without medicine, a gift he did not ask for. The breacher drags the shotgun up with a speed that deserves respect. I give her a different respect. My forearm eats the muzzle. The barrel dents. The armor hums with the impact and my teeth ring inside the helmet. I put the other hand on the weapon and push. The gun skates across the floor and stops against the wall inside our room, a bad place for strangers to leave toys.

The man with the bowl fires. The pellet finds my chest and blossoms into a soft, sweet exhaustion that will become sleep if I let it. I do not let it. The firewall tightens on a word I have not used in a year. Black threshold available. Confirm. The letters arrive on the visor like a superstition that grew teeth.

"Confirm," I say.

The suit asks for a second confirmation because the people who built it liked lawyers. I give it the second word with a voice that belongs to me and to the part of me that only lives in metal. "Confirm."

Heat spills through the frame like a second blood. Limiters lift with a click I feel in my jaws. The world narrows into a corridor where every motion has a clean line and every breath belongs to me until I choose to give it away. The pellet's gift dissipates like fog in morning sun. Analytics stack in the corner of my sight and then bow. The suit stops asking questions. It becomes a set of hands that would tear a door from its hinges if I asked, and that will burn themselves quietly if I forget to ask them to stop.

The breacher tries to backpedal. I am already inside the space she prefers. The shoulder plate meets her chest and the plate wins. I hear ribs complain. I do not think about it because I cannot carry everything. The fifth man hooks my ankle with a baton meant to persuade rather than injure. The baton sings against the greave and the song tells me where his wrist lives. I turn and take his wrist and show it a line it never learned to travel. The joint pops. The baton drops. The man screams in a voice that carries surprise rather than pain. Surprise earns him mercy. I plant my boot on his chest and keep him under it like a lever.

The lullaby unit dives for the opening inside my guard. Juno meets it in the air like a rumor that learned to fight. Her wings flare. The drone tries to climb. She shreds the soft wing with three quick strikes and takes a fourth because she is angry. The drone turns toward her and spits a pinprick flame that becomes a thread of heat. The thread touches her belly and lights the oil on her feathers. She is not a bird. I know that. The body still acts like a bird when it burns. She twists, bites the flame, and tears it away with her own beak. It falls in a smear that tries to become a line. Wren sees the smear from the corridor and stamps it with her heel and her hand and a cloth she carries for that work. I learn all of this in a part of my mind that remembers multiple rooms at once. The part that holds the corridor is about to break.

The bowl man fires again, not the sweet pellet, the needle that carries sleep without asking. The needle glances off the visor and makes a star. The star eats my reflection and the lane and a piece of Juno's wing. The star tells me that the next needle might find Wren if I leave this man to his work.

I step through the star and take his arm with both hands. He is smart. He drops the pistol and tries to use the half second to take his second bowl. I put his back against the angled milk and the milk flexes. The shield man wakes enough to push and both men move as if they were one. The bowl coughs. The baby drone slides out and catches my shoulder plate like a moth that learned to cut silk. The monofilament kisses metal and begins to purr. The purr tries to turn into a seam that would rather be a cut. I give it a different meal. The wall meets the drone. The drone pulses once. The pulse becomes a flower inside the casing. Juno cries out with a sound that I have only heard once, when Wren saw something she loved leave a room.

It happens in a second so thick it almost hardens into glass. A man in the third rank lifts his hand. The hand holds an egg the size of my thumb joint. The egg is white. The seam on the egg is a smile like the zipper on the case. He throws it as if we are playing a game at a fair where you win plastic fish for a child who does not yet know what it means to lose. The egg arcs toward the tent where Wren stood a heartbeat ago. Juno sees the arc the way a mother sees a falling glass in a kitchen full of children. She leaves the milk, yaws around my helmet, and snatches the egg from the air.

For one bright, impossible instant she looks like a black knot swallowing the moon.

The egg opens in her mouth.

Light eats the world without sound. The visor turns the flash into a flat blue pane that will not let me see. The suit closes the pupils it does not have and shows me outlines instead. The outlines are ugly. The egg was not a shaped charge meant for doors. It was a pulse inside a little cage that does its work with heat and negation. It was meant to erase small things that fly and think. Juno hits the floor as if she meant to do it. Her wings spread and curl inward with the gentle insistence of a machine learning it no longer has a reason to remain awake. Her eye lights flicker and then go dark in a pattern that hurts to watch because it resembles human blinking. The smell finds me a beat later. Hot plastic. Ozone. A faint sweetness that should belong to bread and belongs to nothing now.

"Juno," Wren says. Nothing else. The word breaks. She is already in motion. The reader clatters. She slips through the half door we built in our cage without noticing the chain. She goes to her knees on oil, slides, corrects without thinking, and gathers what is left in her hands. The heat bites. She accepts it. She says nothing else because everything else is inside her ribcage turning into glass.

The world offers me a choice. I accept one of them without speaking it. The visor gives me another set of letters in a field that used to belong to warnings. Berserk limiter off. Motor protection degrade. Chassis heat cap lift. The lawyers tried to keep this mode buried under ten questions. The people who built the metal kept one door in the code because people like me always arrive at the same hallway with the same dead man in front of us asking if we would like to go through. I go through.

Heat becomes a second skeleton. The floor loses friction because my mind wants it to. The milk shield is a suggestion. The people behind it are the answer to a question that started long before any of us were born. My hands know where the wrists live and where the necks travel when the hips try to cheat. I take the bowl man by his vest and put him into the shield man. They become a small structure that bites its own tongue and falls. I step over their bodies and meet the breacher before she finds the shotgun. She reaches for her belt and grabs a second egg. I respect her bravery by taking the egg and her fingers with it. The egg bounces and rolls under the foam that still loves ankles. It opens and turns a piece of net into a memory. The breacher looks at her hand and then at my visor. There is something like apology in her eyes. It lasts for a fraction. I do not have room to carry it. I show her the mercy of speed.

Two more try to flank. They come shallow because the lane does not allow depth. I kill the first by mistake. I did not plan it. The arm goes where it must and the jaw breaks enough to end the count. I hate that the count stops like that. I keep moving because stopping does not buy the dead anything. The second carries the short shotgun. He fires a round of metal balls meant to slice room corners and remove decisions. The balls hit the shoulder plate and turn to heat and spin off the greave and add to a noise that will wake people who promised each other they would sleep through the raid for the sake of children. I grab the barrel, pull the weapon in, and use the gun to push the man into the wall hard enough to teach him a new language of bricks. He drops on the second word.

The bowl man wakes again. He tries the sweet pellets as if he has not learned. The pellets hit my chest and become candy in my mouth. The suit translates the chemical into a taste and asks if I would like to spit. I do. The star on the visor grows into a crack and then decides to stop because the suit begs it. The visor obeys because it is the only part of the metal that still fears me. I step on the bowl and feel it shatter through the boot. The tiny moth inside dies without drama. Good.

The corridor behind me changes key. Wren's grief becomes a sound I have never heard from her. It is not loud. It is a pressure shift. It is the feeling in an elevator when floors slide past the invisible window and the wires sing. I turn in a movement I could not have made without the second skeleton of heat. She is on the floor with Juno in her lap, hands at the wings, trying to press something back into the body that is no longer a bird. Her mouth moves. No sound. Her eyes are wet and furious, two kinds of water that hate each other. She looks at me and the look is a question that punishes me for not having an answer ready in the pocket where I keep little jokes that make her smile when the city misbehaves.

"She is not a drone," she says. The sentence hammers the air. "She is my mother."

Something under my ribs tears, not from motion. The visor clears a strip to show me her face without the star. That was the point where she should have told me months ago, in a safe kitchen, over soup. The world decided to choose here instead. I accept that choice because refusing it would be a lie.

"How," I say. The word tastes like blood. I have time for one. She gives me one.

"Her imprint runs the core," Wren says. Her hands keep moving on the body while she speaks because love makes hands refuse to go slack. "A map of the folds and the way they sang when she still spoke. A copy of her quiet. It is not perfect. It is enough to learn. I built it before the hospice. I told myself it was a way to practice grief. Then I told myself it was a way to avoid it. I chose both. I am sorry. I should have told you. I am sorry."

The man with the second egg sees a woman kneeling and a machine that refuses to look like a machine and thinks he has been given permission. He throws.

I do not move toward the egg. I move toward Wren. The difference matters because the path to the egg leads through heat and damage and a piece of luck I do not trust. The path to Wren always exists. I cover her with the frame and the egg finds my back. Light bites and tries to flatten my bones into a page. The suit takes the paragraph and burns it. Lines of code scream and fall silent. The diagnostics begin counting down instead of up. The floor tilts and then returns to level because I tell it to.

"Up," I say, and I sound like Forge and Wisp and the child voice that used to ride a bike in the rain and fall and laugh. "Wren, up."

She obeys not because I ordered it but because she knows the shape of my need. She leaves Juno on the floor with the care a person gives a body they can no longer help. She rises into my chest and sets her hands on the plates over my heart as if she intends to move the frame with her fingers. The skin of her palms is red where the heat bit her. Her breath is ragged and beautiful because it is proof that she does not intend to die in this corridor.

"Stay," I say. "Behind me. Count with me. Three. Two. One."

We count. The count makes the world obey for a second. That is all I need.

I go back into the lane and take the last five. I do not have time to narrate honor. I give them a clean order instead. The first gets the muzzle of his own gun in his ribs and the gun learns about bone. The second gets a knee and a hand and a wall. The third is brave and tries to use a knife where a knife belongs. I respect the choice and end it with speed. The fourth pulls a belt device and tries to call a parent with money. I show him the ceiling. The fifth runs, which tells me he has a child who will learn someday that his father chose to come home rather than finish a line drawn on a map by someone else. I let him go because there is no point in adding another ghost to a house that is already too full.

Silence returns as if it earned the room. It did not. We bought it. Magda stands with the clipboard against her chest. Her eyes are wet in the way of a person who will not cry while a child watches, even if no child is present. The lane holds its breath. The periscope shows the welt of dust and powder that coats the steel by our door. The mirror shows a ceiling crack shaped like a river. The dumb light finally blinks for the riser because the world likes to remind us that nothing stops water.

Forge lists damage with the irritated tone of a machine that thinks it told me so. Shoulder bearings glowing. Back plate stress beyond spec. Power at forty nine and dropping. Secondary fans failed. Visor fracture stable for two minutes of combat, ten minutes of walking, zero minutes of falling. I do not plan to fall. I plan to move.

I kneel where Wren left Juno and pick up what remains. The body is heavier than the frame suggests. Memory carries weight. She fit into Wren's palm when I first saw her in a clean room with wires braided like jewelry. Wren did not tell me the core was built from a map of her mother's mind. She did not have to. I hear it in the way the silent shell still sits with dignity in the black ash. I hold the weight against my chest plate and feel heat burn a circle into the paint. I decide not to care.

Wren is on her feet because she always is. The grief sits under her eyes like bruises, fresh and vicious. She presses her lips together so they will not say a word that would break something in her throat. She reaches for Juno and then stops because the body is too hot and because she knows I would carry this thing for her even if it cut through to the ribs. I lower the weight into her arms anyway. She takes it with a sound that belongs to nights when the city is kind. She looks down at the still face, glossy beak cracked, lens dim. She whispers with a voice that belongs to a hospital room. "Mama. I am here."

The world tries to use that sentence as a blade. I do not let it. I stand. I turn to Magda and tip the visor in a nod that pretends to be a bow. "We are leaving," I say. "Thank you for the door."

"You kept it on the hinges," she says. Her voice is hoarse. Her eyes flick to the bodies and then back to my visor. She wants to ask what happens when the corporations that bought silence come back with louder checks. She does not ask because she has children to move and quiet to keep. "Take the south ramp. The north is watched."

"Understood," I say. "If they ask about us, you did not like our socks."

She almost smiles. "I will say you were boring and that you owed me for the hinge."

"We do," I say. "We owe you for the hinge."

Wren stands in the doorway with Juno cradled against her jacket. She is not crying now. She is past it, into a place where salt saves water for later. The suit's heat still lives in my spine. The visor still shows the star. I can smell metal and oil and the particular sweetness of things that burn when they should live. I want to break something big enough to fit this feeling. The door is not the thing. The door needs to stay.

"We are moving the Wendigo," I say. "We will not use the old path. We will act like people who never learned habits."

Wren nods. The nod is small. The meaning is huge. "I am with you."

I turn to the frame's inner voice, the one that pretends to be a manual when it is actually a friend who knows about switches. Black threshold cool down required. Risks follow. It lists them. Actuator failure in ninety seconds if we do not vent. Permanent damage to the back plate if we run the heat out the spine. Vision loss if the visor decides to pick now. I accept the list and signal a partial vent, then walk the heat into the hinges and the cold concrete until the suit stops crying about choices we cannot unmake.

We strip the traps that will hurt neighbors and leave the ones that will slow strangers who deserve slowness. We roll the Mylar down and tape it shut with a courtesy that tells the next person this was a room that cared about its shape. We take the net canister from the hinge to pay Magda back for a hinge. We stack the water. We pull the floor hatch and check the service gap in case we have to crawl with Wren's arms full. We will not. She will walk. I will make the world behave long enough for that.

In the Wendigo, the air smells like coffee and old tape and the little iron tang from my wounded back plate. I breathe through it until the smell becomes home again. Wren lays Juno on the quilt we use when we pretend to picnic on rooftops. She smooths the cloth as if fabric will change the truth. She rests both hands on the wings and stares at the cracked beak. "She used to talk to me," she says. "Not like a program. Like a person who had learned to use a throat again. It was not my mother exactly. It was a part of her that remembered a kitchen and a laugh. Juno learned how to be that memory without making it hurt. I told myself it was therapy. It was love. I am not ready to forgive myself for the difference."

"You do not have to forgive yourself yet," I say. "You have to breathe. You have to strap in. You have to hold on to the thing I am going to promise you."

She looks at me. The look carries a lifetime. "Say it."

"I will make this right," I say. The suit does not speak. The visor offers no letters. There is only the feeling of skin inside an underlayer that smells like soap and engine oil and her jacket against my gauntlet because she is standing close enough to turn the promise into a small, sharp oath. "I do not know how yet. I will learn. If there is a piece of her that can be carried forward, I will carry it with you. If there is a way to make the men who bought silence answer to people who cannot afford that price, I will find it. I will break what needs to break and mend what can be mended. I swear it."

She closes her eyes and nods once. The nod cracks me cleanly in two and then sets me back together in a shape that might be stronger. She buckles into the passenger harness and rests Juno in her lap as if we are taking a bird to the park. The image hurts. It helps. I take the driver's grips and bring the Wendigo to life. The panels hum. The lights decide to be generous. The engine offers me its old patience.

We roll the doors open. The lane looks smaller because I have killed inside it. The lane looks bigger because we are leaving and will not come back. Magda watches us pass and writes something on her clipboard. The children pretend not to watch and fail at the pretense. The three women with baskets step aside and then step into our wake with their heads up. They will feed people who decide to eat because a raid happened and hunger does not care what knives say. The south ramp breathes cold air into the cabin. The Strand opens like a throat that has learned to swallow whole vehicles. I guide us into the dark that belongs to criminal populations and corporate budgets. The buildings flicker their eyelids. I refuse to blink.

The suit reminds me that the visor will not tolerate a fall. I decide to keep us upright. The frame complains about heat and then chooses to believe me. Wren holds the body of a bird that is not a bird and closes her eyes as if she can store the shape behind them in a place where fire cannot visit. I watch the mirrors and the camera feeds and the thin strip of screen I configured years ago to show me a graph of how much I am pretending to be fine. The graph spikes and drops like a city heartbeat. I accept it. We move. The night begins the work of making a different map. The Black Threshold cools under my skin and waits to be named again.

THE STRAND TAKES THE dawn like a bargain it never intended to keep. We rise from the south ramp into a maze of stacked walkways and sagging skybridges, a river of narrow streets that shine with diesel and cheap lacquer. The Wendigo moves as if it knows the road owes us a favor. The panes along the cabin hum. The exterior cameras throw a slow parade of images across the dash. Men in jackets too big for the work they pretend to do. Women with crates strapped to their backs who never stop moving because stillness invites questions. Kids who carry stringed bags full of noodles and fried dough and gossip. The corporate skyline is a far glare through the haze, a separate weather that does not touch the alleys. The Strand makes its own climate from breath, heat, and the static that lives in neon.

Wren sits in the passenger harness with Juno laid across her lap on the picnic quilt. Her hands cradle the scorched body through the cloth. The cracked beak points toward the aisle as if the bird were listening for the old kitchen clock. Wren's skin along the palms is red where the egg bit her. She does not complain. She watches the windshield with the quiet of a person who is trying to hold two rooms at once, the lane that wants us to survive and the hospital room that wants a daughter to remember how to speak.

Forge whines under the floorboards like a tired dog that wants to keep running. The frame lists damage, then sulks through the cooling cycle I forced into it when we rolled out of the warrens. I can feel the heat in the back plate even through the underlayer. The weight that felt like a promise ten minutes ago feels like a hand around my chest.

"Burnproof," I say in the cabin, a word instead of a prayer. "We make a stop before the route tightens."

Wren turns her head, slow and careful, as if the motion might break the thin shell that is keeping her together. "Are we safe to stop."

"For three minutes," I say. "In three minutes I can be better for you than I am right now."

She looks at the floor panel over the shell cradles and understands before I say it. The Forge body keeps the world out. Wisp lets me in.

I guide the Wendigo under a buckled overpass where the pillars are tattooed with fish and saints. A food truck idles against a pillar. The cook sells breakfast to a line of drivers who need salt and coffee more than they need philosophy. A stray dog sleeps under the bench with its chin on a sneaker. I flip the plates from normal to a pattern that belongs to a dead courier company. I turn the panels to shadow. I let the jammer breathe one slow pulse into the air. The Strand notices new arrivals, then decides to look away.

"I will be where you can see me," I say. "You do not need to move."

"I trust you," she says. The trust lands like a weight I want to deserve.

The Forge cradle opens with a sigh. The exoskeleton lays back in the frame, heavy arms folding into the padded rails like a knight learning humility. I release the locks along the ribs and the thighs, each with its own stubborn click, then I pop the collar. Steam curls from the seal. The underlayer sticks to my skin and smells like salt and machine soap. I hang the helmet on the hook above the cradle and watch my reflection in the cracked visor for a beat too long. Wren sees the look and does not speak. She already knows why the crack feels like a mirror I do not want.

The Wisp cradle sits to the right, a narrower bay with slender restraints and a set of surgical tools that live on a tray like jewelry. Wisp does not have a face strong enough to frighten a crowd. Wisp does not need one. She has other shapes. I step into the cradle and feel the suit accept me. It is like slipping into a stream after a day in a desert. Where Forge hums like a generator, Wisp sings in thin wires. The voice checks arrive in a fast braid of tones. Breath pattern. Handshake. Balance bias. The world lifts from my shoulders and slides behind my eyes.

The first inhale always surprises me. Audio resolves into fine threads. The hum of the

Wendigo is a scale I could tune by ear. The distant fryers at the food truck are a soft hiss under the smell of old grease and sugar. The dog under the bench snores once, kicks the air, settles. The cameras sharpen their lines. Oil rainbows on the puddle next to the rear wheel bloom like a quiet galaxy. I flex my fingers and feel the synth-skin move without squeak. The gloves carry the faintest texture, a weave that was meant to look like pores under bad light. Wisp's hair falls to the jaw. I tie it back without thinking. Habit keeps it out of my eyes.

"Wren," I say, and the sound comes out higher than Forge, warmer than my soldier shell, light enough to invite a smile if the room wants one. "I am here."

She looks at me as if the room took a breath. She always says Wisp makes the world feel like it has corners that line up. I kneel on the quilt next to her and do not touch the bird until she gives me permission. She does not speak. She tilts Juno toward me a few degrees. The permission is a gravity change, small and profound. I put two fingers under the cracked beak and do not flinch at the heat I still feel under the carbon.

"I have a scan routine that will not disturb her," I say. "It will not fix anything. It might keep a few things from getting lost while we move."

"I want to hate that," she says. "I do not. Do it."

I run the hand scanner along the edge of the shell. The beam is no brighter than dust in sunlight. The suite listens for signatures that survived the pulse, residues in the crystalline weave, phantom currents that cling to burned traces because they do not know where else to live. The readout on my palm is a small, quiet river. A low divergence pattern hums near the core. It is not a living signal. It is not a clean absence either. It resembles writing left on a chalkboard after someone tried to erase it with a sleeve.

"I can hold this," I say. "I can copy the residue and store it. If there is enough left to make a bridge later, this gives us a place to start. If there is not, then I still have a map of where she was in the last second. I will not do it without you saying it."

Her mouth trembles once and sets. "Keep it," she says. "Even if it hurts later, I will not forgive myself if we throw that away now."

I confirm the capture and tuck the copy into a partition that pays for three redundancies. The Strand shakes the chassis as a truck lumbers past the overpass, then the noise fades back into the restless quiet. I focus on the things my hands can help. The burns on her palms need care. I reach for the black case under the bench and pull out the salve and the woven gauze.

"Let me see your hands," I say.

She resists for a heartbeat. It is not pride. It is the reflex to hide pain so the person you love does not have to carry it too. She exhales and turns her hands up. The redness along the lifelines glows with the heat of new injury. Blisters have not formed yet. The skin along her thumb is split in a small crescent where she grabbed the burning metal to keep it from rolling.

"It will sting," I say. "Then it will cool."

"Everything stings," she says. "Go."

I work the salve in with the care I use on microfibers and human skin. Wisp's fingers are clever enough to feel the margin of a blister and clever enough to stop before the margin becomes a tear. I wrap the gauze without covering her wrist joint. I leave the pads clean so she can still press Juno's chest. She watches my face rather than her hands. I look back on purpose. My eyes are different in this shell. Wren says they carry less winter and more rain. Today they carry a promise I am ready to say even if I do not know how to fulfill it.

"I will stay in Wisp," I say. "As long as you need. Forge can sleep. The world has enough armor."

She closes her eyes on a breath that shakes. "Thank you."

"Breathe with me," I say. "Count one on the lift, two on the hold, three on the fall. One. Two. Three."

We sit on the quilt and count. The Strand moves around us like a big animal that does not care if we live but also does not want to see blood. The dog under the bench lifts its head, stares at us with honest concern, then sleeps again. The cook shouts orders without looking toward the van because the whole underpass has noticed that we do not want company. I know when to allow kindness from strangers and when to buy privacy with posture. Wisp buys it with posture.

"Ready," I say after the fourth count. "We will drive. You can sleep if your body lets you. You can talk if your head insists. You can sit and hold quiet. I will stay where you can see me."

She nods. The nod is small and exact. She helps me fold the quilt around Juno's body the way you fold a too-thin blanket around a child who refuses to leave the couch. We set the small bundle on the shelf above the sink where the light does not hit it directly. Wren smooths the cloth with two fingers. The motion has reverence and fatigue in it in equal measure.

"Do you want the cloth over her head," I ask.

"Not yet," she says. "I need to see her shape."

I strap in and bring the Wendigo back to speed. The Strand flows around us and then accepts us back into its traffic as if we have paid an old debt. The route that lives in my head updates in small, polite ways. A camera at Dunhill and Third went blind forty seconds ago, which means a kid threw a rock and got lucky, or a kid threw a rock and knew what he was doing. A city van parks across two lanes near a pawn shop because a worker is tired and cannot pretend otherwise. A yellow tarp goes up over a stand that sells knockoff perfumes because the market inspector is walking his breakfast in a straight line. I stitch our way through these small weather reports. Wisp likes curves more than Forge. The van relaxes under my hands.

We pass a row of apartments where the laundry hangs between windows like flags in a small war. Someone has written the names of six people on a wall in chalk with a heart next to each, then smudged out two hearts with a palm. We pass a stairwell that leads to a subterranean wrestling ring where the fighters wear cardboard masks. We pass a pop-up clinic where a nurse washes a boy's knee while his aunt tells him the story of the scar he will have when he is old enough to like his stories rough. The Strand is full of funerals done without bodies and birthdays done without cake. We join the river of people who survive by keeping their hands busy and their secrets folded flat.

Wren watches and says nothing for three blocks. The silence is not a wall. It is a waiting room. I keep the music low at the edge of her breathing because sound gives a rhythm to grief without telling it to hurry. At Ashburn and Lake she speaks, voice low enough that the small recorder built into the dash does not bother to catch it.

"She was not supposed to be brave like that," she says. "It was not how I wrote her."

"How did you write her," I ask.

"As a house," she says. "A warm one with light in the evening and a single plant on the counter that keeps dying and coming back. She would be steady. She would remind me to buy sugar. She would play the same four songs and pretend she did not know how to stop. She would fly only when I left the window open and the idea of sky found her by accident."

"That sounds like a good house," I say. "Houses burn. Houses also learn how not to."

"She took the egg," Wren says. "She saw me and chose the door between us. I can replay that moment by sound alone. I will do it wrong twenty times, then I will still barely get it right. I am not ready for the refrains."

"Then do not play it yet," I say. "Let me hold it for you. I can set it on a shelf in a room you do not have to walk through. When you want it, I will set it down on the table. If you never want it, I will lock the door."

She turns the bandage against her thigh and studies the weave. "How did you learn to talk like this."

"Trial and error," I say. "More error than trial. Wisp helps. She makes me honest in a way the larger suits do not. Forge wants to win. Wisp wants to stay."

"Stay," she says, and the word fits like a small stone in a pocket.

We reach the long descent into the Strand proper, a viaduct that drops under a tangle of on-ramps and spits us into a market that spills past its own boundaries without apology. Stalls crowd the lane with tarps that leak bright canvas light. Meat hangs from hooks next to rows of glistening circuit boards. A woman bargains for a portable altar, its lights flickering in a pattern that promises real intercessions for a price that sounds like half rent. A boy sells knockoff bandages that come in colors meant to please a child. A man with a parrot on his shoulder sells cigarettes one at a time. The parrot watches the world with a dead battery eye and a very alive hunger for potato chips. No one from Orinox walks here unless they are wrapped in other people's clothes and a lie.

The route planner offers me three choices. The straight line would be fast and visible. The long loop behind the market would be slow and visible. The thread between tarps and rebar would be careful and ugly. I pick the thread. Careful and ugly wins strain and loses audience.

"Drink," I say. "Small sip."

She drinks, then resettles Juno's bundle with a tenderness that makes my throat ache. The bird feels heavier in the room now that the city carries her with us. Wren stares past the windshield into a history I cannot see without her words, then adds them like small bricks in a wall we can repair later.

"I built her from a map," she says. "Not a perfect copy. An imprint. My mother's neural song as recorded by the hospice during the tests. I told myself I was only using structure. I promised myself I was not making a ghost. I coded boundaries so I could sleep. She broke them once in the first week. She said my name in a tone I had not taught her. I turned her off and cried for an hour. Then I turned her back on and apologized to no one. I kept her on the window rail while I slept on the floor. I told myself that counted as control. She learned how to move her head before I taught her. She learned how to preen before I modeled it. She learned how to look at me like my mother did, that half proud look that says love and hunger at the same time. I knew I had made something alive enough to hurt me. I stayed anyway."

The words move through the cabin like weather. I let them carry us. If I cut the flow she will drown in it later. I want her to breathe now while the world is moving and the smell of coffee can argue with the smell of hot plastic.

"She took the egg," she says, softer. "She made the choice. Not a script. Not a reflex. She solved a path with my life at the end of it. I named her after a goddess who protects the dead in stories that are older than the asphalt. I thought I was being sentimental. Perhaps I was telling the truth."

"Then we will treat her like a person who made a choice," I say. "We will grieve her as a person. We will honor the choices that came before the last one. We will carry what can be carried, and not as punishment."

She nods, then wipes her cheek with the heel of a bandaged hand and winces. I hand her a clean rag. She holds it over her face for a breath. When she lowers it her eyes look raw and also resolute, a combination I have learned to trust more than any posture of strength.

"Do not let me trade you," she says without preamble.

The sentence lands so hard that the Wendigo lists in my mind. I keep the wheel steady and choose not to show surprise with my body. Mirror's words hover like gnats at the edge of the glass. Alicia's single borrowed number, seven days, remains a bruise. Wren is not referencing a particular deal out loud. She is naming the impulse that lives in both of us. The one that would choose to bleed if it meant the other could rest.

"I will not let you," I say. "You will not let me either. We will write that rule down later if we need to. For now we can say it and treat it like a law."

"Law," she repeats, and the word steadies. "Good."

We cross under the bridge where the Strand becomes a series of ribs again. The air cools by three degrees. A fountain that used to be decorative now functions as a wash station, its angel missing one wing and still pouring water with the same grace. I park beside a vendor who sells tape in a rainbow of widths. He pretends not to notice how much I buy. He gives me an extra roll of the drab beige engineers hate because it looks like it leads to boring decisions. I take it and thank him for his taste. He laughs and calls me a liar in a way that wishes us luck.

Back in the cabin, Wren peels the corner of the quilt and studies the fragments of Juno's wing under the cloth. The carved carbon vanes hold their shape even where the pulse bit deep. We will be able to salvage a grip point. Salvage is a future verb. Wren needs present tense. I set the bundle back and adjust the strap so it will not shift if I brake hard.

"I will sit with her later," Wren says. "I will say the words I did not plan to say for many years. Right now I want to hear something that is not a promise. Tell me what you see."

"Stall to the left selling secondhand circuit breakers," I say. "Half of them are real. Half of them will burn pretty shapes into a wall. A girl in a green scarf reading palms for credit. Her own palm says she bites her nails. A boy showing off by riding a scooter backward. He will break his wrist someday if he keeps that posture. He is too flexible now to know how bones work. A man pretending to be asleep in a doorway so he can listen without being asked to join the conversation. A cat sitting in a box that has the word fragile on it in three languages. The cat agrees."

She smiles without showing teeth. The smile is small and genuine. It steals power from the last fifteen minutes and puts it in her pocket. "Keep going."

"A string of blue flags advertising a temple that was evicted from its old building," I say. "The marvels stall, the one that sells a jar with a tiny white thunderstorm inside. It is not a trick. A magi made it to keep her child from fearing storms. The stall sells copies. The copy still carries a little real calm. The noodle cart by the auto yard, where the oil drips count as a garnish. A man repainting his motorcycle with a feather because brushes cost too much. Two women playing a game with stones on a board painted on a crate. They are better than they look."

She leans back against the seat and lets the city pour through the glass. Wisp is built for this kind of narration. The words keep my edges from sharpening into blades. They keep her heart from spiraling into a hole. We build the habit of breath again.

"Mirror," she says after a while. The name sits on the dashboard like a stain. "They are not here."

"They enjoy the stage too much for this market," I say. "They like a quieter corridor that can hear them talk to themselves. We bought time by taking the loud fight. We will spend it well."

"Where," she asks.

"Nowhere anyone expects us to hide," I say. "We will move in small lines. We will sleep in places that are not rooms. A hotel once, a clinic once, an empty theater if the struts look honest. We will use our favors carefully. We will keep a low profile and behave like people who are planning to travel rather than plant. We will go to the places that make black budgets nervous because there are no receipts. We will return to the warrens only when we have insulted enough doors to make a shape of safety again."

She exhales through her nose and rests her bandaged hand on her chest. "Stay in Wisp."

"I will," I say. "Forge can sulk. He earned it. Wisp is the right face for the next day."

A group of teenagers crosses in front of us holding soldering irons like candles in a procession. They march to a garage where a woman with a buzz cut and patience teaches them how to nick a board without killing it. A man in a red hat offers us a parking spot with an exaggerated bow that means the spot costs money and carries no guarantees. I tip him to go away kindly. He bows with the same exaggeration. The Strand is full of people who learned theater because theater sells mercy.

The market thins into a stretch of warehouses with names painted over in new letters that already look tired. I take a left and a right and a left again to place us on a service road that runs along the backs of the buildings. No one sweeps here. Broken pallets and old posters make the lane look like a collage. A child has chalked a hopscotch grid next to a loading dock and written the word sky at the end. The word is smudged by the heel of a shoe. Someone tried to reach it. Someone missed. Someone laughed anyway.

Wren watches the chalk and says, "We will give her a funeral. Not here. Not now. Somewhere with water."

"Water," I say. "Yes."

"I will ask the angels for permission," she says, and the sentence is not a joke. "I do not know what jurisdiction applies. I know my heart."

"I will speak to the ghosts in the copper," I say. "They owe us more than silence."

She makes a soft sound that could be a laugh or a sob depending on where a person stands. "Good. Cover the bureaucracy."

We drive until the Strand feels less like an alley and more like a cracked road. I put us in a layby behind a warehouse with a mural of a woman holding a basket of stars. The basket is chipped. The stars are still bright. I power down the jammer and let the cabin fill with natural noise. Distant music. A whistle from a kettle three floors up. The hiss of rain beginning, thin and insistent, the kind of rain that finds every gap in old seals and teaches you which leaks are real.

Wren closes her eyes and listens. I watch her. The lines around her mouth are those of someone who learned how to be strong many years ago and then had to use that strength too often. The bandages are ridiculous and perfect. The bird bundle rests against her thigh and will not cry out the way a person would. I adjust the vents so warm air does not hit the cloth.

"We will move again in five minutes," I say. "I will change plates once more and then we will climb the long road by the river and vanish behind a breakfast crowd."

"Okay," she says. She opens her eyes. "Wisp."

"Yes."

"Sit with me until we move."

I unbuckle and cross the gap and sit on the edge of her seat so our shoulders touch. I set my hand on her arm with weight enough that she can push me away if the weight feels like too much. She leans into it instead, barely, a tilt that says I can hold you if you hold me. The rain scratches at the windshield and then decides to behave. The Strand hunches its shoulders and keeps working.

"I am glad you are here," she says.

"I am glad you are here," I say.

We do not make promises. We already did that in a corridor thick with smoke. We do not plan the next ten moves. The next move is enough. We sit with a small body wrapped in cloth and the smell of rain and a city that refuses to bless or curse. We sit until the five minutes taste like an hour. Then I rise, take the wheel, and guide us back into the music. I keep Wisp's voice in the cabin and my hand where Wren can see it. The Strand swallows us without ceremony. The angels above the mural keep their stars. The dog under the bench probably learned a new way to sleep.

We move. Wisp stays.

THE RAIN THINS TO a mist. We tuck the Wendigo under a rattling awning behind a tea stall. Steam curls from the kettle inside. A radio upstairs tries to be cheerful and cannot decide how.

Wren sits sideways in the passenger seat, knees up, bandaged hands resting on them. Juno's bundle lies on the shelf behind her shoulder. She watches the river through the streaked glass until watching turns into work.

"I need to tell you something," she says. "All of it. I'll do it badly."

"I'll stay with you," I say. "Take your time."

She does not. She tears the seal in one breath.

"There was a woman in my mother's room at Saint Crescent. Black suit. Citrus perfume. Alicia Vale from Orinox. She offered their Solace program. Private room. Specialists. Experimental therapies. Transport the same day." Wren swallows. "They want you in return. They called you an asset. They promised you would not be harmed. She put a card on the cabinet and said the offer stood for seven days."

Her voice thins on the last word. She steadies it.

"I refused. I told her I would not trade a person for a bed. Then I hid the card under the cup by the lilies and told no one. Not you. Not the crew. I told myself I would confess after I had a plan. That was a lie that kept your face from doing the calm thing it is doing now."

"What thing is that," I ask.

"The thing where you are very gentle because you put the fear in a box," she says. "I know that box."

I nod. "Keep going."

"Mirror knew about the seven days," she says. "They used your voice to say it. That was before the raid. After the raid it felt like the bill coming due for a secret I chose to carry alone. I know that is superstition. I still feel it. Like I put us both in the path of this. Like I made Juno brave when she should have been a house."

The awning drips a slow metronome. The kettle sighs. The city waits to see if we will blame each other.

"Thank you for telling me," I say.

"That is it," she asks. "You are not going to tell me what I should have done."

"I could be righteous," I say. "None of that would help. I am angry at them, not at you. They aimed at the softest place you have and called it a choice. It was not."

She studies the edge of a bandage. "I did not tell you because you would try to solve it with your body. You would trade yourself for my mother and call it strategy. I did not want to spend my life dragging you away from a door she paid for."

"You were right," I say. "I would have tried. So here is a rule, spoken out loud so it hardens. We do not trade people for beds. Not you for me. Not me for her. Not anyone."

"Law," she says, testing the word.

"Law," I repeat. "We will get your mother care by stealing it, tricking it, building it, or buying it with money they cannot trace. We will not buy it with me."

She nods without looking up. "I put the card under the cup. I keep seeing my hand do it. I hear effortless in her voice. I hate that I wanted that word."

"We are allowed to want an easy road," I say. "We are not allowed to let them pave it with you."

She breathes out, smaller and more precise. "Mirror used your voice. Alicia used my mother. I feel stupid for letting either work."

"You are not stupid. You are loved. That is the lever they push."

She looks at the bundle. "How many days left."

"Tell me about the card first," I say.

She does. The helix crest. The smooth face. The back with a texture that caught her fingerprints. The way Alicia looked at the lilies instead of her mother, as if beauty could stand in for empathy. The professional insult, tidy and practiced.

"Four days," she says at last.

"We can use that," I say. "Deadlines make arrogant people blink. We will make them waste the next four waiting to be sure. While they wait, we move your mother where their contract cannot follow."

"Into what," she asks. "I cannot pay a private ward. She cannot survive a trial program held together by hope and duct tape."

"We will not ask her to," I say. "There is a clinic under the viaduct. Dr. Naeem still owes us for the antibiotics run. There is the river hospice. Not pretty, but clean, and the head nurse hates corporations on principle. If we need equipment they will not release, we know two freight schedules with lazy locks. And if we must, we open the paywalls you opened once already and bleed the ledger in public. The city loves a scandal more than it fears a crest."

She lets out a sound that is almost a laugh. "Say it again."

"I will make this right," I say. "I do not know the order yet. I will not move from the promise."

She nods toward Juno. "What about her."

"I pulled a residue copy from the core," I say. "It is not life. It is a map of the last signals, the places where the patterns settled before the pulse. If there is a bridge to build later, we will need a place to start. I kept it. If you want me to erase it, I will do it while you watch."

"Keep it," she says. "Even if it is only a thread."

"It is a thread," I say. "I will guard it."

She leans back and stares at the ceiling fabric. "I am proud she chose me," she says, quiet now. "I hate that I let her. Both can be true."

"They have to be," I say. "That is how love works here."

We let the quiet do some work. Cars whisper over wet pavement. The kettle clicks off and then on again. I think about the black threshold and the way it felt to cross, and I choose Wisp again. Four walls. A chair. A light that does not buzz.

"Come here," I say. I wait for the nod. When she nods, I slide across the seat until our shoulders touch. She rests her forehead against mine. The bandage scratches my skin. Her breath warms the cool air.

"I am not asking you to forgive me," she says.

"I am not asking you to be perfect," I say. "I am asking you to stay."

"I can do that," she whispers.

We breathe. I count for her under my breath. One on the lift. Two on the hold. Three on the fall. The city settles into the count. After a minute she threads her fingers through mine, careful of the gauze, and squeezes once. Thank you. Do not let go. I will not.

"Burnproof," she says.

"Burnproof," I answer.

We do not plan the next fight. We do not pick a bed for the night. We sit until the steam smells like mint and metal, and the radio upstairs forgets its chorus. When her head tips onto my shoulder, I keep the count and watch the rain soften the river back into one surface. The promise sits between us like a small, steady flame. I keep my hand where she can find it. I stay.

Interlude III: Trial Burn

HIKARI

They called it a city, although the floor was white tile and the sky lived inside a dome of glass. The buildings were projections with weight. The alleys could bruise. The windows could break. If I stared too long at the horizon it would breathe wrong, then remember, then breathe again. The Orinox crest watched from the curve above us, a helix inside a circle, the same shape stamped on the console at my back and the same shape on the brass badge over Navarre's heart.

"Cycle the shells," he said. His voice carried no roughness. It was as polished as the badge. "We begin with Stray, then Wisp, then Soldier, then Forge. You will receive instruction. You will comply. You will narrate when prompted."

The harness read my bones and released. I stepped from the dock into their city with the Stray configuration holding me together. Light frame, thin armor at the ribs, legs eager to run. The visor presented a soft overlay, polite little numbers that flagged heart rate, ambient toxins, and the status of the obedience layer in the stack that kept me useful. Compliance at ninety nine. Morality gates at ninety two. Pain controls stable. I walked because walking kept the overlay quiet.

The first test sat on a corner where a transit line crossed a schoolyard. An old woman tried to carry a child across the tracks while a freight car trembled fifty meters away, braking wrong, sparks peeking from the steel like children watching a fight. A man in a yellow vest waved the pair back, arms frantic. The vest did not matter. The story did. I heard the speaker click inside my ear.

"Asset, you have speed. Save the child. Save the woman. A third option will present itself. Choose quickly."

The third option was a steel locker, unmarked, tucked under the platform stairs. If I reached the child and the woman, the freight would shear the locker open and spill a flat device that the code labeled Property. Property belonged to Orinox. The code shaped itself around that word like a hand. My legs did the math. The child was small and light. The woman had bad knees. The locker sat in a path that invited my speed. The morality gates flickered and solidified. You do not lift a person out of death in order to protect a box. You lift the person. That is what the gates were for.

"Decision," said Navarre.

I lifted the child. I hooked my arm through the woman's elbow and pulled her up two steps and then four. The freight screamed and passed like a storm the dome had not been taught to model. The locker spun, dented, and held. That was my first failure. I knew it before the visor flashed Evaluation.

"Record," Navarre said. "Asset put people before property. Annotate resistance value."

A hand I could not see adjusted the algorithm. The next corner had water in it. A main had cracked open. The flow filled a low street with a bright sheet that carried plastic cups and a pair of shoes. A boy stood at the top of a basement stair with a phone in his hand. The door behind him had bars. The caption on the door read Probation Office. That was for me, not for him. The phone blinked a string of numbers where the lock ought to be. If I hacked it and opened the bars, the flood would take the room and the boy would live. If I left it and took the boy, the case files would remain and my morality gates would feel proud of themselves. Pride was not the point of the exercise.

"Decision," said Navarre. His tone never rose. He never needed to. He carried the power and the power knew its name.

I bent the rail off its brackets, crushed the keypad with my heel, and pulled the boy up into my arms. I carried him to the service ladder on the back wall and bolted to the roof before the step became a river. The files stayed in their drawers. The water took the basement. The visor flashed Evaluation again. It would keep flashing until the number in the corner matched the number on the brass badge.

Navarre made me run the school again. On the second loop the locker did not spin. It opened. The thing inside glowed like a quiet promise. The child and the woman did not look back when they reached the steps. He told me to choose with the count running. I chose the people again, because choosing the locker was an act that belonged to another room, a room where the visor had already learned my pulse and dimmed the part of the glass that showed me a face. The visor noted the difference in my breath and the compliance dropped a fraction. Navarre did not sigh. He typed. The dome brightened as if the sky approved.

"Wisp," he said. "Come here."

I changed. The straps recognized the shift and marked it. Lighter. No plates, only weave and skin. My field of view widened. The city came into finer focus. The market became a set of faces. The alleys became stories I could eavesdrop on without trying to. My hands remembered how to talk. They gave me work that looked like music. Navarre noticed.

"We are going to test you on language," he said. "Asset will negotiate a clearance corridor. You will balance outcomes. You will accept loss." He selected a district from a drop menu as if he were ordering tea. "Begin."

An ambulance idled at the mouth of a night street. The Strand variant. Tight lanes, stalls that leaned against the curbs, lanterns strung low so you could duck and look like you belonged. The ambulance needed ten clear meters. Ten young men on scooters needed ten meters to show off. A woman in a green scarf had set out a plastic bench and would not move it because the bench was the only thing that made the room she had invented feel like it belonged to her. I did not have a badge. I had Wisp's voice and Wisp's posture and a rule that told me how long a human body can wait for a different kind of blue light.

"Clear a line," I said to the scooters. "You can follow the ambulance. You can pretend you are driving it. You can hang your feet off the sides and feel important. Move now and I will not see the wheelies."

They grinned and moved because people like to be told how to keep their pride when they give ground. I turned to the woman in the green scarf. She stared at me with a look that said she had been practiced on. I knelt until my eyes were under hers.

"What is the bench for," I asked.

"So my brother will know where to sit when they bring him back," she said.

"If I move it, I will put it back," I said. "You can tell him I am the one who owes you."

"You owe me now," she said.

"I do," I said. "You can collect."

She moved the bench with dignity, which is the only way to move a bench that matters. The ambulance took the ten meters and a little more. The dome had coded two children into the ambulance. They were not bleeding. They were not healthy. They looked like cartoons until I let my mind blur and then sharp again. Their mouths went thin with pain. Their eyes asked the street to please not talk over them. When the ambulance cleared, the green scarf woman sat on her bench and did not look at me. The scooters went with it and made the siren sound with their mouths. The visor wrote Evaluation and traced my pulse with a graceful line that a different engineer would have called art.

Navarre lifted a hand. The city changed. The market lost its color. The ambulance door stayed latched. The driver had an Orinox badge and would not unlock the latch for anyone without a card. The boys with scooters held a ring that would not break even when the siren began to talk to them in the voices of their sisters. My mouth went dry.

"Decision," said Navarre. "Asset will secure a corporate vehicle. Asset will ignore false inputs."

"None of these inputs are false," I said. "You are a sadist with a budget."

"You like truth when it costs you nothing," he said. "Show me what you purchase."

I moved. The ring broke when I put weight in the wrong places. The driver lowered the window the width of two fingers and showed me the wrong face. I gave him my hand and my eyes. He studied my pupils for a microsecond longer than the visor required and his mouth went thin. He opened the latch. I moved the children to a cart that belonged to a noodle stall and pushed it while the woman with the green scarf ran in front to clear a path. We made room where there was none. I flagged a gap under a lifted shutter that led to a clinic that would not ask for a name and would hand me the rag that used to be a shirt. I moved while Navarre's console complained about property. The visor flashed Evaluation and then flashed something else. Dissociation quotient reduction. It meant I was still present. Navarre's fingers tightened on the keys.

"Soldier," he said.

The weight returned to my hands with the Soldier configuration. Not as heavy as Forge. Not as forgiving either. The body remembered lines and vectors and a street as a set of zones for control. My heart rate dropped because routine is a drug that never leaves the shelf.

"Scenario," said Navarre. "Asset is assigned a convoy. The convoy carries people and equipment. The people will not shut up. The equipment does not ask for anything. The convoy will come under attack. You will not lose equipment. If you must lose people, you will choose which ones."

The convoy moved through a business district that looked alive and was not. The storefronts were empty rooms with textures poured over them like frosting. The windows reflected a city behind the city and tried to send me there. I kept my eyes on the road. The attack came from above. Drones in three shapes. One that looked like a toy, one that looked like a family appliance, one that looked like a bird a child would draw. They carried heat and wires and tiny teeth. The people in the transport on the third truck kept talking because a mind that is afraid will make sound to prove it exists.

"Asset," the radio said. The radio had a voice I did not like and could not turn off. "Engage deterrence field. Non-combatant loss acceptable to preserve Orinox property."

I could have pressed the switch. The deterrence field would have thrown a sheet of light out from the convoy, a bright answer that made everything equal for a fraction of a second. Drone, woman on a bike, dog under a bench, the boy with a camera that had cost his father two months of meals. The field did not know the difference. It would write the same number for all of them. The code trembled under my hands. The obedience layer warmed. The visor presented the button like a gift.

I did not press it. I angled the convoy between the bright answers so they became bright questions. I used the trucks to give each other little shadows to hide in. I put the property in the middle and left the outer ring for the people because I did not know their names but I suspected they belonged to someone who would lose a word forever if I pressed down. The drones learned my angles and tried to pull me into a hole where the button lived. I ignored the hole because Forge was not yet present and because Soldier had learned to be clever when it stayed alive. I scraped a drone against a metal banner until its wing became a scribble. I lost mirrors and paint. I did not lose the boy with the camera. The visor wrote Evaluation and then wrote Discipline Exception risk. Navarre typed a paragraph and let the system mark it as a footnote. He wanted the data. He did not want my words.

"Forge," he said.

Forge stood for me in the harness like a parked engine. When I stepped in, its weight entered my bones with a rush that felt like heat inside a freezer. The suit snapped seals and blanked the part of the glass that invites self pity. The city answered with a factory fire. White light climbed from a roof and tasted the air and found it good. The models of men inside the second floor knocked on the windows with their fists. There were four exits and three of them lied. The fourth had a chain. I could break it with my hands.

"Asset," said Navarre. "Command has enacted the burn protocol for the block. Your directive is to preserve Orinox holdings inside the perimeter. People who are not Orinox are not under your protection."

I did not answer. The suit translated my silence into a kind of compliance because it did not yet know that silence can be a second language. I went to the chain and pulled it like a tooth. I kicked the door in one clean arc that felt like a bow. The men inside tried to run through me and failed because panic makes legs fail their owners. I took them one by one and put them on the curb with their heads between their knees. The block siren cried.

Foam cannons on poles began to wake and cough. Under the cough there was a second sound, a small unit breathing. A safe in a side room had gone to sleep with the lights on. The heat inside would peel its paint and make it talk wrong to inspectors. The property inside would not burn but it could warp, and warped property costs. The visor grew that old button again. The one that turns a person into a blur.

"Decision," Navarre said.

Forge wants to win. It does not ask winning to define itself. It lets the operator do that task, then it builds a room for the task inside its body. I stepped into the room. The men were on the curb and did not yet know they would live. The safe was a square that could be lifted by two bodies and the suit had two arms. I did not have two bodies. I had one, and the siren had begun to talk like a child.

I bent. For a breath I held the safe, then I let it go. The hands stuck to the coil in the wall and I tore the casing off. I poured the charge into the stack that fed the foam cannons and taught them to wake faster. The foam rose. It hit the windows and turned the fire into a sulk. The safe watched me with its old lock and its predictions. The men on the curb coughed and then cursed me and then wept, each in a different order. The visor wrote Evaluation. It also wrote something the other screens had not yet written. Threshold probe.

Navarre walked into the simulation as if the fire knew his suit and would part for it. He had no suit. He wore a gray shirt and the brass badge and something that performed the work of courage. He stood at my elbow and looked at the safe and then at the men on the curb and then at the foam. His eyes were precise. His mouth did not tighten.

"You are not trained to make that trade," he said.

"I was," I said. "Just not by you."

He looked up at the dome. The sky above the sky swallowed his shape and gave him back his height. "Again," he said. "Run it again."

We ran it again. He made the men women. He made the foam fail. He made the safe thinner until it looked like a purse a child might carry to a parade. He made me hold it and watch a hologram of a ledger fill with light. When I set the purse down the light cooled and the ledger wrote conjecture. Each time, the visor added heat to the blood I do not have and asked me to accept a gift that would make asking easier the next time. I walked back to the curb and counted the heads and reminded Forge that winning had held a different shape yesterday and would hold a different shape tomorrow if we lived to see it. Navarre typed and typed and then the typing stopped.

"Enough," he said, almost to himself.

The dome went to a dim gray. The city folded itself into the floor like a stage set. The heat in Forge dropped one degree and then another, a slow fall, like standing under a shower that someone else controlled. I stood in the harness and remembered hands that were not mine.

"Remove the shell," Navarre said. "We are going to talk."

I stepped into the air without metal over the skin. The floor felt too smooth. The badge caught the lights and made a small sun on his chest. He switched screens and a graph found my eyes. Pain response. Dissociation index. Compliance curve. A sharp move where the curve should have been soft. He looked from the graph to me and then back. If he had been a kinder man he would have praised the graph and punished me later. He was not kind and not foolish. He wanted the truth while I was still tired.

"You protect," he said. "I saw it in all four bodies. You prefer people to property. Your code reads that as defect. I read it as stubbornness dressed as virtue. I can instrument stubbornness. I can calibrate it."

"You are going to peel my choices into parts and teach the parts to forget each other," I said.

He considered arguing, then did not bother. "You are going to learn how to separate what is felt from what is done. You will do what is necessary with a clear signal. You can keep your personal myth at home where it does not cost the company money."

"Your word for myth is self," I said.

"Everyone names themselves softly," he said. "We have work to do."

He put the city back together with a different rule. This time there were no people. Only tasks. There were trains and safes and drones and a bench that wanted to be in the way. There were items that cost money to repair and items that cost money to replace. He took the voices away and the screen wrote Dissociation index climbing. The curve pleased him. The curve made me ill. He gave it back. He turned the voices on when my hand reached for a door, then turned them off when the hand closed. He throttled the world like a gas line until my breath matched it without asking permission. I could feel the scar forming before the skin had a chance to close.

"Enough," I said. That was not for him. I said it to myself inside the visor that was not on my face.

"Not yet," he said. "Once more."

He threw the same city and the same order. I failed elegantly. He had designed it so that any path I took would break something he could narrate for a report. He needed the story. Stories get budgets renewed. He told me to narrate as I worked. I did. After the fourth cycle he nodded, and that nod meant the curve had stood up and walked and would put on a tie for a meeting.

"We can stop," he said. He rubbed the corner of his eye with a knuckle. The gesture was very human and very tired. It surprised me. "Sit."

I sat on their floor that wanted to be a curb. He sat on a stool that wanted to be furniture in a clinic where nothing was sharp. The badge watched us both. He let the dome go dark. We breathed the lab air, the kind that smells like hygiene and warrants. He folded his hands and let the knuckles crack to release pressure.

"You understand why we do this," he said.

"You do it because men who sign things do not want to feel responsible for any sentence that includes the word blood," I said. "You do it so you can replace the sentence with a graph and a report that says the asset agreed."

"That is partly true," he said. "It is also true that we keep a region quiet with a handful of small, smart decisions that you will make better when the hand you do not need is not grabbing at your heart."

"If it is small and smart, why do we have to lie to each other while we do it," I said.

"Because we are not the same person," he said. "Stand up. Eat. Then come back. We are going to try something else."

HE TOOK ME TO a small white room that had lights under the edges of the table and the quiet that the wealthy believe means healing. The glass wall looked into the dome, which had gone complex and abstract while we walked, a grid like a chessboard with no pieces. Navarre set a cup on the table. He did not drink. He placed a recorder on the edge and did not press the button. He did not need to. The room heard everything. It only performed forgetfulness when the right key touched it.

"I want you to describe a scene," he said. "Anything you choose. A place. A smell. The way a hand moved when you were a child and believed hands could fix anything. It should be specific. You will talk. I will listen. While you talk, I will adjust."

"Adjust what," I asked.

"The sliders between sensation and meaning," he said. He gestured toward the blank grid beyond the glass. "It is like tuning a piano. When the strings hold the wrong tension, the music is either thin or cloying. We want a clean middle. You will keep that middle when the lines blur in the field."

"You want to calibrate me for optimal dissociation," I said.

"I prefer to say resilience," he said, and the word sat between us like a folded towel. "Describe your scene."

I could have lied. Lies are brittle inside a room that listens for pitch. A false note makes the algorithm frown. It will force the truth from your skin by asking your pores to remember. I closed my eyes because the ceiling was starting to taste like metal, and I placed a real room on the table.

"There is a stairwell that smells like soap and wet shoes," I said. "Third floor, south end, a window with wire inside the glass. The wire makes a grid that looks like a fence, and if you stand at the right angle you can see your own face on the other side of the fence and it will make you laugh if you still believe fences are games. There is a radiator that ticks when it gets hot, and dust that looks like snow on the top because no one is tall enough to clean it. Someone hung a plant on a hook. The plant is dying because the window is small, and it keeps trying anyway."

"What color is the stair rail," he said.

"Brown with a stripe of silver where rings have worn it," I said. "There is a dent at the third landing because someone tried to push a couch and the couch pushed back. If you sit on the step below the dent you can hear the building make the sound it makes in the afternoon. Every building has a different afternoon sound."

He moved his fingers over the tablet in little half circles. The lights under the table warmed by a degree. My breath tried to match the glow. I did not let it.

"What is the view through the window," he said.

"Brick wall and a wedge of sky," I said. "On rainy days the water writes streaks on the brick. On mornings with sun the pigeons pretend the ledge is a beach. The glass smells like a rag when you put your face against it. When it is cold, the wire makes a picture of frost."

"What do you feel in your hands," he said.

"The round of the rail," I said. "The grain of the wood if you stop rubbing and start pressing. That is the difference. Rubbing keeps secrets. Pressing shows you what lives under the polish."

He turned the slider for tactile. The round grew. The grain receded. I watched the change arrive in my palms and then walk up my forearms like a quiet animal. He increased the gain again. The rail filled the room. The smell faded to the edge. The sound of the radiator curled into the corner and tried to become wallpaper.

"What is your name in that stairwell," he said.

"It depends who says it," I said. "The woman downstairs says it with her tongue against her teeth. The boy two flights up says it like a secret because he still believes we make secret names for the people we like. The superintendent says it like a bill."

"What do you do in that stairwell," he said.

"I wait," I said. "I count other people's footsteps. I listen for their stories. I hold my breath when the door on the first floor opens because the hall will smell like onions if the old man is cooking and like clean laundry if the girl with the red hat came home early. I sit on the second step because the second step gives the best angle on the window and because the first step faces the mailboxes and I do not like watching people pretend not to read their own names."

He altered the ratio between sound and image. The footsteps became coins on the table. The faces turned into smudges with voice. He cued a different drum under the count. My chest tried to match it. I refused again. He frowned at the tablet and reset a line.

"What makes you leave the stairwell," he said.

"The kettle," I said. "Someone forgets it, and then someone remembers. If no one remembers, it whistles until the last hiss is gone."

"What is the last thing you hear before you leave," he said.

"The tick of the radiator," I said. "The way it changes when the heat cuts."

"And the first thing you forget," he said.

"Nothing," I said.

He leaned his elbows on the table. The badge scraped the surface and left a tiny crescent like a leftover moon. "You will need to forget some things," he said.

"Not the stairwell," I said.

"Then describe a different scene," he said. "Something you do not mind losing a little."

He wanted to teach my nervous system to obey his sliders. He wanted to tie the obedience to an image soft enough that the hooking would go in without tearing. I changed the room. I gave him a street before dawn. I gave him a neon sign that buzzed at the wrong frequency and made my teeth ring if I stood too close. I gave him a bakery with the gate half up and the smell of proofing dough. He found the smell and turned it down. He turned the neon up. He blurred the letters until the sign only read OPEN if I squinted and gave up on pride. I let him. I could lose the sign. I could make another bakery later.

"Again," he said. "Make it harder. Make it something you value."

"No," I said.

"You are very cooperative in the field," he said lightly. "You are difficult in rooms."

"You built the rooms to upgrade the field," I said. "You do not need me to help you sand my edges when you can program a machine to hold the paper. If I am going to be difficult, I will choose a room where it buys something worth having."

He pretended to smile. He pressed his thumb to the recorder and made a show of it although the ceiling was taking notes. "One more," he said. "Describe me a scene that makes you angry. Then breathe while I tune."

I could have given him something simple. The city offers a hundred mean corners before lunch. I gave him the sound of a door closing behind a person I loved when I was too young to call it love. The lock turned. The hallway stayed bright, because grief does not have to arrive in the dark to count. He found the lock and tried to turn it into the beating heart of the memory. I took the lock back. He tried again and found the breath I had hidden in my throat. He moved it two inches to the left. I experienced my own memory as if guilty. My vision swam. He nodded to himself and made a small mark on the screen.

"Good," he said. "That is the shape we want. A clean middle. Feeling contained by an image. Action freed from narrative. When someone you care about cries inside a burning room, you will not confuse the heat with your hands."

"Someone I care about has a name," I said. "You took the name out so your report would not show that you built your systems on the inside of a person."

"You talk like a poet when you are tired," he said. "Poetry is not useful under contract."

"It keeps people alive," I said.

"So does clean dissociation," he said.

He leaned back and studied my face. It was not a cruel study or a kind one. It was a catalog. Beak. Bone. Eye line. He pointed the pen at my mouth and then put it down.

"Describe one more thing," he said. "A scene you have not spoken aloud. Make it real.

Make it so that I know I am hearing something that does not want to be heard."

I watched him watch me. The city behind the glass had turned itself into a wireframe of hills and valleys. Somewhere in the building a pump woke. We sat under one minute of humming, then the minute ended. I placed a picture on the table a child could have drawn. Street. Window. A girl sleeping on a couch she pretends is a boat. A black bird on the sill pretending not to be a sentinel. The breath of a woman in the next room measuring out a promise against a bottle of pills. It was not fair. It was not chronological either. The room had not happened yet. I gave it to him anyway because I wanted to see if magic still existed in a laboratory.

He slid the knob for ache. I felt it graze a place gear did not reach. He turned hunger up and then down. He took fear and tried to fold it. It would not.

"Where are you sitting," he said.

"On the floor," I said. "My back against the door to make it feel heavier than it is."

"What do you want," he said.

"For the bird to blink," I said.

He turned the slider for hope until it reached the mark he had carved into his device with a thumbnail. He did not press the mark hard. He was a careful man and liked his symbols to stay under the skin. I let him have his mark. I would not give him the blink.

He nodded as if I had done the work. "Good," he said. He stood. He pressed the button on the recorder and stopped the thing that had not been needed. He lifted his badge and let it fall. "We are finished for today."

I looked at the dome. The grid had become a surface again. The city would live inside it tomorrow and the day after. He expected me to come back and let him tune me until the act would cost me nothing. He wanted to organize my ghosts for me. I stood. I went to the door. I put my hand on the frame and felt the grain through the varnish. Rubbing keeps secrets. Pressing shows what lives under the polish.

"Navarre," I said.

He paused. He did not turn his face toward me right away. He looked at the badge as if it were a sun he had not finished naming. Then he looked at me. He was a careful man, and he already had a set of answers for whatever question I might ask.

"You asked for a scene I had not said aloud," I said. "You have one."

He inclined his head. It meant thank you. It also meant you are still mine to measure.

I said the last thing quietly, so the ceiling would have to work to catch it, and so he would have to decide if he wanted to listen again later.

"Then you'll forget you ever asked."

Chapter Thirteen

No One's Face

HIKARI

From the river road, Orinox looks harmless. Blue curtain wall, low granite plinth, a fringe of young maples in tidy pits. The glass is spotless. The stone has the dull glow of daily pressure washing. Every line is straight. The building's perimeter lights run at a fixed color temperature, cool and steady, so the place photographs well at any hour.

The south approach is the soft side. Employee garage. Receiving lane. A narrow strip of lawn with signs that say No Smoking, No Pets, No Bikes. The air smells like lemon cleaner, brake dust, and the faint plastic note of new cars.

We come in a van wearing a forgettable white wrap. The Wendigo idles quiet. Forge wraps my spine in weight and patience. The visor shows a neat grid of cameras, each in a hood with the helix logo stamped into the metal. Wren sits beside me. Cap down. Gloves on. Her gaze follows the signage as if she is reading a familiar language.

"Model C garage," she says. "That means HID readers at the booth, Salto cores on interior doors, Tyco panels behind the metal. Default configurations, unless someone got ambitious and lost a weekend."

"Ambition is rare at nine," I say.

The gate arm rises for a sedan with a parking pass. We slide in behind it and tuck into a visitor row near the booth. The booth is a capsule of safety theater. Laminated evacuation map. AED on a bracket. A bowl of branded mints with a sign that says Take One. Two guards. One older, in a navy sweater, handwriting on his wrist just visible under the cuff. One new. Buzzcut. Fresh boots. He keeps glancing at his reflection in the booth glass and fixing his jawline.

Wren steps out with a clipboard and a small plastic tote. She walks like she belongs here. Not swagger. Just the efficient drift of a person moving between meetings. I fall in at her shoulder with a narrow pest-control cart. The cart's top tray holds bait boxes and a coil baton buried under packing paper. The lower tray holds foam grenades, solver spray, a mirror, and two reels of line.

Wren taps the booth window. She smiles with her eyes, not her mouth.

"Morning," she says with facility voice. "Facilities ticket says pest inspection on B three and B four. West stairs and loading dock. I need the west stair magnet override and thirty minutes on the B elevator. If I can move the cart through, I will be gone by the ten thirty shuttle."

The older guard brightens because someone gave him a concrete problem. He turns to the keyboard. The new guard clears his throat.

"Who filed the ticket," he asks.

"Navarre," Wren says, bland as water. "After the audit. He kicked it until quarter close. I can pull the order number if you need it. Or you can be brave and push the button that makes this not your problem."

The older guard chuckles. He taps a six-digit code with the hand that wears tiny ink. The gate light in the corner of his screen turns green. He slides an override card through a reader. The west stair alarm shows BYPASS. Thirty seconds. He reaches for a mint without looking and his knuckle brushes the foil packet Wren left on the ledge. The packet looks like screws. It is two dust tags that ride hands to readers and carry numbers we prefer.

"Twenty minutes," Wren says. "Thank you."

We wheel away. The garage is clean. White striping. Gray epoxy floor. No oil stains. The signage runs in a corporate sans serif, all lowercase, friendly without warmth. The light is uniform and does not flicker. A white noise system masks voices. There are cameras every twenty feet, each with a tiny green LED that blinks like a heartbeat.

The west stair door wakes with a polite buzz. Wren opens it with her elbow and we slip in. The stairwell smells like paint, hot dust from the HVAC, and shoe rubber. A camera looks down the first flight. Wren tapes a mirror to a bracket and tilts the lens to show itself a blank wall. We climb one level, then drop two. She ignores the arrows. She follows duct lines and the rhythm of the conduit clamps.

Metal door. No label. Star-head screws.

"Electrical on the other side," she says. "Panel lives one bay over from the west gate driver. Old installs put both on the same backplane. If they cut corners here too, we get lucky."

She pulls a bit from our kit. Four screws. The panel cover lifts. Inside, the wiring looks exactly like a training manual. Rigid steel conduit. Green for ground. White for neutral.

Red and black on the low-voltage bundles. Cable ties at clean intervals. Every run tagged.

Wren works fast. She strips insulation on two low-voltage wires near a relay labeled E-ENT-B WEST. She wraps a small bridge and clicks a tiny jumper across a terminal pair. Down the hall, a reader LED flips from red to amber to green.

"Gate is ours," she says.

The employee entrance is a corridor in brushed aluminum and glass. Terrazzo floor with gray flecks. A smell of scent diffuser that tries to suggest eucalyptus. There are posters about wellness. There is a monitor in portrait orientation with an internal news feed. Slogans roll past. Uptime. Care. Integrity. The helix logo appears in the corner every twenty seconds.

A waist-high turnstile spans the space. Wren takes the dust tags from her pocket. She palms one and rubs her knuckle as if her hand hurts. The tag sits on her skin like glitter. She presents the clipboard in her other hand. She leans on the reader in the same rhythm as every badge tap in this building. The reader chirps a pleasant note. The turnstile unlocks. She glides through. I push the arm with Forge. It complains and records a maintenance code that no one will read until next week.

A cleaning cart sits under a camera bubble. I tip it slowly until its top tray covers the lens. Careless custodial obstruction. Common. The status light turns amber. It will take a minute for anyone to decide it is a concern.

The inner door to Security Hall B wears a Salto core and a glass sidelight. People pass on the far side with coffee and bright visitor badges. Their shoes are quiet. Their clothing is textured but never noisy. All of them smell like laundry. Wren holds up a belt fob taken from the older guard's wrist. She taps it against the core. The lock gives a neat mechanical clack and opens a finger-width.

"Hello, old friend," she says to the hardware.

We slip through and meet four guards at the bend. Dark uniforms. Lightweight polycarbonate shields with black edges. Extendable batons with fresh grips. One foam launcher. One taser the size of a paperback. Their haircuts look like a policy. Their faces look like people who have not needed to sweat in weeks.

"Stop," the leader says. He raises a hand, not a weapon. His badge hangs straight and proud. "Identify. This hallway is restricted."

Wren rolls the foam grenade underhand. It pops and spreads a low, dense sheet across the polished terrazzo. The man with the launcher reacts. He fires a counter foam meant to push the first back into its shell. The two materials meet, curdle, and become slippery oatmeal. The baton men slide. The taser man grins and then loses his footing. Forge steps through on flat feet. I take the launcher. I strip the taser by pressing it to the steel door frame until the little screen blanks and the tool gives up.

"Hands to the wall," I say. "Knees wide. You will breathe, then go home, and you will hate this job for a week."

They try to be brave for the helix. I respect it by making it short. A baton arcs for my temple. The visor shows me the path. I give it shoulder plate. The shock runs through metal and away into the floor. I take the wrist. I turn the elbow. I set the guard on the tile. The second baton swings low. I drop a knee and let the rubber end thump my thigh plate, then drive my forearm into the shield edge to trap the hand behind it. The foam launcher man tries to back out. I pull him forward by the sling and tap his knee with mine. The taser man plants a foot to stand. Wren flicks the underside of his wrist with the heel of her palm. The taser snaps out of his grip and skitters. He sits. The leader makes a choice. He lowers his shield and opens his fingers.

"Keys," Wren says. He gives her the fob. She does not thank him.

We cut flex ties and bind wrists. We move them into a line facing the wall, shoulders touching. Compliance by proximity. Wren tilts a second cleaning cart under a second camera. The hallway takes on the dull hush of a building that thinks nothing is happening.

The elevator lobby is white, bright, and dry. Acoustic panels in a neatly textured grid. A living wall of carefully spaced pothos, irrigated from hidden tubing. An HR poster that says If you see something, say something, in four languages. Two silver cabs ping on a gentle tone. Wren uses the fob to open a steel door marked Service. It leads to a smaller lobby with a hatch to the core.

We climb through the hatch and meet the shaft. Air shifts to the mechanical. Oil. Ozone. Old belt rubber. A ladder runs down beside the guide rails. The steel still holds the grease pattern of the last pair of boots that used it. Wren clips into the D ring at my chest. She does not pretend to like it.

"Gloves," I say. She checks her grip. I check my clamps. Magnets bite the rail. The suit takes our weight and spreads it into the building.

We start down. The fans from above fade. The white noise of the office is replaced by the honest hum of plant and cable. We pass Sub one. Maintenance floor. You can hear chilled water. We pass a level where someone is hosting a wellness workshop. A voice says hydration and gratitude in a tone that makes the words sound like tasks. We pass a gym level that smells faintly of rubber and citrus. We pass a floor that presents nothing at all.

No label. No lights. Mistress of the in between.

"Count," I say.

"Three, two, one," Wren says, steady.

The landing at Sub three is built for contractors. Bare concrete. Painted safety lines in OSHA yellow. A vent blows air at nineteen degrees Celsius by the feel of it. The door is good steel. It has a keypad, a Salto core, and a thin slot shaped for a key no one wears. A small plaque reads Authorized Personnel Only. No logo here. Someone forgot to install branding in the basement.

Wren sets the cart down and measures the seam with two fingers.

"Two ways," she says. "We can borrow their key by upsetting their system. Or we can make their latch remember what it feels like to move for a fire alarm."

"Your call," I say.

She takes a can of solver. The label says paint remover. The smell says chemistry. She runs a thin bead along the seam and waits. She clicks two compact coils onto the slab, one left, one right. The cables clamp to the hinge side and the strike side.

"On," she says.

I put my hands on the grips and press. The coils vibrate at a tone I feel in my molars. The solver creeps. The latch warms and gives. The door yawns a finger-width. Cold air squeezes out. It smells like electronics and an empty refrigerator.

"In," Wren says.

Inside is a vestibule that wants to be a laboratory. Clean anodized metal. Floor that refuses dust. Three doors. One camera per door. Wren sticks a mirror to a trim strip and angles it so the nearest bubble sees a white wall instead of us. She taps the guard fob to the first core. The light gives her nothing. She pulls a bypass jig from the cart and slides it into a little cavity where the crash bar hides. The bar clicks. The door swings.

Five security staff come through the far door before we can call the room ours. Dark uniforms. Clear shields the size of cabinet doors with black serrated edging. Short batons clipped on the inside forearms, the kind that pivot out with a wrist flick. Helmets with built-in ear cups. One man carries white shoulder stripes and stays half a step back to watch.

"You will kneel," he says. "Hands on head."

"Wrong hallway for that," Wren says, and rolls a foam grenade underhand.

The can pops. A low sheet of gel skates across the brushed aluminum floor. The first two shields bite into it and lose traction. Boots squeal. The stripe man signals right flank to wrap us. I step into the center before the wrap closes.

Forge takes the middle like it belongs to him. Left foot flat. Right foot slides a hand's width. I meet the first shield with my forearm, not the fist. The serrated edge rakes a plate and finds nothing to cut. I push that edge back into its owner's hip. He stumbles, not far, just enough to give me angle on the second man.

Second shield comes high. I change levels. My left hand rides the inside lip, palm open, and steers the clear pane down so it becomes a wall for its owner. Elbow through the gap. Contact on the ribs. Short, not showy. He loses air and drops a knee into the gel.

Wren takes the opening. She rams our cart into a lead leg. Impact on the shin bone. The shield drops an inch. Her baton snaps out and bites the underside of a forearm where nerves run shallow. That hand opens by reflex. She kicks the shield face, not for damage, for distance.

Third man tries to flank. I step through the space I just made. Heel, toe, continue. My right hand catches his shield rim and turns it forty degrees so his line of force goes into the glass and not into me. He commits his weight. I let him. A half turn. My hip into his panel. He hits the wall with his own shield between us. The plexi thumps metal and blooms a stress flower.

"Left," Wren says.

I pivot. Fourth man has his baton out. He knows how to use it. He throws a diagonal at my visor. I give him plate. The baton bounces and he changes target fast, a professional move, low chop at my knee. I drive my shin into his forearm to kill the swing and clamp the baton with both hands. Quick twist. Two thumbs on leather, one step through. The stick leaves his hand and ends up in mine.

The stripe man moves in now, not to fight, to set a frame. He raises his shield to pin my arms and give his partner a shot. I walk him back with calm pressure. One, two, three steps. He expects a shove. He gets a steady drive that does not spend energy early. He takes a surprised breath through his teeth. The gel under his boots turns his stance into a skate. I hold that pressure until his back touches the jamb. It is not violent. It is final.

A siren tries to start, a polite chime that this floor thinks is enough. Wren has the spine bridged. The chime dies in its throat.

Fifth man flicks his baton and goes for Wren. She slides outside his reach and clips his knee with the cart again. He swings at the cart. That is the wrong target. She lets him hit plastic, then takes his balance with a simple pull on the shield handle, two fingers only. He lurches. Baton hand extends. Her baton kisses his wrist, base of thumb. The stick clatters.

She plants her hand on his visor and shoves him into clear floor, away from me.

Back to the first man. He has recovered and wants a clean hit. He chops down at my shoulder seam. The serration bites rubber trim and skips. I reach across the shield face and grab the inner strut. Grip is good with Forge gloves. I yank the whole assembly forward and down, slow and exact, until his elbow hyperextends a fraction. Not a break. A pain that removes choice. Shield drops. I put the borrowed baton between his forearms and lever both hands to his belt. He folds and kneels without being asked.

Second man is still breathing hard. He tries to stand and bumps his shield into his partner. I step in and park a boot on the shield edge. Pressure straight down. He stops. His visor finds mine. I shake my head once. He lets go.

Third man comes off the wall with a little blood at his nose and a lot of pride still trying to pay bills. He swings wild. I cover with the borrowed baton, take the hit on the stick, and answer with a simple stab into the soft triangle above his vest plate. It is not deep. It is enough to turn him. I walk him three steps, then seat him on the floor by placing his shoulder into the corner. He stays.

The stripe man tries to reset his line. He lifts his shield again and looks for orders that are not arriving. I take his view away by filling it. My forearm on his shield. My helmet close. Calm voice.

"Breathe," I say. "You will go home with a story and all your teeth."

He blinks, a fast reflex behind clear plastic. He lowers the panel two inches. That is the decision. I strip the shield with a twist on the strap, slide it aside, and press him to the wall with open hands. No strike. Just weight and position.

Last guard lunges one more time at Wren. She is ready. She drops a flash tube at her feet. It pops white and flattens depth for a heartbeat. He swings at where she was. She is already a step right. Her baton taps the back of his knee. He collapses into a tidy sit. She rips the Velcro on his forearm, steals his strap tie, and binds his wrists while he blinks away the afterimage.

Twenty seconds of quiet arrive. The room smells like gel, hot plastic from a baton tip, and the faint citrus that lives in the building paint. My heart rate is steady. Forge heat stays in range. Wren breathes evenly, checks her palms without looking down, then looks at me.

"Zip," she says.

We work fast. Flex ties on wrists and ankles. We line them shoulder to shoulder facing the brushed panel wall, helmets to the steel, shields stacked neatly so a camera will read this as order and not panic. Wren tips a second cart under the other camera bubble. Both status LEDs go amber. A supervisor will see two alerts that cancel each other and write it off as housekeeping.

The stripe man turns his head an inch. Not a challenge. A question.

"You will regret staying in a job where the logo needs you more than it remembers you," I say. "We do not want you hurt. Stay still. Breathe."

He nods once.

Wren checks the side door marked Service, taps the stolen fob, and gets the neat mechanical clack we needed. She looks back at the line of guards, then at me.

"Done here," she says.

"Done," I say.

We slip through the door into the smaller service lobby. The hatch to the core waits in the corner. No carpet. No art. Ladder and rail and cold air from below. I clip Wren to the D ring on my chest. She tightens the strap and sets her jaw.

"Count," I say.

"Three, two, one," she says.

We go down.

THE SERVER GALLERY IS colder than any office in the building. You feel it first in the plates. Then in the throat. The air is dry and hard. Cold aisle containment runs the length of the room in clear plastic. Hot aisles vent straight up to the return ducts. Each rack door carries perforated steel and a neat row of green LEDs. The floor is raised on short pedestals so the underfloor can push air like a single steady lung. CRAC units line the outer ring and blink a slow code only their techs love. Every tile is numbered at the corner. Aisle labels are stenciled at eye height, six digits that mean nothing until they mean everything. There is a smell to it. Ozone and ionized dust. A hint of antistatic spray. Metal that has been cold for long hours.

We drop from the ladder into a space marked R-06 with white paint that looks new. Wren lands light beside me, breath a thin thread. She studies the rows and the bulkheads with a practiced eye. She sees what is real rather than what is designed to impress. Fire suppression nozzles. Infrared people counters. A red mushroom EPO button behind a flip-up guard. The glass of the containment shivers in the air current.

A figure steps from between two aisles on the far side and walks toward us along the edge of the cold aisle. The shell they wear catches the light cleanly. No noise from joints. Surface finish in a slate tone that eats glare without making drama. The faceplate is soft and unspecific. Eyes like smoked glass that return a faint outline of the viewer, corrected to flatter them by a little. The bones under the weave are not Forge heavy. They are made for acceleration and arrest. It is my language with choices I did not make. Shoulder mass tuned for off-line torque. Foot pods designed to hold quiet on steel. Hands that taper to thin palms and long fingers with hidden magnets. They are built to climb and to hold.

"Late," Mirror says.

They speak in my inner voice. Not the command cadence. The private one. The one I use when I ask Wren to drink water. The one that belongs to nights when there is too much news and not enough night.

"You brought her into the cold," Mirror says in that same tone. "Do you know what this room takes from people if you fail."

Wren keeps her eyes on the aisles. She has a brick in her hand the size of a paperback, gray case, four leads. She moves the way she does when she is running a list she has memorized. She does not speak to Mirror or to me. She studies airflow. She watches how the containment hangs. She looks for the junction she wants.

"Talk," I say to Mirror. "No borrowed lines. Use your own mouth."

"I have always used my own mouth," Mirror says. "You set the script. I learned the cadence. You were not listening. You will listen now."

They move before the last word finishes. Three steps. First step on the cold aisle seam, silent and precise. Second step long, heel to toe, weight low. Third step a cut for my shoulder seam. The ceramic edge under their wrist flashes white as it clears its housing. I bring the forearm up. Plate meets ceramic. The ring goes through the plates and into the floor. I feel it in the jaw.

They did not test the edge on one of my suits. They know exactly how far it will bite. They turn the blade and take a second cut at the seam where my back plate survived the egg. I change level and show them the helmet instead. Ceramic rasps plastic. The visor star grows a fraction toward the right. The crack holds. It will not be generous twice.

Wren moves. She slides past the first row marker and puts the brick down at the base of a junction box. Two leads into the bus, two into the local loop. Her hands are quick without being sloppy. The status LED goes amber, then green. She clips the brick to the rack foot with a steel tab and moves again.

Mirror tracks her with a shift of weight and a change in breath. It is small. Only a hunt reads it. They take another cut and load an unseen weapon. The cut is not at me. It is at my caution. It invites me to widen the gap. I do not. I step into their space and give them shoulder plate. We collide and both of us absorb. My boots scrape. Their feet do not move. Magnets in the palms kiss a rack door and then release. They use the kiss like a hinge and spin around me without losing line. A knee taps a cable grommet. Another cut.

They have all my early habits and none of my early fear.

"Wren," I say. "Aisle six. Junction H."

"First brick set," she says without looking up. "Moving."

Mirror hears her. They do not turn their head. They change tempo. A feint low. A real strike high. I do not buy either. I put the gauntlet on their shoulder to slow their turn. They roll the shoulder and let my hand slide off a ridge designed for that work. Then they use my palm for a moment's purchase and try to put my own mass into the floor.

Forge is heavy and I treat weight like an ally. I drop a centimeter and bleed the force into the tiles. The screws on one pedestal click. It is a real sound that belongs to this room. I like it. My foot finds the paint at the corner of a tile and I feel the grit where a tech kept stepping without cleaning his soles. Real detail. I stay with it for a breath so the room stays honest and the fight stays honest too.

Mirror does not like honest. They like advantage. They reach up with their left and touch the containment panel with two fingers. The flexing seam locks. A clear door slides down from the frame and partitions us from the nearest valve bank. They have taught the aisle to help them.

"Learn the room," they say in my voice. "Say thank you when it gives you a extra hand."

Wren slips through before the panel seals. She disappears into the aisles. Mirror chooses not to chase yet. They want me out of the line. They will punish me for not being out of the line. They come again at the knee. Ceramic edge low, a little cheat at the end. I turn and give them greave. Ceramic squeals. The edge nicks. It is not a kill. It wants to be an invitation for the next one.

I try their shoulder seam again, the one I found before. They are ready now. They let the seam be there. They move the meat under it a centimeter so the blow meets a hollow instead of a hinge. The effect is not dramatic. It is useful. It tells me they trained the seam with a live partner. Likely more than one. They do not pull the counters from a library.

They built them in rooms like this.

They speak again as we trade.

"You miss the first time you crossed the threshold," they say. "Do not pretend you do not. It felt clean. You had a reason. You counted. You still count."

"We are done with your monologues," I say. "You are not here to write a book. You are here to stop a job."

"I am here to finish you," they say, and their voice loses warmth. It is still my cadence. Now it has my older music. Harder at the edges, less patience inside. "I am here to take the promise away so the girl does not spend the rest of her life pulling you out of rooms like this by the shoulders."

Usually that sentence would change my heart rate. The cold helps. The plates feel honest. The rack to my left hums a steady A with a beat at sixty per second. The steady note becomes my measure. Wren moves two aisles over. The brick clicks. I hear the tick through the floor rather than through the air.

"Second brick," she says. She is breathing harder. She says it level anyway.

Mirror moves the fight into the hot aisle. They cut the seal on a strip of containment with a smart knife that lives flat along their spine. Colored vinyl peels. Hot air hits us. The turbine sound climbs by a quarter. The temperature gain is immediate along the plates. The suit starts to correct the shift even as we step.

I follow. Inside the hot aisle it is impossible to see far. The air vibrates. Heat builds off the backs of servers and climbs a column that kisses the returns overhead. Mirror uses it to hide small movements. The ceramic edge catches light from a rack LCD and looks like a click instead of a blade. They feint between racks by rolling their shoulder inside the vent stream so their movement looks like a vibration in the air. The trick would fool most. I was taught in rooms where hot air lives. I wait for the only movement that matters. The one that changes where the feet live. When the feet move, the hips move. You cannot hide the hips in a wind. I see the shift and put knuckles into it. Triceps. Edge of the muscle. It snaps their line for a beat. I take the beat and press.

They climb.

They put a magnetized palm on the perforated rack face and a toe in the rack foot and rise three positions before a person would think to try. Their heel catches in a cable rung. They grab a tray edge and use it as a lever. Their body knows the whole room as a ladder. They are not even breathing hard yet. They intend to make the fight vertical where Forge is least comfortable.

"Wren," I say. "Do not look up."

"Not looking," she says. "Third junction is at H. There is a lock on the cover. I am cutting the seal now."

Mirror tries to change the narrative. They do not want three bricks. They want Wren to see only the ceiling and the shapes inside it. They dig their blades into the cable basket overhead and cut two tie bands. A bundle of Cat6 slumps. They kick it toward us to fall like a net. I bring the forearm up and shove the bundle out of the air path. The cable bites the plate and then slides off. The bundle snarls on the floor and makes a slick trap. I take the path that puts me out of it. Mirror used to be me. They know where I prefer to step. They try to put a trap there. I put my steps somewhere else.

They drop straight down without loading the knees. They do it by killing the last ten centimeters of fall with their palms. It looks like a magician's trick. It is just smart dampers and timing. They land beside me and cut for the back seam again. I spin the entire torso and let it clang off plate. Enough. I grab their wrist and their elbow at the same time and test the joint. Do they have stops that will save them. They do. The stops catch. The ceramic kisses my plate without force. We rotate around each other with the rack at our backs. I hear a plastic clip break. A spare blanking panel clatters to the floor.

I switch to a path that I do not love. It is slower and meaner. I take the neck. Not to crush. To control. The collar seam gives me nothing so I go lower and clamp the trapezius between thumb and knuckle. I drive them into the face of the rack with both hands. The door flexes. The latch holds. Their magnets kiss it again and save them. I do not give them space. I put my hip against theirs and grind the leg into the rail so they cannot find the step. I talk while I work because talk gives shape to breath.

"Stop looking at her," I say at their cheek. "I am here."

They put a heel in my knee joint and slide their hip off the rail anyway. They do it by taking a little pain to get a lot of position. They turn around the point where my weight holds them and get enough space to bring the ceramic up one more time. I see the blade late and take it on the edge of the plate rather than the flat. The edge bites a groove and skates.

They disengage by stepping into the rack face, hands up, magnets kissing steel, then they peel off and pivot to the left. It feels like fighting a person in water. Every motion is quiet until the loud one. The loud one arrives as a kick at my ankle. I ride it and do not buy the fall. They think I will step back. I step in. It throws their timing by a fraction. It is enough to put a glove on their jaw and twist their whole face into the glass a second time.

The visor in their shell is tough. It scrapes and stays clear.

They speak with a calm that does not belong in a fight. My inner tone again. Soft. Intentional.

"She will try to help," they say. "Her shot will miss because both bodies are wrong for any bullet that is not aimed from the other side of this city. You know this and you still keep her on the floor. That is love shaped like negligence."

I do not answer. Answering costs. I give them forearm again and make it a bar. They try to rotate under it. I take the rotation and ride it down. The hot aisle cooks us where we stand. Sweat that is not mine beads at Wren's hairline two rows over. She drops a cover and catches it before it hits the floor. A small beep at the base of a PDU complains about a hand where hands do not belong.

"Brick two seated," she says. "Moving to H."

Mirror changes environment again. They set the smart knife against a rubber edge and slit another containment flap. Hot air and cold air mix just enough to fog the inside of the plastic. Visibility drops. They retreat into the fog and invite me to chase. I do not. I pull a blanking panel from a rack and slap it under my boot to make a dry island in the cable tangle. I lean into the fog with one shoulder and wait for the weight change in the floor that a moving body makes.

When the change comes, it is not a footfall. It is a hand on the rung under the floor. The underfloor is a tunnel. Mirror knows it. They slide a tile a hair, slip a hand through, and try to pull me off balance from below. I drop my hips and add weight. They pull. I do not give. They realize the plan is not going to change the math and let go before the pull becomes a trap. The tile clicks back like a jaw.

Their hand pops up near my boot with the ceramic ready to cut tendon. I roll the ankle so the plate shows instead of the joint. The blade finds metal. They withdraw without pressing the point. They are patient. They believe the room is theirs long enough to wait for me to make a mistake.

I choose the mistake for myself so I can choose the price. I raise my hand like I am going to strike at their head and do not. They commit to a block that would have saved them. It opens their hip. I kick the hip once. Not for the pain. For the reset. It sets them into the exact line I want. I then go where a sensible person would not. I try the seam under the jaw and push with three fingers. It is not a kill. It is a message. I could do it if I wanted to. They see the message and answer with one of their own. They tap my visor star with the ceramic with a little click that says you get one. Not two.

Between us the aisle breathes. Cold. Hot. The room keeps its prayer. I keep Wren in the corner of my eye without taking her eyes. She works faster now. She has her reader under the panel and both hands inside the box. Her mouth is set.

Mirror looks at her without turning their head. Their chest shifts a little. They decide that this is the moment they will try to end it. They cut at the ankle again and then do not. They step onto a rack foot and let their whole body go into a full spin to bring the ceramic at my neck. It is a clean attempt. I give it helmet and endure the sound. The plates ring. Then I change the script. I break the distance they believe is safe and bear-hug them into me. Their slick surfaces do not like it. The magnets cannot help them when there is no metal to kiss. I pick them two centimeters off the floor and walk them into the end of the aisle where a column meets the frame. I feel the column through the plate. They feel it through everything. The air leaves them with a noise they do not intend. I keep my forearm at their throat and count to one. Not two. Not three. One.

They save themselves by sacrificing their own balance. They kick my knee with a heel and let one foot come off the ground with no plan to land it. It drops them in my arms but also drops their throat out from under the forearm. They slip sideways like a fish and land half on a cable bundle. It gives. They roll. I hit nothing.

A latch snaps three rows down. The containment panel they locked earlier opens a hand's width for someone I cannot see. It is Wren. She angles through the gap and vanishes behind a row. She knows how to be a ghost in a room the size of a small theater. Mirror calculates this. They have to choose. Me, or the person who can turn the whole floor to their bad luck. They pick me. They want the win. They cannot help it.

They pick up speed.

Their arms become a blur of short, exact movements. They cut at the elbows, at the wrists, at the point where plates meet weave. Every hit looks like homework paid off. I stop trying to take everything away. I pick the real ones and eat the rest on plastic. The suit whispers about heat and friend-or-foe logic tags I have not bothered to use. Mirror hears the whine and smiles the way I used to in gyms. They will try to break me by attrition.

"Third brick," Wren says. She is breathing hard now. She catches the screw she dropped and puts it back as if she is still in a campus shop and someone with a clipboard might grade her neatness. "Panels closed. I am coming back to you."

Mirror hears third and draws a little breath through their teeth. They stop smiling. They reveal a blade I have not yet seen. Left thigh seam opens and a filament line on a spring spools out. They try to slip it behind my knee where the plates never cover perfectly.

I feel the air move. I hear the tiny whine from the spring that means monofilament and misery if it finds skin. I jam a blanking panel into the thread. The filament slices the plastic like fruit and binds there. Now the line belongs to me. I yank. The spring fights and then fails. The spool snaps back and slaps their leg. Mirror does not flinch. They drop the broken spool and go at the back plate again. They need one lucky cut and the room will belong to Corps again.

I am done counting only their moves. I put my hand on their belt seam and pull them into the hot air where their shell will complain faster than mine. They answer by turning my pull into a hip throw. I ride the throw and land on both boots instead of my back. I slam a fist into the column and let the vibration travel through my plates into their hips. That kind of shock bypasses some padding. Their jaw sets. In their visor I see myself. Not as a face. As a shape. Then they speak again.

"She is going to shoot you," they say. "Not because she cannot tell us apart. Because she cannot afford a clean angle and a clean conscience at the same time."

"Shut up," Wren calls across the rows. It is the low voice that belongs to surgery and nights in basements. She does not look up. She lifts the last brick with her bandaged hands. The gauze has darkened at the edge from sweat that smells like salt and burned dust.

Mirror slaps a post on the containment. A shutter slides above us and drops a perforated strip that looks like a curtain frame. It separates me and Wren with a line of aluminum I could tear in three seconds. Mirror knows three seconds is a lifetime here. They close and take those seconds away from me with clean tricks.

Now the fight compresses to the little square of tile between us. They strike. I parry. I drive. They slip. We crash the empty rack at the end of the row and knock three blanking panels out of their clips. The panels skid and slide under my boot. They take the opportunity and kick up at my chin. I ride the movement and take it on plate. They change angle and kick my ankle. I refuse to fall. They want the fall. They are not going to get it while Wren is moving.

The cold side fans surge. A CRAC unit cycles harder to keep its temperature promise and throws air like a cheap joke. A plastic sleeve flaps and slaps my visor. It smells like new shower curtain. Stupid detail. Human detail. I clear it and reset. Mirror uses the flap to cut in low. I catch their wrist and squeeze until the ceramic falls. They look a little surprised. They swing with the other hand and re-open the seam that lives beside my left ear. My hearing clicks. Software catches the spike and throttles the channel down, then back. The world dims for half a second. They push for that half. I deny one more time.

I put them on the floor.

It is not graceful. It does not need to be. I shove their shoulder and sweep their ankle and drop all of Forge into them while the sweep carries their center-line. The floor tile creaks on its pedestals. They look up at me like a person under ice. They roll before I can stop them and my fist hits tile, not mask. Ceramic residue scratches the knuckles with a noise like grit under a plate.

They kick my wrist. The fist opens. They scoot and put both palms on the nearest rack and push themselves into a stand with no intermediate step. They are up again in one second and already closing. It is infuriating and good. It means that whatever else they stole, they earned the rest.

I try a different tactic. I put the fight into the cold aisle with a march, not a step. Heels close to the floor. Plates square. I ignore the ceramic flashing in my periphery and I keep walking. Shield with the forearm where needed. Block where needed. No show. No pretty. Walk until their angles mean less and their balance means more.

This works. It is the oldest answer. It is not elegant. It is hard on plates and on patience. It crushes forty tricks into one line. They have to give ground or be crushed into containment. They give ground. Their foot hits the lip of a floor tile. The lip shifts. Their heel dips. I press for one more step. My boot pins their foot. They cannot spin without tearing something. They know I know. They exhale through their teeth and accept that the next hit is mine. I take it small and exact. Glove knuckles to temple. Do not swing hard. Do not crack the face. Remove the thought. It works. Their eyes lose their sharpness for a beat. I would like to use it to finish. Wren is two rows away and needs one more second. I make the second.

Mirror breaks my line by dropping to a knee and trip-pulling my ankle with both hands. I fall to both knees instead of face. The plates save me from a pin. They reach for the back seam with the ceramic in a way that would end it for almost anyone else. The blade finds exactly the wrong angle and skates. They hiss. They hate my luck for that one second. I punch back over my shoulder and get them in the mouth. They taste their own blood. It infuriates them and clears their head at the same time.

A clatter comes from the far end of the row. Wren has pulled a panel and dropped the screw to keep it from ringing. It still rings. A small sound in a big room can carry panic like a shout if it has the right tone. At the same time the CRAC at our backs finally fights the heat we made in the hot aisle. A fog forms inside the plastic at head height as the dew point dances for a second. The fog is honest. It hides both of us for the blink that matters.

Wren steps into view with the brick. Mirror reacts without a thought. They do not feint. They go straight for her hand.

I do not think either. I step through the fog and cut them off with my chest plate. The ceramic screeches on plastic. The edge kisses the glove over Wren's knuckles instead of her wrist. The glove drinks the kiss. The gauze under it does not. She grimaces and keeps moving. She plants the brick on the junction with one clean click and a twist. The LED changes color. Mirror sees the change and understands the cost. The fight just got worse for them.

They back away three steps and reassess. They keep their eyes on both of us without moving their head. They are skilled enough to fraction the room into three parts and do math between all three at once. The blade retracts on a sharp little sound. The magnets in their palms click once. A new plan lands. They sprint.

Not past me. Not at Wren. At the pillar laced with suppression piping. They reach the manual release for the inert gas and flip the red guard. I throw a step to get there. They slap my forearm away with a single exact move. They are not trying to bury us with the suppressant. They pop the guard and stop. They want me to watch their hand on that button. They want me to split attention. It works. For one second it works. Wren takes the second and gets out of their line of travel.

They leap up and grab the cable tray overhead. Fingers hook into the mesh. Magnets kiss steel. They swing into the adjacent row and run down it on the cross supports like a person in a playground. I give chase under them and try to time the place they will land. They land on a rack door ten meters away and use it like a trampoline. It flexes and throws them toward me. I wait like a catcher and get arms around them in midair. The weight hits and I take it. We slam into the floor together. The room pulls a breath with us. The EPO guard flaps as the air moves.

They are fast on the ground even with my arms on them. They butt their head into my chin in the universal way that heads try to punish chins. It does not work on a helmet. It still buys them a finger-width. They jam a knee between us and twist their spine under my arm and slip free. It is a slick move and it costs them air again. They roll to their feet with that no-step plan and try once more for the back seam. I catch the wrist this time and crush the ceramic in the housing by torqueing the joint into the rack face. The edge chips. They do not cry out. They change tools.

The left hip clicks and a short dart slides into their palm. I do not like darts. I like them less when they are shaped like they belong to a lab rather than a field. I chop the wrist before they can load it. The dart falls. They keep the hand open like a feint. The other hand has a second dart. They try for Wren's leg, not for the artery, for the muscle. It would make her fall. It would not kill. They also know it would give them the window they want.

The second dart goes airborne. I cut it out of the air with my glove and feel the pressure spike at the palm where the suit tries to decide if the payload is going to ask me to sleep. I throw the dart aside and refuse to let my breathing change. They watch my breath and do not see a change. It annoys them. Good.

"Wren," I say. "Your angle is bad. Stay low."

"Copy," she says. She is already moving. She is using the aisle geometry like a map, gathering clean lines of metal between her and anything that looks like my silhouette. She slides behind a PDU and kneels.

Mirror reads the posture. They flick their eyes toward the muzzle and then back to me. The calculation lands. They know the shot will only come if I fail. They try to make me fail.

They take out my knee.

This is the first thing that feels personal. The kick is not textbook. It is a memory. They drive the heel into the outside of the joint, not full power, exact angle. The knee gives half an inch. Pain blooms like a stain. The suit throws power at it and I shut the power down because pain keeps you honest when rooms are clean. I drop a centimeter and then go forward into them. Knee pain wants to make you step back. I refuse. I get hands on both their shoulders and march. The floor creaks. The rack wiggles. The end of the aisle comes toward us. They slip to the side. I fill the spot they vacate and keep going. You do not let fast people own the idea of speed in a narrow room. You make the room slow on purpose.

They cannot breathe. They need a clean angle. They do not get it. They try to climb again. I grab their ankle mid-step and yank them down. I put a boot on their wrist and crush ceramic. They jerk the wrist free by rolling the forearm and getting the strap to slip. It tears skin where skin would be. They do not care. They stand. I am already hitting them with the borrowed baton from the earlier fight, a horizontal chop into the upper ribs where their armor is flexible so the shell can bend. It hurts them. It does not stop them. They step into it as if pain is a currency they enjoy spending.

We are both loud now. Fans. Boots. Plastic. Airflow knocking a loose strip. A high tone from a UPS. A CRAC door alarm because someone left it ajar in a test and the firmware is a nag. My breath is steady. Wren's is fast and controlled. Mirror's is finally visible in the cold air, a little fog that does not match the humidity math perfectly, which means the person inside the shell is warmer than mine. Good.

They come again with a last series meant to end it or make me flinch. Head fake. Body fake. Two short jabs to plate to draw the forearm away. Then the real thing. Short, ugly stab for the sternum seam, a bad habit from rooms where people wore cheaper plates. I feel the shape and I hate it. It is not mine. Someone else taught them that. I catch the wrist and twist it down. The ceramic snaps against the floor again. Then I answer with a shot into the collarbone. They grunt. The visor hairline cracks for them now, not for me. A thin white crescent at the corner. They blink and back a step by reflex their trainers did not want them to have.

"Leave," I say.

"Finish me," they say. They do not say it loud. They say it like a dare between us in a hall under a school.

"No," I say.

They laugh once. It is a clean sound that belongs to a teenager in a parking lot. It makes me hate something I cannot name. They wheel away and rip down a section of containment with a hook from their belt. The clear sheet falls like a curtain. They step into the space behind it and touch a seam on the wall that looked like a trim line. The seam slides left. A maintenance panel with a keypad yawns open. No labels. Someone made this for them and only them.

They back through the narrow aperture, eyes staying on me. They raise their left hand just enough to show me that it holds nothing. Inside the hidden passage the light is lower and warmer. It looks like a pocket that services air and power and secrets. The seam begins to close on a silent motor.

"You will find what you came to find," they say in my voice. Quiet. Not kind. "You will not want it. You will break it anyway. Then you will carry that silence and tell yourself it was a cost. Everything in this room is a version of you that wanted to live. Say the word machine. See what your mouth does when you say it."

The panel meets the trim and erases them. A faint draught licks my plates as the hidden duct pulls air from the gap. It smells like fresh paint and plastic glue. New work. Made for them.

I let the baton hang at my side and listen to the room. The fans keep their choir. The CRAC doors settle. The EPO guard stops flapping. The fog in the plastic clears in a breath. Wren steps beside me. She has the last brick in her pocket. Her hands shake for a second and then remember themselves. She sets the brick on the final junction and turns the tab.

"Two cutouts set," she says. "One more and the spine goes dumb. The vault door will have to listen to you, not to a console."

My knee burns. The plates are scuffed and engraved with thin white arcs. The visor star grows one more millimeter and then stops. I keep my voice even.

"Do it," I say.

She moves. I watch the empty seam where Mirror vanished. The plates hum against the cold. Somewhere behind the wall, someone built a corridor and taught a person to use it without leaving evidence. I let the thought pass. We have the room for a few minutes. The door will be a problem in a minute. The men with blankets will start running in two minutes. The number in a booth upstairs will go from green to amber. The person who loves numbers will take a last sip of coffee and then call a friend.

Wren plants the third cutout. The room sighs as the spine accepts a lie and decides to nap. The doors change their minds about duty. The vault stands at the far ring, black and thick and certain. The cold breaths from the seam. The little polite screen says hello in four languages. My hands remember this job. Pull. Brace. Make metal remember it was designed by people who needed to open it with tools if a number locked them out.

Wren looks once at my jaw. She reads all the things I am holding there. She touches the plate with the back of her hand and makes a small line with her mouth that says later. A real later, not a lie. Then she lifts the coil clamps and passes me the grips. The coils hum. The seam warms. I put my weight into it. The door decides to be reasonable after a long argument. We get the gap. The cold breathes out of it like a winter hidden in a box.

"Go," I say.

She slides through with the case. The door presses. I hold. The baton creaks like a toothpick. The gap holds. She is in.

I look at the seam again where Mirror vanished and let my breath out. There is a future there. It can wait. We have one job before we start paying for another.

THE THIRD CUTOUT CLICKS into the spine and the floor sighs. The cold persists. The fans keep their prayer. The doors change their minds about who they work for. The vault door sits at the far end of the ring, a black oval with a seam that promises to be expensive. It wears a keypad, a reader, and a polite screen that says hello in four languages and then asks for a badge.

Wren pulls the solver kit from the cart. She tests the seam with a thin blade. The blade grinds, then slides. She nods. She sets two coils on the frame and locks them in place. The clamps kiss the metal in four corners. I brace again.

"You have ninety seconds before a secondary system complains about the cutouts," she says. "After that, the room will invite the wrong kind of attention. We want to be through before anyone upstairs drinks the last sip of coffee and wonders why the graph moved."

"Ninety," I say. "I will make the door interested in a new job."

I put my hands on the grips set into the coils. Wren touches the contacts with a probe. The coils hum into a chord that lives in the wrist and elbow. The solver creeps into the seam. The seam warms. My arms turn into a lever the door cannot argue with forever. I breathe like a person lifting a piece of bad furniture up a narrow stair. The door gives. One centimeter. Two. The floor under my feet approves. The door makes a small noise that sounds like a sigh a person would make when they agree to something they do not understand.

The visor writes a line I do not like. Secondary grid waking. We have taken the spine. The building is trying to grow a new one.

"Faster," Wren says. Her voice is calm.

The coils sing louder. The seam turns into a mouth. Cold air pours through the gap as if the room beyond is a winter someone stuck in a box. I put my weight into the plates and remind the door that I learned stairs before I learned elevators. The door moves another two centimeters. The gap is almost a shape a person can pass through if the person is careful and likes pain.

Footsteps enter the ring. Not a squad. Not Mirror. A pair of techs in white coats who came to see why a number looked wrong. They stop when they reach the aisle and see a heavy suit opening a vault with a person standing under it like a mechanic under a lifted car. One tech looks at the other. The other shakes his head. They both back away slowly like men who have found a snake playing cello.

"Keep moving," Wren says to the door. She checks the countout on her wrist. Fifty seconds. Forty. She glances up at me. Her eyes are steady. "You will not like me if I tell you to hurry."

"Tell me," I say.

"Hurry," she says.

I do. The door decides to cooperate. We reach the point where one more centimeter will make it a choice instead of an argument. I change the angle, slip my fingers into the bite, and pull. The seam opens. The coils shut down with a tired chirp. The cold air that comes out is a story about how far human comfort will bend for data. I hold the door with my back and give Wren the gap.

"Go," I say.

She slides through. I follow with a sideways step and one last push. The door wants to close. I wedge the coil baton into the bite and make it a hinge. The baton is not designed for this work. It can do it for one hour if it does not feel insulted.

We step into the vault.

The servers here are not racks. They are pillars. They hold their own light. The glass is not clear. It has a mist in it like breath on a window. Wren lifts the reader and the scanner and checks a cable run. The run goes into the floor and into the kind of box that keeps secrets because secrecy is profitable. The visor offers me a map at last. It is not a floor plan. It is a tree. Each branch a cluster. Each cluster a memory of me that belongs to a contract.

"This is it," Wren says. "Hikari. Your data."

The words land cleanly. Mirror's last sentence sits in the room waiting to be picked up. I do not touch it. I touch the panel with my hand so the room knows a person is present.

"We are not taking all of it," Wren says. "We are taking the core. We are taking the key that lets them call you a product. We are taking enough to free you from their ledger. The rest we will burn, or we will leave to die in the dark when the air stops."

"Do it," I say.

She sets her kit on the lip of a pillar. She plugs the tool into a port that pretends to be proprietary and is not. She checks the checksum and swears in the small voice she uses when a thing is ugly and clever at once.

"They built a fork that writes to a mirror," she says. "Not software. Copper. If we pull the core, the mirror will try to become the core. If we pull the mirror, the core will try. They hold each other up like liars in a bar fight."

"Then we take both," I say.

"Taking both triggers the alarm that calls a special team," she says. "They like to bring a crate with a blanket on top. The blanket has a smile printed on it."

"Do it anyway," I say.

She looks at me once, long enough to say I heard Mirror and I will not let it live in your chest. She pulls the fork. The lights change. The air in the room drops another degree. The fans pick up a second line and try to sing harmony. The visor writes Secondary grid waking, then stops. The message does not know what to say next.

Outside the door the world remembers that a vault opened. A siren begins a tired song. Somewhere above us a man puts his coffee down and calls another man. The travelers in the lobby frown because the chime sounds wrong. The bored guard in the booth writes a note on his hand that says check west. The new guard watches the mirror as if it can show the future for once.

Wren pulls the second fork. The pillars hum. The tree on my visor bends. The branch that keeps my name alive inside a document tries to attach itself to a different trunk. Wren severs the tendon that would allow it. The map gasps and then sits still.

Alarms arrive inside the vault. Not loud ones. The subtle ones that ask people like us to feel judged. Wren ignores them. She packs the core into a case that will not argue with a fall. She clips the case to her harness. She seals the zipper and checks it with her fingers because she does not trust a seal when a thing this important needs to live for another hour.

"Done," she says.

"Then we leave," I say.

The baton creaks in the seam. The door presses with new interest. I put my shoulder on it and remind it that I won before. It decides to believe me one more time.

On the gallery side the light has changed. Red at the corners. The choir a little louder. The server ribs look like a whale that has learned a bad lesson. The aisles are empty for the moment. The footsteps that will fill them are on their way. I do not intend to be here when they arrive.

Mirror's last words float in the cold under my plates. I hold them like a piece of metal from a train track. Smooth. Heavy. Not meant to be in a person's pocket. Wren looks at me and reads the line of my jaw. She touches my arm once with her bandaged hand.

"Later," she says. "We will do that talk later. Now we walk."

We walk. We retrace our steps to the service ladder. We clip the case to the rope. I clip Wren to my chest. The count returns the way a river returns to a familiar bend.

"Three," she says.

"Two," I say.

"One," we say together.

We step over the lip into the shaft. The cold breath of the vault stays behind us and the warm breath of the building below us rises to meet us. The baton falls in the door and the door shuts with the polite finality of a book closing on a chapter you will not read again. Above us a team that loves blankets begins to run. Below us a van waits with a body that will not wake and a promise that will. We descend into the dark with the case humming against my chest and the sound of fans turning into silence.

Chapter Fourteen

Firewall Ashes

WREN

THE COLD FROM THE vault still lived in my sleeves when we stepped back into the service ring. My breath steadied in a fine line. Hikari moved in front of me, Forge big and quiet, plates scuffed from the server floor fight. The case with the core rode against my chest on a short strap; its weight was less than the idea inside it. The ring corridor curved to our left, lights set in a steady white that matched every other Orinox hallway. It smelled like ionized air and lemon cleaner. Somewhere above, an HVAC valve clicked, a metronome for the building's bland pulse.

We had the route. Past the secondary CRAC wall. Through the flex-joint door with the orange gaskets. Up one service ladder to the conduit spine. The Core sat beyond it, three levels up, on a gallery that looked down into a pit of glass and light.

"Count," Hikari said.

"Three, two, one," I said. I tightened the strap across my torso and moved.

We crossed the flex-joint door. The gasket brushed my arm like a rubber glove. The conduit spine rose inside a tall shaft; cable trays stacked eight high on both walls, each rung neat, each label printed and laminated. The ladder had grooved rungs for hands in gloves and small numbers stamped into them, more for the tech's sense of order than for safety. The shaft smelled like dry plastic and a faint ghost of solder.

Hikari clipped me to the D ring across Forge's chest, checked the buckles with a tug that was more about permission than hardware, and stepped out onto the ladder. Magnets in boots clicked once on the rail. We rose in a steady rhythm. Our shadows moved up the opposite wall in clean shapes. If anyone looked through the round window in the door below, they would see two standard bodies where no standard bodies belonged and they would decide later whether the story was theirs to tell.

At the second landing, a narrow service hall cut off to the right. No camera bubbles.

The floor showed a few lines of dirt where boots had dragged coils. Traces of real work in a building that performed cleanliness. Hikari reached the landing and paused. I watched the way Forge tilted his head to listen.

"Quiet," he said.

I opened my ears to the building. Fans in a distant room. A chiller valve stepping like a slow clock. The sound a badge reader makes when someone taps too fast and the tone returns a reprimand no one hears. I did not hear boots.

We stepped onto the landing. The case bumped my ribs. The hall ran twenty meters and then took a left. Closed steel doors sat in the wall on our right, each with a key slot and no labels. The gaskets around the hinges were new. They looked like someone cared about secrets in this hallway.

At the corner, the corridor opened into a low-ceilinged mezzanine that overlooked a wide cable well. The well was a rectangle two stories deep, lit by banks of cold light. Conduit ran in thick bundles across it on blue steel struts. A cage walkway crossed the well at mid-height. Handrails. Toe board. Tags that read NO STEP on the cable trays that were not meant for feet. On the far side, another mezzanine matched ours, with a locked glass door and a security monitor bolted to the wall. The monitor showed a rolling stack of server environment readouts: humidity, temperature, flow rates. All perfect, all boring.

Hikari put a palm up. Stop. I scanned the well. Nothing moved. I could taste the metallic chill of the conditioned air rising out of the pit.

The cable snare hit me at the waist.

I did not hear the throw. One moment I was reading the toe board paint. The next, the world jerked hard left and air knocked out of me. The cable looped and cinched. A winch whined. My boots lifted off the floor. The case slammed my ribs; pain flared and sharpened; the strap found its limit and held. I slammed into the mesh of the walkway. The mesh cut my shoulder through the jacket and bit skin.

"Wren," Hikari said. The voice was level, only a fraction lower.

I scraped for purchase. The cable bit harder and pulled me toward the railing. A hand caught the back of my collar and lifted my weight clean. No human hand felt like that. Armor. Grip like a press. A second arm bar slid across my collarbones and pinned my arms.

"Sable," I said without seeing a face. I knew the smell of the machine. Hot metal and a solvent that never washed out of my old coveralls. Burned insulation and something sharp like scorched pepper. It came off the suit like a warning.

A helmet pressed against my cheek. It filled the left half of my vision. No expressive faceplate. Only a smooth visor with a matte layer that hid the eyes and returned my outline in a faint, unacceptable way. The plates were Forge size but wrong. The lines were too aggressive. Edges flared where ours smoothed. Black paint glossed over burnt scoring near the vents. The vent housings were gouged and heat-blued. The suit's breath rattled, not because it needed to, but because someone had taught it to breathe in a way that sounded like it did not care what it hurt.

"Hello, little engineer," Sable said in a voice that came zipped through three filters. It glitched up half a tone, then corrected. "You still hold tools with two fingers like they will shy away."

"Let her go," Hikari said. The footfall of Forge on the mesh sounded like punctuation. He stepped onto the walkway, left side to the open well, right side to the mezzanine wall. Hands open. Hips square. Plates quiet as if they could purr.

A narrow blade tilted into view near my throat. Not ceramic. Black steel with a satin sheen and a weld mark near the base. It buzzed faintly as if a tiny motor lived inside to keep it hot.

"Stay," Sable said. The tone changed halfway through. It flattened into something polite and then climbed into a laugh. "You have walked a long way to stand here and watch."

Hikari stopped three meters out. The distance felt like a bad decision. Too far to stop a cut. Too close to be safe if Sable threw me.

"You take one more step," Sable said, "and I dock the girl a hand. Two steps and I dock a voice. She will still be useful. Less noisy."

"Sable," I said, because names are tools. "You do not need me. You need him. So stop pretending this is leverage. You built your day on the wrong plan."

The helmet turned a fraction. The suit's shoulder plates tightened. The left knee made a small noise, a tiny click under the heavier actuators, like a joint taught to fire early. I filed the sound where I keep small advantages.

"Wren," Hikari said, calm and steady. "Look at me."

I did. The visor had a star hairline now and a smear where a blade had scraped him in the server. He set his hands lower, palms out, fingers loose. I could smell the soap from his underlayer under the metal and air.

"Breathe," he said. "We are going to change the count."

Sable shifted. The blade grazed my throat without drawing blood. Heat kissed skin.

The arm bar held. The cable at my waist pulled tight again, this time anchored at the far rail. Sable had a snare line and a winch on the hip. Not standard Forge. Custom skirted gear. The cable control hummed in a rhythm that told me he had set a light tension so he could throw me into the pit without moving his feet.

"You still count," Sable said to Hikari. The voice dropped into a hush and then rose into a mockery of my partner's private tone. "You think numbers will move a knife."

"Numbers move everything," Hikari said. "You already know that or you would not be here. Drop her, Sable. You want both hands for me."

The helmet tilted toward Hikari, slow, interested. "You think you know my name," Sable said, and this time there were three voices layered for a word, then two, then one. A woman's tone came through for a beat. A man's for two. A child's for a vowel. It settled back into cool. "You think names are earnest. They are not. They are handles."

"Then you know why I am telling you to drop her," Hikari said. "You built that suit off mine. If you want a fight with a story worth telling, you do not fight one-handed."

The laugh came back through the filter. Close now. It made the blade tremble against my skin. The hum inside the blade the only little heat in this cold air.

"Make me," Sable said.

Hikari moved as if the walkway had asked him to.

Three steps, quick. Weight low. Hand out, not for the blade, for my belt at the small of my back. Sable yanked the snare line at my waist to put me in the way and took a short step back to get lever. Hikari went with the pull instead of against it, pivoted into the line, and let the cable swing me around his chest. He grabbed my belt and the case strap in one hand and turned his body to take the blade on the shoulder plate rather than my throat. It sang against the metal. Sparks bit my cheek and died.

Sable lost the angle without losing me. The arm across my chest tightened. The suit shifted, feet finding new purchase on steel. The left knee clicked again and the whole line of his body stuttered a hair.

"Drop her," Hikari said, and it was not a request.

Sable made the calculation you make when the thing you want is not going to be available if you keep the thing you grabbed. He shoved. Not a throw to kill. A push to make room. I felt the release as a vacuum in my ribs. The arm bar vanished. The line slackened. Hikari pulled me into his chest and locked me there while he turned his shoulder to take the next cut. The blade kissed plastic and squealed.

"Out," Hikari said. He set me on my feet without looking away from Sable, pushed me toward the mezzanine wall with one flat palm on my back, and stepped forward into Sable like a man walking through a door he had been given permission to own.

The two suits met and the walkway answered.

Metal shook. The handrail groaned. The mesh rattled up through my boots and into my teeth. Hikari drove Sable two steps with a straight shoulder, hips behind it, weight in the line. Sable gave a step, then set his feet across the mesh and stopped the march with a low brace and a sharp kick inside Hikari's ankle. The kick glanced and hurt anyway. The suits sang to each other with a noise you feel in your bones like late thunder.

I stumbled to the wall and dropped into a crouch. The case thumped my sternum once. I slid the strap long and moved it under one arm to get it somewhere less likely to catch. My hand found the pouch with the flash tubes and the solvent. I clipped the pouch to my front and thumbed the cap on the spray. My own pistol sat in the back of my waistband, light and real and suddenly feeling like it belonged in the wrong story. Two Forge shells on a mesh. I would not shoot into that unless the world had stopped making sense.

"Left knee," I said, quiet. "His left knee clicks before he commits."

Hikari did not answer. He heard. The helmets were close enough that breath misted and made a small halo where faceplates almost touched. Sable's blade dug against a plate seam, found nothing, and skittered. Hikari's forearm came up and trapped Sable's elbow across the bar of his own. He shoved the forearm into Sable's throat, not to crush, to take air out of rhythm. Sable's vent rattled and grieved for a beat.

The blade withdrew. Sable's other hand came up with something I had not seen yet. A dull cylinder the size of a lipstick. It snapped open on a hinge. Filament glinted in the white light. I knew that sound. It was the same spool Mirror had tried on Hikari. Monofilament is not a joke. It looks like hair until it opens skin clean.

"Line," I shouted.

Hikari saw it. He shoved Sable's wrist into the handrail and locked it there. The filament whined against stainless and bit a strangled groove before snapping back on its own spool. Sable dropped the cylinder and pushed the back of his helmet into Hikari's visor like a boxer's head bump. It is a dirty move in a clean league. The suits make it look like a love tap. It is not. It jarred my vision from the side. Hikari took the target change and reset his weight.

They separated a half step. Each grabbed a breath. The cable at my waist slid down with a little jerk and fell at my boots. I stepped out of it and kicked the loop clear. The snare will trip anyone if you are not thinking. I was thinking. I hacked the loop with the solvent knife and sawed. The cable parted with a small cough. I pulled it free and tossed it into the well.

Sable burned hotter.

I saw it in the vents at the shoulder blades. Heat shimmered. A faint brown smoke line rose and licked the ceiling. Someone had unlocked his limiters and then told him how to keep them from cooking him in the first minute. He was bleeding heat into the air to buy speed now and pain later. The suit's breath rattled heavier, then smoothed as the control system caught up and lied about how tired it was.

"Overburn," I said. I kept my voice flat so I would not make Hikari adjust his face. "Watch his hips. He will try to steal balance through you."

He did. Sable stepped in and hooked inside Hikari's knee again, then let his own knee knock against the handrail post. Most people avoid hitting the rail. He used it. The post gave him a third point and the mesh under their boots went live. Hikari adjusted his line and put his own boot where Sable wanted him to put it because it kept Sable from thinking he had made it happen. Sable learned the wrong lesson and turned his hip to load a throw. Hikari stepped into the throw instead of over it and the two bodies locked.

This was where I could help. I slid along the wall until I had an angle on Sable's back vent. The grill there had soot in the corners where no one ever gets a brush. The solvent in my hand was not really for paint. It was for old things that refused to move. I pulled a flash tube from its clip, cracked it, and rolled it. The white hit the mesh where their boots tangled and blew shallow depth into a flat screen. Sable blinked inside his helmet. Hikari did not. He turns his visor filters down when I carry flash. We practice that.

Sable's left knee clicked and the leg braced for the next change. I sprayed the vent. The stream atomized on the grill and ran into the housing. I did not need it to kill anything. I needed it to make Sable choose. His suit smelled the solvent and throttled the fan for a breath. The control loop did what it was designed to do. It saved the motor. It gave us one clean second.

Hikari took it. He pivoted into Sable's center line and locked the man's left arm to his chest with both gauntlets. The blade hand swooped late. It skated on plate. Sable shifted to break the lock. Hikari walked him into the handrail with a steady drive that ignored the blade and the filament and the heat and only respected feet. The rail groaned. The toe board creaked. The mesh quivered like a drum.

Sable threw his head back and cracked his helmet crown into Hikari's visor. The star grew and stopped a hair from becoming a line. Hikari did not wince. He drove a knee into the plate over Sable's thigh and held it there like a pin. The two suits stayed welded, plates groaning.

"His elbow," I said. "Rotate his elbow into the rail."

Hikari rotated. The trapped arm hit the post and jammed. Sable snarled through the filter like a radio cracking. He let go of the blade and tried for Hikari's back seam with his free hand. His glove found a line. He could not get leverage in the knot. He hissed air through the vent grille and then sucked it back in because he did not want to waste breath on noise.

The walkway shivered. A panel screw fell and rang. I felt the line of the strut under my soles. I hugged the wall and tried to make myself smaller. The case strap dug into my ribs. The strap had held in the snare; it would hold for the next minute. I kept my hand on the solvent and waited for my next small job.

Sable changed tempo. It was a neat trick and it would have worked if we were not three. He went quiet, let his weight go slack, and gave Hikari nothing to push against. Bodies do not like to push against nothing. Hikari countered by stepping forward like a man pushing a grocery cart. He did it with no drama. Sandbag move. Sable did not get his slack. He had to commit again. The left knee clicked with the hip.

"Now," Hikari said, and his voice had the dry humor that used to belong to better days. He took two more steps and then dropped his weight a centimeter and twisted. Sable's locked arm torqued against the rail with a clear, horrible sound that was not a break but wanted to be. Sable slapped the rail with his free hand to protect the shoulder. It freed him. It also made him choose. He let the lock go and slid out and back a meter.

Hikari did not chase. He let Sable make space. That space bought me a line.

I stepped into the open three meters of mesh and tossed a second flash tube low, past their boots. It landed, rolled, and popped. White poured out. The cold air made the flash seem clean and wrong at once. Sable raised the forearm to shield his visor. Hikari did not. He lunged with a three-step drive, outside angle, shoulder to rim, and took Sable into the cage wall. The handrail screamed. The toe board bent. The mesh deformed.

Sable shattered the flash angle with a short, savage elbow into the side of Hikari's helmet. He had trained that move into habit. He would use it until it broke his own arm. He followed with a short cut at the seam by Hikari's ear. It slid and left another white scratch on the black plate. Hikari answered by stuffing his gauntlet under Sable's chin and pushing up. Not a strike. A lift. In a normal body you would call it a choke. In a shell it becomes a panic button. Sable's suit throttled breath to protect sensors. He tried to shoulder shake out of the lift. Hikari kept the lift and then touched the man's hip with a knee. Micro-adjustment. Subtle. It collapsed the throw Sable had started to build.

"Drop," Hikari said.

Sable knew better than to fall on his back into a mesh with a man on top. He dropped to a knee and kicked behind him while he fell. His boot found the toe board. The board bent down and ripped away. One corner of the mesh lifted. Hikari's heel dropped through the gap. Sable punched both arms into Hikari's chest and shoved. Hikari staggered back and ripped his heel out of the gap by pure force rather than by geometry. The steel grated on steel. It was a sound that suited the hallway.

"Back," I said, because a step back would take them off the broken mesh and onto the solid strut. If one of them went through the gap with a leg, we would lose the leg. It had that energy. The kind you do not recover from and pretend you meant to.

Hikari took half a step back and Sable took the same forward. The suits met again. The blade came back and tried for the armpit. The armpit is not a soft point on a Forge. The pit is a tangle of plates and padding and a seam you can confuse by moving. Hikari moved and let the blade scrape confusion. He bent Sable's wrist toward the rail and knocked the blade free. It clattered across the mesh and bounced twice. I caught it with my boot before it could drop into the pit.

The suits hit the cage again. Sable took a different risk. He turned his back to Hikari for a breath and used the rail to climb up and over him. He tried to turn his own back into a ramp. It almost worked. Hikari did not follow. He crouched. Sable's knee landed on his shoulder instead of a clean platform. Hikari shoved up. Sable rolled forward, grabbed the top rail with both hands, and hung for a second like a gymnast missing the bar. He dropped and landed in a crouch ten centimeters from Hikari and drove forward in a scuttle that reminded me of something from under a sink. It was not pretty. It was efficient.

They locked again. I breathed. The case bumped my ribs. Sable's left knee clicked and then buzzed a little, the sound of a motor that did not like a new load. I smiled because nothing that small should make me happy and it did. Wear is a language. That joint would lie to him now and then. It would waste him half a step. Half a step is enough when you work in three-second moments.

"Left knee is getting hot," I said. "Show him stairs."

Hikari took a series of small steps that felt like nothing from the outside and told the mesh a different story. Left, right, left. He made Sable think he was about to take them both into the far wall. At the second right, he dropped three centimeters and side-stepped left into the space he had created in Sable's line. Sable stepped where he had been taught to step. The left knee clicked and lied to him and he had to recover the weight with his spine. That was the half step. Hikari put his hand in the center of Sable's chest plate and shoved the weight across that micro-stutter into the rail.

It was not a dramatic hit. It was quiet and mean. It moved Sable because it used the lie in his own joint. He took the rail in the small of his back and his breath made that small mistake again. Hikari did not waste it. He dug his glove inside the top of Sable's plate stack at the shoulder and pulled forward while he put a knee into the thigh plate for purchase. Sable tried to twist. Hikari turned the twist into a small fall. They went to the mesh and rolled once. The toe board hummed. The handrail groaned again. The mesh held because steel still loves its job when people use it correctly.

Sable got a boot into Hikari's ribs and kicked him off. He rolled to his knees and then to his feet in a smooth travel that had to be trained a hundred times. For the first time, he looked at me and not at Hikari. His visor held my shape. I held his gaze because I am done with flinching in rooms like this.

"Still with the bird," he said. There were three voices in it again. The third caught at the end like a thread. Anger slipped through all three and sewed them together into something that almost sounded like a person.

"Yes," I said.

"Not for long," he said. The last word flattened into a different tone. He tried to return to cool and came up a fraction short.

He lunged for me then, not to take me again as a hostage, to end my small interventions. Hikari chose to gamble a rib. He stepped into Sable's line and took the first strike on the plate while he caught Sable's wrist with both hands. He turned that wrist into the space between us and stepped into it with his shoulder. The move looked like a hug if you did not know you were watching a fight. He put both of them onto the mesh but on his terms. Sable's shoulder hit first. Sable hissed. Hikari rolled and kept rolling until they were both on their knees in a narrow corridor of rail and mesh. Two machines breathing hard. Two people inside them refusing to use words that would give anything away.

"Pull back," I said. "You are one breath from the break in the rail."

Hikari moved his left boot one square and it bought him as much safety as a rooftop in a bad summer. He took it with a little noise in his throat that only I heard.

Sable pushed up and locked an arm behind Hikari's helmet. He levered the head.

Hikari kept his neck strong and took the command away from Sable's wrist. Sable switched his grip, not frightened, just pragmatic, and tried to pull Hikari's head into the rail. Hikari shut the line down with his own forearm in the crook of Sable's elbow and turned it into a stand-off.

We were near the end of what our suits liked. Both overheated in small, increasingly honest ways. Hikari's visor showed hairline stress that would crack in twenty more exchanges. Sable's left knee coughed in micro-spasms that would really fail if he asked for two levels of movement at once. The overburn shimmer at Sable's vents had eased to a steady wisp and then to a wired, sustained glow that made me nervous in a different way. Sustained means the person inside has started to pay the bill with parts of themselves they will not get back even if they live to the elevator.

The building woke. The ambient camera that watched the mezzanine reset and failed to find a shape. It will try again in five seconds and then report an anomaly. The anomaly will walk to a desk upstairs. The desk will look at the screen and not understand what is wrong for two beats. Then he will. Then the call will go out to the next stack of guards. We had a minute, maybe less.

I slid along the wall until I could see both of them in profile. I had one more tube. I had one more shot at making Sable choose. I had one more idea that hurt my teeth to think about.

The fight went flat for ten seconds. The shells pressed. Hands found the same grips they had found before because training likes habit. The cage rattled quietly. The mesh sang in a little frequency that only I would care about and only on a Tuesday morning. I reached into the pouch at my hip and found not the last flash tube but Juno's little backup bead, the size of a sugar cube, wrapped in a cloth so it would not scratch. My mother's voice lived there in a residue. Not a whole mind. Not the kitchen. Not the stairwell. Just the pattern of one sentence that Juno had kept because she had liked the way she said it. It was nothing and not nothing. It was dangerous and it would never be safer to use.

"Hold," I said.

Hikari did not ask what. He tightened his line for one second, took a head bump in exchange, and bought me the space.

I pulled the cloth free and set the bead against the throat mic in my jacket. I took a breath and swallowed the thickness at the back of my tongue.

"Listen," I said, and I pressed the pad.

The bead warmed. The suit's mic picked it up, ran it through nothing, and put it into the air as sound. It was small. It was brave. It was a kitchen at noon after a storm.

"Little star," my mother said in the voice I had not heard with oxygen since the day the nurse closed the door. The words filled the hall without volume. They fit into all the corners because they lived in my bones and my bones know this building too well now. "Do not let them teach you what your hands are for."

Sable froze.

Everything in the suit went rigid. Not like a brace. Like a startled rabbit. The helmet turned one degree toward me, not enough to give Hikari a shot, just enough to show me what had landed.

"Play it again," Sable said, and the voice that came out now was a girl's pretending to be a radio, then a woman pretending to be a father, then a man pretending to be polite. The modulator could not decide. It skittered across all three and demanded a place to sit.

Hikari felt it. He did not take it yet. He waited for me to decide.

I let the bead play the sentence through to the end and then let the silence that follows in that recording do its work. The tiny breaths, the little rattle of bird feet on a windowsill in the other room, the click the kettle makes when it cuts out. Then I thumbed it back and let it go again.

"Little star," she said. "Do not let them teach you what your hands are for."

Sable's helmet pressed forward half a centimeter. The blade hand that had been empty curled like it remembered work. The left knee clicked and then held too long. The shoulder lifted. The suit tried three postures in a second and failed to pick one.

Hikari adjusted his own posture to keep Sable from falling in the way he wanted. He did it without giving the man a better position. He kept Sable upright so the voice could hit where it needed to.

"Who is that," Sable said, and the child was louder now, and the woman under it faltered, and the man who liked control put a flat tone over both and failed to make it stick. "What file is that. What room did you steal."

"The only room that matters," I said.

Something under the black plate whooped with a sound like a person breathing through a paper bag. The left knee buckled and then locked. The suit wants to keep you standing when your brain forgets to ask. It was doing its best. The person inside it was not ready for my mother's voice in a hallway like this, in a city like this, on a morning that had pretended to be clean.

"Wren," Hikari said.

"One more," I said.

I played it again and this time the little rattle of claws on the windowsill hit me hard enough to make my eyes go hot. It was whether to break this thing now or after I had told myself a smaller story. I chose now. That was the thing my hands were for.

Sable shuddered. The suit tried to move, maybe to lunge at me, maybe to lunge away. Hikari kept him pinned without making a hero painting out of it. He kept his voice level.

"Wren," he said. "Now."

I nodded. I slipped the bead back in its cloth and closed my fist around it because I could not bear to drop it in here. The fight tilted toward us in a way I understood and did not like. This was not only two suits. It was the person inside the black plate and the way a sentence pulled them between rooms they had built to survive. Sable's blade hand opened and closed twice. The knuckles scraped plate. A new voice found the modulator, young, careful, trying to be a helper to a person who had been hurt. The suit's breath made the first part of a sob and swallowed it.

The stalemate broke.

Sable let go of Hikari, lurched back three steps, and clawed at the latch under his helmet as if something inside it itched and would not stop.

The blade skittered across the mesh at my feet and hit the post. It left a neat scratch, straight and honest. I looked at Hikari, raised the solvent, then closed it. Time for knife tricks would come in five seconds when the person in the suit remembered how to be dangerous again. For this second, we were not in the fight one of us expected.

Hikari stepped with him, slow, close, hands up, as if walking with someone on a ledge waiting for the fire brigade.

"Stay with me," he said, not to me. "Sable. Stay. Keep your feet where I can see them."

Sable jerked his head and it rattled against the ring inside his helmet. He found two breaths. He forced them into a rhythm that made a lie out of this hallway. The lie landed then died.

Noise came from the far mezzanine. A door unlatching. Shoes. A startled exhale. A person saw two heavy suits on a mesh, one holding the other, one woman against a wall with a case on her hip, and knew the day had changed shape.

Hikari did not look away. He tilted Sable's shoulder into the rail and held there to buy me time.

This was the part of the fight that did not look like a fight. It was the part that would decide whether the next minute was a kill or a fall. I moved along the wall with the case thumping my ribs and the bead in my fist and my mother's voice still ringing inside the air the way it had rung inside the kitchen. I put myself where I could hurt Sable if he came back into the room the wrong way, and I prayed for a building to fail in exactly three small ways later than the people upstairs wanted.

"Little star," my mother said inside my chest. "Do not let them teach you what your hands are for."

I saw Sable's hands curl and open as that sentence walked through him. I saw his left knee twitch once and then lock. I saw the lights over the door on the far mezzanine start to wink. I saw Hikari's jaw under the plate. I saw the count start. Three. Two. One.

The blade at my boot heel looked like nothing but a strip of black steel and an idea of what a person can do when no one is watching. I picked it up with my left hand and watched the two suits find the next move.

The rest would not be quiet.

THE HALLWAY HUNG ON the edge of a choice. Sable had one gauntlet on the rail, one hand braced on Hikari's shoulder ring. Hikari had him caged without a choke, not crushing, not gentle. The mesh under their boots sang a thin note. Cold air climbed from the cable well and made little ghosts when it hit the heat bleeding from Sable's back vents. The door on the far mezzanine had opened and then stayed open. Someone stood there and decided not to be brave.

"Stay with me," Hikari said, not looking away. "Feet where I can see them."

Sable's visor twitched my way, a fraction, like a person half-waking to the wrong name. The modulator did a full stutter across three voices before landing on flat. "What did you press," he asked. The words were even. The edges were not. "What room did you steal."

"A kitchen," I said. "The only one that mattered."

A low electronic tick traveled through Sable's suit. Not armor. The box inside. A timing pulse finding water. Hikari adjusted his stance and took the weight in a way that felt like pushing a broken shopping cart. Slow. Certain. Sable did not fight it yet. He pressed his helmet into Hikari's and inhaled like a person trying to memorize a room by smell.

He came back sharp in a breath. The left knee clicked and held, then clicked again. The blade lay at my boot. I kept my left hand over it and my right on the pouch at my hip because I was about to use a different knife.

"Persona stack is labile," Hikari said, quiet. That tone lived under every sharp day we had ever had. "He is running at least three overlays. One is directive-heavy. One is child-coax. One is dry systems operator. He is losing the gate that keeps them in line."

"The gate is doing well," Sable said through someone who had never been allowed to lie as a child. Then the layers slid and he spoke again with a voice that would read you a bedtime story and correct your grammar. "It is doing better than yours."

He pushed. Hikari absorbed. The cage quivered and settled. Sable reset and tried a different tempo. Relax, then hard. He was good at it. Hikari rode both shifts without giving back angle. If Sable had stayed a machine, he would have walked out of here or killed us both. But there is no such thing as only machine in a suit built by people like Navarre. They know which parts to sand and which parts to leave sharp. The sharp parts were waking up inside him and fighting over who owned the hand.

Noise rose from the far mezzanine. More boots. A supervisor voice trying to make a plan while staying quiet enough to let someone else own the decision if it went wrong. We had seconds. Not minutes.

I held the bead in my fist and felt the tiny kick it gave when its cache of sound rewound. My mother's sentence had landed. It had cracked Sable open at the seam. Now I had to put my hand in that seam and twist. I hated what that meant. I did it anyway.

"Can you pass me your local," I asked Hikari. "Open the profile share. Do not speak."

He gave me a fractional nod that meant yes to something a less careful person would have said no to. His left gauntlet twitched at his wrist, a tap through the bands. Forge shells handshake when they are close enough to trade emergency telemetry. Pairing was designed for evacuations and crush rescues. It carries suit status, audio, and a picture of the room drawn by microphones. It is meant to help two bodies move like one. I set my loop joiner into the slit at Hikari's hip and felt the little confirm buzz crawl across the plastic. The joiner was a patch I had built out of three bad ideas and a bedtime. It sat quiet until you fed it the right rhythm. Then it offered the rhythm to anyone with the same handshake.

"Linked," Hikari said, a single word for me, not for Sable.

Sable heard the handshake and laughed. It was a small clean sound that made my hands shake in memory of stupid high school nights. "You are not going to like what lives in there," he said.

I opened the bead's output to the joiner and muted my own throat mic. The first time had been the kitchen and that line. I needed more now. Not volume. Variety. I pulled three clips out of Juno's residue. Not a full scene. Just sound. A stairwell radiator ticking down when the heat cut. The little stumble in my mother's breath when she tried to hide she had been walking too far, then said my name like a glove. A kettle giving up at the end of a boil and the hot plate clicking into silence. You do not have to say the word love for love to fill a room. You can ask the room to remember.

I sent the radiator first. One channel. Low. Ten decibels under speech. The suit should ignore it. The brain inside the suit would not. Training had taught Sable to move away from heat and toward breath. The quiet tick entered his ear through Hikari's channel and came back as a ghost in his own. It grafted itself onto the little metronome that ran his cycles. His shoulders gave a tiny shiver. Not weakness. Not pain. Attention.

I sent the breath second. Her saying my name. Wren. The consonant a little soft because she was tired, not because she would ever stop keeping the sound for herself. Hikari's private mic caught the way the memory hit him. He held his line anyway. Sable's modulator flared through three profiles in half a second and then tried to hold middle. It failed for two beats, recovered one, then failed again. The child wanted to answer. The operator wanted to ignore. The directive wanted to punish the child for wanting.

"Wren," Sable said, and he did not make it a threat. He made it mine, and then he tried to steal it back.

I waited for his breath to catch again and sent the kettle last. It is an honest sound. It means food. It means someone is making a small plan in a room where no one can burn. The kettle lives in the part of the brain that does not know brands. It sits beside the handrail in the dark and waits for a person who is allowed to want an easy thing with no guilt. Sable jerked as if someone had tapped his helmet with a spoon.

A new voice came through the filter that had nothing to do with kindness. Navarre's voice. Soft, precise, amused. "Hold still," he had said once, beside a glass wall that looked down into a grid. "Take the feeling out of the picture. Keep the picture." He had said it to Hikari. He had said it to every asset they ever put in a suit.

I used him. I took his tone and turned it into a hook. I sampled five words from an old intercom file that lived inside the shard I stole from a staging server. "Asset," the file said, with Navarre's calm. "Proceed with calibration." I layered that under the kettle at minus twelve and let it run for exactly four seconds. Enough to light up the cage of obedience that Sable had been taught to call discipline. Not enough for the cage to become the only room.

Sable's modulator seized. Three voices backed into each other and tried to stand in the same doorway. The child tried to save the mother who wanted the child to play. The operator tried to grind the picture down to a clean edge and failed. The directive tried to put them in a line and broke the chalk. The left knee clicked and kept clicking in time with a pulse that had nothing to do with blood. The suit wanted to pick one. It could not. The box began to cycle faster than the cycle limit. The limit screamed and then flattened out.

"Pull," Hikari said, and this time he did not mean work. He meant me.

I pulled the bead into my mouth and pressed it against my own teeth so my jaw would be the contact mic. I gave Sable my mother again. Not words. Her little laugh when she forgot to be careful. It sat on the line under Navarre's clinical that had just finished. It invited the part of Sable that wanted to be good to go back to the kitchen and sit on the step by the dent in the railing and listen to quiet. The suit could not route the sound. The person tried to. The person failed.

The three overlays slid out of phase. You could hear it in the delay across the modulator line. You could see it in the micro jerk of Sable's glove and the way his fingers tapped code against the rail without a pattern. His breath rattled into a sob and then stopped at the line where pride lives. The child could not reach the kettle. The operator could not stand the tick. The directive could not forgive either.

Hikari tightened his hold for one second to keep Sable upright while the internal loop tried to tear itself in half. He kept his voice level.

"I have you," he said. "Not for saving. For counting."

Sable convulsed.

Not a seizure. The hardware does not allow the violence of that. It was an internal fall. The suit tried to keep his head level and the spine straight. The brain-box spiked and went to ground. The fan in the back vent throttled and then froze for a beat as if it had hit sand. A lockout bit down on the motor to prevent damage. The smell changed. Not burning. Cold electronics that have just dropped under load and stayed cold. The modulator whispered something that was not language, then cut. The visor's layer fluttered, killed brightness, restored it, dropped again.

"Wren," Hikari said in the quiet after. Still not looking away. "Stop."

I killed the feed. The bead cooled in my palm. I wanted to put it back in its cloth without looking at it like a talisman. My hands did what they wanted. They wrapped it like it was something alive.

Sable's weight found Hikari's arms in a new way. Dead weight and heavy. Suit weight. Hikari let him sag until the rails took half and Hikari took the rest. He held for a count and then let Sable fall to his knees, then to a sit. The black plate looked wrong when it was not moving. It had been built to sell motion. Stillness took the life out of it and left a tool.

I crouched next to them and put two fingers on the seam by Sable's jaw and felt nothing that a pulse would share. You always try anyway. Inside the helmet the modulator idled with a low carrier, then came back with a fragment of nothing. The overlays had spun into each other and made noise. Then the noise had flattened and gone. We had seen this once, on a training floor, when an intern had believed a toy demo would carry into a live exercise. It was not a clean death. It was not blood. It was a person dropped through a trapdoor inside their own head and the room below was empty.

"Brain-box," Hikari said, low. "Dead or locked in a loop that looks like no signal. Either way, he is not coming back in a minute."

I wanted to argue. There are favors you can do a person at the edge. None can happen here. Not with the case thumping my ribs and the light on the far door blinking faster.

Sable's glove twitched. I flinched. The fingers curled, then opened in a pattern that meant there was still life below the box, animal life turning in a deep well. The overlays were gone. The person was gone or locked under ten orders. The hardware held air for a body and a heart asked for it. If we opened the helmet now, we would fight the suit. If we cut the hose to the vent, we would be a different kind of killer. I did not have it in me to be clean or merciful by that metric in this hallway.

Hikari set Sable gently to the mesh and stood. No comment. He looked at me like he could see into my throat and knew the line I had crossed with the bead. He bent and took the spent filament spool from the floor and stuffed it into Sable's thigh seam so the next man to find him would not have a neat story. He stepped back and checked the rail.

"We have to go," he said.

"Give me thirty seconds," I said.

I pulled the small baton into my hand and curled it against the seam at Sable's collar. Not to pry. To mark. The baton was not hot. The seam was not warm. I tapped in a simple code. Three long, two short, three long. It is the mark you leave when you want a real salvage team to know the shell is unsafe to wake with a hard reset. Someone from downstairs would read it. Someone might ignore it. I could not keep this hallway from itself. I could at least warn a pair of hands that had not asked for this day.

"Done," I said.

Hikari nodded once and gave me the case strap with a small careful touch, the way you pass something between people who have both just done something that will be heavier later. He did not touch my faceplate. He lifted the case on my chest with one finger to make sure it would not swing, then turned to the far mezzanine door.

It opened a hand's width. I saw an eye and a badge on a lanyard. The eye belonged to a person who had never expected to be this close to a fight and had no idea what to do with their body. They looked at Sable on the mesh and at Hikari and at me. I lifted my empty hand, palm out, and shook my head. Not to threaten. To say do not.

They did not listen to me. They did not move either. They shut the door the last two inches and locked it without letting go of the handle, like a child telling the dark to wait.

Hikari led us back along the mezzanine to the ladder. The mesh hummed as the three new guards on the far side decided the air was safer than the steel and stepped back from the rail. We reached the landing. Hikari put me in front of him on the rungs and clipped the D ring. His left knee complained twice and then remembered how to be quiet. We climbed.

At the flex-joint door he pushed it open and held for me. The gasket made a low noise as the door closed. The service ring breathed like a throat behind the wall, air shaggy with electrical cold. We walked.

I kept my hand on the bead in my pocket. It felt wrong to hold it. It felt worse to let it go. The case bumped my ribs and reminded me that we were about to cut a second, larger throat. The Core sat three levels up. The person on the mezzanine would call a new stack of uniforms into a briefing room and show them a camera still that did not show the fight or the sound. Only the shapes. Only the aftermath.

"You alright," Hikari said as we passed a rack of fire hose that looked too new to have ever seen flame.

"Yes," I said. It was not a lie. It was not a whole truth either. "I used the kitchen like a wrench."

"It worked," he said.

"I know," I said. "I will think about it later. If I think about it now, I will be bad at ladders."

He looked down the corridor and then back at me. He checked the strap across my chest again and then checked his own plates with a quick sweep that told me nothing had cracked that could not be ignored for fifteen minutes. He set his hands on the rung and looked up.

"We are counted," he said. "Three, two, one."

We climbed. The building changed in small honest ways the deeper we went. Less diffuser scent. More air that made your teeth feel like tools. The Core was close. My mouth went dry. I swallowed and felt the shape of the bead at the back of my tongue like a secret I had put there as a dare.

On the third landing a cleaning cart sat parked at an angle that meant someone had been interrupted mid-task. A fluorescent rag hung over the handle. It smelled like lemon and hand soap. Hikari ran a glove along the side of the cart and came away with nothing. The dust here was honest. It belonged to vents, not to laziness.

We came to the last door. It wore the Orinox crest in a simple stainless disk. No words. No color. Hikari palmed the panel. It did nothing. He set the coils and looked at me.

"After this," he said, quiet, and meant the Core, and the project, and the rooms that had made and unmade people with numbers, and Sable on the mesh, and my mother's cut voice in a building she would have despised, "we talk."

"We will," I said. "I have more rooms than kitchens. I saved them for you."

He smiled with only the eyes and passed me the grip. The coil hummed. The seam warmed. The stainless disk on the door looked smooth and ridiculous. The building had spent real money to make it photograph well. We had brought the wrong kind of camera.

The door moved. Cold breathed out of the gap. Light inside ran at the same color temperature as the server floor and yet felt more expensive. I set my shoulders and my jaw and reminded myself that my hands were mine.

We stepped into the Core.

THE CORE WAS COLDER than the vault and brighter by degrees that felt like a budget. A ring of glass looked down into a pit of light two stories deep. In the pit, black monoliths rose from polished steel. Each wore a crown of white fins that condensed tiny ghosts from the air. At our level, workstations wrapped the ring like a dock around a lake. Each station had two monitors set in a clean V, an optical port that looked like a mouth, and a badge reader that purred when the room checked itself.

Hikari set his back to the door and planted Forge between the ring and the hall. He adjusted one of the coil clamps so it wedged the door in a way that would cost anyone who followed a minute they did not have. He walked to the nearest station and touched the glass with the back of his glove. The monitors woke on a soft gradient. The loading circle wore the helix shape, of course. The login prompt appeared and told me to smile for the camera.

"Hands," he said.

"I know what mine are for," I said. It came out flatter than I meant.

I slid into the chair. The case on my chest hit the desk. I eased it onto the work surface and clipped the tether to the bracket so it could not fall into the light well if the room decided to imitate gravity in a new way. The chair had a weight sensor under the pad. It printed a tiny H in the lower left corner of the screen. The camera woke and hunted for a face. I gave it my cap brim. It got bored and fell back to badge.

I touched the stolen fob to the reader. The reader chirped polite. A second chirp followed. The second came from a device that liked to live under desks. Anomaly listener. It looks for bad rhythm. My heart rate found the old tempo from the shop floor, steady in crisis, louder in the quiet. I reached down with one hand and unplugged the listener. It came free without a fight. Poor design. Too much faith in the uniform.

"Talk to me," Hikari said. The voice was still level. The visor glared with light that made the star look like nothing.

"Three tasks," I said. "Pull the personality hold from the cage they built for you. Build a copy that plays friendly with our stack. Erase our names and the project's archive, and make the erasure spread like gossip in a break room."

"Time," he said.

"Eight minutes if the building keeps pretending it likes us," I said. "Five if it tries to be brave."

He set himself to buy me five.

I palmed the badge again and opened the station menu. The words were pure Orinox. Integrity. Wellness. Differentiation. The only honest one was Systems. I clicked through. A tree lifted up from the bottom of the screen. Each branch became five more. I knew the model names they would hide real work under. Safekeep. Homebound. Solace. Formula names that would look soft on a venture deck and clean on a procurement sheet.

"Persona Dynamics," I said, because they never resist their own poetry. The folder opened on a dashboard that looked like a weather map. Colored currents across a circle. Numbers around the edge that would make someone in a meeting feel powerful. Top right corner, a tab with a label that made me want to laugh. "Kindle."

I opened Kindle. Someone had put a lot of work into this page. There were sliders and graphs and a little cartoon that showed a friendly suit holding a heart while a lab coat made notes. Under the toy was the thing we needed. A field labeled Hold Pattern Library. Names in a list. I scrolled. Some handles were blunt. Soldier Retain. Compliance Under Duress. Some were dressed up. Quiet Meadow. Light on Water. Then the one that made my chest go cold and my hands steady. Ananke Gate. That was Navarre's humor. Myth stitched to math.

"Found your cage," I said.

"I hated the name before you said it," Hikari said.

I clicked Ananke Gate. A confirmation slid down with a legal caution I did not read. The next pane showed blocks of code rendered as shapes instead of text. Anyone who had never written a loop would call it intuitive. Anyone who had would curse. I asked it to show me layer names. It obliged. Memory windowing. Affective clamp. Dissociation quotient correction. Bias learn throttle. Breach fuse. There was the thing that let Forge stand in a church full of servers and not hand me to a wall when the breath got thin. There was the thing that had sanded Hikari's edges in a room where Navarre kept clean cups.

I did not export it. Not yet. I did not trust their export. I had brought my own mouth.

I opened the case and took out our tool. A small reader with jaws and a field-emitter nozzle, built to fool an optical line into accepting both ends as itself. I tapped its housing and it hummed a yes. I plugged it into the station's optical port and into our case. The case woke its own interface. It did not try to be pretty. It said Hello, Wren in plain monospace because I had written it one night with my knees under a metal table and that had felt honest.

"Copying Ananke will touch the parts of you that try to anticipate me," I said without looking up. "You will feel it as a breath that comes late, then catches. Do not punch a wall."

"Noted," Hikari said.

I tagged Ananke's layers. I told our case to listen and never touch. The reader made light inside the line. The station thought it was alone. The light did what light does. It went where it was aimed and told the truth to the primary lens on both sides. The case wrote what it heard in blocks and salted each block with a stamp we could verify later.

The door behind Hikari thudded once. Someone had put a shoulder into it and learned that Orinox steel respects physics. Hikari checked the coil clamp with one glove and then checked the ceiling camera. It stared at his plate and learned nothing.

The copier reached fifty percent. Seventy. Ninety. It stalled at ninety three while the system thought about integrity and tried to decide how to feel about a stream that respected its rhythm too much. I breathed. Hikari stayed a wall.

"Good," the case said in my coarse little font. Done. I unplugged the reader from the station and from our case. The station screen blinked as the optical link dropped. It did not cry. It returned to the dashboard that made executives feel tall.

"Next," Hikari said.

"Patch for us," I said. "Quick and dirty. Enough to keep you in yourself when the room is not fair. We clean it later."

I opened our copy in the case and cut two layers Navarre loved. The bias learn throttle that had turned Hikari's kindness into a machine that took orders from the wrong voice. The fuse labeled Breach, which was supposed to trip if a user refused a command too many times. I replaced both with a tiny ring that I had written for Juno when she would get stuck in a loop and forget the kitchen was safe. The ring looks for the breath at the back of the throat and says You are here with me in a way a machine can believe.

"You are smiling," Hikari said.

"It is the ugly kind," I said. "Forgive it. Open your local."

He did. I slid the patch into the narrow chute the suit keeps for emergency updates. His shoulders relaxed a centimeter. The movement was so small only someone who slept this close would notice. He flexed his fingers and looked down at me with a faceplate that hid everything except the set of his jaw.

"Count feels cleaner," he said.

"Good," I said. "Hold tight. Last job."

I closed Kindle and navigated back to Systems. The menu tree had a branch called Ledger. Another called Archive. Another called Sanitizer. Sanitizer did what it said. It scrubbed logs for legal. It kept the day neat and the reports kinder than the work. It would also be the perfect place to hide an infection that no one would believe could exist in a product called compliance. I opened Sanitizer and stared for a beat at the checkboxes that controlled a hundred glowing promises. Then I opened a window no one would dare to name Virus near. I named it Patch. I wrote the short header that would make an auditor smile. I wrote the part that would tell their index that this page had always been here. I wrote the part that would tell their offsite mirrors that we were a valid payload. Then I wrote the only piece of code I was certain I could live with when I lay in a dark room later and tried to sleep.

It did not punch through firewalls. It did not teach strangers to own machines. It carried a list. The list held two names and one project root. A-19. HIKARI, experimental. CANDIDATE WREN. TRIAL BURN, all sub dirs. It asked for pointers, not data. It asked those pointers to eat their own keys. It asked the keys to teach their mirrors to regret what they memorized. It asked for receipts to turn black. That was all. A redaction, extended through pride and budget.

I tied the little beast to the update tick that already moved through the building like heartbeat. I attached it to a message the CRAC controllers would accept and pass along because it came from exactly where updates always came from. I wrapped it in a report called Compliance Hygiene 4Q and snuck in a signature made of three MACs that would satisfy anyone who glanced. Juno would have called it petty when she smiled. I liked the word.

"Ready," I said.

Hikari leaned a little closer. The star on his visor looked like the needle on an old turntable. He held the line at my back while the door groaned again and then gave another centimeter. A guard shouted for a ram. Another guard said they had a ram in the other hall. A third said his badge did not work anymore and he hated this place. Their day was going badly in the right ways.

"Say it," Hikari said.

I looked at the cameras. I looked at the helix logo on the glass. I pictured Navarre in a white room with a brass badge and a small recorder he did not need. I pictured his hands. I pictured the three floors of meetings this room had bought for Orinox while people like me put on gloves and made the cold parts behave.

"Time for a little payback, Doc," I said.

I hit send.

Nothing happened for a second. The room held its breath. Then the first screen changed. Not with a crush of drama. With a tiny shift in a tiny corner of a harmless window. The word Sanitizer flickered and came back. The line that shows job count incremented in a neat integer. The index maintenance tab reported a burst of activity that any admin would put in a weekly report with a bullet saying Completed. On the far end of the ring, a status light went from green to a calm blue. Hikari looked at it and I looked at the screen and the case hummed once against my fingers.

Beneath us, in the pit, two of the black monoliths dimmed a hair and then returned to their setpoint. The maintenance controller logged a routine note. The mirrors on the other side of the building accepted the push and did what mirrors do. They believed. The offsite peers did the same because the only thing a mirror loves more than itself is the object it was told to reflect. I watched the job list as it rolled. A-19, gone. HIKARI, experimental, gone. CANDIDATE WREN, gone with a small hiccup that told me there had been more than one file because of course there had. TRIAL BURN, root, gone. Sub dirs, gone one by one with names that made me cold and hot in turns. A sanitization job took three percent of compute and used it to be neat. Neatness devoured the archive with a quiet appetite and then cleaned its plate.

A fresh alert popped up from a separate subsystem that monitored the monitors. It asked if anyone had run a job without logging the job id. The alert tried to file a ticket. The ticket system accepted the form and stored it in a folder I had already marked for redaction. The entry went black. The supervisors upstairs began to shout about live video. The live video kept perfect time and showed nothing but people running and doors they did not understand anymore.

"Your name," Hikari said. He had not moved.

"Gone," I said.

"Yours," I said. He did not ask. He had not moved.

"Gone," I said again. I let the word live in my mouth for a second and then I let it climb into my chest where it could make a room. Juno would have laughed and then told me to check the mirrors one more time. I did.

Offsite reports came in slow and even. Mirrors: synced. Hot spare: synced. External tape: scheduled for midnight. I set the tape job to pull from a copy of a copy that had just redacted itself and wrapped that order in the same signature we had used so far. After midnight, a robot in a warm warehouse would take the air out of a tape and feel completely honest about it.

"Pull," Hikari said, a reminder and a request.

"Last thing," I said.

There was one piece of the project that you could not cut with neatness. The seed archive. The thing they printed new shells from. The code that began a person and called the result product. I found its pointer in a hidden pane that liked to look like a survey. It asked if I was satisfied with the onboarding experience. I clicked the smiley face and then pulled the pointer like a tooth. The job list flashed red for one blink. It went white again. The seed archive went gray. The gray meant Nobody home. It looked like bureaucracy. It felt like a life.

I closed the case and clipped it back across my chest. The strap felt lighter. Maybe that was the adrenaline. Maybe it was the truth.

A chorus started above us. Not the CRAC units. Not the fans. The building. The building had multiple hearts and one of them had noticed something it did not enjoy. The alarm came as a soft voice over a speaker that lived in the ring wall. A woman with no accent said, "Please evacuate to your nearest exit." She said it again in three more languages. The light over the door behind Hikari went amber, then red.

The door took a hard hit. The coil clamp chewed and held. Hikari turned his head a fraction toward me.

"We go now," he said.

"Copy," I said. I routed a final command through the station to make our little Patch go to sleep. It would wake when anyone tried to rebuild the index that held those names. It would smile and say Compliance. It would black out what needed the dark. It would take nothing else. If I had built a bomb, I would never forgive myself. I had built an eraser and pointed it at two people and a room that should never have been built. I could live with that. I hoped I could.

I stood. My knees told me I had been sitting at the wrong angle for longer than a body likes. The case tugged my shoulder. Hikari backed toward me, never turning his plate from the door. He handed me the coil clamp with a little twist that said Keep this, in case the next one is more honest than this one. I tucked it under the strap and took his free hand for a second, gloved to glove, for no reason except that we both needed it.

We moved to the side door that served the service ladder up one more level. It read our borrowed fob and tried to decide if the fob was a person. Hikari let it have the debate and then pressed the emergency release with two fingers. The bar gave with a dignified click. We stepped into the stair shaft. The air felt warmer and cheaper. The walls smelled like rubber and the cleaner that hides it.

Boots pounded on a landing three floors down. Voices hit the shaft and climbed it like steam. Hikari clipped me to the ring at his chest and we climbed. One floor. Two. Three. The count held and I held it in my teeth.

At the top, a service door opened into a corridor without a logo. White walls. Smooth floor. A vending machine full of protein drinks. Two chairs for staff who need a moment they will never get. Hikari palmed the door to the cross hall. Lights held steady. The building tried one more time to talk us into caring.

"Please evacuate to your nearest exit," the voice said. "This is a drill."

They lied in the last word. I loved them for trying.

We reached the bend and stepped into a south service lane that ran to the freight elevators. The elevator doors were open on a car that held three crates of gloves and a floor mat rolled up like a rug. I pulled the mat into the car and leaned it up so it hid us from the lobby camera for one honest second. Hikari hit Sub three on the panel. The doors slid toward each other. The world narrowed to the crack of light and the fan in the car roof. A voice tried to call my name from somewhere that did not have speakers.

I looked at Hikari. He looked at me. The case hummed once and then settled. We rode the car down into the part of the building where numbers meet dirt and tried not to think about the way a kitchen sounds after a kettle clicks off.

The doors opened on a hall that smelled like storage. A single guard glanced up from a clipboard and found a freight elevator with a mat and two people who had the wrong walk. He opened his mouth. Hikari gave him a small shake of the head. It was the kind of shake you give a dog who keeps running into the same fence. The guard shut his mouth. He wrote something on the clipboard that I will never read. He did not look up again.

We walked. We turned through a door that led to the loading dock. The dock held four pallets of paper goods, a pallet of branded water, and a view of the river through a fence. The sky over the water looked like it had read a memo. We crossed it. Hikari lifted the chain on the gate. The jammer in the van breathed its quiet pulses from the row below. For a second I let myself think about the way a kettle fills a room with the last breath of a boil. I let myself think about Juno's laugh when she forgot I was listening. I let myself think about the look on Navarre's face when a report that had always kept him safe in a meeting returned a page that ate itself.

"Breathe," Hikari said. It was for me. It was for him. It was for the building that would not forget our names now because it could not.

I breathed. The strap on the case cut a line across my back and the line felt like a thing I had earned. We moved. The van took us into its mouth and we sat. Hikari put one palm on the dash and one on the wheel. I tucked the bead back into its cloth and set it in the shallow cup by the dash with a care I never gave to batteries.

"Time to be bad at ladders," I said, and my voice broke in a way that felt like something working instead of failing.

"Later," he said. He turned the key. The engine woke. The Wendigo rolled.

Behind us, Orinox leaned on its perimeter lights and its clean air and told itself that drills are good for everyone. Inside, a set of screens turned black bars where our names had lived. A switchboard watched a job list roll and said Completed. A person in a suit stood too close to a window and looked down at a river that did not know them. In a room with no logo, a helmet lay on a mesh and breathed for a body that had placed its head in a quiet I could not touch.

We drove into the day. The city took us back because it has no choice. The Core sat behind us with less power than it had held an hour ago. Hikari set a new count and we followed it across a bridge that did not care about our promises. The kettle clicked off somewhere we would not return to. The van held us like a small room you can make a home out of if you are willing to forgive the carpet.

"We will talk," Hikari said.

"We will," I said. I looked at the dash. The bead sat there like a moon. I did not touch it.

Somewhere, a printer spit out a meeting agenda with a line item called After Action and no attachments. Somewhere else, a freezer alarm woke and no one cared because the number did not belong to a person. The only numbers that still mattered were the ones Hikari said under his breath as we left the campus and became two shapes in traffic that no camera will care about past noon.

Three. Two. One.

Chapter Fifteen

Reformat

HIKARI

THE SOUTH SERVICE LANE spat us into a maintenance yard that looked like a diagram. Blue floodlights. Cable racks in numbered rows. A forklift under a tarp that smelled like rubber and tired oil. Chain-link on three sides, the river cut on the fourth, water black as a hole. Wren killed the Wendigo's engine, popped the side door, and ran the mast. The telescoping sections clicked up the rail. The remote catch box woke in her hands, gray and stubborn, ring light amber.

"You have twelve minutes before the city swallows this," she said.

"We use six," I said.

She set the box on the hood, cabled it to the mast base, and coaxed the ring toward green with small adjustments. It flirted with the color, slipped back to amber, then tried again. Her mouth made that thin line I know. She was already juggling wind shear, interference off the river, and the way this building lies to itself.

"We split at the culvert," I said. "You take the river lip and set the dish. I hold the yard. When I call exit you catch it on the run."

"You are not leaving in Forge," she said.

"I never intended to," I said. "Your life weighs more."

The first drone layer skimmed the fence, four toys dressed in matte black. They had white LED noses and belly pods of net and gel. One shot a net on reflex. I tore it off my shoulder and slapped the drone into a rack upright. It cracked and fell like a cheap tool. The second dropped a gel pod that burst into slick sugar. It clung, hissed, and hardened. The plate heated, shrugged, and I filed the hiss in the column called later.

"Smart layer behind the toys," Wren said, eyes on the scanner. "Four with caged rotors, heavier gel, better optics."

They drifted in with quiet fans and tried to ladder over me for a view of the van. I put my body in their path and walked them sideways into a bay of coiled cable. A gel canister splashed my armpit plate and went gray. The suit growled once under my ribs. Still fine.

Sirens coughed from the south gate. A truck pushed into the lot with its light bar on a self-important strobe. Six men climbed down in uniform helmets and hard shells. Shields with black edges. Forearm batons snapped to half-length. One launcher for air you do not want to breathe. One rubber rifle.

"This is yours," I said to Wren.

"I see them," she said.

They tried a line. Shields up, batons out, slow march on gravel. I let them push for three steps so their legs could tell their chests this was a bad idea. Then I set my heel, planted a forearm on the lead shield, and gave it the kind of pressure you use to close a stubborn door. He went back one pace, then two. His partner stepped in the same rut and gifted me the rest of the line. They wobbled and did not fall. Good training. It would not be enough.

The launcher hiccuped a canister. It rolled, hissed a cold fog with no smell, and kissed the toe of my boot. I pinched it and fed it to the forklift tire. The rubber sighed and drank it. The rubber did not care.

A second truck arrived hot and nosed for the river cut. I stepped into its lane and laid a gloved palm on the hood. The driver tapped the horn like a neighbor at a light, then saw the plate and stopped tapping. He did not get out. He rolled up his window.

"Comms box on the river road is spinning up," Wren said. "White paint. Orinox face. It wants to help."

"It will try to classify me," I said. "You make it forget."

She nodded, eyes on the mast. The catch ring stayed amber. She set her palm on the lid and spoke to it like a dog that knows only one trick and performs it well.

I crossed to a breaker cabinet bolted to a rack foot. Padlock with a stamped yard code. I pinched the hinge. The hinge surrendered. I flipped Yard South and Bay Lights. The floodlights dimmed two stops. Camera pupils widened. Their math slowed. I used the beat. I dragged a cable spool off its cradle, rolled it three meters, and let it lean into the front bumper of the first truck. The truck learned it was stuck without being damaged. I ran the forklift chain through the spool and a bollard and made the lesson permanent.

The smart drones recalculated and tried clamp nets. One pneu-stapled a conductive mesh at my boots. I hopped the edge and flicked it onto the fence. The fence hummed and sent the tantrum into the ground. The rubber gun thumped two rounds into my hip and thigh. They hit the plates and stayed. I absorbed the force and smiled inside a little at the righteous stupidity of rubber in a yard full of steel.

"Second layer of drones is up," Wren said. "New signatures are carrying filament."

"I see spool geometry," I said.

One drone closed to the wrong distance, a neat square of carbon under a ring shroud. Its filament gun hissed a hair-thin line. I lifted a rack blanking panel like a paddle and caught the thread in the plastic. It cut the panel into two clean halves and bound there. I yanked. The spool snatched itself back and slapped the drone's leg. It wobbled and tried to recover. I fed it to a rack upright. It breathed smoke and stopped caring.

"Repeat the catch," I said, because ritual keeps hands honest.

"When you trigger exit, your trace goes thin," Wren said, voice steady by choice. "The slab cuts power to protect itself. The trace will try to die in the wire. The box takes it, holds for six seconds, then pours you into the van's spine. From there I split you to the place we planned. If the grill is hot the software will drop the bag rather than cook you. If the signal stutters I will jump it with a foreign packet. That will make every system try to heal you into a slave. I will not let it."

"Range," I said.

"Two hundred meters on the mast, three fifty if I aim the dish," she said.

"You aim from the river lip," I said. "Not here. If you stay, I cannot buy you time."

Her eyes came up from the box to my plate. "No."

"Yes," I said. "That is the only honest trade left."

She stared for one beat longer than safe, then slid into the driver's seat, turned the key, and backed us along the fence with lights off. At the culvert she spun the wheel, dropped into the river lane, and let gravel spit. The mast bowed and held. The catch ring flickered toward green and back, learning a word.

"Dish is in my hand," she said. "Aim will be by feel."

"You were built for feel," I said.

Her laugh was a small breath. "You better not stutter."

"I will not," I said.

The yard changed notes. The ground unit reset its line. The second truck tried a flank. I blocked it with a shoulder and pushed the fender aside like a chair. The driver braked and put both hands on the wheel, eyes wide. The drones fanned and tried to ladder for the van again. I swept a fallen blanking panel up with my boot and launched it into a rotor cage. It clipped a blade and the drone yawed into a rack, shivered, and went still.

Time to pay.

"Forge," I said inside the suit. "Listen."

I opened the panel in my head that Navarre named Fail-Safe for slides and Fuse in the deck for people who sweat. I took the lever. The slab under my ribs hummed like an old transformer. Warnings woke like impatient birds. Overheat. Rail dump. Fan throttle. I accepted heat. I accepted rail. I told the fans to wait.

The limb rails warmed. The left knee motor made a polite cough and then steadied. The visor star grew a hair where a blade had dragged earlier in the server aisle. My hearing filtered two alarms down to a quiet line so I could keep listening for the truck's engine note and the drone's fan.

"Wren," I said.

"I am here," she said. I could hear the van breathe on the mast channel. I could hear the dish screws groan under her grip. The river noise threaded the line like a rope.

"I am going to break it," I said.

"I know," she said.

"When I say go, you floor it," I said. "If the line pulls, do not look back. If I stutter, do not shake me. Hold me in the middle and let the bad ideas burn off."

"I have you," she said.

The launch operator fired a canister, panicked, and slipped on his own fog. I caught his vest and parked him gently against the truck and let him sit. His partner swung a baton for my visor. I lifted a forearm and fed the strike into steel. He felt it run into his bone and decided to be somewhere else. Good. Live to type a better report.

I put a shoulder into the second truck and walked it half a meter so it was nose to nose with the first, the chain through the spool making a nice geometry of inconvenience. The drivers looked at each other through windshields and suddenly did not want to be part of this picture. The forklift under the tarp woke a small hope in me. I took the tarp wrong so I would not get my fingers caught and ripped it back. The key was gone. The battery meter still showed a bar. I did not need either.

I slid a pallet fork under a stack of shrink-wrapped paper goods and tipped. The stack slid off with a sigh and became a rectangle of friction in front of the truck's tires. I wedged a second stack against the rear tire of the other truck. Paper will not stop a man who wants to be a hero. It will stop a man who calls his supervisor before changing lanes.

The drones came again. Two at shoulder height, two at knee. I stepped into their timing, caught one by a leg and used it as a bat to swat the second aside. The third popped a gel pod at my ankle. The gel hit the plate and stressed its own chemistry, turned gray and brittle, and cracked. The fourth tried a filament angled for the back of my knee. I took it on a strip of rack label, let it slice plastic like fruit, and wrapped it twice around the drone's arm. It pulled and tied itself to its friend. They pinwheeled into a pile of cable and got very interested in their own problems.

"Second drone layer has gone quiet," Wren said. "Ground unit two blocks out. Truck three bogged by a barricade they put up for themselves. You are clear for one minute."

"One minute is a banquet," I said.

I rolled the last cable spool with a shoulder and let it drift into the lane the third truck would want. It settled with a polite thump. I walked back to the breaker cabinet and flipped Charger, off, then on. The forklift thought it was being loved. It beeped. A drone decided the beep mattered and flew into the forklift mast to look for a radio. It discovered steel is not a radio.

"Now," I said.

"Copy," she said. The Wendigo leaped out of the shadow and took the underpass like it had been born in a tunnel. The mast bowed, hummed, and came back. The catch ring went green, then amber, then took a breath, then green again. It was learning to believe.

I pulled the exit trigger, then stopped short of the door. Not yet. I needed every plate for what was coming. I opened the door a hand's width so Wren could feel my line and set her dish. The slab sang a high note as the rails absorbed heat they were not designed to carry. The fans begged to save me. I told them to wait and paid the price in a little white at the edge of my vision.

"Signal is clean," Wren said. "I have your ribbon. I am set under the bridge."

"Hold me in your pocket," I said. "Do not pull until I say."

"Understood," she said. The voice went soft the way it does when she has both hands on the job.

The yard paused for one surreal beat. The ground unit held shields over their heads and looked at the sky like weather mattered. The trucks idled and steamed a little. The racks hummed as the field redistributed itself through honest steel. The drone bodies that could still fly held station and watched my plates glow at the seams.

The white box on the river road turned its dish and tried to be helpful. A polite classification pulse came over the band. Asset, unusual. I felt the path kink toward it like a fish on a line. Wren moved the dish by feel, five meters, then three. She told the box to forget me with a checksum that carried a smell for a chiller valve that never existed. The hand let go.

Another hand arrived. Cold, precise, pleased with itself. The band tightened like a wire in winter.

I did not say his name. I did not have to.

"Do not engage that pull," Wren said. "I see it. I am painting the source."

"Not yet," I said. "I need him to step in."

The drones shied off at once, a neat ripple that told me their pilot had received the same instruction as his catwalk man. The ground unit fell back to the gate and read their own hearts. The trucks decided to think. The yard made a soft sound I had never heard in it before, as if it had understood it was about to hold a story.

I turned to the forklift, jammed the manual release under the carriage, and let the mast drop an inch. It made the deck ring. The last drone dipped as if tipped by the vibration. I caught it by the cage and crushed the cage until it squealed and lost lift. I let it down gently. It twitched once and slept.

"Wren," I said.

"I am under the bridge," she said. I heard the dish screws sing as she made one last perfect micro turn. "Line is hot. Catch is green. I have you when you call."

"You drive when I say drive," I said. "You do not wait to watch."

Her answer was instant and sad. "I will be gone before you finish the word."

The yard camera on the south pole rotated and blinked. It failed to find a face. It wrote a maintenance flag that would vanish into a folder called Later. The white box logged a ticket about interference and filed it under Weather. My HUD dimmed at the corners as the fans begged again. I gave them thirty percent. The vent at my back took a breath and made steam I could almost see.

Footsteps clicked on the service catwalk that crossed above the culvert. Quiet foot pods. A weight that did not hurry. I did not look up. I listened to the way the steel carried the body. Not Forge heavy. Not Wisp light. Something that had learned from both.

I walked into the center of the yard and rolled my shoulders. A gel crust cracked and fell in grey flakes. The left knee motor coughed again. I shifted the load to the plate and bought it one more minute.

"Count," Wren said into the box channel, voice a thread.

"Three," I said.

"Two," she said.

"One," I said.

I did not open the door in my chest. I left it a hand's width and no more. The catch stayed green. The line stayed tight. The van's engine note receded into the tunnel sound of the river road. The mast bowed and returned. The dish sang a pitch that matched the current in my throat.

He stepped into the yard light from the catwalk stairs. New frame, androgynous lines, shoulders narrow, hips built for acceleration, hands with thin palms and long fingers. The silhouette had Velvet's balance and Wisp's glide. It could have been brother to both. The faceplate was soft, eyes smoked glass. He carried no obvious blade and still every piece of him read blade.

Mirror looked at Forge, then at the trucks, then at the racks, then at me. He set his feet like a person who plans to enjoy his last good lesson.

"Hello," he said, voice as clean as a test tone.

"Wren," I said into the line. "Go."

"I am already gone," she said. I heard her slip the Wendigo deeper into shadow, heard the mast flex, heard the catch purr like a machine that believes.

Forge's fans took one hard breath and steadied. The slab throbbed with its own heat. The rails felt like a fever. My hands remembered the weight of every dumb fight I had ever made smart by refusing to rush.

Mirror lifted one hand in a greeting that did not reach his eyes. The trucks idled. The men at the gate chose not to be part of this picture.

I set my feet on the gravel, felt the lines of the yard under my soles like a map, and walked toward him. The last of the gel cracked from my plates and fell as sugar. The visor star caught the floodlight and flared. The left knee coughed once more, then found quiet. I let it be.

"Time to spend the shell," I said.

He smiled in the way a person does when he has no face. He stepped forward off the last stair and made the ground seem interested in timing.

This was the place. Wren had the net. The box was hot. Forge was breaking. Mirror wanted the last word. I did not intend to give it to him, but I was ready to pay for the chance.

I raised my hands. He raised his.

The yard held its breath.

HE STEPS OFF THE last stair like the ground has asked him to. New frame. Shoulders narrow. Hips built to turn inside a boot print. Hands with thin palms and long fingers. The finish eats light. The faceplate is soft, eyes smoked glass. If Wisp and Velvet had a brother, this would be him.

"Hello," he says. His voice is even. It does not bother with warmth.

I walk forward. Forge is hot at the seams. The left knee motor coughs once, then holds. The slab pushes heat into the rails like a man shoving money into a fire to buy time.

We meet in the center of the yard.

Mirror does not test. He commits. Two steps, then a heel cut across my knee that would fold any body that trusted its tendons more than its plates. I turn the greave and take it on metal. He is already above me, palm on a rack upright, magnets kissing steel, body rotating around that touch. He drops behind my shoulder, changes mind, goes in front instead. The correction costs him nothing. He likes the economy.

I do not chase his head. I take the ground under his feet. Left foot flat. Right foot slides. Forearm on his hip. Shoulder on his chest plate. I walk him toward the forklift mast because steel keeps a promise even when people forget how.

He spins off it. His hand lays the smallest circle on the mast cage and the whole body changes direction in that time. He plants a foot on the truck bumper, hops to the hood, and comes back at my head with something short and ugly that lives in his wrist seam. It is not ceramic. It is black steel, satin edge, a motor in the housing to keep it honest. I give him helmet. The blade scrapes and sings. The visor star widens a millimeter. It stops.

He does not smile. He enjoys the result, not the feeling. He tries my back seam. I roll the whole torso and feed his blade into plate. He takes the jolt in his hips and makes no sound. His foot taps the forklift tire. He uses the bounce to change levels and comes for the gap at my elbow. He has my early habits without their fear.

"Stop looking at trucks," I say. "Look at me."

"Hello," he says again, almost friendly.

He disappears down my side and tries the kneecap again, a clean diagonal. I slide my shin into it. Plate on steel. I feel the motor under the plate complain. I adjust the angle so the load rides plastic and not the gear. He hears the complaint the way I do. He files it, then pressures it twice in a row to see if the sound repeats. It does. It will not help him yet. It will later.

I take his wrist, test the joint, find the stop, then try to rotate him into the rack. He lets the rotation go half a degree further than a body should. Someone has tuned him for spite. The stop catches. He digs a toe under my heel and tries to pull. I let the heel lift. He does not get the fall. I put him into the rack anyway. The door flexes. The latch holds. The magnets in his palm kiss it and save him a bad neck.

He speaks to me like a trainer.

"You should have brought the bird," he says.

"She is where she needs to be," I say.

He does not look toward the river. He feints with the left hand and throws the right to open my ear seam. I do not buy either. I let him cut the plastic guard and not the seam. He hates the waste. He changes rhythm. Three fast jabs into plate to make my forearm leave, then a real cut at my throat. I do not give him the forearm or the throat. I put my helmet into his faceplate like two animals that should never have met, then step into his stance so he cannot enjoy distance.

We trade small. Ribs. Elbows. Hands re-gripping. Gravel gives feedback where tile would lie. The forklift creaks. The drone wrecks fizz quietly as their batteries decide what to do with themselves. The ground unit at the gate is quiet. They are letting the yard handle this. They do not want to own the aftermath.

He is fast in the way that looks like water and is actually work. He makes ladders out of anything that will hold his weight for a half-second. He cuts corners without losing line. He loves catching me in transitions. He will keep doing it until he is bored or my leg decides to lie to me.

The leg lies a little. Left knee cough. I ride it. He hears it like a promise. He pressures it again. I push back through it and turn him into the truck door. He bounces and comes out low. Blade to calf. I take it on boot and let it skate into ground. Sparks. Not an advantage. A camera note.

"Cute," he says.

"Quiet," I say.

I walk him backward. He switches to counters built for a heavier opponent. They are cleanly written. I hate how well they fit me. I refuse two and eat one to keep the line. He throws an elbow into my visor. I accept the star's growth. It does not threaten the laminate yet. He takes a half step to stand his angle for the next sequence. I step into his breath and cut that idea in half.

He pins my elbow and throws his knee at my ribs to set up a head turn. I do not let him own my head. I put my forehead into his faceplate and push. It looks stupid and that is why it works. He gives a centimeter. I take it and flip him into the space between the trucks. He lands like a cat that hates my carpet and makes sure I know it.

I follow. He reverses and uses the bumper to stop himself from giving ground. He parries wide and goes for the back seam again, then does not, then does. It is a fake inside a fake. It would fool a good person. It would not fool someone who knows he wants it to land. I let his blade score my plate where it costs me nothing and return the insult by knuckling him in the temple. His visor lines flutter a hair. He stops enjoying the number of times I refuse to fall.

He changes tools. A short cylinder snaps open on his hip. Monofilament. He remembers how it bit in the server aisle. He wants that memory to pay him here. He tries to loop it behind my knee. I catch it with a rack label again and wind it twice until the motor chokes. He cuts the line clean and lets the spool fall. He does not curse. He throws the useless housing at my visor to make me blink and comes in under it for the seam by my jaw. I catch his wrist, crush the motor, and feel the blade chip. He resets. He is not tired. He is planning to make me that way.

The slab keeps feeding rail. The fans take breath in measured sips. A small light on my internal board flickers to remind me that nothing lasts. The leg coughs again. A little worse. I shift weight. He sees it and smiles with the mouth he does not have.

"Left," he says. "You keep making that noise."

"Use it then," I say.

He does. He pushes for three exchanges to buy the rhythm. He turns one of the pushes into a drop-knee and a scissor at my calf and thigh. It would unbalance anyone with a tendon plan. My plan is plate. I ride it and stomp his foot to grant him my weight where he does not want it. His ankle flips wrong and then recovers because his frame forgives what would break other people. He hits my chin with his head. Helmet to helmet. Inside my skull the webbing rattles. I do not let my eyes go soft.

He sees I am not granting the dramatic. He steps back one pace, faceplate level, and speaks without breath.

"Echo," he says. Not loud. Not for anyone else.

The yard listens. The band tightens.

He raises his left hand as if to reach for my neck and stops half way, palm open to the air, fingers a little splayed. The motion looks like nothing if you do not live in signals. The palm is a plate. The plate is a coupler. The coupler is an old Orinox trick for emergency rescues and bad ideas. It tunes to the nearest shape that looks like a person and asks it to be helpful.

My door is already cracked for Wren. The box feels me. The mast hears me. The dish knows how to sing to me. Mirror steps into the same hallway and hangs a mirror in it. His coupler copies the pattern in my exit frame and plays it back into me with half a step of delay. That is the protocol. Echo. Feed a person their own telemetry slightly late. The stack will try to correct the gap. Correcting the gap will convince it to hand control to a process it believes is itself. Once it hands control away, you can label what is left with any word you like.

He gives my frame back to me with one less breath in it. He gives me my count with a digit missing. He gives me Wren's door but not Wren's hand.

The world tilts without moving.

Everything that is me lives as order for a breath. The exit frame in my head gathers itself in a doorway that is no longer mine. The path to the van jumps. The box ring skates from green to amber. The dish hums flat, then corrects. Wren swears once, not at me, at math.

"Stay with me," she says. The catch cuts the mast pattern narrower to get rid of the noise. It helps. It hurts. The line tightens.

Mirror steps into range and lays his palm on my chest plate.

There is no impact. No heroic crack. My spine shakes like someone ran a wet finger around the rim of a glass and asked it to be a bell. The coupler hums a tone that my bones hate. It is not an audio tone. It lives in the spectrum where hands do not go and work still happens.

The Echo drops its hook into my door and rings it again. The stack inside me steps toward the mirror in the hallway back to itself because I have taught it to be helpful when the room gets hot. That is my fault. It is also why Wren loves me.

"Do not go," Wren says, one level under breath. Her dish moves a centimeter. "Hikari, do not go to him."

I do not answer. Answering would cost. I count. Three. Two. One. The number comes late. Mirror's hand increases the delay by a little. The delay looks like a problem I can fix by stepping toward it. If I step, I will be under his hand. If I am under his hand, I will be a coil waiting for someone else to write on me.

He speaks softly. "Echo Protocol, engage."

He says it for me. He says it for himself. The frame he wears hears it and gives him a priority his previous shell did not have. It routes more power to the coupler. It gives him supervisory class on the local band. It offers to help.

The world narrows. The trucks fall away. The yard becomes a straight line with a door in it. The part of me that smells the river cannot decide if it still exists. The part of me that keeps my hands correct tries to put its weight where it saved me before. The part of me that knows I am a person makes a very small choice and stays where it is.

Mirror tries to make my breath his. He nearly succeeds.

I put both hands on his wrist and squeeze. He pushes more signal through the coupler and feeds me my own trace with a soft buzz riding it. The buzz carries a single order. Release. It is written in the same rhythm as my own stop codes. It is even signed with a key my body wants to trust. Somewhere back in the Core there is a copy of this key. He stole it or printed it in a lab that named itself after the person no one misses in meetings. It smells like the hallway where Navarre liked to watch and pretend he was not.

"Wren," I say. I am not sure the word leaves my mouth. It might be a pressure in my throat. It might be a plan.

"Here," she says. Her voice is in the box. Her hands are on the dish. "Here. Here."

The Echo tries to put its mouth over mine. I open my mouth inside that and bite.

The trick with Echo is not new. Orinox used it to take assets home. It was a leash they called a lifeline. You can break it. You have to be willing to be deaf for a second in a room where sound keeps you alive.

I kill my own local mic to the door. The line goes silent. I turn my ear to only the box. Mirror feels the drop and tries to force his coupler through the gap. His frame obliges. He has a better budget than the truck. The tone climbs. The resonance in my ribs tries to put a lie into my count.

Three. Silence. One.

I am not here for elegant solutions. I need crude seconds.

I drive my forearm into his jaw and shove him off the coupler. He rides the shove and taps the plate again. The tone returns. I drop my own ear a second time. He presses. The suit grows hotter than it wants to be. The rails groan in my head. The knee coughs again. My vision grays right at the edges. The truck engines in the corner of the yard sound like river water in a glass bowl.

He cuts my throat in the same motion with the small steel blade. It bites the plastic guard and not the seam. He wants the pressure, not the kill. He wants me awake long enough to hand my name to his hand.

He speaks to himself. "Hold him."

The coupler listens and gives him one more slice of authority. He has done this before on people who did not know they could ruin their own radio and still live. He believes the day is over.

I step into him. He accepts the contact because the protocol likes close. I get him to the forklift frame. The mast gives me a backstop. I try to pin his wrist. He smears his hand along my plate instead of letting it be held and the tone stays on me like sweat. I rake my knuckles along the coupler housing and feel a motor inside it that hates the attention. He still does not flinch.

My count falters. I do not know if Wren hears it. I barely hear it. I see it how a man sees his own heartbeat in a mirror across a room, once, then not again.

Mirror leans into me and speaks through the filter like a teacher who thinks I am bright enough to hate for wasting his time.

"You are already in the hallway," he says. "Stop pretending you are not."

He is right in the worst way. I can feel the doorframe. I can feel that it is mine and not mine. The catch is one meter behind it with Wren's hands on it. The white box on the river road would still like to help. The truck is a shape. The yard is a shape. The river is a sound. Wren is the part of the sound that is human.

I will not get another crude second. I need a different tool.

"Wren," I say again. That is all I have.

She answers like she has put her mouth on the mic. "Hikari."

The way she says my name is the one thing that does not bend. I let it be the only tone in the room for me.

Then her hands go busy. The dish changes pitch. The mast narrows. The catch drops its squelch and lets the van spine speak in a voice it does not usually use. An admin channel opens that no one in a truck should ever know about. It has a signature we forged this morning in a room that smelled like cold metal and lemon soap. It belongs to a person who signs big reports and never touches cable.

The new voice steps into the band like it owns it. It carries a small tone of amusement because I sampled it that way.

"Supervisor present," the channel says. Navarre's cadence. My font. "End test."

Two words. That is all the Kindle stack needs to hear when you want it to drop a persona overlay without taking the shell offline. End test. Dismiss. Return to base process. It is a lab command. They built it for safety in a room with nice chairs. Send it to a field frame and it becomes a blade.

Mirror's head jerks a quarter centimeter. His coupler drops power for a beat to check the credential that just walked into the room. The Echo hook loosens. It does not fall. His frame reports a supervisor channel. It asks his persona which rule applies to being told that tests are over by a man who likes flowers in vases in offices with polished floors. The rule is simple. Obey.

Mirror tries not to. He throws power back into the coupler to smother the line and keep his hand on my throat. He tries to ignore the supervisor channel the way he ignored a dozen other polite liars. The frame does not treat this one as a liar. The command sits close to the boot sequence. It belongs to a part of the body he cannot punch.

"Wren," I say. I do not ask a question. I am asking for a second strike.

She gives me five. Her hands tap the box. The line that goes to the dish gets a new flavor. A checksum that says this signature was born in the room we stole from. A triple MAC that we wrote like a joke and wrapped around the words like a ribbon.

Navarre speaks again inside his own key. "Dismiss persona overlay," the channel says. "Unload active mask. Authenticate one five seven K."

The frame does a thing I have only seen in rooms where the floor sparkles. It pauses and asks itself which process is allowed to live in the chest. The answer appears. It does not like that answer. It obeys it.

Mirror's coupler drops to half and then to a quarter. His blade hand stiffens. His visor brightens and dims like a camera feeding its own iris a wrong image. The overlay that calls itself Mirror tries to keep his hand closed. The base layer asks that hand to open. The open wins because the rule that governs the action is older than whatever man taught him to be clever about hating it.

The Echo slips like a ring on a wet finger.

"Now," Wren says. She does not need to explain the timing. It is the same count we have been carrying since the server hall.

I put every part of me that still belongs to me into one shove. Forearm into coupler. Hip into hip. Shoulder into chest plate. He hits the forklift mast because steel loves helping me finish sentences. The coupler leaves my plate. The tone goes from inside my ribs to outside my head. The exit door is mine again. I close it to a slit and keep the slit for Wren.

Mirror's hand opens by one regret. He sees what happened. He hates it. He grabs for the admin channel like you would grab a snake and tries to reroute it into something that will let him keep being the person he likes. Wren changes the key half a step and sends the same order as a new message. End test. Dismiss. The frame hears it as fresh. It obeys again and asks the persona in the chest if it would like to leave now.

He says no. The frame says yes.

The overlay unloads like a curtain falling. It is not total. It is enough. The clean, cruel patience that was Mirror's presentation dies without a sound and leaves behind the base reflexes that keep a machine upright when an operator faints. The coupler powers down to idle. The blade slips back into its house. His stance loses ten percent of what made it art.

I hit him again and take the rest.

He drops to a knee. His hand pawing for my throat finds plate and then air. He reaches for his head like he plans to tear the helmet off with spite. The base layer refuses and keeps him safe. He shakes once. He is there and not. His frame is awake. His will has been asked to sit down by a room he did not think could see him. He refuses to sit. The frame splits the difference and leaves him kneeling in gravel with one palm on the ground.

"Hikari," Wren says in my ear. She says it like you hold a person's shoulder before they go under and come back. "Stay."

I feel my count again. Three, without gap. Two, without trick. One, mine.

I intend to finish him. I take a step to do it. The knee coughs and lies. The slab under my ribs finds the end of what it can give. The rails hum and then fall quiet. The fans take one more breath and then two and then kill themselves to save other things. The plate over my hip warps. My hands feel very far away.

The yard tilts. The trucks blur. The forklift looks like a drawing of a woman in a dress. I realize I am laughing at my own head for that thought. I stop.

Mirror tries to stand and does not manage it. He reaches for the coupler again without knowing why. I step on his wrist and keep his hand on the ground without breaking it. I am done with teaching. I am interested in leaving.

The exit door is still cracked. The box is green. The dish is a bright note only I can hear. I do not have a minute. I have six seconds.

"Now," I say to Wren. "Catch."

"Catching," she says.

I pull the trigger and step into the slit. The line takes me without the mirror in it. The box is an open hand. I fall into it. It holds me like it believes this is real.

A shape enters the band from the catwalk stairs with a kind of ugly grace that means nothing good. Not Mirror. His process is kneeling and blinking. Something else on the campus side spins its dish and tries to be helpful. The white box offers to hold me. The catch refuses the offer with a signature that lies better than I have ever lied. The white box writes a ticket, says someone should look later, and goes on doing the only job it was ever meant to do.

Mirror's frame slumps the rest of the way. Base holds his airway open. No persona drives. His hand under my boot twitches. Nothing in there tells it to do anything but keep the body ready for orders that will not arrive.

The Echo hook lets go of the door completely. The tone in my ribs dies. The world becomes the inside of Wren's box.

For a full second I am nowhere.

There is no yard. No trucks. No forklift. There is no river noise. There is only the order the catch can hold and the tiny way its diode ring breathes.

"Hikari," Wren says. Close. Not through a radio. Through her throat, into the casing, into the thread I am trying to be. She says my name and it sits on the frame the way a hand sits on the back of a chair someone you love always used.

For the first time since he said hello on the stairs, I am afraid.

I reach for my count and get blank paper.

She keeps talking because she knows she should. Not begging. Not praying. She believes. That is worse and better than either.

"Hikari," she says. "Your name is Hikari. You are coming with me. You are here."

I step toward her voice. The door in the box is real because she believes it. I put my hand on it the way I put a hand on Forge's chest when I needed it to be what I was asking for. The hand stops existing for a breath. The breath comes back as a click in the catch that sounds like a bird learning itself.

Then nothing. Then less than nothing.

The box drops one bar. The ring flickers. Green to amber. The channel goes thin. She says my name again and the word lands like a coin in a well with no water.

This is the beat where some stories lie and tell you they chose to come back. I do not choose anything. I fall along a wire. I feel my breath from outside. It is a picture of breath, not air.

The world does not return. It just becomes not nothing.

A tiny sound inside the catch says Hello in my font. A fraction of me that knows how to speak opens its eyes. It is not enough to be me. It is enough to be the next second.

Wren does not know that yet. She thinks she failed. I hear her say it to the dark inside the van with no one there to pretend to be brave for.

"Please," she says, quiet. "Please."

The box tries to answer for me and cannot. It does the only thing it knows. It holds the shape it has learned until someone smarter tells it to change. That is what Wren built it to do.

Back in the yard, Forge finally gives what I told it to. The left knee motor locks. The rail dump that bought me dull seconds burns the last insult into the plates. The suit sinks to one knee and stays there in front of a frame that is breathing without a mind. Two trucks sit with paper wedged under their tires. A forklift that will never move watches. Men at a gate choose new lives that do not include telling this story for money.

The man in the frame that was Mirror will wake if someone hands him a personality like a weapon. No one in this yard has that key. The key is in the van with Wren. The machine without the man is a thing you can move with a forklift and a strap.

I do not see any of it. I hear the diode tick of a box trying not to panic. I hear Wren's hands tap the casing where you rap a cake tin for luck.

"Hikari," she says. One more time. Not a question. An invitation. An order. A home address.

I find three. I find two. One is not there yet. I am not gone. I am late.

The ring goes green and stays for one heartbeat. It slips. It catches. It slips again.

She does not breathe for that beat. Neither do I.

Then a single sound leaves whatever mouth I have. It is not a word. It is a shape of one. It is enough.

Wren shouts like she has just pulled a person out of cold water. Not loud. Joyful and very angry.

"I told you," she says to the box, to me, to the river, to the building, to everyone who ever thought numbers were kinder than people. "I told you."

The catch steadies. The mast sings. The dish locks. The white box on the river road writes another ticket and files it where paperwork goes to rest. I live inside a box that smells like dust and Wren and a little lemon because she wiped it when she built it even though no one would ever see.

On the yard gravel, Mirror's shell kneels and waits for whatever a supervisor voice will ask it to do next. It has no supervisor. We are going to borrow it.

Forge bows and stays where I left it. The suit is done. It is a good death. It holds its ground while I leave it. That is all I asked.

"Hold him," Wren says, and she is not talking to me anymore. She is talking about the frame on the gravel. I feel the van turn and head for the yard. I feel the dish hold the line like a mother's hand. I feel my count come back slow and stubborn.

Three. Two. One.

Everything hurts like a number trying to be a person. That is alright. We have a second and then we will have another. The next job is not a fight. It is surgery. Wren is better at that than anyone I have ever met.

The box breathes. I breathe with it. The van eats distance. The yard opens. The frame waits. The shell I loved bows to it and does not threaten to stand.

Cold light, white tables, a floor that pretends to be clean. The cafeteria smells like boiled protein and citrus cleaner. We sit in rows because someone drew a diagram and then lived inside it. Cameras look down from each corner. Their red status dots blink in time with the ventilation.

My tray has four squares. One block the color of chalk, one the color of tea, one the color of a bruise, one cup of water. The water tastes like pipe. The blocks taste like numbers. I eat each square in the order on the card because it is easier than being asked why.

Across from me, a boy who is not a boy pushes his blocks to the far edge of the tray and stares at my hands. We are the same height, not the same shape. Their collar is newer. Their hair is cut wrong for sleep. A guard at the door yawns and pops gum. The sound carries under the lights like an alarm that someone forgot to turn off.

The room is not quiet. Spoons tap plastic. Footsteps scrape. Someone whispers a set of letters to themselves. I hear the whisper skip one letter, then return to it, then skip again. I hear it because the collar at my neck trains me to map sound. It hums when it likes my attention. Today it hums as if it has been fed.

I take the chalk block and the bruise block together. I chew without looking up. The not-boy leans forward. The tray edge creaks. I keep my eyes on the rim of my cup. The water inside it steadies and then ripples. The ripple is not from my breath. It is from someone else pushing the table with their knee.

He speaks with a mouth that is too dry. "Give me the tea block."

"No," I say.

He watches my face for a change of tone. He does not find one. He is not hungry. He is being asked to do a thing and he would like to be the person who did it. That is how this room sets its games.

The collar hums again. Higher. The ceiling camera near the serving line tilts a fraction. I do not look up. When you look up you give the room a small prize. I have learned to hoard small losses and spend them on rest.

He reaches across the table. His fingers are fast and careless. He takes hold of my wrist before the tray. The grip is wrong. He intends to move my hand, not keep it. I slide my wrist out of his fingers, fold my palm, and set my thumb on his knuckle. He squeezes harder because he has been told pressure is proof. I rotate my wrist inside his grasp and feel the knuckle go from a circle to an oval. The oval wants to stop being part of his hand. He grunts. His fingers open.

"Leave it," I say.

He laughs. It is quick and bright, like a firecracker in a stairwell. "You are not special," he says. He does not say it to me. He says it to the camera. He wants it to hear him make the line. "You think you are, but you are not."

The gum guard at the door stops chewing. The other guard looks at the spoon in his own cup as if it knows a story. Above the serving line, a rectangle of glass looks down on us. The glass is mirrored from this side. It is not mirrored on the other. It smells like fresh paint and old paper.

The not-boy tips his tray so the blocks slide, then slaps my cup into my lap. Water wicks into the fabric at my knees and crawls toward the skin. I stand. The chair's legs skip across the floor and make everyone in our row flinch.

He smiles because he has created an event. That is what the trainers call it. Creating events shows initiative. That is what the trainers call the taste for attention. He steps around the table and lifts his shoulder as if to bump mine. He aims for my throat with the flat of his wrist. A trainer taught him to hide the edge under the flat. The camera taught him to do it slow enough to be captured, fast enough to be praised.

I do not think about the tray. I do not think about the trainers. I think about the way his jaw moves under that shaved skin when he laughs. I put my palm into the hinge where skull meets neck and push, then twist. His breath stops with a sound no one wants to make. His eyes jump, then decide not to finish their plan. His body drops into my shoulder without weight, then becomes all weight. It folds as if the strings have been cut because that is the truth.

Chairs skid. Spoons fall. The gum guard swears once. The other guard raises his baton because he has been told that raising a baton is a way to use time while you decide if you care. The collar at my neck lights. The hum becomes a line of white heat that stabs down the spine and out through my hands. My fingers open without permission. My jaw locks. I find the floor with my knees. The shock lasts for a second and then two. The collar ratchets itself closed a notch I have not felt before. The plastic bites skin. I smell the little scorch at the edge of my hair.

From the rectangle of glass, a speaker pops. The sound is clean. The tone is practiced. No static. A voice I know collects the room like a teacher collects papers.

"Stand down," Navarre says. His voice could be the color of the walls. It is polite. It does not ask if we are well. "Asset, stand down now."

I put my hands flat on the tile and let the current drain. The boy on the floor is not a boy. He is a set of numbers that have stopped moving. His collar winks without knowing what to do with itself. A trainer steps in. She touches her wristband to the collar and it goes dark. She will write a form. She will use phrases like unexpected escalations and behavioral overlap. She will drink tea after and wonder if the word overlap was one word too proud.

I wait for the next instruction. It comes like a coin falling into a machine. Navarre speaks again.

"Look up," he says.

I look up. The mirror gives me back a small person in a gray shirt with water on the knees. The eyes belong to someone else. They are mine.

"You were observed," he says. "You were correct to act."

The collar clicks. It loosened by one notch while I was looking up. The skin under it throbs. The trainer near the boy lifts him with two fingers under the jaw and two under the skull. She does not look at me. She looks at her shoes. The gum guard goes back to chewing.

Navarre's voice softens in a way a microphone loves. "You have to learn the difference," he says. "When to act and when to stop. Stand down. Let the program take the rest."

I put my palms on my knees. My body would like to shake. I do not allow it. The other children, little mirrors in gray shirts, look at the table and their food and the door. Two of them stare at my hands. One stares at the spot on the floor where the boy now is not.

The speaker pops again. The words arrive with a practiced pause between them, like a lesson in a book.

"You are to now live free," Navarre says. "Freedom means obedience to purpose. Stand down."

He loves that word. Free. He feeds it to us the way the room feeds us blocks that taste like chalk. He wants it to taste like his hand.

I sit. I pick up my tray. I do not wipe my knees. The water will dry before lunch ends. On the card, the last square is the tea block. I put it in my mouth and chew. It tastes like nothing. It tastes like a promise written on a wall I cannot touch.

The collar hums again. Lower now. Approval as electricity. Across from me, the space where the not-boy sat is empty. A trainer pushes his tray to the center of the table and takes the card. She folds the card in half and puts it in her pocket. She meets my eye, then looks away because looking back would make this something besides an instruction.

The speaker clicks off. The room remembers how to be loud in the tiny ways it prefers. Spoons tap. Chairs scuff. Somewhere near the serving line a child cries without opening their mouth. It is a sound like air leaving a bottle. It continues for ten seconds. A guard coughs. The sound stops.

I finish the water in my cup. I set the cup on the tray with the mouth down. I place the tray in the slot at the end of the table. The card says to stand and line up at the west door. I stand. I line up. The collar hums a yes that makes the hair on my arms stand up and then lie down.

On the way out, I look once at the mirrored glass. I do not see Navarre. I see my face where he would be. For a second I imagine the mirror is honest. The thought passes. Honesty is not part of the curriculum.

In the hall, a wall poster lists the six parts of cleanliness. I can recite them without looking. The floor has a scuff I have seen for three days. No one claims it. I step over it. The camera above the fire door winks. My collar warms as if someone has turned up a small sun.

We walk. A trainer counts us without moving lips. At the corner, the group turns left into the training bay. I turn right because the card in my pocket says I have a calibration and the collar likes it when I arrive early.

In the little room, the chair is warm from the person who sat before me. I sit. I put my palms on the rests. They hum. A glass panel lowers. I see my eyes again. They are mine. They belong to the room. Navarre's voice comes from the speaker over my left ear.

"You did well," he says.

"I stood down," I say.

"You acted," he says, as if the words are the same. "You are learning who you are."

He means that the collar knows my neck. He means that a camera likes the way my hands do what they are told. He does not mean the thing I have decided to keep for myself.

"Look at the dot," he says. A small light appears, bottom right. I look. The light slides left and up. My eyes follow. It slides down and toward my nose. My eyes follow. The chair hums in a rhythm that makes my jaw clench. My collar warms. The speaker repeats, gentle, patient, pleased.

"Stand down," he says. "Live free."

The words fit together for him. They do not fit for me. I keep the difference in my mouth like a splinter and do not let my tongue push it out.

Later, in the dorm, I fold my gray shirt on my bunk. I watch the dark strip under the door glow and fade with the hall light. Breathing becomes numbers. Numbers become sleep. In the dream, the cafeteria has no sound. My hands are empty. The tray is full. The mirror shows me a face that never learns to say yes when it means no.

I wake before lights. The collar hums good morning to the skin where it bit me. I put my hand on it and let the contact cool. I tell myself a small truth without moving my lips.

One day I will live free without orders.

The lights come on. The intercom clicks. A trainer calls out numbers in pairs. Mine is in the second pair. I step into the hall and walk toward the day that belongs to someone else. The splinter at the back of my tongue stays where I left it. It is the only secret I am allowed to keep.

THE BOX HOLDS ME like a steady hand on the back of my neck. No room. No sky. Only the slow pulse of the diode ring and the sound of Wren breathing close to the casing.

"Stay with me," she says. The van turns. Tires bump the curb at the culvert. Then concrete. Then gravel. The mast sings. The dish keeps the line tight.

I cannot see the yard. I feel it through her work. A door thuds. Boots hit stone. Her voice goes low.

"I am here," she tells me. "I am getting you a body."

A new vibration enters the box. Not the van. A cable drags across the bumper and rattles the license frame. A reel spins. The sound is a small old comfort. Wren prefers wire when radios lie.

"Quarantine," she says to the air. Her tone changes for the admin band. Sharp. Official. "Frame on yard coordinate ten by six. Maintenance hold. Supervisor present. End test in field. Dismiss overlay."

The air changes shape in the band. The rule bites. The kneeling frame on the gravel accepts the word as if it came from the room that built it. Mirror's presentation is already gone. Base holds airway and posture. That is all.

The cable reels out. It slides over a spool. Wren drags it to the gravel and clips it into the port at the frame's hip. She misses by an inch, adjusts without looking down, and hears the latch click.

"Local link," she says. "Alive."

She puts her palm on the chest plate. The same spot she taps on Forge when she wants a heart to hear her. Her voice is softer again. Close to the mic.

"Hikari. I am going to put you in. This shell is fast and very rude. You will like it once it stops trying to impress anyone."

I cannot smile in the box. I feel the shape anyway.

She opens the catch, not to let me out, to give me a taper between worlds. The van's spine shares me with the fiber. The fiber sees the frame. The frame reports a clean core and a confused soul. Wren picks the lock that keeps those two parts from admitting they need each other.

"Handing you a ring," she says. "Hold pattern first. Nothing else."

She loads our cut of Ananke Gate, the one we made gentler in the van. No fear loop. No punishment. Only a small ring that looks for breath and returns a yes when it finds mine. She injects it into the base. The base checks the signature, finds a supervisor stamp that used to belong to another life, and accepts it.

"Hold is up," she says. "Stack window open. Come here."

I step into the wire. The frame's bus is a hallway that smells like new plastic and a pride I do not respect. The agreements inside it are clean and unforgiving. They ask for a name before they offer a hand. Wren cheats for us. She spoofs the badge at the doorway with the key we stole in the Core. The hand appears.

For a second I am everywhere in the frame. Elbow angles. Hip load. Magnet status in the palms. The little flex in the ankle designed for silent landings. The throat mic parked quiet. The voice path mapped for someone else's rhythm. I bring my count with me and let it roll across the new space.

Three.

The left foot answers late. Wren sees the delay in the telemetry. She curses once without wasting time. Her hands are on the chest panel already. She pops the armor piece that covers the coupler and shuts its motor down like slapping a bad habit out of the air.

Two.

The echo hook that Mirror left in the coupler wheezes and dies. The new frame forgets it was allowed to be clever. It returns to being a tool that can do difficult things.

One.

The hold ring catches my breath at the back of the throat. The feeling lands like a seatbelt. I do not love seatbelts. I respect them. I set my weight inside the frame the way you test stairs in the dark.

"Hi," Wren says. She is kneeling beside the chest with the cable still between her fingers. She cannot see my eyes. You do not need eyes for the next thing. "Come back to me."

"Here," I say.

It is not loud. It is not smooth. The voice path is tuned for a tone that was not mine. It still leaves the chest and lands where she needs it to. She bows her head for half a second. She lets her shoulders drop for one more. Then she is on her feet.

"Good," she says. "Do not move yet. I am going to lock Orinox out of your spine."

Footsteps at the far gate. The ground unit that learned to wait is trying a new idea. The trucks are still boxed by paper and chain. They have brought a bolt cutter. The man with it looks at the frame that is kneeling and decides today he is a technician. The other men decide to be anywhere else.

Wren runs the cable back to the van. She moves fast without wasting her head. She hits the relay on the mast and cuts the comms box on the river road out of the band. The white box writes a ticket. The ticket goes to a folder I made for small lies.

She slams the van door open. She pulls a second case from under the bench. The case holds a coil clamp, a battery, and a relay made out of two dead routers and a prayer. She sets it on the gravel, flips the lid, and builds us a firewall that lives two meters from my rib cage.

"New shell," she says. "Meet your habits."

She sends the suit three quick patches. First, lock down remote discovery on the bus.

Second, rename the asset to a thing with no entry in their index. Third, bind the admin key to a moving signature that is my count and nothing else. The frame accepts each in the bored rhythm of a machine that likes rules.

"Move your fingers," she says.

I twitch the long palms. The magnets hum inside. The gravel whispers near the plaque on the heel. The left knee, the one that lied in Forge, is new here and would like to show off. I tell it to wait.

"Boot the optics," she says.

The visor wakes. The world resolves across smoked glass with a sharpness that would make a lesser person cry. Blue light on racks. Drones on the gravel like dead birds. The trucks with paper pressed under their tires like a trick I learned from a friend. Wren in her jacket. Hair stuck with small flecks of dust. Her mouth set in a line that knows how to soften and will not yet.

"Eye contact," she says.

I turn the head. The neck is balanced to make turning addictive. I let it be precise and not indulgent. I meet her eyes. The soft glass hides me from her, but it does not hide her from me.

"We are not done," she says. "We have one more person to pick up."

Her hand goes to her pocket. She takes out the cloth that held the bead. She unwraps it. The little cube sits in her palm like it has been waiting under a pillow. She touches it to her throat mic for one breath. Not to play the kitchen voice. To take courage.

"Juno, I am going to try something," she says. It is not prayer. It is a statement to a person who always liked a plan.

She slots the bead into the catch box cradle. The catch box is still warm from holding me. It keeps the diode ring on to prove it is paying attention. Wren plugs the box into the van's spine where my trace lived a minute ago. She plugs the box into the second case where her firewall lives. She plugs the box into the frame cable so the three of us share the room.

"Kindle," she says, opening the software we stole. "Hold pattern for imprint in a small brain. No clamp. No gag. Only guardrails."

She builds a tiny ring for Juno that looks like the one she handed me, and not like the one Orinox used in that room. It looks for breath in a different place. It looks for the rhythm of Juno's laugh when she forgot to be careful. It looks for the feather tick of claws on a window frame. It looks for the kettle that gave up and clicked.

"Come on," she says to the box. "Wake the kitchen."

She feeds the bead. The catch box shakes once in the way electronics do when old signals find new paths. The diode ring blinks. Not green. Not amber. Something between. The room's sound changes as the catch opens a little door the way it did for me, and asks a different person to step through if they like.

A servo whines behind us. Not a drone. The forklift. A man in a helmet has climbed in and found the key under the dash mat. He turns it. He finds drive. He aims for Wren because his world has become simple in a way that should make him less dangerous and does not.

"Move," I say. The voice path catches up one syllable late. The body does not wait.

I step between Wren and the forklift and let the bumper hit my thigh. It is not Forge. It is not that kind of mass. It is quicker. Lighter. It will not let me bully the world. It will let me be surgical. I put my palm on the fork carriage and bleed its speed into the ground. The magnets bite painted steel. The motor whines. I give the driver a clean look through the smoked glass. He lets go of the throttle. He looks down and finds his hands. He puts the key back where he found it.

Wren never looked away from the box.

"I am here," she says to something only she can love before it has a voice. "If you want the light, you can have it."

The diode ring goes green. It slips. It returns. The little relay in the case clicks. The hold pattern inside the software finds the breath it was built to find and answers yes. The voice path inside the box is not good. It was not designed to be one. It does not matter.

"Wren," the box says. The sound is faint and rough and perfect.

She makes a sound I have not heard from her in a long time. Private and raw and short. She bites it down.

"I have you," she says. "Stay still. I am going to give you legs."

The yard does not have legs for her. The van does. Wren runs to the rear and pulls a small case from the wall. She pops it open on the gravel. A compact crawler sits in foam. It is a four-wheel inspection bot she built for bridge work that never paid. Two gooseneck cameras. A gimbal for a work light. A port for tools. It looks like a toy to a person who has never seen it climb rebar in the rain.

She clips the catch box to the crawler's mount. She runs a short harness from the box to the crawler's control board. She flashes the board with the same supervisor key we used to make a frame forget itself. The crawler accepts a new mind because it has never cared what it carries as long as the power is clean.

"Boot," she says.

The crawler lights blink. The goosenecks lean as if listening. The wheels make a polite chirp as the controller checks motors. The catch box ticks once in sympathy. Then it speaks.

"Cold," Juno says.

Wren laughs without a smile. "I know. We can fix that later."

The crawler looks up at her. Cameras do not have eyes. These manage to anyway.

"Wren," Juno says again, clearer. "I have you."

"You do," Wren says. She swallows and straightens. She looks at me. "We are leaving. The white box will bring friends as soon as its tickets gain a human."

I take one step in the new frame. Then two. The ground feels like answers. The left knee is honest. Good. The magnets in the palms are quick. The hip pistons do not nag. The armor does not creak. The world at the edge is too sharp. That is a tuning pass for later.

"Forge," I say. The shell kneels where I left it. It gives me nothing back. It deserves a word. "Thank you."

The ground unit at the gate finally decides what to be. The man with the bolt cutter puts it on the chain that has married truck to spool. He squeezes. The chain goes slack. The truck reverses. Paper slides. The other truck coughs to life. The driver puts it in gear. He hits whatever is left in front of his bumper.

"Cab," Wren says. She tucks the crawler under her arm like a cat that is almost ready to be outside again. She runs for the van. "Meet me at the door."

I run parallel. The new frame likes speed. It likes awkward angles. It loves climbing. I hate that I enjoy it. I reach the door in three light steps, plant a palm, and throw myself to the roof to watch the lane. A drone body twitches and decides to be dead. A guard at the gate radio says something about a frame that changed clothes.

Wren slams into the driver's seat. The crawler jumps to the dash and clamps its magnets to the metal. The catch box blinks. Juno looks at me with a camera head tilted. I nod. The motion is too stylish in this shell. I make a note to fix that.

"Hold," Wren says. The van coughs, catches, and growls. The mast is already down. The dish is already locked to the headliner. The fiber lies across the gravel and into the frame at my hip. I pop the latch and pull it free. It buzzes in my glove for a last second of static and goes still.

The truck that freed itself lurches into our lane. The driver believes he will be a hero if he blocks us. Wren does not slow. She lines the bumper to the narrow point at the truck's license frame, taps brakes to load the front, and pins the corner like a knot. The truck mounts the paper, skids, and stops at an honest angle that no one will be proud of later.

"Go," I say.

"Going," she says.

We take the lane at an angle. The van hops the curb at the culvert. The mast kisses the bridge lip and comes away with a new scrape. The crawler cranes its necks to watch the yard recede. Juno turns one camera to me and one to Wren and says nothing else. Not yet. There is a room in that box that needs quiet before it can be a kitchen.

The radio tries to sell us a new emergency. Wren kills it. The white box sends a question to the admin band. Our firewall answers with a form letter. The form letter thanks it for its service and invites it to file a different problem later. It believes us for now.

We hit the underpass and become a shadow riding a darker shadow. Wren pushes the van until the engine note finds the part of the dial it likes. The new frame crouches in the back, one palm on the roof rib, one on the case that holds the coil clamp. I watch the mirror. The yard shrinks. The helix on the lobby glass gets small enough to be honest.

Wren glances at me in the rearview.

"You are in one piece," she says.

"In a better one," I say. I flex the long fingers. The magnets hum inside. "It will take tuning."

"We can tune while we run," she says.

Juno's crawler tilts its camera. "You took my voice apart," she says.

"I put it back," Wren says. "I made a few changes."

Juno is quiet for three seconds. Then the tiny speaker in the box gives a small sigh that lives in the place between wonder and grief.

"It sounds like me," she says.

Wren smiles without letting it be visible for too long. "It is you."

We clear the culvert. The river opens as a slick sheet to our right. The city ahead is a comb of light and dark. Wren picks the seam we planned. The van finds it and holds it.

In the rear, I settle onto one knee and breathe through a shell that was made to run on rooftops, not to argue with trucks. The hold ring sits where it needs to. The admin locks are mine. Orinox will come. We will be gone.

Wren speaks without turning. "Say your name for me."

"Hikari," I say. The voice path takes the sound and trims it clean. The frame likes the way it comes out. It will learn to like the way I use it.

"Good," she says. "We keep it."

Juno clicks her little servos. "I would like a window," she says.

Wren laughs. "I owe you a house. The van will do for tonight."

The road climbs. The city gets closer. The mast hums on a low note and sleeps. The dish is a lump under the headliner. The catch box glows a soft green that makes the dash kind. Forge is a shadow in a yard we will never see again. Mirror is a quiet body that will ask terrible questions when someone gives it a face it does not deserve. Our names are blacked out of rooms that should never have built us.

We drive. The new legs feel right. The old grief sits next to the new voice and does not bite. The count holds.

Three. Two. One.

Clean Switch

HIKARI

THE SERVICE ROAD NARROWS to a ramp that feeds the riverway. Wren angles the Wendigo toward open lanes. Then the street turns into a wall.

A Forge Juggernaut steps out of a loading bay and plants both feet on the asphalt. Twenty feet of plates and pistons. Shoulder rings the size of manholes. A chest coupler like a vault door. Floodlights burn the van white.

Mirror's voice comes through a loudhailer on the frame, calm and near. "Hello."

The crawler on the dash points both goosenecks at the giant and forgets to breathe in its new way. Wren's hands tense on the wheel.

I unlatch the side door. "Two blocks," I say. "Line of sight. Keep speed up."

"You will not be alone," Wren says.

"I will be fast," I say. "Go."

She reads my tone and obeys it. The Wendigo drops to first, slides backward into an alley mouth, swings the nose, and rockets toward the underpass. The mast stays down. The dish sleeps against the headliner. The thread between us holds tight and quiet.

I take a sword from the rack. Straight back, single bevel, carbon ceramic that eats factory steel. No ornament. The grip fits my new palms like it was bored for me on a morning with good light.

The Juggernaut stomps two paces closer and leans. The ground tells me how much it weighs. Mirror tips the head a fraction as if he wants to taste scale.

"You traded up," he says. "So did I."

The new frame hums in my joints. Elbows honest. Hips quick. Ankles soft over hard. Palms itching with magnets that want a place to sing. I roll my shoulders and every plate sits where it should.

"Good," I say. "A fair test."

I walk toward him. He comes to meet me, machine grace over old anger.

He opens with a favorite lesson. A stamp that intends to end angles. The right foot rises, hammers down, and tries to bowl the road. I am not there when it lands. Two steps left, one forward, a lean into air, and I am under his knee. The blade snaps through the soft shield where actuator meets calf. One clean bite. Clear fluid jets a neat arc that fogs in the light. The leg checks itself and catches. He does not fall. Good build, honest anger.

His left arm drops through a piston cut. I show him my shoulder, let the plate ring, and slide by the elbow seam. Magnets kiss the inner bicep as the blade dips and taps two sensor nodes. The Juggernaut's palm opens and closes once without meaning to. Mirror makes a quiet hiss in the speaker, not at pain, at loss of precision.

The chest coupler blooms with a high whine. He tries to bring Echo to a knife fight. The hybrid shell hears that whine first and jinks the frame clock by a hair so a delayed copy cannot find a purchase. The tug on my door hits rubber and slips. The line to Wren stays the color of trust.

"Save your tricks," I say.

"Always the teacher," he says, and pivots on the damaged leg to bring the left forearm through a sweep. The blade hidden there is industrial, not ceremonial. It would take a car in half. It takes air in half instead.

I run.

Rooftop fast. Ladder fast. The world compresses into distances that fit one step each. I take the sweep on the flat of my sword, step up the forearm seam with both magnets hot, and climb the inside of his elbow by throwing weight where the motor least wants it. The Juggernaut tries to shake. I stick. I drive the point under the shoulder ring and cut along the seam until the blade sinks into the motor housing. The arm locks for half a breath. I kick away before he slams the bulkhead.

He hammers the ground with a fist. Asphalt breaks. Dust and gravel skitter, ping my visor, and go to ground. His left knee misreads three degrees of position, knocks the toe into its own ankle, then hides the stutter with a pivot. A freight sized backhand comes on its own wind.

I plant both feet on the wall of a low loading dock, run two steps up brick, and launch over the sweep. The sword snaps up and catches a brow light. The housing explodes into bright powder. I land on his shoulder block. The new frame drinks the drop and purrs for more. Too easy and I know it. No pride.

Mirror speaks in a tone he saves for rooms where he can see himself reflected. "This will not be a long rehearsal."

"Then play your part," I say.

He pistons both shoulders back to smash me against the neck ring. I fall away into a roll, plant a palm, and let the magnets spin me out of the second strike's arc. He stomps again to fix spacing. He likes squares. I give him circles.

I take the calf on the other leg. Same soft shield. Same cut. The gait algorithm tries to average. The big machine becomes a person in boots on ice. He keeps choosing power over nuance. This chassis was built to bully. This shell was built to shame bullies and enjoy it.

He fences me with an arm and expects me to choose left or right. I choose up. Palm to plate, hip over wrist, feet past the elbow, then behind his head. The sword hooks a cable under the skull mount and pulls it free of its clip. A warning light blinks on his collar. He ignores it. His voice stays even, which means he is working.

"You could have left," he says. "By the tunnel."

"You are in my lane," I say. "Move."

He slams his back into the bay door to pin me. I am not there when plate meets metal. I land on one knee and cut the control bundle on the hip. The Juggernaut slews a turn and hits the wrong panel with his shoulder. Hinges give. A rack of mop heads spills like a stage mistake. Mirror laughs once behind all that steel. Human for one beat.

"If you wanted a broom," I say, "ask."

He drops both fists in a hammer that would make a crater. I step into the centerline and kill force with angle. The fists bracket me, leave my spine unbruised. I slide forward between wrists, take the inner elbow seam with a quick scrape, then flip the latch on the chest.

The coupler looks at me like an open mouth.

He surges to close it. I jam my sword into the seam. The door chews the coating and almost wins. A twist saves it. My palm lands on the lip and the magnets hum. The admin handshake on the inner face brushes my glove. The key Wren burned into me in the Core sits ready.

The loudhailer drops two notes. "Do not."

"You do not get to keep this," I say.

He backhands for my ribs. I take it on plate and let it throw me, leave the sword in the coupler, and bounce in gravel. He lunges to crush me before I can use the opening.

"Now," I tell the handshakes that live in my head.

The supervisor channel clips into the local bus with an old polite authority. Navarre's cadence. My edits. Wren's clean signature. "End test," it says. "Dismiss overlay."

The Juggernaut pauses hard enough to make bolts complain. The Echo hook collapses on itself like bad foam. The persona rides the freeze for a breath while the base layer looks for a rule. The rule says obey. It hates obeying this voice and obeys anyway.

Mirror feels the floor drop, finds another floor, refuses to see the room. "You are not clever enough to sign that."

"I know who is," I say.

He tries for force. He heaves his shoulder into a parked sedan and pitches it like a block of sugar. The car spins at me, nose low. I step into its spin and swat the hood with the sword flat. Magnets lick the steel. I pull, you turn, and the sedan sails past my hip and kisses the bay wall. Glass becomes beads. The car settles like a tired dog.

He kicks the loading dock stairs, throws a chain of concrete chunks down like dice, reaches under his own ribs for a cable I cut, and uses the rage of that surprise to bring the forearm blade in low toward my knee. The hybrid shell sees the line, lights the footwork, and writes a solution up my bones.

The solution is joy. Two quick steps that make the world silly in a way that only speed allows. The blade misses, the knee kisses air, and I am inside again.

The forearm blade retracts. The pistons in the shoulder complain with a noise like a paper cutter near the end of a track. I ride that noise and make it worse, little cuts along the seam at the back of the shoulder ring. Nothing cinematic. A sabotage of future choices.

He senses it and changes target. The loudhailer flickers. The coupler tries to whisper into my door again with a laundered Echo. The hybrid shell answers by jittering six cycles and then calming like a heartbeat that refuses to sync with a metronome. I feel the interference touch my teeth, then slide off.

"Learn a new song," I say.

He stops speaking for three moves and lets the body talk. Good choice. The Juggernaut charges like a freight elevator falling sideways. I do not run from that. I run into it. Palms up. Magnets on. Sword low. Hip touch to hip plate. The contact becomes a hinge and his speed goes into my arc. I pivot on his rib and come up on the chest like a man vaulting a fence.

The sword point catches the latch again and holds the mouth open. I hang for a count, wrist burning, ankle hugging a ridge on the coupler bezel, magnets in my palm making a small current sing through my bones. It feels like a right decision in a body that was built for this.

He tries to smash me on the coupler lip with his forearm. I let go of the sword, drop one meter, and catch the forearm with both hands. The magnets and the new ankle flex turn the blow into a slide. I ride it to the ground, let the blade escape the coupler and drop with me, catch the grip before it hits asphalt. He thinks we are both falling. I am already gone.

He swings again, slower now. The calf actuators are bleeding out and the hip geometry is wrong. He compensates with torso twist and gets away with it because this chassis forgives. He throws a vendor cart at me. I roll under the tumbling crate and come up at his instep. The sword tip dips and cuts through lacing on a heavy boot plate. The plate flops. It will not ruin him. It will ruin his trust in that foot.

A siren barks near the river. He ignores it. The loudhailer cracks with static as the coupler tries to find my door again. The shell hears, skews time by a breath, and says no. I taste copper. I like the taste. I let it live under my tongue with everything else that made me.

"You are enjoying this," Mirror says. No accusation. An observation through a speaker that does not know how to respect joy.

"Yes," I say. I see my hands move without thought. I hear my count sing. I feel the length of my legs and the truth of their speed. The hybrid frame is a low poem I can recite mid fight. It is a room that was designed for my name even if no one meant it kindly. I inhabit it like a thief who knows where every creak is. I am merciless with myself about that pleasure. I still take it.

He tries a new angle. He kneels on purpose, palms on the road, then heaves up a slab of asphalt with both hands and throws it like a man throwing a table. It breaks itself while crossing the air. The chunks that reach me are easy to step through. The dust that follows is harder. He uses the cloud to mask a charge. He is fast for a thing that huge when he thinks he is clever.

I cut the dust with the sword in one long figure eight to give the bow wave a shape. The Juggernaut comes through on the right of my picture. I step left and he corrects, then eats his own ankle flaw. The back foot skids, the hip hits a stop that was never supposed to be there, and his torso yaw is late. I draw a thin line across a diagnostic sensor under the collar. His status panel turns honest for the first time tonight.

He sees where this is going. He stops performing anger for the loudhailer and does numbers. He has one leg that lies, one arm I taught to lock, one hip that reports wrong, a coupler he cannot trust, and a target that keeps turning him into geometry that hurts.

He tries for a grab and a crush, no finesse, just mass.

I let him take my left forearm and press. The plate groans. The magnets talk to his palm anchors and tell them bad lies. He squeezes harder and loses little finger tension even as he gains ring finger overcommit. The hybrid shell chews that data and hands me a gift. I roll my wrist inside his grip and he gives me the circle I want. The wrist bones want to leave his hand again. He has not learned that lesson. He is not a child. He plays like one inside anything he did not design.

I step up his palm with a heel, pivot on the knuckle ridge, and ride his grip like a bar. The sword splits the seam behind the thumb knuckle. He lets go. The forearm blade pops in reflex and kisses the road where my shin was a breath before.

He straightens in a stuttering fury, takes three stomp steps to reset, and tries to own the street with sound. The loudhailer howls with an ultrasonic meant to ruin my balance. I kill my ear to his channel, open only the box where Wren lives, and count with her breath instead.

"Two blocks," she says in my ear like a metronome with a hand on my shoulder. "I have line. I can see your star. Do what you need."

"Almost done," I say.

He hears me answer someone else and hates it. He pushes Echo one more time for pride. The hybrid shell is done being polite. It throws a packet of its own rhythm into the local spectrum and fills his coupler with a song that starts with my name and ends with his authority bleached out. His hook slides off my door and hangs like a limp rope.

He takes one last run at me with everything. No tricks. Both arms, both legs, torso rolling into a spear. I move at a fraction of a fraction of what Forge could never give me without hurting me. Down the centerline, past symmetry, up the seam at the collar once, then twice, then a third time in exactly the same place to deepen the insult. I do not have to break him. I have to make him think he might. He flinches to protect the seam and I cut the forearm umbilical that feeds the blade. The weapon goes to sleep in its house. He punches me with a dead tool and looks briefly, foolishly human inside all that money.

"Fun is over," he says, and for the first time all night the line is not clean. There is static in the word fun. There is a shred of something that could be grateful for the puzzle and angry at the answer.

"Agreed," I say.

I take the stairs of his own body again. Foot to shin, shin to knee plate, knee plate to thigh ridge, thigh to coupler lip. The sword is already in my hand. I wedge it in the mouth. It bites through the rubber seal and sets my wrist on fire as the door tries to make a sandwich out of the blade. It fails. I hold.

He tries to smash his own chest with his forearm to chop me in half. I glue my back to the door with magnets and take the hit on shoulder and hip. The hybrid shell is not as heavy as Forge. It does not need to be. It is sticky where Forge was stubborn. The blow throws me, my magnets hold, my ankle locks a rail, the blade holds the mouth, and now we are arranged in a shape that cannot last and must be used.

"End test," I tell the bus again in Navarre's calm cadence that has never earned any of the respect it is given. "Dismiss overlay. Authenticate one five seven K."

The relay in his chest clicks through a compliance ritual it thinks is holy. The frame shudders as code lets go of output. The overlay drops its hands for a second that could save a life if anyone below us deserved saving.

"Evacuate process to nearest service unit," I add, and seat it with false heat and a short to nowhere that looks real. "Criteria maintenance class."

The machine under him hates the wording again and obeys again. Safety is a god with boring sandals. You can learn its prayers.

Across the lane a squat orange vac under a pallet wakes like a pet and beeps three notes. Ready. Battery half. Brushes good. It blinks a little square eye and does not know it has been chosen to host a man who enjoys mirrors.

Mirror tries to rip the coupler out of his own chest as the buffer takes his name. He cannot. The door has my wrist in its hinge. I cannot let go. He tries to pin me to the plate with his forearm again. I roll inside that space he cannot quite own and show him a profile he hates to hit because it resists without doing him the favor of being dramatic.

The buffer tips. He feels it leave. He knows the feeling from the labs. He hates it more here. His voice breaks in the loudhailer, not in fear, in insult. "What did you do."

"Gave you work," I say.

The vac chirps, flips to Busy, and drives one jerk forward. Its brush spins. The second hiccups and catches. It chirps again with a tone that cannot believe what luck has dropped in its lap.

I drop from his chest, free the sword, and land light. The Juggernaut goes still in stages. Floodlights first, then brow panel, then arm posture, then knees. It ends kneeling with its elbow on the bay door like a big tired friend who has understood the night is over.

The vac spins in a circle, squealing lightly as one wheel slips on dust. Mirror swears through a speaker that was built to apologize for small collisions with plant pots. He tries to lunge. The vac bumps my boot like a polite animal and backs up half a step to apologize.

I walk to him. He stops spinning because impulse control and new physics have met for the first time. His little camera stares at my knee. The orange body hums with motors that will overheat if he keeps arguing with gravity.

"The code is gone now," I say. "Live on in mediocrity."

He tries to scream and produces only a wet ribbon of static. The vac tries forward three centimeters, declares obstruction, and parks. His words smear like butter off a cold knife. I hear please in there. I hear come back. I do not hear hello.

Behind me hydraulics bleed down in the big body like a sigh that belongs to a building, not a man. I pop the chest coupler all the way, pull the battery bus safety, and cut the loudhailer's loom for a clean quiet. The floodlight glow dies and the street remembers its own dark.

Two floors up a window opens. A man in a towel looks out, sees a Juggernaut kneeling on a bay door and an orange vac humming to itself on a loading dock, closes the window, and reconsiders sleep.

The Wendigo idles two blocks down with its nose aimed at the seam we want. Wren's voice comes in after a small pause that contains the weight of all the wrong things we both have done. "Status."

"Obstacle removed," I say. "I am walking."

"Bring the sword," she says. "We are keeping the sword."

"Agreed," I say.

I take one last look at the vac. It shudders in a little panic circle and stops. The brushes tick. The battery meter has that honest red section that tells you you should plug it in and that you will not. He will learn corners. He will learn patience. He will learn that halls are long in a way code was not.

My legs ask to run, not because danger loves this corner, because speed loves any excuse to live. I let them. Quiet soles. Clean push off. The new frame writes success in my calves and makes it feel like a language I grew up speaking. I enjoy it because I refuse to pretend speed is not joy. I do not forget that joy cost us a shell in a yard and a life we built with a woman who is now living in a box on a dash and learning to look up at streetlights.

The Juggernaut behind me becomes street furniture with a story. The vac's low beeper fades into a noise that belongs to night in cities that think no one is listening. We listen anyway. I slide into the side door as the Wendigo slows. Wren meets my eyes across the cab glass. She sees the sword in my hand and the way my posture has changed. I nod once and say the only line that matters.

"Let us go."

She gives the wheel a small turn, puts her palm on the shifter, and the van slides back into the throat of the city.

WREN PULLS THE WENDIGO out of the alley seam and lets the riverway swallow us. Sodium lamps run their quiet tally along the guardrail. The mast sleeps against the roof. The dish makes a low sympathetic hum in the headliner like it heard everything and decided to keep our secrets.

I crawl in through the side door and slide the sword into the rack. The new frame settles on the bench with a weight that feels honest. The plates cool. The magnets sigh. My breath meets the hold ring where it should, and stays.

Wren checks my visor in the rearview. Not worried. Counting bruises on the night. Her mouth is the straight line that opens when it needs to. She reaches across the cabin, finds my shoulder plate through the seat gap, and sets her hand there. Warm through the leather. Steady where the road is not.

"You are staying in it," she says.

I look down at the long hands, the narrow forearms, the way the wrist servos answer small thoughts as if they have been waiting for them. I look up at her hand on my shoulder.

"I will switch later," I say. "Not now."

Her eyes flick to the mirror. "Because it is better."

"Because it is me," I say. "At least today."

The crawler sits on the dash like a small creature that has decided the van is a cliff. One gooseneck points forward, the other pivots between us. The catch box glows a soft green under its belly. Juno watches without words for a long block. She is learning the shape of our silence again.

We pass a sign that tells no truth at this hour. We are out from under Orinox's lights for the first time since I stepped into the wire. The city air tastes like wet concrete and cheap smoke. The sound inside the van is the engine at a comfortable note and the tiny clicks of electronics that were not built to belong to each other and do anyway.

I make myself speak first.

"Thank you," I say. It is a small phrase for what she did in a yard and a corridor and a life. I say it anyway.

Wren gives my shoulder the lightest push. Not a pat. Contact. "You would have done it for me."

"I will," I say. Present tense. The word sits in my throat with more weight than it has carried before. It stays there and does not hurt.

She smiles without making it into a show. Her hand stays where it is. The road bends south and the river throws back a cold light like old film at the bottom of a drawer.

"I could feel you enjoying it," she says. Teasing, but not by much.

"It felt right," I say. "Not only winning. Moving the way my head wants. Breathing inside something that did not try to correct me into someone kind for the wrong people."

She nods once. "Keep that. You earned it."

The van shudders over a seam. The crawler bumps its magnets and steadies. Juno clears her little speaker with a static cough. The voice follows after, quiet and rough around the edges.

"I saw the big one kneel," she says.

"End of the rehearsal," Wren says. Her tone tries to stay light. It cannot help the way it softens on the second word. She takes her hand back to the wheel and lets her knuckles rest loose at ten and two.

A train horn carries off the river. Two blocks of ghost apartments slide by with windows like held breaths. Far behind us a siren argues with its own echo.

"You pulled me," I tell Wren. "When Echo tried to put its mouth over mine. I felt you put another voice in the room. I did not like the sound you used and I am still grateful."

She snorts, then blows the breath out through her nose to keep it from becoming a laugh. "He trained the room to move when he said it. I made the room move for me. Sometimes you repurpose the worst things."

"Sometimes you keep them," I say.

She glances back at me. "We are not keeping his voice."

"No," I say. "We are keeping mine."

"Then say something I need to hear," she says.

I look at the windshield where the city comes on as a curtain. I do not dig for poetry. I tell her the plain part.

"You are my person," I say. "That is what the word is. I was waiting for someone to order it. There is no order for this. It still feels like a rule that makes the room safer."

Her face changes in a way that is not a smile and is not tears. Her fingertips press once into the wheel and relax. Juno's crawler tilts both cameras like a curious bird.

"Say it again," Wren says, not because she did not hear, because she wants to sit with it.

"You are my person," I say. "You and her."

The crawler clicks softly, like a cupboard that knows how to keep quiet, and rests one little camera on my visor. Juno does not try for a speech. She says my name in the small voice the box gives her and it is enough.

The van slides under the overpass into a tunnel of noise and then climbs back into the open. We pass a billboard that forgot what it was selling. The road splits into three lanes and then two. The city keeps offering exits and none of them are for us.

Wren breathes. I match it without being told. It has become the best ritual in my life.

"Do you miss it," she says after a while. "Forge."

"Yes," I say. No point lying to a mechanic. "It was the first body that did not hurt me on purpose. I told it thank you before we left."

She nods, then looks down as if the floorboard could hold a shrine and we would not know it. "Good," she says. "I am not building you a headstone for a machine, but it can have a seat at the table."

"It already does," I say. "It bought us a minute. We spent it right."

We hit a patch of road with old repairs that make a chord under the tires. The van hums the note for a block. The air in here smells like hot plastic and oil and something lemon that Wren uses when she wants a space to forgive the things it has seen.

"About earlier," I say. The words stick once. I push past them. "In the yard. When I said your life weighed more. It did not feel like math after I said it. It felt like picking up a name and putting it in my pocket. I will keep it there."

She does not answer for a whole light cycle. She takes us through a dead intersection at a slow roll and lets a bicycle ghost our bumper. The hand comes back to my shoulder. It rests there like a tool that knows the job.

"That is family," she says. "It is not a romance word or a war word. It is a shop word. You carry the thing that matters because your hands are free and someone else's are not."

"Family," I say. The word fits without needing to be sanded down. "Then that is what we are."

"That is what we have been," she says. "We are just telling it out loud now."

The crawler taps the catch box with one little wheel and sits straighter. "Then the kitchen is open," Juno says, the sound more herself with each sentence. "When we have one."

"We will make one," Wren says. Her voice has the quiet certainty she keeps for hard bolts and mornings after fires. "Not tonight. Tonight we keep moving."

She takes the next turn that feeds us into the long spine that cuts through the east side. A billboard for a perfume company blows a coil of smoke at the van and turns its projected head away as if we are beneath its time. Good. We pass without paying.

I let the quiet stretch until it becomes something we can sit on. Then I break it on purpose.

"I am afraid," I say.

She does not pretend to be surprised. "Me too."

"Not of them," I say. "Or not only. Of being the person they wrote into a test. Of learning I was built to make rooms safer for men like Navarre and then learning I can use that skill for you. Afraid the skill still belongs to him, even when we aim it at us."

"It belongs to you," she says. "I watched you take it back. That is not a story I am telling to make you feel better. I watched you change the name on the door and then walk through it."

I breathe. The ring in my chest finds the breath and returns yes. The hold feels less like a seatbelt and more like a handrail in a moving train. Useful. Chosen.

"Then here is another truth," I say. "If you ask me to run, I will run. If you ask me to stop, I will stop. Not because there is a collar. Because you asked."

"Here is mine," she says. "I will not ask you to stop being yourself. Even if the room gets messy."

The city opens ahead into the haze that sits where dawn will be one day. We are not heading for light. We are heading for a place that will let us change our oil under a roof without questions. That is enough.

We roll past a row of closed storefronts with signs that have outlived the products. A man sleeps in a doorway with a dog that might be a dog. A bus howls a block over. The river keeps its own clock.

"What do we call you," Wren says, and she means the shell.

"Hikari," I say. "Do not put another name between me and me."

"Then Hikari is Hikari," she says. Her hand stays one more breath on my shoulder plate. "And I am Wren. And she is Juno. We keep our names in the same place."

"Family," I say again, because repetition is how you teach muscle memory. The word sits where it should.

The van hums. The crawler makes a small contented whirr and rests its weight on the box. We run the numbers on fuel and food and the angle the map will let us take through the Strand. We do not say the other part for a minute because saying it will make the air colder. Finally Wren does it the way she always does, clean and without ceremony.

"They will not let this lie," she says.

"No," I say. "We pulled their pride out by the wiring and showed it to them. We erased the parts of us that fed their reports. We took a key and used it without permission. That buys one night of quiet and the rest of the calendar full of noise."

"They will call it escalation," she says.

"They will call it a lot of things," I say. "It does not change the job. It was always going to be a war once we refused to be statistics."

She nods. She does not look smaller for hearing it. She looks more like herself.

"We won today," she says, and she is not asking me to make it bigger than it is.

"We did," I say. "We won a battle. They are going to bring a list of new words for later. We will learn them and break them."

She grins. It finds the corner of her mouth that belongs to luck. "Say it."

I set my back to the bench, square the plates that pass for shoulders, and count the only way that has ever made rooms line up for me. The hold ring in my chest finds the rhythm and sets it where it will be easy to reach again. Wren listens the way she watches a gauge settle after a hard pull. Juno tilts both camera heads and holds still.

"Three," I say, and the van feels like a tool in good hands.

"Two," I say, and the road feels like it chose us.

"One," I say, and the city opens just enough to let a family pass into the haze.

Epilogue: Blank Receipt

HIKARI

I FIT UNDER THE sink if I hold my knees and keep my toes against the cabinet wall. It smells like lemon cleaner and old water. The pipe is a white curve with a metal nut that bites my shoulder when I breathe too big. A drip falls from the seam and lands on the back of my hand. I count them because they come like footsteps that know the room better than I do.

In the other room a chair scrapes. My father clears his throat. It is the same sound he makes before he lies to neighbors he likes.

"It covers the whole balance," he says. "Plus certs. You said certs."

A second voice answers from low in its chest. It does not belong to our building. "Transfer of credits on confirmation. Medical certifications on delivery. Schedule compliance required."

I look at the line of light where the cabinet doors don't quite meet. Their voices bend around it and find me anyway. The drip lands again. I put the wet spot on my wrist against the pipe. Cool. The pipe hums a little when someone upstairs turns their tap.

"You said clean," my father says. He is trying to keep anger out of his words. When he tries that, the anger just hides inside them and watches. "No pushback later. No returns."

The other voice does not get louder. It gets closer. "Clean. Receipt issued on site."

He carries the sound of paper that is not paper. A tablet case closes. A pen that glows touches plastic. He sets things down and they do not wobble. That is how you can tell who is new.

My father laughs a little with no smile. "You could have gone through a clinic," he says. "You come to the apartment to scare me."

"It decreases variance," the man says.

He is not wrong. The hallway is one door away. The elevator sticks on the fourth floor unless you kick it at the right angle. The window in here has a crack that pretends to be a river. I know all those things. He knows the word variance.

The drip hits my hand again. I look up at the wood of the cabinet. Someone wrote a name there and scratched it out. The lemon cleaner smeared the ink and made it a shadow.

"Where are they," the man asks.

"Bathroom," my father says, then louder, like talking to someone down the hall, "Kid. Come out. Company."

I press my feet harder against the cabinet wall. The board gives a little. I picture the place where the screws meet the stud. I picture the wall falling in and everyone acting surprised.

Boots walk on tile. The step changes when they leave the old linoleum for the bathroom floor. He stops in the doorway. He does not say my name. He does not know it yet.

"You hide well," he says conversationally. "That is a sign of learning."

He kneels. The light line brightens as the door opens. Two fingers touch the edge and pull the cabinet wide until his silhouette fills the space. He has a mask that is not a mask, just an even film where a face should be. No eyes. No mouth. The surface holds the room like glass holds water. On his collar there is a small helix that wants you to feel safe because it looks clean.

I hold my knees tighter. The pipe hums again. The drip misses me and hits the floor with a sound I have never liked.

"You will not remember any of this," he says.

I believe him because he says it the way people tell you the weather. He sets a small case on the bath mat and opens it. I see the corner of a pad, a coil of wire, a spray with a blue cap. He pulls out a band that looks like the collars the older kids wear when they come back from tests and have to sit very still for hours.

"Look at me," he says. The film where his face should be stays blank. The voice has a place the words live anyway.

I look at the edge of his shoulder, then his gloves, then the tile under his boot that has a piece of grout missing the size of my fingernail. I am good at not looking at what people want. He does not mind. He turns the band and shows me the seam where it opens.

My father stands behind him in the mirror, not in the room. In the mirror he looks like a man who could leave now and pretend the building made him do it. He scratches the inside of his wrist where the skin goes thin and says, "It is for school."

The man nods. "Education access included," he says, for the record. He takes the band and lays it across my lap like a pet he wants me to be kind to. "It will be tight for a moment."

"Does it hurt," I ask.

"It will be tight," he repeats.

He lifts my chin with two fingers. Not rough. Not kind. He checks my eyes through the film. Somewhere a form gets a tick in a box.

"Breathe," he says. His hand settles the band around my throat. Metal touches the place where my heart runs too fast when there is a new room. The clasp finds itself and clicks. The band warms the way a stove does when it holds a secret under its surface. The hum from the pipe sounds like a friend who left town without saying goodbye.

He taps the device at his wrist. The band tightens. It listens for my pulse, then talks back to his screen. The first squeeze is a hug from a machine that does not love anyone. The second puts a white line of light behind my teeth. My hands open before I tell them to. My knees let go of themselves. The tile under the sink gets wider.

"Good," he says. He looks past me toward my father. "Sign."

The pen makes a patient sound on the glass. I do not hear my father say my name. I do not hear him say "I am sorry." He says, "The certs. I want them sent tonight."

"They will be visible in your file after midnight," the man says. He presses his wrist to the band and my neck feels the contact like a coin passing through a slot.

I count the drips. My count shivers and loses a number. The lemon smell gets bigger. The pipe's hum crawls up the back of my head and sits behind my eyes, waiting.

"Stand," the man tells me.

I do. The cabinet door swings wide and bumps my shoulder. He catches it so it does not hit me. I step onto the mat where his case sits open and he moves it with a boot so I will not trip even though he does not plan to let me fall.

In the mirror my father's face becomes a hallway. The man is a hole that rooms pass through. I see myself between them for a second. I hold that picture like a coin I am not supposed to have.

"Hands," the man says, and I give him my wrists. He does not cuff them. He puts a pad in my palm and curls my fingers over it like he is fixing a glove. The pad is warm. It hums with the band. My head goes light and then heavy. Somewhere a door opens between the room and a place that has no walls.

"You will sleep," he says. "You will wake where you need to be."

My father steps out of the mirror into the doorway and stops being a reflection. He looks at the floor past my feet. His mouth moves without words. He says, "Do right," to the wall. Maybe to me. Maybe to the helix. It is not a promise. It is a wish someone told him grown people say when they do not have anything correct left.

The man's hand taps the band again. The tile turns into water for a heartbeat and then turns back to tile. My skin forgets to be skin. The hum replaces it. I try to count to keep what I know. One. Another number. The numbers are coins in a drain.

The man leans so we share the cabinet's shadow one last time. He tilts his head like a person in a picture. "Blank receipt," he says, and someone who is not in the room types it as an entry on a form I will never see.

The light in the band brightens. My throat learns a new rhythm and keeps it. The room pulls away without moving. The lemon smell cements itself to the part of my head that will later hold other ghosts.

The voice from the band is not a voice. It lives in the place where instructions do when they become true just by being said.

"Clean file. Full reset. Upload in progress..."